The *Summer Wedding*

DEBBIE MACOMBER

HARLEQUIN®MIRA®

Published in Great Britain 2015
by Harlequin MIRA, an imprint of Harlequin (UK) Limited,
Eton House, 18-24 Paradise Road,
Richmond, Surrey, TW9 1SR

THE SUMMER WEDDING © 2015 Harlequin Books S.A.

The publisher acknowledges the copyright holder of the individual works as follows:

The Man You'll Marry © 1992 Debbie Macomber
Groom Wanted © 1993 Debbie Macomber

ISBN 978-1-848-45399-9

58-0715

Harlequin (UK) Limited's policy is to use papers that are natural, renewable and recyclable products and made from wood grown in sustainable forests. The logging and manufacturing processes conform to the legal environmental regulations of the country of origin.

Printed and bound by
CPI Group (UK) Ltd, Croydon, CR0 4YY

CONTENTS

For Jenny and Kevin

One

Jill Morrison caught her breath as she stared excitedly out the airplane window. Seattle and everything familiar was quickly shrinking from view. She settled back and sighed with pure satisfaction.

This first-class seat was an unexpected gift from the airline. The booking agent had made a mistake and Jill turned out to be the beneficiary. Not a bad way to start a long-awaited vacation.

She glanced, not for the first time, at the man sitting beside her. He looked like the stereotypical businessman, typing industriously on a laptop, his brow furrowed with concentration. She couldn't tell exactly what he was doing, but noticed several columns of figures. He paused, and something must have troubled him, because he reached for a calculator in his briefcase and punched out a series of numbers. When he'd finished, he returned to his computer. He seemed impatient and restless, as though he begrudged the travel time. Not a good sign, in Jill's opinion, since the flight to Honolulu was scheduled to take five hours.

He wasn't the talkative sort, either. In her enthusiasm before takeoff, Jill had made a couple of attempts at light conversation, but both tries had met with minimal responses, followed by cool silence.

Great. She was stuck sitting next to this grouch for the beginning of a vacation she'd been planning for nearly two years. A vacation that Jill and her best friend, Shelly Hansen, had once dreamed of taking together. Only Shelly wasn't Shelly Hansen anymore. Her former college roommate was married now. For an entire month Shelly Hansen had been Shelly Brady.

Even after all this time, Jill had problems taking it in. For as long as Jill had known Shelly, her friend had been adamant about making her career as a producer of DVDs her highest priority. She'd vowed that men and relationships would always remain a distant second in her busy life. For years Jill had watched Shelly discourage attention from the opposite sex. From college onward, Shelly had carefully avoided any hint of commitment.

Then it had happened. Shelly met Mark Brady and the unexpected became a reality. To Shelly's way of thinking, her mother's great-aunt Millicent—known to everyone in the family as Aunt Milly—was directly responsible for her present happiness. She'd met her tax-accountant husband immediately after the elderly woman had mailed Shelly a "magic" wedding dress. The same dress Milly had worn herself more than sixty years earlier.

Both Shelly and Jill had insisted there was no such thing as magic, especially associated with a wedding dress. Magic belonged to wands or fairy godmothers, not wedding dresses. To fairy tales, not real life. They'd scoffed at the ridiculous story that went along with the gown. Both refused to believe what Aunt Milly had written in her letter; no one in her right mind, they told each other, could possibly take the sweet old woman seriously. *Marry the next man you meet?* Preposterous.

Personally, Jill had found the whole story amusing. Shelly hadn't been laughing though. Shelly, being Shelly, had overreacted, fretting and worrying, wondering if there wasn't some small chance that Milly could be right. Shelly hadn't *wanted* her to be right, but there it was—the dress arrived one day, and the next she'd fallen into Mark Brady's arms.

Literally.

The rest, as they say, is history and Jill wasn't laughing anymore. Shelly and Mark had been married in June and to all appearances were blissfully happy.

Four weeks after the wedding, Jill was flying off to Hawaii. Not the best month to visit the tropics, perhaps, but that couldn't be helped. Her budget was limited and July offered the most value for her money.

Her seatmate leaned back and sighed deeply, pinching the bridge of his nose. Whatever problem he'd encountered earlier had persisted, Jill guessed. She must have been correct, because no more than ten seconds later, he reached for his calculator again. Jill had the impression this man never stopped working; even during their meal he continued his calculations. Not a moment of their flight time was wasted. If he wasn't studying papers from his briefcase, he was typing more columns of figures into his computer.

An hour passed. A couple of times, almost against her will, she found herself watching him. Although she assumed he was somewhere in his mid-thirties, he seemed older. No, she decided, not older, but…experienced. His face managed to be pleasing to the eye despite his rugged, uneven features. She wondered fleetingly how he'd assess *her* appearance. Except he hadn't looked at her once. He seemed totally unaware that there was anyone in the seat next to him. His eyes were gray, she'd noted earlier, the color of polished steel. There was nothing soft about him.

This was obviously a man who had it all—hand-tailored suits, Italian leather shoes, gold pen and watch. She'd bet even his plastic was gold! No doubt he lived the way he flew—first class. He was the type who had all the answers, too. The type of man who didn't question his own attitudes and beliefs....

He reminded Jill of her father, long dead, long grieved. He, too, had been an influential businessman who'd held success in the palm of his hand. Adam Morrison had fought off middle age on a gym floor. Energy was his trademark and death was an eternity away. Only it was just around the corner, and he hadn't known it.

Ironic that she should be sitting next to him thirteen years after his death. Not her father, but someone so much like him it was all Jill could do not to ask when he'd last seen his family.

He must have felt her scrutiny, because he suddenly turned and stared at her. Jill blushed guiltily, bowing her head over her book, reading it with exaggerated fervor.

"Did you like what you saw?" he asked her boldly.

"I—I don't know what you mean," she said in a small voice, moving the paperback close to her face.

For the first time since he'd taken the seat next to her, the stranger grinned. It was an odd smile, off center and unpracticed, as if he didn't often find anything to smile about.

The remainder of the flight was uneventful. Jill held her breath during the descent, until the tires bumped down on the runway in Honolulu. She wished again that Shelly was taking this trip, too. With or without her best friend, though, Jill intended to have the time of her life. She had seven glorious days to laze in the sun. Seven days to shop to her heart's content and to go sightseeing and to swim and relax and eat glorious meals.

For months Jill had dreamed of the wonders she would see and experience. Tranquil villages, orchid plantations— oh, how she loved orchids. At night, she'd stroll along lava-strewn beaches and by day there'd be canyons to explore, tumbling waterfalls and smoldering volcanoes. Hawaii was going to be a grand adventure, Jill felt sure of it.

The man beside her was on his feet the instant their plane came to a standstill. He removed his carry-on bag from the storage compartment above the seat with an efficiency that told her he was a seasoned traveler. The smiling flight attendant handed him a garment bag as he strode off the plane.

Jill followed him, watching for directions to the baggage pickup. Her seatmate's steps were crisp and purposeful. It didn't surprise her; this was a man on the go, always in a rush to get somewhere. Meet someone. Make a deal. No time to stop and smell the orchids for her friend the grouch.

Jill lost sight of him when she purchased a lei at a conces-sion stand. She draped the lovely garland of orchids around her neck and fingered the delicate flowers, marveling at their beauty.

Once again the reminder that adventures awaited her on this tropical island moved full sail across her heart. She wasn't the fanciful sort, nor did she possess an extravagant imagination. Not like Shelly. Yet Jill felt something deep inside her stir to life....

Shelly had become a real believer in magic, Jill mused,

smiling as she bought herself a slice of fresh pineapple. For that matter, even she—ever the practical one—found herself a tiny bit susceptible to the claims of a charmed wedding dress. Just a tiny bit, though.

Jill's pulse quickened the way it did whenever she thought about what had happened between Shelly and Mark. It was simply the most romantic thing she'd ever known.

Romance had scurried past Jill several times. Currently she was dating Ralph, a computer programmer, but it was more for companionship than romance, although he'd been hinting for several months that they should start "getting serious." Jill assumed he meant marriage. Ralph was nice, and so far Jill had been able to dissuade him from discussing the future of their relationship. She didn't want to hurt his feelings, but she just wasn't interested in marrying him.

However, Jill fully intended to marry someday. There'd never been any question of that. The only question was *who*. She'd dated frequently in college, but there hadn't been anyone special. Then, when she'd been hired as a pharmacist for PayRite, a drugstore chain with several outlets in the Pacific Northwest, the opportunities to meet eligible men had dwindled dramatically.

Prospects weren't exactly crowding the horizon, but Jill had given up worrying about it. She'd done a fair job of pushing the thought of a husband and family to the far reaches of her mind—until she'd made one small mistake.

She'd tried on Aunt Milly's wedding dress.

Shelly had hung the infamous dress in the very back of her closet. Out of sight, out of mind—only it hadn't worked that way. Not a minute passed that Shelly wasn't keenly aware of the dress and its alleged powers.

On impulse, Jill had tried it on herself. To this day she

didn't know what had prompted her to slip into the beautiful hand-sewn wedding dress. It was so elegant, so beautiful, with row upon row of pearls and delicate lace layered over satin.

That it fit as though it had been specifically designed for her had been as much of a surprise to Shelly as it had to Jill. Shelly had seemed almost giddy with relief, insisting her aunt had made a mistake and the dress was actually meant for Jill. But by that time, Shelly had already met Mark....

No, Aunt Milly hadn't made a mistake—the wedding dress had been meant for Shelly all along. Her marriage to Mark proved it. And really, she'd have to attribute Shelly's meeting and marrying Mark to the power of suggestion, the power of expectation—not to *magic*. She shook her head and hurried off to retrieve her luggage.

Then she headed outside, intent on grabbing a taxi. As the driver loaded her bags, she stood for a moment, savoring the warm breeze, enjoying the first sounds and sights of Hawaii. She couldn't wait to get to her hotel. Through a friend who was a travel agent, Jill had been able to book a room in one of the most exclusive places on Oahu at a ridiculously low rate.

The hotel was everything the brochure had promised and more. Jill had to pinch herself when she got to her room. The first thing she did was walk to the sliding-glass doors that led to the lanai, a balcony overlooking the swimming-pool area. Beyond that, the Pacific Ocean thundered against the sandy shore. The sight was mesmerizing, the beauty so keen, it brought tears of appreciation to Jill's eyes.

She tipped the bellhop, who'd brought up her luggage, and returned to the view. If she never went beyond this room,

Jill would have been satisfied. She stood at the railing, the breeze riffling her long hair.

The hotel was U-shaped, and something—a movement, a figure—caught her eye. A man. Jill glanced across the swimming pool, across the tiki-hut roof of the bar until her gaze found what she was seeking. The grouch. In a lanai directly opposite hers. At least she thought so. He wore the same dark suit as the man with whom she'd spent five of the most uncommunicative hours of her life.

Jill didn't know what prompted her, but she waved. After a moment, he waved back. He stepped farther out onto the lanai and she knew beyond a doubt. Their rooms were in different sections of the hotel, but they were on the same floor, their lanais facing each other.

He held a cell phone to his ear, but slowly lowered it.

For several minutes they simply stared at each other. After what seemed like an embarrassingly long time, Jill tried to pull herself away and found she couldn't. Unsure why, unsure what had attracted her attention to the man in the first place, unsure of everything, Jill looked away.

A knock at the door distracted her.

"Yes?" she asked, opening her door. A bellhop in a crisp white uniform stood before her with a large wrapped box.

"This arrived by special courier for you earlier today, Ms. Morrison," he explained politely.

When he'd gone, Jill studied the package, reading the Seattle postmark and the unfamiliar block printing. She carried it to the bed, still puzzled. She had no idea who would be mailing her anything from home. Especially since she'd only left that morning.

Sitting on the edge of the bed, she unwrapped the package and lifted the lid. Her hands froze. Her heart froze. Her breath jammed in her throat. When she was able to move again, she inhaled sharply and closed her eyes.

It was Aunt Milly's wedding dress.

A letter rested on top of the tissue-wrapped dress. With trembling hands, Jill reached for it.

Dearest Jill,

Trust me, I know exactly what you're feeling. I remember my own emotions when I opened this very box and found Aunt Milly's wedding dress staring up at me. As you know, my first instinct was to run and hide. Instead I was fortunate enough to find Mark and fall in love.

I suppose you're wondering why I'm mailing this dress to you in Hawaii. Why didn't I just give it to you before you left Seattle? Good question, and if I had a reasonable answer I'd be more than happy to share it.

One thing I've learned these past few months is that there's precious little logic when it comes to understanding any of this—love, fate, the magic within Aunt Milly's wedding dress. Take my advice and don't even try to make sense of it.

I suppose I should tell you why I'm giving you the dress. I was sitting at the table one morning last week, with my first cup of coffee. I wasn't fully awake yet. My eyes were closed. Suddenly you were in my mind, standing waist-deep in blue-green water. There was a waterfall behind you and lush, beautiful plants all around. It had to be Hawaii. You looked happier than I can ever remember seeing you.

There was a man with you, and I wish I could describe him. Unfortunately, he was in shadow. Read into that whatever you will. There was a look about you, a look I've only seen once before—the day you tried on the wedding gown. You were radiant.

I talked to Mark about it, and he seemed to feel the same way I did—that the dress was meant for you. I phoned Aunt Milly and told her. She said by all means to make you its next recipient.

I should probably have given you the dress then, but something held me back. Nothing I can put into words, but a feeling that it would be too soon. So I'm sending it to you now.

My wish for you, Jill, is that you find someone to love. Someone as wonderful as Mark. Of the two of us, you've always been the sensible one. You believed in logic and common sense. But you also believed in love, long before I did. I was the skeptic there. Something tells me the man you'll marry is just as cynical as I once was. You're going to have to teach him about love, the same way Mark's taught me.

Call me as soon as you get back. I'll be waiting to hear what happens. In my heart I already know it's going to be wonderful.

Love,
Shelly

Jill read the letter twice. Her pulse quickened as her eyes lifted and involuntarily returned to the lanai directly across from her own.

The frantic pace of her heart slowed to normal.

The grouch was gone.

Jill recalled Aunt Milly's letter to Shelly. "When you receive this dress," she'd written, "the first man you meet is the man you'll marry."

So it wasn't the grouch, it was someone else. Not that she really believed in any of this. Still, her knees went unaccountably weak with relief.

After unpacking her clothes, Jill showered and lay down for a few minutes. She hadn't intended to fall asleep, but when she awoke, a rosy dusk had settled. Flickering fires from the bamboo poles that surrounded the pool sent shadows dancing on her walls.

She'd seen him, Jill realized. While she slept. Her hero, her predestined husband. But try as she might, she couldn't bring him into clear focus. Naturally it was her imagination. Fanciful thinking. Dreams gone wild. Jill reminded herself stoutly that she didn't believe in the power of the wedding dress any more than she believed in the Easter Bunny. But it was nice to fantasize now and then, to pretend.

Unquestionably, there was a certain amount of anticipation created by the delivery of the wedding dress and Shelly's letter. But unlike her friend, Jill didn't expect anything to come of this. Jill's feet were firmly planted on the ground. She wasn't as whimsical as Shelly, nor was she as easily influenced.

True, at twenty-eight, Jill was more than ready to marry and settle down. She knew she wanted children eventually, too. But when it came to finding the man of her dreams, she'd prefer to do it the old trial-and-error way. She didn't need a magic wedding dress guiding her toward him!

Initially, Shelly had had many of the same thoughts herself, Jill remembered, but she'd married the first man she'd met after the dress arrived.

The first man you meet. She was thinking about that

while she changed into a light cotton dress and sandals. She was still thinking about it as she rode the elevator down to the lobby to have a look around.

There must have been something in the air. Maybe it was because she was on vacation and feeling free of her usual routines and restraints; Jill didn't know. But for some reason she found herself glancing around, wondering which man it might be.

The hotel was full of possibilities. A distinguished gentleman sauntered past. An ambassador perhaps? Or a politician? Hmm, that might be nice.

Nah, she countered silently, laughing at herself. She wasn't interested in politics. Furthermore she didn't see herself as an ambassador's wife. She'd probably say the wrong thing to the wrong person and inadvertently cause an international incident.

A guy who looked like a rock star strolled her way next. Now, there was an interesting prospect, although Jill had a minor problem picturing herself married to a man who wore his hair longer than she did. He was cute, though. A definite possibility—*if* she took Shelly's letter seriously.

A doctor would be ideal, Jill decided. With her medical background, they were sure to have a lot in common. She scanned the lobby area, searching for someone who looked as if he'd feel at home with a stethoscope around his neck.

No luck. Nor, for that matter, did she seem to be generating any interest herself. She might as well be invisible. So much for that! These speculations were all in fun anyway....

Swallowing an urge to laugh, she headed out the back of the hotel toward the pristine beach. A lazy evening stroll among swaying palms sounded just the thing.

She walked toward the ocean, removed her shoes and

held them by the straps as she wandered ankle-deep into the delightfully warm water. She wasn't paying much attention to where she was going, thinking, instead, about her hopes for a family of her own. Thinking about the few truly happy memories she had of her father. The Christmas when she was five and a camping trip two years later. A picnic, once. But by the time she was eight, his success had overtaken him. It wasn't that he didn't love her or her mother, she supposed, but—

"I wouldn't go out much farther if I were you," a deep male voice called from behind her.

Jill's pulse soared at the unexpectedness of the intrusion. She saw the silhouette of a man leaning against a palm tree. In the darkness she couldn't make out his features, yet he seemed vaguely familiar.

"I won't," she said, trying to see who'd spoken. Whoever it was stayed stubbornly in the shadows of the tree.

From the distance Jill noted that he had the physique of an athlete. She happened to appreciate wide, powerful shoulders on a man. She stepped closer, attempting to get a better look at him without being obvious. Although his features remained hidden, his chin was tilted at a confident angle.

She'd always found confidence an appealing trait in a man....

"I wondered if you were planning to go swimming at night. Only a fool would do that."

Jill bristled. She had no intention of swimming. For one thing, she wasn't dressed for it. Before she could defend herself, however, he continued, "You look like one of those helpless romantics who can't resist testing the water. Let me guess—this is your first visit to the islands?"

Jill nodded. She'd ventured far enough onto the beach

to actually see him now. Her heart sank—no wonder he'd seemed familiar. No wonder he was insulting. For the second time in a twenty-four-hour period she'd happened upon the grouch.

"I don't suppose you took time to eat dinner, either."

"I...had something earlier. On the plane." That had been one of the benefits of her unexpected move to first class.

"I was there, remember?" He snickered softly. "Plastic food."

Jill didn't agree—she'd enjoyed it—but she wasn't going to argue. "I don't know what concern it is of yours," she said.

"None," he admitted, shrugging.

"Then my going without dinner shouldn't bother you." She bristled again at the intense way he was studying her. His mouth had twisted into a faint smile, and he seemed amused by her.

"Thank you for your advice," she said stiffly, turning away from him and heading back toward the water.

"You're not wearing your lei."

Jill's fingers automatically went to her neck as she stopped. She'd left it in her room when she changed clothes.

"Allow me." He stepped forward, removed the one from his own neck and draped it around hers. Since this was her first visit to the islands, Jill didn't know if giving someone a lei had any symbolism attached to it. She didn't really want that kind of connection with him. Just in case.

"Thank you." She hoped she sounded adequately grateful.

"I might have saved your life, you know."

That was a ridiculous comment. "How?"

"You could've drowned."

Jill couldn't help it. She laughed. "Not very likely. I had no intention of swimming."

"You can't trust the tides here. Even this close to shore, the waves are capable of jerking your feet right out from under you. You might easily have been swept out to sea."

"That's absurd."

"Perhaps," he agreed, amicably enough. "But I was hoping you'd realize you're in my debt."

Ah, now they were getting somewhere. This man wasn't given to generosity. She'd bet a month's wages that he'd initiated the conversation for his own purposes. He'd had plenty of time on their flight from Seattle to advise her about swimming.

No, he was after something.

"What is it you want?" she asked bluntly.

He grinned that cocky, unused smile of his and nodded. Apparently this was high praise of her finely honed intuitive skills.

"Nothing much. I was hoping you'd attend a small business dinner with me."

"Tonight?"

He nodded again. "You did mention you hadn't eaten."

"Yes, but…"

"It'll only take an hour or so of your time." He sounded impatient, as if he'd expected her to agree to his scheme without question.

"I don't even know who you are. Why would I want to attend a dinner party with you? I'm Jill Morrison, by the way."

"Jordan Wilcox," he said abruptly. "All right, if you must know, I need a woman to come with me so I won't be forced to offend someone I can't afford to alienate."

"Then don't."

"He's not the one I'm worried about. It's his daughter.

She's apparently set her sights on me and doesn't seem capable of taking a hint."

"Well, then, it sounds as though you've got yourself a problem." Privately Jill wondered at the woman's taste.

He frowned, shoving his hands into the pockets of his dinner jacket. He'd changed clothes, too, but he hadn't substituted something more casual for his business suit. Quite the reverse. But then, that shouldn't have surprised her. It was always business, never pleasure, with people like him.

"I don't know what it is about you women," he said plaintively. "Can't you tell when a man's not interested?"

"Not always." Jill was beginning to feel a bit smug. She swung her shoes at her side. "In other words, you need me as a bodyguard."

Clearly he didn't approve of her terminology, but he let it pass. "Something like that."

"Do I have to pretend to be madly in love with you?"

"Good heavens, no."

Jill hesitated. "I'm not sure I brought anything appropriate to wear."

He reached inside his pocket and pulled out a thick wad of cash. He peeled away several hundred-dollar bills and stuffed them in her hand. "Buy yourself something. The shop in the hotel's still open."

Two

"I'll pay for the dress myself," Jill insisted for the tenth time. She couldn't believe she'd agreed to attend this dinner party with Jordan Wilcox. Not only didn't she know the man, she didn't even like him.

"I'll pay for the dress," he said, also for the tenth time. "It's the least I can do."

They were in the ultraexpensive dress shop located off the hotel lobby. Jill was shifting judiciously through the rack of evening gowns. Most were outrageously overpriced. She found a simple one she thought might flatter her petite build, ran her hand down the sleeve until she reached the white tag, then sighed. The price was higher than any of the others. Grumbling under her breath, she dropped the sleeve and continued her search.

Jordan glanced impatiently at his watch. "What's wrong with this one?" He held up an elegant cocktail dress. It was made of dark green silk, with a draped bodice and a slim skirt. Lovely indeed, but hardly worth a week's salary.

"Nothing's wrong with it," she answered absently as she flipped through the row of dresses.

"Then buy it."

Jill glared at him. "I can't afford eight hundred dollars for a dress I'll probably wear once."

"I can," he returned from between clenched teeth.

"I *won't* allow you to pay for my dress."

"The party's in thirty minutes," he reminded her sharply.

"All right, all right."

He sighed with relief and put out a hand for the dress. Jill stopped him.

"Obviously nothing here is going to work. I'll check what I brought with me. Maybe what I have is more suitable than I thought."

Groaning, he followed her to the elevator. "Wait in the hall," she said as she unlocked her door. She wasn't about to let a strange man into her room. She stood by the closet and rooted through the few dresses she'd unpacked that afternoon. The only suitable one was an antique-white sleeveless dress with large gold buttons down the front. It wasn't exactly what one would wear to an elegant dinner party, but it was passable.

She raced to the door and held it up for Jordan. "Will this do?"

The poor man looked exasperated. "How do I know?"

Leaving the door open, Jill ran back to her closet. "The only other dress I have is Aunt Milly's wedding gown," she muttered.

"You packed a wedding dress?" His gray eyes lit up with amusement. It seemed an effort not to laugh out loud. "You apparently have high hopes for this vacation."

"I didn't bring it with me," she informed him primly, sorry she'd even mentioned it. "A friend had it delivered."

"You're getting married?"

"No. I— Oh, I don't have time to explain."

Jordan eyed her as if he had plenty of questions, but wasn't sure he wanted to ask them.

"Wear the one you showed me, then," he said testily. "I'm sure it'll be fine."

"All right, I will." By now Jill regretted agreeing to attend the dinner party. "I'll be ready in five minutes." She closed the door again, but not before she got a glimpse of the surprised look on Jordan's face. It wasn't until she'd slipped out of her sundress that she realized he probably wasn't accustomed to women who left him waiting in the hallway while they changed clothes.

Although she knew Jordan was impatient, Jill took an extra few minutes to freshen her makeup and run a brush through her shoulder-length brown hair. Using a gold clip, she pinned it up in a simple chignon. Despite herself, she couldn't help feeling excited about this small adventure. There was no telling whom she might meet tonight.

Drawing in a deep breath to calm herself, she smoothed the skirt of her dress, then walked slowly to the door. Jordan was waiting for her, his back against the opposite wall. He straightened when she appeared.

"Do I look okay?"

His gaze narrowed assessingly. His scrutiny made Jill uncomfortable, and she held herself stiffly. At last he nodded.

"You look fine," was all he said.

Jill heaved a sigh of relief, returned to her room to retrieve her purse and then joined Jordan.

The dinner party, as he'd explained earlier, was in a

private room in one of the hotel's restaurants. Jordan led the way to the elevator, his pace urgent.

"You'd better tell me what you want me to do," she said.

"Do?" he repeated with a frown. "Just do whatever you women do to let one another know a certain man is off-limits, and make sure Suzi understands." He hesitated. "Only do it without fawning all over me."

"I wouldn't dream of it," Jill said, gazing up at him in mock adoration and fluttering her lashes.

Jordan's frown deepened. "None of that, either."

"Of what?"

"That thing with the eyes." He motioned with his hand, looking annoyed.

"Should I know something about who's attending the party?"

"Not really," he said impatiently.

"What about you?" He shot her a puzzled look, and Jill elaborated. "If I'm your date, it makes sense I'd know who you are—something beyond your name, I mean—and what you do."

"I suppose it does." He buried his hands in his pockets. "I'm the CEO for a large development company based in Seattle. Simply put, we develop projects, gather together the financing, arrange for the construction, and then once the project's completed, we sell."

"That sounds interesting." If you thrived on tension and pressure, that is.

"It can be," was his only response. He looked her over once more, but his glance revealed neither approval nor reproach.

"I didn't like you when we first met." Jill wasn't sure why she felt obliged to tell him this. In fact, she still didn't like him, although she had to admit he was a very attractive man indeed. "When I sat next to you during the flight, I thought you were very unfriendly," she continued.

"I take it your opinion of me hasn't changed?" He cocked one brow with the question, as if to suggest her answer wouldn't trouble him one way or the other.

Jill ignored him. "You don't like women very much, do you?"

"They have their uses."

He said it in such a belittling, negative way that Jill felt a flash of hot color invade her cheeks. She turned to look at him, feeling almost sorry for a man who had everything yet seemed so empty inside. "What's made you so cynical?"

He glanced at her again, a bit scornfully. "Life."

Jill didn't know what to make of that response, but luckily the elevator arrived just then.

"Is there anything else I should know before we get there?" she asked once they were inside. Her role, Jill understood, was to protect him from an associate's daughter. She had no idea how she was supposed to manage that, but she'd think of something when the time came.

"Nothing important." He paused, frowning. "I'm afraid the two of us might arouse some curiosity, though."

"Why's that?"

"I don't generally associate with…innocents."

"Innocents?" He made her sound like one of the pre-school crowd. No one she'd ever known could insult her with less effort. "I am over twenty-one, in case you didn't realize it."

He laughed outright at that, and Jill stiffened, regretting—probably not for the last time—that she'd actually agreed to this.

"I think you're wonderful, too," she said sarcastically.

"So you told me before."

The elevator arrived at the top floor of the hotel, where the restaurant was located. Jordan spoke briefly to the maître d', who led them to the dinner party.

Jill glanced around the simple, elegant room, and her heart did a tiny somersault. All the guests were executive types, the men in dark suits, the women in sophisticated dresses that could all have been bought at the little boutique downstairs. Everyone had an aura of prosperity and power.

Jill's breath came in shallow gasps. She was miles out of her league. These people had money, real money, whereas she'd spent months just saving for this vacation. Her money was invested in panty hose and frozen dinners, not property and office towers and massive stock portfolios.

Jordan must have felt her unease, because he turned to her and smiled briefly. "You'll be fine."

It astonished Jill that three little words from him could give her an immeasurable boost of confidence. She smiled and drew herself up as tall as her five-foot-three-inch frame would allow.

Waiters carried trays of delicate hors d'oeuvres and narrow etched-glass flutes filled with sparkling, golden champagne. Jill reached for a glass and took her first sip, widening her eyes in surprise. Never had she tasted anything better.

"This is excellent."

"It should be, at three hundred dollars a bottle."

Before Jill could comment, an older, distinguished-looking gentleman detached himself from a younger colleague and made his way across the room toward them. He looked close to sixty, but could have stepped off the pages of *Gentlemen's Quarterly*.

"Jordan," he said in a hearty voice, extending his hand, "I'm delighted you could make it."

"I am, too."

"I trust your flight was uneventful."

Jordan's gaze briefly met Jill's. "It was fine. I'd like you to meet Jill Morrison. Jill, Dean Lundquist."

"Hello," she said pleasantly, giving him her hand.

"Delighted," Dean said again, turning to smile at her. He held her hand considerably longer than good manners required. Jill had the impression she was being carefully inspected and did her utmost to appear composed.

Finally, he released her and nodded toward the entrance. "If you'll both excuse me for a moment, Nicholson's just arrived."

"Of course," Jordan agreed politely.

Jill waited until Dean Lundquist was out of earshot. Then she leaned toward Jordan and whispered, "Suzi's dad?"

Jordan made a wry face. "Smart girl."

Not really, since few other men would have had cause to inspect her so closely, but Jill didn't discount the compliment. She wasn't likely to receive that many, at least not from Jordan.

"Who was that standing with him?" She inclined her head in the direction of a tall, good-looking young man. Something about him didn't seem quite right. Nothing she could put her finger on, but it was a feeling she couldn't shake.

"That's Dean, Junior," Jordan explained.

Jill noticed the way Jordan's mouth thinned and the thoughtful, preoccupied look that came into his eyes. "He's being groomed by Daddy to take my place."

"Junior?" Jill studied the younger man a second time. "I don't think you'll have much of a problem."

"Why's that?"

She shrugged, not sure why she felt so confident of that. "I can't picture you losing at anything."

His gaze swept her warmly. "I have no intention of giving Junior the opportunity, but I'm going to have a real fight on my hands soon."

"Just a minute," Jill said. "If Suzi is Dean Senior's daughter, then wouldn't a marriage between you two secure your position?" It wouldn't exactly be a love match, but she couldn't envision Jordan marrying for something as commonplace as love.

Jordan gave her a quick, unreadable look. "It'd help, but unfortunately I'm not the marrying kind."

Jill had guessed as much. She doubted there was time in his busy schedule for love or commitment, just for work, work, work. Complete one project and start another. She knew the pattern.

Jill couldn't imagine falling in love with someone like Jordan. And she couldn't picture Jordan in love at all. As he'd said, he wasn't the marrying kind.

"Jordan." A woman's shrill voice sent a chill up Jill's spine as a beautiful blonde hurried past her and straight into Jordan's unsuspecting arms, locking him in a tight embrace.

"This must be Suzi," Jill said conversationally from behind the woman who was squeezing Jordan for all she was worth.

Jordan's irate eyes found hers. "Do something!" he mouthed.

Jill was enjoying the scene far too much to interrupt Suzi's passionate greeting. While Jordan was occupied, Jill took an hors d'oeuvre from a nearby silver platter. Whatever it was tasted divine, and she automatically reached for two more. She hadn't recognized how hungry she was. Not until she was on her third cracker did she realize she was sampling caviar.

"Oh, darling, I didn't think you'd ever get here," Suzi said breathlessly. Her pretty blue eyes filled with something close to hero worship as she gazed up at Jordan. "Whatever took you so long? Didn't you know I'd been waiting hours and hours for you?"

"Suzi," Jordan said stiffly, disentangling himself from the blonde's embrace. He straightened the cuffs of his shirt. "I'd like you to meet Jill Morrison, my date. Jill, this is Suzi Lundquist."

"Hello," Jill said before helping herself to yet another cracker. Jordan's look told her this was not the time to discover a taste for Russian caviar.

Suzi's big blue eyes widened incredulously. She really was lovely, but one glimpse and Jill understood Jordan's reluctance. Suzi was very young, early twenties at most, and terribly vulnerable. She had to admire his tactic of putting the girl off without being unnecessarily rude.

Jordan had made Dean Lundquist's daughter sound like a vamp. Jill disagreed. Suzi might be a vamp-in-training, but right now she was only young and headstrong.

"You're Jordan's date?" Suzi asked, fluttering her incredible lashes—which were almost long enough to cause a draft, Jill decided.

She smiled and nodded. "We're very good friends, aren't we, Jordan?" She slipped her arm in his and looked up at him, ever so sweetly.

"But I thought—I hoped…" Suzi turned to Jordan, who'd edged himself closer to Jill, draping his arm across her shoulders as though they'd been an item for quite some time.

"Yes?"

Suzi glanced from Jordan to Jill and then back to Jordan. Tears brimmed in her bright blue eyes. "I thought there was something special between us...."

"I'm sorry, Suzi," he said gently.

"But Daddy seemed to think..." She left the rest unsaid as she slowly backed away. After three short steps, she turned and dashed out of the room. Jill popped another cracker in her mouth.

Several people were looking in their direction, although Jordan seemed unaware of it. Jill, however, keenly felt the interested glances. Not exactly a comfortable feeling, especially when one's mouth was full of caviar.

After an awkward moment, conversation resumed, and Jill was able to swallow. "That was dreadful," she muttered. "I feel sorry for the poor girl."

"Frankly, so do I. But she'll get over it." He turned toward Jill. "A lot of help *you* were," he grumbled. "You were stuffing down crackers like there was no tomorrow."

"This is the first time I've tasted caviar. I didn't know it was so good."

"I didn't bring you along to appraise the hors d'oeuvres."

"I served my purpose," Jill countered. "But I'm not happy about it. She's not a bad kid."

"Believe me," Jordan insisted, his face tightening, "she *will* get over it. She'll pout for a while, but in the end she'll realize we did her a favor."

"I still don't like it."

Now that her mission was accomplished, Jill felt free to examine the room. She wandered around a bit, sipping her champagne. The young man playing the piano caught her attention. He was good. Very good. After five years of lessons herself, Jill knew talent when she heard it. She walked over to the baby grand to compliment the pianist, and they chatted briefly about music until she saw Jordan looking for her. Jill excused herself; their meal was about to be served.

Dinner was delicious. Jill was seated beside Jordan, who was busy carrying on a conversation with a stately-looking gentleman on his other side. The man on her right, a distinguished gentleman in his mid-sixties, introduced himself as Andrew Howard. Although he didn't acknowledge it in so many words, Jill knew he was the president of Howard Pharmaceuticals, now retired. Jill pointed out that PayRite Pharmacy, where she worked, carried a number of his company's medications, and the two of them were quickly engaged in a lengthy conversation. By the time dessert was served Jill felt as comfortable with Mr. Howard as if she'd known him all her life.

Following a glass of brandy, Jordan seemed ready to leave.

"Thank you so much," she told Mr. Howard as she slid back her chair. "I enjoyed our conversation immensely."

He stood with her and clasped her hand warmly. "I did, too. If you don't mind, I'd like to keep in touch."

Jill smiled. "I'd enjoy that. And thank you for the invitation."

Then she and Jordan exchanged good-nights with her dinner companion and headed for the elevator. Jordan didn't speak until they were inside.

"What was all that with Howard?"

"Nothing. He invited me out to see his home. Apparently it's something of a showplace."

"He's a bit old for you, don't you think?"

Jill gave him an incredulous look. "Don't be ridiculous.

He assumed you and I knew each other. He just wanted me to feel welcome." She didn't mention that Jordan had spent the entire dinner talking with a business associate. He seemed to have all but forgotten she was with him.

"Howard invited you to his home?"

"Us, actually. You can make your excuses if you want, but I'd really like to take him up on his offer."

"Andrew Howard and my father were good friends. My father passed away several years back, and Howard likes to keep track of the projects I'm involved with. He's gone in on the occasional deal."

"He's a sweet man. Did you know he lost his only son to cancer? It's the reason his company's done so much in the field of cancer research. His son's death changed his life."

"I had no idea." Jordan was obviously astounded that he'd known Andrew Howard for so many years and hadn't realized he'd lost a child. "You learned this over dinner?"

"Good grief, dinner lasted nearly two hours." She sighed deeply and pressed her hands to her stomach. "I'm stuffed. I'll never sleep unless I walk off some of this food."

"It would've helped if you hadn't eaten half the hors d'oeuvres all by yourself."

Jill decided to ignore that comment.

"Do you mind if I join you?" Jordan surprised her by asking.

"Not in the least, as long as you promise not to make any more remarks about hors d'oeuvres. *Or* lecture me about the dangers of swimming at night."

Jordan grinned. "You've got yourself a deal."

They walked through the lobby and out of the hotel toward the beach. The surf thundered against the shore, slapping the sand, then retreating. Jill found the rhythmic sounds relaxing.

"What sort of project do you have planned for Hawaii?" she asked after a few minutes.

"A shopping complex."

Although he'd answered her question, his expression was preoccupied. "Why the frown?" she asked.

He shot a quick glance her way. "The Lundquists seem to have some sort of hidden agenda," he said.

"You said Daddy's grooming Junior to take your place," Jill prompted.

"It looks like I'm headed for a proxy fight, which is an expensive and costly proposition for everyone involved. For now, I have the controlling interest, but by no means do I have control."

"This trip to Hawaii?"

"Is strictly business. I just wish I knew what's going on behind my back."

"Good luck with it." This was a world far removed from Jill's.

"Thanks." He grinned and suddenly seemed to leave his worries behind.

They strolled for several minutes in companionable silence. The breeze was warm, the moon full and bright, and the rhythm of the ocean waves went on and on.

"I suppose I should go back," Jill said reluctantly. She had a full day planned, beginning first thing in the morning, and although she didn't feel the least bit tired, she knew she should get some sleep.

"Me, too."

They altered their meandering course in the direction of the hotel, their shoes sinking into the moist sand.

"Thanks for your help with Suzi Lundquist."

"Anytime. Just say the word and I'll be there, especially if there's caviar involved." She felt guilty, however, about the young and vulnerable Suzi. Jordan had been gentle with her; nevertheless, Jill's sympathy went out to the girl. "I feel kind of bad for Suzi."

Jordan sighed. "The girl just won't take no for an answer."

"Do you?"

"What do you mean?"

Jill stopped a moment to collect her thoughts. "I don't understand finance, but it seems to me that you'd never get anywhere if you quit at the first stumbling block. Suzi takes after her father and brother. She saw what she wanted and went after it. Rather an admirable trait, I guess. I suspect you haven't seen the last of her."

"Probably not, but I won't be here for more than a few days. I should be able to avoid her during that time."

"Good luck," she said again. She hesitated when they reached the pathway, bordered by vivid flowering shrubs, that led to the huge lighted swimming pool.

Jordan grinned. "I have a feeling I'm going to need it."

The night couldn't have been more perfect. It seemed such a shame to waste these romantic moments, but Jill finally forced herself to murmur good-night.

"Here," Jordan said just as she did.

Jill was startled when he presented her with a single lavender orchid. "What's this for?"

"In appreciation for all your help."

"Actually, I should be the one thanking you. I had a wonderful evening." It sure beat sitting in front of her television and ordering dinner from room service, which was what she'd planned. She held the flower under her nose and breathed in its delicate scent.

"Enjoy your stay in Hawaii."

"Thank you, I will." Her itinerary was full nearly every day. "I might even see you...around the hotel."

"Don't count on it. I'm headed back to Seattle in two days."

"Goodbye, then."

"Goodbye."

Neither moved. Jill didn't understand why. They'd said their good-nights—there seemed nothing left to say. It was time to leave. Time for her to return to her room and sleep off the effects of an exceptionally long day.

She made a decisive movement, but before she could turn away, his hand at her shoulder stopped her. Jill's troubled eyes met his. "Jordan?"

He caught her chin, his touch light but firm.

"Yes?" she whispered, her heart in her throat.

"Nothing." He dropped his hand.

Jill was about to turn away again when he stepped toward her, took her by the shoulders and kissed her. Jill had certainly been kissed before, and the experience had always been pleasant, if a bit predictable.

Not this time.

Exciting, unfamiliar sensations raced through her. Jordan's mouth caressed hers with practiced ease while his hands roved her back, moving slowly, confidently.

Jill was breathless and weak when he finally broke away. He stared down at her with a perplexed look, as if he'd shocked himself by kissing her. As if he didn't know what had come over him.

Jill didn't know, either. There was a sinking feeling in

the pit of her stomach, and then she remembered something Shelly had told her—the overwhelming sensation she'd experienced the first time Mark had kissed her. From that moment on, Shelly had known her fate was sealed.

Jill had never felt anything that even came close to what she'd just felt in Jordan's arms. Was it possible? *Could* there be something magical about Aunt Milly's wedding dress? Jill didn't know. She didn't want to find out, either.

"Jill?"

"Oh, no," she moaned as she looked up at him.

"Oh, no," Jordan echoed, apparently amused. "I'll admit women have reacted when I've kissed them, but no one's ever said that."

She barely heard him.

"What's wrong?"

"The dress…" Jill stopped herself in time.

"What dress?"

Jill knew she wasn't making any sense. The whole thing was ridiculous. Unbelievable.

"What dress?" he repeated.

"You wouldn't understand." She had no intention of explaining it to him. She could just imagine what someone like Jordan Wilcox would say when he heard about Aunt Milly's wedding dress.

Three

Jill glared at Jordan. He had no idea how devastating she'd found his kiss. And the worst of it was, *she* had no idea why she was feeling this way.

"Jill?" he said, eyeing her suspiciously. "What does my kissing you have to do with a dress?"

She squeezed her eyes shut, then opened them. "It doesn't have anything to do with it," she blurted without thinking, then quickly corrected herself. "It's got everything to do with it." She knew she was overreacting, but she couldn't seem to help herself. All he'd done was kiss her! There was no reason to behave like a fool. She had a good excuse, however. It had been a long and unusual day compounded by Shelly's letter and the arrival of the wedding dress. Who *wouldn't* be flustered? Who wouldn't be confused—especially in light of Shelly's experience?

"You're not being too clear," Jordan told her.

"I know. I'm sorry."

"What dress are you talking about?" he asked patiently. "Could you explain yourself?"

Jill didn't see how that was possible. Jordan wouldn't understand. Not only that, he was cynical and scornful. The man who placed power and profit above all else would laugh at something as absurd as the story about the wedding dress.

She drew in an unsteady breath. "There's nothing I can say."

"Was my kiss so repugnant to you?" It didn't appear that he was going to graciously drop the matter, not when his male ego was on the line.

Forcing her voice to sound carefree, Jill placed a hand on his shoulder and looked him square in the eye. "I'd think a man of your experience would be accustomed to having women crumple at his feet."

"Don't be ridiculous." His habitual frown snapped into place.

"I'm not," she said. Best to keep Jordan in the dark, otherwise he might misread her intentions. Besides, he wouldn't be any more enthusiastic about a romance between them than she was. "The kiss was very nice," she admitted grudgingly.

"And that's bad?" He rubbed a frustrated hand along his blunt, determined-looking jaw. "Perhaps you'll feel better once you're back in your room."

Jill nodded eagerly. "Thank you. For dinner," she added, remembering her manners.

"Thank you for joining me. It was…a pleasure meeting you."

"You, too."

"I probably won't see you again."

"That's right," she agreed resolutely. No reason to tempt fate. She was beginning to like him and that could be dangerous. "You'll be gone in a couple of days, won't you? I'm here for the week." She retreated a couple of steps. "Have a safe trip home, and don't work too hard."

They parted then, but before she walked into the hotel, Jill turned back to see Jordan strolling in the opposite direction, away from her.

Jill awoke late the following morning. It was rare for her to sleep past eight-thirty, even on weekends. The tour bus wasn't scheduled to leave the hotel until ten, so she took her time showering and dressing. Breakfast consisted of coffee, an English muffin and slices of fresh pineapple, which she ate leisurely on her lanai, savoring the morning sunlight.

Out of curiosity, she glanced over at Jordan's room to see if the drapes were open. They were. From what she could discern, he was sitting at a table near the window, talking on his phone and working with his computer.

Business. Business. Business.

The man lived and breathed it, just like her father had. And, in the end, it had killed him.

Dismissing Jordan from her thoughts, she collected her purse and hurried down to the lobby, where she was meeting the tour group.

The sightseeing expedition proved excellent. Jill visited Pearl Harbor and the U.S.S. *Arizona* memorial and a huge shopping mall, returning to the hotel by three o'clock.

Her room was cool and inviting. Jill took a few minutes to examine the souvenirs she'd purchased, a shell lei and several colorful T-shirts. Then, with a good portion of the day still left to enjoy, she decided to spend the remaining afternoon hours lazing around the pool. Once again she glanced over at Jordan's room, her action almost involuntary. And once again she saw that he was on the phone. Jill wondered if he'd been talking since morning.

Changing into her bathing suit, a modest one-piece in a—what else—Hawaiian print, she carried her beach bag, complete with three different kinds of sunscreen, down to the swimming pool. With a large straw hat perched on her head and sunglasses protecting her eyes, she stretched out on a chaise longue to absorb the sun.

She hadn't been there more than fifteen minutes when a waiter approached carrying a dome-covered platter and a glass of champagne. "Ms. Morrison?"

"Yes?" Jill sat up abruptly, knocking her hat askew. "I…I didn't order anything," she said uncertainly as she reached up to straighten her hat.

"This was sent compliments of Mr. Wilcox."

"Oh." Jill wasn't sure what to say. She twisted around and, shading her eyes with her hand, looked up. Jordan was standing on his lanai. She waved, and he returned the gesture.

"If that will be all?" the waiter murmured, stepping away.

"Yes… Oh, just a moment." Jill scrambled in her beach bag for a tip, which she handed to the young man. He smiled his appreciation.

Curious, she balanced the glass of champagne as she lifted the lid—and nearly laughed out loud. Inside was a large array of crackers topped with caviar. She glanced up at Jordan a second time and blew him a kiss.

Something must have distracted him then. He turned away, and when Jill saw him again a few minutes later, he was pacing the lanai, phone in hand. She was convinced he'd completely forgotten about her. It was ironic, she mused, and really rather sad; here he was in paradise and he'd hardly ventured beyond his hotel room.

Jill drank her champagne and savored a few of the caviar-laden crackers, then decided she couldn't stand his attitude a minute longer. Packing up her things, she looped the towel around her neck and picked up the platter in one hand, her beach bag in the other. After that, she headed back inside the hotel. She knew she was breaking her promise to herself by seeking him out, but she couldn't stop herself.

Muttering under her breath, she took the elevator up to Jordan's floor, calculated which room was his and knocked boldly on the door.

A long moment passed before the door finally opened. Jordan, still talking on his phone, gestured her inside. He didn't so much as pause in his conversation, tossing dollar figures around as casually as other people talked about the weather.

Jill sat on the edge of his bed and crossed her legs, swinging her foot impatiently as Jordan strode back and forth across the carpet, seemingly oblivious to her presence.

"Listen, Rick, something's come up," he said, darting a look in her direction. "Give me a call in five minutes. Sure, sure, no problem. Five minutes. See if you can contact Raymond, get these numbers to him and call me back." He disconnected the line without a word of farewell, then glanced at Jill.

"Hello," he said.

"Hi," she returned, holding out the platter to offer him an hors d'oeuvre.

"No, thanks."

She took one herself and chewed it slowly. She could almost feel his irritation.

"Something I can do for you?"

"Yes," she stated calmly. "Sit down a minute."

"Sit down?"

She nodded, motioning toward the table. "I have a story to tell you."

"A story?" He didn't seem particularly charmed by the idea.

"Yes, and I promise it won't take longer than five minutes," she added pointedly.

He was obviously relieved that she intended to keep this short. "Go on."

"As I've mentioned before, I don't know a lot about the world of high finance. But I'm well aware that time has skyrocketed in value. I also realize that the value of any commodity depends on its availability."

"Does this story have a point?"

"Actually I haven't got to the story yet, but I will soon," she announced cheerfully.

"Can you do it in—" he paused to check his watch "—two and a half minutes?"

"I'll hurry," she promised, and drew a deep breath. "I was nine when my mother signed me up for piano lessons. I could hardly wait. The other kids dreaded having to practice, but not me. From the time I was in kindergarten, I loved to pound away at the old upright in our living room. My heart and soul went into making music. It was probably no coincidence that one of the first pieces I learned was 'Heart and Soul.' I hammered out those notes like machine-gun blasts. I overemphasized each crescendo, cherished each lingering note. Van Cliburn couldn't have finished a piece with more pizzazz than I did. My hands would fly into the air, then flutter gently to my lap."

"I noticed you standing by the piano at the dinner party. Are you a musician?"

"Nope. For all my theatrical talents, I had one serious shortcoming. I could never master the caesura—the rest."

"The rest?"

"You know, that little zigzag thingamajig on sheet music that instructs the player to do nothing."

"Nothing," he repeated slowly.

"My impatience was a disappointment to my mother. I'm sure I frustrated my piano teacher no end. As hard as she tried, she couldn't make me understand that music was always sweeter and more compelling after a rest."

"I see." His hands were buried deep in his pockets as he studied her.

If Jordan was as much like her father as she suspected, she doubted he really did understand. But she'd told him what she'd come to say. Mission accomplished. There wasn't any other reason to stay, so she got briskly to her feet and scooped up her beach bag.

"That's it?"

"That's it. Thank you for the caviar. It was a delightful surprise." With that she moved toward the door. "Just remember what I said about the rest," she said, glancing over her shoulder.

The phone pealed sharply and Jill grimaced. "Goodbye," she mouthed, grasping the doorknob.

The phone rang again. "Goodbye." Jordan hesitated. "Jill?"

"Yes?" The way he said her name seemed so urgent. She whirled around, hope surging in her heart. Perhaps he didn't intend to answer the phone!

It rang a third time, and Jordan's eyes, dark gray, smoky with indecision, traveled from Jill to the telephone.

"Yes?" she repeated.

"Nothing," he said harshly, reaching for the phone. "Thanks for the story."

"You're welcome." With nothing left to say, Jill walked out of his room and closed the door. Even before the lock slid into place she heard Jordan rhyming off lists of figures.

Her room felt less welcoming than when she'd returned earlier. Jill slipped out of her swimsuit and showered. She was vain enough to check her reflection in the mirror, hoping to have enhanced the slight tan she'd managed to achieve between Seattle's infamous June cloudbursts. It didn't look as though her sojourn in the tropics had done anything but add a not-so-fetching touch of pink across her shoulders.

She dressed in a thick terry robe supplied by the hotel and had just wrapped a towel around her wet hair when her phone rang.

"Hello," she said, breathlessly, sinking onto her bed. Her stomach knotted with anticipation.

"Jill Morrison?"

"Yes." It wasn't Jordan. But the voice sounded vaguely familiar, although she couldn't immediately place it.

"Andrew Howard. I sat next to you at the dinner party last night."

"Yes, of course." Her voice rose with pleasure. She'd thoroughly enjoyed her chat with the older man. "How are you?"

He chuckled. "I'm fine. I tried to phone earlier, but you were out and I didn't leave a message."

"I went on a tour this morning."

"Ah, that explains it. I realize it's rather short notice, but are you free for dinner tonight?"

Jill didn't hesitate. "Yes, I am."

"Good, good. Could you join me around eight?"

"Eight would be perfect." Normally Jill dined much earlier, but she wasn't hungry yet, thanks to an expensive snack, compliments of Jordan Wilcox.

"Wonderful." Mr. Howard seemed genuinely pleased. "I'll have a car waiting for you and Wilcox out front at seven-thirty."

And Wilcox. She'd almost missed the words. So Jordan had accepted Mr. Howard's invitation. Perhaps she'd been too critical; perhaps he'd understood the point of her story, after all, and was willing to put business aside for one evening. Perhaps he was as eager to spend time with her as she was with him.

"I wondered if you'd be here," Jordan announced when they met in the lobby at the appointed time. He didn't exactly greet her with open enthusiasm, but Jill comforted herself with the observation that Jordan wasn't one to reveal his emotions.

"I wouldn't miss this for the world," he added. That was when she remembered he was hoping to interest the older man in his shopping-mall project. Dinner, for Jordan, would be a golden opportunity to conduct business, elicit Mr. Howard's support and gain the financial backing he needed for the project.

Jill couldn't help feeling disappointed. "I'll do my best not to interrupt your sales pitch," she said sarcastically.

"My sales pitch?" he echoed, then grinned, apparently amused by her assumption. "You don't have to worry. Howard doesn't want in on this project, which is fine. He just likes to keep tabs on me, especially since Dad died. He seems to think I need a mentor, or at least some kind of paternal adviser."

"Do you?"

Jordan shrugged. "There've been one or two occasions when I've appreciated his wisdom. I don't need him holding my hand, but I have sometimes looked to him for advice."

Remembering her dinner conversation with the older man, Jill said, "In some ways, Mr. Howard must think of you as a son."

"I doubt that." Jordan scowled. "I've known him all this time and not once did he ever mention he'd lost a son."

"It was almost thirty years ago, and as I told you, it's the reason his company's done so much cancer research. Howard Pharmaceuticals makes several of the leading cancer-fighting drugs." When Andrew Howard had told her about his son's death, a tear had come to his eye. Although Jeff Howard had succumbed to childhood leukemia a long time ago, his father still grieved. Andrew had become a widower a few years later, and he'd never fully recovered from the double blow. Jill was deeply touched by his story. During their conversation, she'd shared a little of the pain she'd felt at her own father's death, something she rarely did, even with her mother or her closest friend.

"What shocks me," Jordan continued, "is that I've worked on different projects with him over the years. We've also kept in touch socially. And not once, *not once,* did he mention a son."

"Perhaps there was never a reason."

Jordan dismissed that idea with a shake of his head.

"Mr. Howard's a sweet man. I really like him," Jill asserted.

"Sweet? Andrew Howard?" Jordan grinned, his eyes

bright with humor. "I've known alligators with more agreeable personalities."

"Apparently there's more to your friend than you realized."

"My friend," Jordan repeated. "Funny, I'd always thought of him as my father's friend, not mine. But you're right—he *is* my friend and— Oh, here's the car." With a hand on her arm, he escorted her outside.

A tall, uniformed driver stepped from the long white limousine. "Ms. Morrison and Mr. Wilcox?" he asked crisply.

Jordan nodded, and the chauffeur ceremoniously opened the back door for them. Soon they were heading out of the city toward the island's opposite coast.

"Do you still play the piano?" Jordan asked unexpectedly.

"Every so often, when the mood strikes me," Jill told him a bit ruefully. "Not as much as I'd like."

"I take it you still haven't conquered the caesura?"

"Not yet, but I'm learning." She wasn't sure what had prompted his question, then decided to ask one of her own. "What about you? Do you think you might be interested in learning to play the piano?"

Jordan shook his head adamantly. "Unfortunately, I've never had much interest in that sort of thing."

Jill sighed and looked away.

Nearly thirty minutes passed before they reached Andrew Howard's oceanside estate. Jill suspected it was the longest Jordan had gone without a business conversation since he'd registered at the hotel.

Her heart pounded as they approached the beautifully landscaped grounds. A security guard pushed a button that opened a huge wrought-iron gate. They drove down a private road, nearly a mile long and bordered on each side by rolling green lawns and tropical flower beds. At the end stood a sprawling stone house.

No sooner had the car stopped than Mr. Howard hurried out of the house, grinning broadly.

"Welcome, welcome!" He greeted them expansively, holding out his arms to Jill.

In a spontaneous display of affection, she hugged him and kissed his cheek. "Thank you so much for inviting us."

"The pleasure's all mine. Come inside. Everything's ready and waiting." After exchanging a hearty handshake with Jordan, Mr. Howard led the way into his home.

Jill had been impressed with the outside, but the beauty of the interior overwhelmed her. The entry was tiled in white marble and illuminated by a sparkling crystal chandelier. Huge crystal vases of vivid pink and purple hibiscus added color and life. From there, Mr. Howard escorted them into a massive living room with floor-to-ceiling windows that overlooked the Pacific. Frothing waves crashed against the shore, bathed in the fire of an island sunset.

"This is so lovely," Jill breathed in awe.

"I knew you'd appreciate it." Mr. Howard reached for a bell, which he rang once. Almost immediately the house-keeper appeared, carrying a tray of glasses and bottles of white and red wine, sherry and assorted aperitifs.

They were sipping their drinks when the same woman reappeared. "Mr. Wilcox, there's a phone call for you."

It was all Jill could do not to gnash her teeth. The man was never free, the phone cord wrapped around his neck more tightly than a hangman's noose.

"Excuse me, please," Jordan said as he left the room, his step brisk.

Jill looked away, refusing to watch him go.

"How do you feel about that young man?" Mr. Howard asked bluntly when Jordan was gone.

"We met only recently. I—I don't have any feelings for him one way or the other."

"Well, then, what do you think of him?"

Jill stared down at her wine. "He works too hard."

Sighing, the old man nodded and rubbed his eyes. "He reminds me of myself more than thirty years ago. Sometimes I'd like to take him by the shoulders and shake some sense into him, but I doubt it'd do much good. That boy's too stubborn to listen. Unfortunately, he's a lot like his father."

Knowing so little of Jordan and his background, Jill was eager to learn what she could. At the same time, a saner part of her insisted she was better off not hearing this. The more she knew, the greater her chances of caring.

Nevertheless, Jill found herself asking curiously, "What made Jordan the way he is?"

"To begin with, his parents divorced when he was young. It was a sad situation." Andrew leaned forward and clasped his wineglass with both hands. "It was plain as the nose on your face that James and Donna Wilcox were in love. But, somehow, bitterness replaced the love, and their son became a weapon they used against each other."

"Oh, how sad." Just as she'd feared, Jill felt herself sympathizing with Jordan.

"They both married other people, and Jordan seemed to remind his parents of their earlier unhappiness. He was sent to the best boarding schools, but there was precious little love in his life. Before he died, James tried to build a relationship with his son, but..." He shrugged. "And to the best of my knowledge his mother hasn't seen him since he was a teenager. I'm afraid he's had very little experience of real love, the kind that gives life meaning. Oh, there've been women, plenty of them, but never one who could teach him how to love and bring joy into his life—until now." He paused and looked pointedly at Jill.

"As I said before, I've only known Jordan for a short time."

"Be patient with him," Mr. Howard continued, as though Jill hadn't spoken. "Jordan's talented, don't get me wrong— the boy's got a way of pulling a deal together that amazes just about everyone—but there are times when he seems to forget about human values, like compassion. And the ability to enjoy what you have."

Jill wasn't sure how to respond.

"Frankly, I was beginning to lose faith in him," Mr. Howard said, grinning sheepishly. "He can be hard and unforgiving. You've given me the first ray of hope."

Jill took a big swallow of wine.

"He needs you. Your warmth, your gentleness, your love."

Jill wanted to weep with frustration. Andrew Howard was telling her exactly what she didn't want to hear. "I think you're mistaken," she murmured.

He chuckled. "I doubt that, but I'm an old man, so indulge me, will you?"

"Of course, but—"

"There's a reason you've come into his life," he said, gazing intently at her. "A very important reason." Andrew closed his eyes. "I feel this more profoundly than I've felt anything in a long while. He needs you, Jill."

"No...I'm sure he doesn't." Jill realized she was beginning to sound desperate, but she couldn't help it.

The old man's eyes opened slowly and he smiled. "And

I'm just as sure he does." He would have continued, but Jordan returned to the room then.

From the marinated-shrimp appetizer to the homemade mango-and-pineapple ice cream, dinner was one of the most delectable, elegant meals Jill had ever tasted. They lingered over coffee, followed by a glass of smooth brandy. By the end of the evening, Jill felt mellow and warm, a dangerous sensation. Jordan had been wonderful company—witty, charming, fun. He seemed more relaxed, too. Apparently the phone call had brought good news; it was the only thing to which she could attribute his cheerfulness.

"I can't thank you enough," she told Andrew when the limousine arrived to drive her and Jordan back to the hotel. "It was a lovely evening."

The older man hugged Jill and whispered close to her ear, "Remember what I said." Breaking away, he extended his hand, gripping Jordan's elbow. "It was good of you to come."

"I'll be in touch soon," Jordan promised.

"I'll look forward to hearing from you. Let me know what happens with this shopping-mall project."

"I will," Jordan said.

The car was cool and inviting in the warm night. Before she realized it, Jill found her head resting on Jordan's broad shoulder. "Oh, sorry," she mumbled through a yawn.

"Are you sleepy?"

She smiled softly to herself, too tired to fight the power of attraction—and exhaustion. "Maybe a little. Wine makes me sleepy."

Jordan pressed her head against his shoulder and held her there. His hand gently stroked her hair. "Do you mind telling me what went on between you and Howard while I was on the phone?"

Jill went stock-still. "Uh, nothing. What makes you ask?" She decided it was best to pretend she didn't know what he was talking about.

"Then why was Howard wearing a silly grin every time he looked at me?" Jordan demanded.

"I—I don't know. You'll have to ask him." She tried to straighten, but Jordan wouldn't allow it. After a moment she gave up, too relaxed to put up much of a struggle.

"I swear there was a twinkle in his eye from the moment I returned after my phone call. It was like I'd been left out of a joke."

"I'm sure you're wrong."

Jordan seemed to ponder that. "I doubt it," he said.

"Hmm." She felt sleepy, and leaning against Jordan was strangely comforting.

"I've been thinking about what you said this afternoon," he told her a few minutes later. His mouth was against her ear, and although she might have been mistaken, she thought his lips lightly brushed her cheek.

"My sad but true tale," she whispered on the end of another yawn.

"About your trouble with the musical rest."

"Ah, yes, the rest."

"I'm flying back to Seattle tomorrow," Jordan said abruptly.

Jill nodded, feeling inexplicably sad, then surprised by the intensity of her reaction. With Jordan in Seattle, they wouldn't be bumping into each other at every turn. Wouldn't be arguing, bantering—or kissing. With Jordan in Seattle, she wouldn't confuse him with the legacy behind Aunt Milly's dress. "Well...I hope you have a good flight."

"I have a meeting Tuesday morning. It would be impossible to cancel at this late date, but I was able to change my flight."

"You changed your flight?" Jill prayed he wouldn't hear the breathless catch in her voice.

"I don't have to be at the airport until evening."

"When?" It shouldn't make any difference to her, yet she found herself wanting to know. Needing to know.

"Eight."

Jill was much too dazed to calculate the time difference, but she knew it meant he'd arrive in Seattle in the early morning. He'd be exhausted. Not exactly the best way to show up at a high-powered meeting.

"I was thinking," Jordan continued. "I've been to Hawaii a number of times but other than meetings or dinner engagements, I haven't seen much of the islands. I've never explored them."

"That's a pity," she said, meaning it.

"And," he went on, "it seemed to me that sightseeing wouldn't be nearly as much fun alone."

"I enjoyed myself this morning." Her effort to refute him was feeble at best.

His fingers were entwined in her hair. "Will you come with me, Jill?" he asked, his voice a husky whisper. "Share the day with me. Let's discover Hawaii together."

Four

"I can't" was Jill's immediate response. She'd already lowered her guard—enough to be snuggling in his arms. So much for her resolve not to get involved with Jordan Wilcox, she thought with dismay. So much for steering a wide course around the man.

"Why not?" Jordan asked with the directness she'd come to expect from him.

"I've...m-made plans," she stammered. Even now, she could feel herself weakening. With his arm around her and her head nestled against his shoulder it was difficult to refuse him.

"Cancel them."

How arrogant of him to assume she should abandon her plans because the almighty businessman was willing to grant her some of his valuable time.

"I'm afraid I can't do that," she answered coolly, her determination reinforced. She'd already paid for the rental car as part of her vacation package, she rationalized, and she wasn't about to let that money go to waste.

"Why not?" He sounded surprised.

Isn't being with him what you really want? The question stole into her mind, and Jill wanted to scream out her response. A resounding NO. Jordan Wilcox frightened her. It was all too easy to envision them together, strolling hand in hand along sun-drenched beaches. He'd kissed her that first time, that only time, on the beach, and the memory stubbornly refused to go away.

"Jill?"

At the softness in his voice, she involuntarily raised her eyes to his. Jill hadn't expected to see tenderness in Jordan, but she did now, and it was nearly her undoing. Her feelings for him were changing, and she found herself more strongly attracted than ever. She remembered when she'd first seen him, the way she'd been convinced there was nothing gentle in him. He'd seemed so hard, so untouchable. Yet, right now, at this very moment, he'd made himself vulnerable to her. *For* her.

"You're trembling," he said, running his hands down her arms. "What's wrong?"

"Nothing," she denied quickly, breathlessly. "I'm…a little tired. It's been a long day."

"That's what you said last night when I kissed you. Remember? You started mumbling some nonsense about a dress, then you went stiff as a board on me."

"Nothing's wrong," she insisted, breaking away from him. She straightened and lowered her hand to her skirt, smoothing away imaginary creases.

"I don't buy that, Jill. Something's bothering you."

She wished he hadn't mentioned the dress, because it brought to mind, uninvited and unwanted, Aunt Milly's wedding dress, which was hanging in her hotel-room closet.

"You'd be shaking, too, if you knew the things I did," she exclaimed, instantly regretting the impulse.

"What are you afraid of?"

She stared out the window, then slowly her lower lip began to quiver with the effort to restrain her laughter. She was actually frightened of a silly dress! She wasn't afraid to fall in love; she just didn't want it to be with Jordan.

"For a woman who drags a wedding dress on vacation with her, you're not doing very much to encourage romance."

"I did not bring that dress with me!"

"It was in the room when you arrived? Someone left it behind?"

"Not exactly. Shelly did. She, uh, enjoys a good laugh. She mailed it to me."

"It never occurred to me that you might be engaged," he said slowly. "You're not, are you?"

"No." But according to her friend, she soon would be.

"Who's Shelly?"

"My best friend," Jill explained, "or at least she used to be." Then, impulsively, her heart racing, she added, "Listen, Jordan, I think you have a lot of potential in the husband category, but I can't fall in love with you. I just can't."

A stunned silence followed her announcement.

He cocked his eyebrows. "Aren't you taking a bit too much for granted here? I asked you to explore the island with me, not bear my children."

She'd done it again, blurted out something totally illogical. Worse, she couldn't make herself stop. Children were a subject near and dear to her heart.

"That's another thing," she wailed. "I bet you don't even like children. No, I can't go with you tomorrow. Please don't ask me to…because it's so hard to say no." It must be the wine, Jill decided; she was saying far more than she should.

Jordan relaxed against the leather upholstery and crossed his long legs. "All right, if you'd rather not go, I'm certainly not going to force you."

His easy acceptance astonished her. She glanced at him out of the corner of her eye, feeling almost disappointed that he wasn't trying to persuade her.

Something was drastically, dangerously wrong with her. She was beginning to like Jordan, really like him. Yet she couldn't allow this attraction to continue. She couldn't allow herself to fall in love with a man so much like her father. Because she knew what that meant, what kind of life it led to, what kind of unhappiness it caused.

When the limousine stopped in front of the hotel, it was all Jill could do to wait for the chauffeur to climb out of the driver's seat, walk around the car and open the door for her.

She hurried inside the lobby, needing to breathe in the fresh air of reason. Wait for sanity to catch up with her heart.

She reached the elevators and pushed the button, holding her thumb in place, hoping that would hurry it along.

"Next time, keep your little anecdotes to yourself," Jordan said sharply from behind her. Then he walked leisurely across the lobby.

Keep her little anecdotes to herself? The temptation to rush after him and demand an explanation was strong, but Jill made herself resist it.

Not until she was in the elevator did she understand. This entire discussion had arisen because she'd told him her story about the caesura and her lack of musical talent. And now he was turning her own disclosure against her! Righteous anger began to build in her heart.

But by the time Jill was in her room and ready for bed, she felt wretched. Jordan had asked her to spend a day with him, and she'd reacted as if he'd insulted her.

The way she'd gone on and on about his potential as a husband was bad enough, but then she'd dragged the subject of children into their conversation. That mortified her even more. The wine could be blamed for only so much.

She cringed, too, as she recalled what Andrew Howard had said, the faith he'd placed in her. Jordan needed her, he'd said, apparently convinced that Jordan would never experience love if she didn't teach him. She hated disappointing Andrew, and yet...and yet...

It didn't surprise Jill that she slept poorly. By morning she wasn't feeling any enthusiam at all about picking up her rental car or sightseeing on the north shore.

She reviewed the room-service menu, ordered coffee and toast, then stared at the phone for several minutes before conceding there was one thing she still had to do. Anxious to get it over with, Jill rang through to Jordan's room.

"Hello," he answered gruffly on the first ring. He was definitely a man who never ventured far from his phone.

"Hello," she said with uncharacteristic meekness. "I'm... calling to apologize."

"Are you sorry enough to change your mind and spend the day with me?"

Jill hesitated. "I've already paid for a rental car."

"Great, then I won't need to get one."

Jill closed her eyes. She knew what she was going to say, had known it the night before. In the same heartbeat, she realized she'd regret it later. "Yes," she whispered. "If you still want me to join you, I'll meet you in the lobby in half an hour."

"Twenty minutes."

She groaned. "Fine, twenty minutes, then."

Despite her misgivings, Jill's spirits lifted immediately. "One day won't hurt anything," she said out loud. What could possibly happen in so short a time? Certainly nothing earth-shattering. Nothing of consequence.

Who was she kidding? Not herself, Jill admitted.

She thought she understood why moths ventured close to the fire, enticed by the light and the warmth. Against her will, Jordan was drawing her dangerously close. She knew even as she came nearer that she was going to get burned. And yet she didn't walk away.

He was waiting for her when she stepped out of the elevator and into the lobby. He stood there grinning, his look almost boyish. This was the first time she'd seen him without a business suit. Instead, he wore white slacks and a pale blue shirt with the sleeves rolled up.

"You ready?" he asked, taking her beach bag from her.

"One question." Her heart was pounding because she had no right to ask.

"Sure." His eyes held hers.

"Your cell phone—do you have it?"

Jordan nodded and pulled a tiny phone from his shirt pocket.

Jill stared at it for a moment, feeling the tension work its way down her back. Jordan's cell phone reminded her of the pager her father had always carried. Always. All family outings, which were few and far between, had been subject to outside interference. Early in life, Jill had received a clear message: business was more important to her father than she was. In fact, almost everything had seemed more significant than spending time with the people who loved him.

Jordan must have read the look in her eyes because he said, "I'll leave it in my room," and then promptly strolled to the elevator. Stunned, Jill watched as he stepped inside. Bit by bit, her muscles began to relax.

While he was gone, Jill filled out the paperwork for the rental car. She was waiting outside by the economy model when Jordan appeared. He paused, staring at it with narrowed eyes as if he wasn't sure the car would make it to the end of the street, let alone around the island.

"I'm on a limited budget," Jill explained, hiding a smile. The car suited her petite frame perfectly, but for a man of Jordan's stature it was like…like stuffing a rag doll inside a pickle jar, Jill thought, enjoying the whimsical comparison.

"You're positive this thing runs?" he muttered under his breath as he climbed into the driver's seat. His long legs were cramped below the steering wheel, his head practically touching the roof.

Jill nodded. She remembered reading that this particular model got exceptionally good gas mileage—but then it should, with an engine only a little bigger than a lawnmower's.

To prove her right, the car roared to life with a flick of the key.

"Where are we going?" Jill asked once they'd merged with the flow of traffic on the busy thoroughfare by the hotel.

"The airport."

"The airport?" she repeated, struggling to hide her disappointment. "I thought your flight didn't leave until eight."

"Mine doesn't, but ours takes off in half an hour."

"Ours?" What about the sugarcane fields and watching

the workers harvest pineapple? Surely he didn't intend for them to miss that. "Where is this plane taking us?"

"Hawaii," he announced casually. "The island of. Do you know how to scuba dive?"

"No." Her voice was oddly breathless and high-pitched. She might have spent the past twenty-odd years in Seattle—practically surrounded by water—but she wasn't all that comfortable *under* it.

"How about snorkeling?"

"Ah…" She jerked her thumb over her shoulder. "There are pineapple fields on the other side of this island. I assumed you'd want to see those."

"Another visit, perhaps. I'd like to try my hand at marlin fishing, too, but we don't have enough time today."

"Snorkeling," Jill said as though she'd never heard the word before. "Well…it might be fun." In her guidebook Jill remembered reading about green beaches of crushed olivine crystals and black sands of soft lava. These were sights she couldn't expect to find anywhere else. However, she wasn't sure she wanted to view them through a rubber mask.

A small private plane was ready for them when they arrived at Honolulu Airport. The pilot, who apparently knew Jordan, greeted them cordially. After brief introductions and a few minutes' chat, they were on their way.

Another car, considerably larger than the one Jill had rented, was waiting for them on the island of Hawaii. A large, white wicker picnic basket sat in the middle of the backseat.

"I hope you're hungry."

"Not yet."

"You will be," Jordan promised.

He drove for half an hour or so, until they reached a

deserted inlet with a magnificent waterfall. He parked the car, then got out and opened the trunk. Inside was everything they'd need for snorkeling in the crystal-clear aquamarine waters.

Never having done this before, Jill was uncertain of the procedure. Jordan patiently answered her questions and waded into the water with her. He paused when they were waist-deep, gave her detailed instructions, then clasped her hand. His touch lent her confidence, and soon she was investigating an undersea world of breathtaking beauty. Swimming out of the inlet, they came upon a reef, with colorful fish slipping in and out of white coral caverns. After what seemed like only minutes, Jordan steered them back toward the inlet and shore.

"I don't think I've ever seen anything more beautiful," she breathed, pushing the mask from her face.

"I don't think I have, either," he agreed as they emerged from the water.

While Jill ran a comb through her hair and put on a shirt to protect her shoulders from the sun, Jordan brought out their lunch.

He spread the blanket in the shade of a palm tree. Jill knelt down beside him and opened the basket. Inside were generous crab-salad sandwiches, fresh slices of papaya and pineapple and thick chocolate-chip cookies. She removed two cold cans of soda and handed one to Jordan.

They ate, then napped with a cool, gentle breeze whisking over them.

Jill awoke before Jordan. He was asleep on his back with his hand thrown carelessly across his face, shading his eyes from the glare of the sun. His features were more relaxed than she'd ever seen them. Jill studied him for several minutes, her heart aching for the man she'd loved so long ago. Her father. The man she'd never really had a chance to know. In some ways, Jordan was so much like her father it pained her to be with him, and at the same time it thrilled her. Not only because in learning about Jordan she was discovering a part of her past, of herself, but because she'd rarely felt so *alive* in anyone's company.

As she recognized this truth, a heaviness settled over her. She didn't *want* to fall in love with him. She was so afraid her life would mirror her mother's. Elaine Morrison had grown embittered. She'd been a young woman when her husband died, but she'd never remarried; instead she'd closed herself off, not wanting to risk the kind of pain that loving Jill's father had brought her.

Sitting up, Jill shoved her now-dry hair away from her face. She wrapped her arms around her bent legs and pressed her forehead to her knees, gulping in breath after breath.

"Jill?" His voice was soft. Husky.

"You shouldn't have left your pager behind, after all," she told him, her voice tight. "Or your phone." Without them, he was a handsome, compelling man who appealed to all her senses. Without them, she was defenseless against his charm.

"Why not?"

"Because I like you too much."

"That's a problem?"

"Yes!" she cried. "Don't you understand?"

"Obviously not," he said with such tenderness she wanted to jump to her feet and yell at him to stop. "Maybe you'd better explain it to me," he added.

"I can't," she whispered, keeping her head lowered.

"You'd never believe me. I don't blame you—I wouldn't believe me, either."

Jordan frowned. "Does this have something to do with your reaction the first time I kissed you?"

"The only time!"

"That's about to change."

Her head shot up at the casual way in which he said it, as though kissing her was a foregone conclusion.

He was right.

His kiss was gentle. Jill resisted, unwilling to give him her heart, knowing what became of women who loved men like this. Men like Jordan Wilcox.

Their kiss now was much more potent than that first night. His touch somehow transcended the sensual. Jill could think of no other words to describe it. His fingers brushed her temple. His lips moved across her face, grazing her chin, her cheek, her eyes. She moaned, not from pleasure, but from fear, from a pain that reached deep inside her.

"Oh, no…"

"It's happening again, isn't it?" he whispered.

She nodded. "Can you feel it?"

"Yes. I did the other time, too."

Her eyes drifted slowly open. "I can't love you."

"So you've told me. More than once."

"It isn't personal." She tried to break free without being obvious about it, but Jordan held her firmly in his embrace.

"Tell me what's upsetting you so much."

"I can't." Looking into the distance, she focused on the smoky-blue outline of a mountain. Anything to avoid gazing at Jordan.

"You're involved with someone else, aren't you?"

It would be so easy to lie to him. To tell him about Ralph

as though the friendship they shared was one of blazing passion, but she found she couldn't do it.

"No," she wailed, "but I wish I was."

"Why?" he demanded gruffly.

"What about you?" she countered. "Why did you seek out my company? Why'd you ask me to attend the dinner party with you? Surely there was someone else, someone more suitable."

"I'll admit that kissing you is a...unique experience," he confessed.

"But I've been rude."

"Actually, more amusing than rude."

"But why?" she asked again. "What is it about me that interests you? We're about as different as two people can get. We're strangers—strangers with nothing in common."

Jordan was frowning, his eyes revealing his own lack of understanding. "I don't know."

"See what I mean?" She spoke as if it were the jury's final decree. "The whole thing is a farce. You kiss me and...and I feel a certain...feeling."

"So do I. And it's something I can't explain. But I've seen electrical storms that unleash less energy than we did when we kissed."

Suddenly Jill found it nearly impossible to breathe. Jordan couldn't be affected by the wedding dress and its so-called magic—could he? Jill swore the minute she arrived in Seattle she was returning it to Shelly and Mark. She wasn't taking any chances.

"You remind me of my father," Jill said, refusing to meet his eyes. Even talking about Adam Morrison was painful to her. "He was always in a hurry to get somewhere, to meet someone, to make a deal. We took a family vacation when

I was ten. My dad, my mom and me. We saw California in one day, Disneyland in an hour. Do you get the picture?" She didn't wait for a response. "He died of a heart attack when I was fifteen. We were wealthy by a lot of people's standards, and after his death my mother didn't have to work. We had no financial worries at all. And yet we would've been happier with far less money if it meant my father was still alive."

An awkward moment passed. When Jordan didn't comment, Jill glanced at him. "You don't have anything to say?"

"Not really, other than to point out that I'm not your father."

"But you're exactly like him! I recognized it the first minute I saw you." She leaped to her feet, grabbed her towel and crammed it into her beach bag.

Jordan reluctantly stood, and while she shook the sand off the blanket and folded it, he loaded their snorkeling gear into the trunk of the car.

They were both quiet during the drive back to the airport, the silence strained and unnatural. A couple of times, Jill looked in Jordan's direction. The hardness was back. The tightness in his jaw, the harsh, almost grim expression...

Jill could well imagine what he'd be like in a board meeting. No wonder he didn't seem too concerned about the threat of a takeover. He would withstand that, and a whole lot more, in the years to come. But at what price? Power demanded sacrifice; prestige didn't come cheap. There was a cost, and Jill could only speculate what it would be for Jordan. His health? His happiness?

She found it intolerable to think about. Words burned in her heart. Words of caution. Words of appeal, but he wouldn't listen to her any more than her father had heeded her mother's tearful pleas.

As the airport came into view, Jill knew she couldn't let their day end on such an unhappy note. "I did have a wonderful time. Thank you."

"Mmm," he replied, his gaze focused on the road ahead.

Jill stared at him. "That's it?"

"What else do you want me to say?" His voice was crisp and emotionless.

"Like, I don't know, that you enjoyed yourself, too."

"It was interesting."

"Interesting?" Jill repeated.

They'd had a marvelous adventure! Not only that, he'd actually *relaxed*. The lines of fatigue around his eyes were gone. She'd bet a month's wages that this was the first afternoon nap he'd had in years. Possibly decades. It was probably the longest stretch of time he'd been away from a telephone in his adult life.

And all he'd say was that their day had been "interesting"?

"What about the kissing?" she demanded. "Was *that* interesting?"

"Very."

Jill seethed silently. "It was…interesting for me, too."

"So you said."

Jill tucked a long strand of hair behind her ear. "I was only being honest with you."

"I admit it was a fresh approach. Do you generally discuss marriage and children with a man on a first date?"

Color exploded in her cheeks, and she looked uncomfortably away. "No, but you were different…and it wasn't an approach."

"Excuse me, that's right, you were being honest." The cold sarcasm in his voice kept her from even trying to explain.

They'd almost reached the airport when she spoke again. "Would you do me one small favor?" She nearly choked on the pride she had to swallow.

"What?"

"Would you... The next time you see Mr. Howard, would you tell him something for me? Would you tell him I'm sorry?" He'd be disappointed in her, but Jill couldn't risk her own happiness because a dear man with a romantic heart believed she was Jordan Wilcox's one chance at finding love.

Jordan stopped the car abruptly and turned to glare at her. "You want me to apologize to Howard?"

"Please."

"Sorry," he said without a pause. "You'll have to do that yourself."

Five

For days later, Jill stepped off the plane at Sea-Tac Airport in Seattle. Her skin glowed with a golden tan, accentuated by the bold pink flower print of her new sundress. She hadn't expected anyone to meet her, but was pleasantly surprised to see Shelly and Mark. Shelly waved excitedly when she located Jill in the baggage claim area.

"Welcome home," Shelly said as she rushed forward, exuberantly throwing her arms around Jill. "How was Hawaii? My goodness, your tan is gorgeous. You must've spent *hours* in the sun."

"Hawaii was wonderful." A slight exaggeration. She'd hardly slept since Jordan's departure.

"Tell me everything," Shelly insisted, taking Jill's hands. "I'm dying to find out who you met after we mailed you the wedding dress."

"Honey," Mark chided gently, "give her a chance to breathe."

"Are you with someone?" Shelly asked, looking around expectantly. "I mean, you know, you're not married, are you?"

"I'm not even close to being married," Jill informed her friend dryly.

Mark took charge of the beach bag Jill had brought home with her, stuffed full of souvenirs and everything she couldn't fit into her suitcase. She removed one of the three leis she was wearing and looped it around Shelly's neck. "Here, my gift to you."

"Oh, Jill, it's beautiful. Thank you," Shelly said, fingering the fragrant lei of pink orchids. As they walked toward the appropriate carousel, Shelly slipped her arm through Jill's. "I can't wait a second longer. Tell me what happened after the dress arrived. I want to hear every detail."

Jill had been dreading this moment, but she hadn't thought she'd face it quite so soon. "I'm afraid I'm going to have to return the dress."

Shelly stared at her as if she hadn't heard correctly. "Pardon?"

"I didn't meet anyone."

"You mean to tell me you spent seven days in Hawaii and you didn't speak to a single man?" Shelly asked incredulously.

"Not exactly."

"Aha! So there was someone."

Jill tried not to groan. "Sort of."

Shelly smiled, sliding one arm around her husband's waist. "The plot thickens."

"I met him briefly the first day. Actually I don't think he counts...."

"Why wouldn't he count?" Shelly asked.

"We sat next to each other on the plane, so technically we met *before* I got the wedding dress. I'm sure he's not the one." Jill had decided to play along with her friend's theory, pretend to take it more seriously than she did. Logical objections, like this mistake in timing, *should* convince Shelly—but probably wouldn't.

"In fact," she continued, "I've been thinking about that dress lately, and I'm convinced you and your aunt Milly are wrong—it's not for me. It never was."

"But it fit you. Remember?"

Jill didn't need to be reminded. "That was a fluke. I'm sure if I were to try it on now, it wouldn't."

"Then try it on! Prove me wrong."

"Here?" Jill laughed.

"When you get home. Right now, just tell me about this guy you met. You keep trying to avoid the subject."

"There's nothing to tell," Jill insisted, sorry she'd said anything. She'd tried for the past few days to push every thought of Jordan from her mind, with little success. He'd haunted her remaining time on the islands, refusing to leave her alone. If she did sleep, he invaded her dreams.

"Start with his name," Shelly said. "Surely you know his name."

"Jordan Wilcox, but—"

"Jordan Wilcox," Mark repeated. "He doesn't happen to be a developer, does he?"

"He does something along those lines."

Mark released a low whistle. "He's one of the big boys."

"Big boys," Shelly echoed disparagingly. "Be more specific. Do you mean he's tall?"

"No." Mark's smiling eyes briefly met Jill's. "Although he is. I mean he's a well-known corporate giant. I've met him a few times. If I understand it correctly, he puts together commercial projects, finds backers for them, works with the designer and the builders, and when the project's complete, he sells. He's made millions in the last few years."

"He was in Hawaii to put together financial backing for a shopping mall," Jill explained.

"Well," Shelly said, eyeing her closely, "what did you think of him?"

"What was there to think? I sat next to him on the plane and we stayed in the same hotel, but that was about it." It was best not to mention the other incidents; Shelly would put far too much stock in a couple of dinners and a day on the beach. Heaven help Jill if Shelly ever found out they'd exchanged a few kisses!

"I'm sure he's the one," Shelly announced gleefully. Her eyes fairly sparkled with delight. "I can *feel* it. He's our man."

"No, he isn't," Jill argued, knowing it was futile, yet compelled to try. "I already told you—I met him *before* the dress arrived. Besides, we have absolutely nothing in common."

"Do Mark and I?" Shelly glanced lovingly at her husband. "And I'm crazy about him."

At first, Jill had wondered what Mark, a tax consultant with orderly habits and a closetful of suits, could possibly have in common with her zany, creative, unconventional friend. The answer was simple. Nothing. But that hadn't stopped them from falling in love. Jill couldn't be in the same room with them without sensing the powerful attraction they felt for each other.

However, there was little similarity between Shelly's marriage to Mark and Jill's relationship with Jordan. What she'd learned from her father's life—and death—was the value of balance. Although her career mattered to her, it didn't define her life or occupy every minute of her time.

"In this case I think Jill might be right," Mark said, his voice thoughtful.

"He's the one," Shelly said for the second time.

"I've met him," Mark went on to say. "He's cold and unemotional. If he does have a heart, it was frozen a long time ago."

"So?" Ever optimistic, Shelly refused to listen. "Jill's perfect for him, then. She's warm and gentle and caring."

At the moment Jill didn't feel any of those things. Listening to Mark describe Jordan, she had to fight the urge to defend him, to tell them what Andrew Howard had told her. Yes, Jordan was everything Mark said, but there was another side to him, one Jill had briefly encountered. One that was so appealing it had frightened her into running away, which was exactly what she'd done that day on the beach. He'd kissed her and she'd known immediately, intuitively, that she'd never be the same. But knowing it didn't alter her resolve. She couldn't love him because the price would be too high. He would give her all the things she craved, but eventually she'd end up like her mother, lonely and bitter.

"I just can't imagine Jordan Wilcox married," Mark concluded.

"I can," Shelly interrupted with unflinching enthusiasm. "To Jill."

"Shelly," Mark said, grinning indulgently, "listen to reason."

"When has falling in love ever been reasonable?" She fired the question at her husband, who merely shrugged, then turned back to Jill. "Did you tell him about Aunt Milly's wedding dress?"

"Good heavens, no!"

"All the better. I'll bet you really threw the guy for a loop. Was he on this flight?"

"No, he returned four days ago."

"Four days ago?" Shelly asked suspiciously. "There's something you're not telling us. Come on, Jill, fess up. You did a whole lot more than sit next to him on the plane. And Mark and I want to know what."

"Uh…" Jill was tired from the flight and her resistance was low. Under normal circumstances she would've side-stepped the issue. "It isn't like it sounds," she said weakly. "We talked, that's all."

"Did you kiss?" The question came out in a soft whisper. "The first time Mark kissed me was when I knew. If you and Jordan kissed, there wouldn't be any doubt in your mind. You'd know."

Sooner or later Shelly would worm it out of her. By telling the truth now, Jill thought she might be able to avoid a lengthy inquisition later. "All right, fine. We did kiss. A couple of times."

Even Mark seemed surprised by that.

"See?" Shelly cried triumphantly. "And what happened?"

Jill heaved an exaggerated sigh. "Nothing. I want to return the wedding dress."

"Sorry," Shelly said, her eyes flashing with excitement, "it's nonreturnable."

"I don't plan on ever seeing him again," Jill said adamantly. She'd more or less told Jordan that, too. He was in full agreement; he wanted nothing to do with her, either. "I insist you take back the wedding dress," Jill said. Shelly and Mark's eyes met. Slowly they smiled, as if sharing a private joke.

But in Jill's opinion, there was nothing to smile about.

* * *

The first person Jill called when she got home was her mother. Their conversation was friendly, and she was relieved to find Elaine less vague and self-absorbed than she'd been recently. Jill told a few anecdotes, described the island and the hotel, but avoided telling her mother about Jordan.

She was strangely reluctant to call Ralph, even though she knew he was waiting to hear from her. He was terribly nice, but unfortunately she found him…a bit dull. She put off calling; two days later, he called her, leaving a message.

They'd kissed a few times, and the kisses were pleasant enough, but for her there wasn't any spark. When Jordan took her in his arms it felt like a forest fire compared to the placid warmth she experienced with Ralph.

Jordan. Forgetting him hadn't become any easier. Jill had assumed that once she was home, surrounded by everything that was familiar and comfortable, she'd be able to put their brief interlude behind her.

It hadn't happened.

Wednesday afternoon, Jill returned home from work, put water on for tea and began reading the paper. Normally she didn't glance at the financial section. She wasn't sure why she did now. Skimming the headlines, she idly folded back the page—and saw Jordan's name. It seemed to leap out at her.

Jill's heart slowed, then vaulted into action as she read the article. He'd done it. The paper was reporting Jordan's latest coup. His company had reached an agreement with a land-management outfit in Hawaii, and construction on the shopping mall would begin within the next three months.

He must be pleased. Although he hadn't said much, Jill knew Jordan had wanted this project to fly. A hundred questions bombarded her. Had he heard from Andrew Howard? Had the older man joined forces with Jordan, after all? Had he asked Jordan about her, and if so, what had Jordan told him?

Jill had thought of writing Mr. Howard a note, but she didn't have his address. She didn't have Jordan's, either; however, it was a simple matter of checking the Internet for his company's address.

Before she could determine the wisdom of her actions, she scribbled a few lines of congratulation, addressed the envelope, and the next morning, mailed the card. She had no idea if it would even reach him.

Two days later when Jill came home from work, she noticed a long luxury car parked in front of her apartment building. Other than giving it an inquisitive glance, she didn't pay any attention. She was shuffling through her purse, searching for her keys, when she heard someone approach from behind.

She turned her head to see—and nearly dropped her purse. It was Jordan. He looked very much as he had the first time she'd met him. Cynical and hard. Detached and unemotional. His smoky gray eyes scanned her, but there was nothing to indicate that he was glad to see her, or if he'd spared her a moment's thought since they'd parted. Nothing but cool indifference.

"Hello, Jill."

She was so flustered that the newspaper, which she'd tucked under her arm, fell to the floor. Stooping, she retrieved it, then clutched it against her chest as she straightened. "Jordan."

"I got your note."

"I—I wanted you to know how happy I was for you."

He was staring pointedly at her door.

"Um, would you like to come inside?" she asked, un-latching the door with fumbling fingers. "I'll make some tea if you like. Or coffee..." She hadn't expected this, nor was she emotionally prepared for seeing him. She'd figured he'd read the card and then drop it in his wastebasket.

"Tea sounds fine."

"I'll just be a minute," she said as she hurried into the kitchen. Her heart was rampaging, pounding against her ribs. "Make yourself at home," she called out, holding the teakettle under the faucet.

"You have a nice place," he said, standing in the doorway between the kitchen and the living room.

"Thank you. I've lived here for three years." She didn't know why she'd told him that. It didn't matter to him how long she'd lived there.

"Why'd you send me the card?" he asked while she was setting out cups and saucers.

She didn't feel comfortable using her everyday mugs; she had a couple of lovely china cups her mother had given her and decided on those instead. She paused at his question, frowning slightly. "To congratulate you."

"The *real* reason."

"That was the real reason. This shopping mall was important to you and I was happy to read that everything came together. I knew you worked hard to make it happen. That was the only reason I sent you the note." Her cheeks heated at his implication. He seemed to believe something she hadn't intended—or had she?

"Andrew Howard decided to invest in the project at the last minute. It was his support that made the difference."

Jill nodded. "I was hoping he would."

"I have you to thank for that."

Nothing in his expression suggested he was grateful for any assistance she might unwittingly have given him. His features remained cold and hard. The man who'd spent that day on the beach with her wasn't the harsh, unrelenting businessman who stood before her now.

"If I played any part in Mr. Howard's decision, I'm sure it was small."

"He seemed quite taken with you."

"I was quite taken with him, too."

A flicker of emotion passed through Jordan's eyes, one so fleeting, so transitory, she was sure she'd imagined it.

"I'd like to thank you, if you'd let me," he said.

She was dropping tea bags into her best ceramic teapot. "Thank me? You already have."

"I was thinking more along the lines of dinner."

Jill's first thought was that she didn't have anything appropriate to wear. Not to an elegant restaurant, and of course she couldn't imagine Jordan dining anywhere else. He wasn't the kind of man who ate in a burger joint.

"Unless you already have plans…"

He was offering her an escape, and his eyes seemed to challenge her to take it.

"No," she said, almost gasping. Jill wasn't sure why she accepted so readily, why she didn't even consider declining. "I don't have anything planned for tonight."

"Is there a particular place you'd like to go?"

She shook her head. "You choose."

Jill felt suddenly light-headed with happiness and anticipation. Trying to keep her voice steady, she added, "I'll need to change clothes, but that shouldn't take long."

He looked at her skirt and blouse as if he hadn't noticed

them before. "You look fine just the way you are," he said, dismissing her concern.

The kettle whistled and Jill removed it from the burner, pouring the scalding water into the teapot. "This should steep for a few minutes." She backed out of the kitchen, irrationally fearing that he'd disappear if she let him out of her sight.

She chose the same outfit she'd worn on the trip home—the Hawaiian print shirt with the hot pink flowers. Narrow black pants set it off nicely, as did the shell lei she'd purchased the first day she'd gone touring. Then she freshened her makeup and brushed her hair.

Jordan had poured the tea and was adding sugar to his cup when she entered the kitchen. His gaze didn't waver or change in any way, yet she could tell he liked her choice.

The phone rang. Jill darted a look at it, willing it to stop. She sighed and went over to check call display.

Shelly.

"Hello, Shelly." She hoped her voice didn't convey her lack of enthusiasm.

"How are you? I haven't heard a word from you since you got home. Are you all right? I've been worried. You generally phone once or twice a week, and it's not like you to—"

"I'm fine."

"You're sure?"

"Positive."

"You seem preoccupied. Am I catching you at a bad time? Is Ralph there? Maybe he'll take the hint and go home. Honestly, Jill, I don't know why you continue to see that guy. I mean, he's nice, but he's about as romantic as mold."

"Uh, I have company."

"Company," Shelly echoed. "Who? No, let me guess. Jordan Wilcox!"

"You got it."

"Talk to you later. Bye." The drone of the disconnected line sounded in her ear so fast that Jill was left holding the receiver for several seconds before she realized her friend had hung up.

No sooner had Jill replaced it than the phone rang again. She looked at call display, cast an apologetic glance toward Jordan and snatched up the receiver. "Hello, Shelly."

"I want it understood that you're to give me a full report later."

"Shelly!"

"And don't you dare try to return that wedding dress. He's the one, Jill. Quit fighting it. I'll let you go now, but just remember, I want details, so be prepared." She hung up as quickly as she had the first time.

"That was my best friend."

"Shelly?"

"She's married to Mark Brady." Jill waited, wondering if Jordan would recognize the name.

"Mark Brady." He spoke slowly, as though saying it aloud would jar his memory. "Is Mark a tax consultant? I seem to recall hearing something about him not long ago. Isn't he the head of his own firm?"

"That's Mark." Jill nearly told him how Shelly and Mark had met, but stopped herself just in time. Jordan knew about the wedding dress—though not, of course, its significance—because Jill had inadvertently let it slip that first night.

"And Mark's married to your best friend?"

"That's right." She took a sip of her tea. "When I said I'd met you, Mark knew who you were right away."

"So you mentioned me." He seemed pleasantly surprised.

He could have no idea how much he'd been in her thoughts during the past two weeks. She'd tried, heaven knew she'd tried, to push every memory of him from her mind. But it hadn't worked. She couldn't explain it, but somehow nothing was the same anymore.

"You ready?" he asked after a moment.

Jill nodded and carried their empty cups to the sink. Then Jordan led her to his car, opening the door and ushering her inside. When he joined her, he pulled out his ever-present cell phone...and turned it off.

"You don't need to do that on my account," she told him.

"I'm not," he said, his smile tight, almost a grimace. "I'm doing it for me." With that he started the engine.

Jill had no idea where they were going. He took the freeway and headed north, exiting into the downtown area of Seattle. There were any number of four-star restaurants within a five-block area. Jill was curious, but she didn't ask. She'd know soon enough.

When Jordan drove into the underground garage of a luxury skyscraper, Jill was momentarily surprised. But then, several of the office complexes housed world-class restaurants.

"I didn't know there was a restaurant here," she said conversationally.

"There isn't."

"Oh."

"I live in the penthouse."

"Oh."

"Unless you object?"

"No...no, that's fine."

"I phoned earlier and asked my cook to prepare dinner for two."

"You have a cook?" Oddly, that fact astounded her, although she supposed it shouldn't have, considering his wealth.

He smiled, his first genuine smile since he'd shown up at her door. "You're easily impressed."

He talked as though *everyone* employed a cook, and Jill couldn't help laughing.

They rode a private elevator thirty floors up to the penthouse suite. The view of Puget Sound that greeted Jill as the doors glided open was breathtaking.

"This is beautiful," she whispered, stepping out. She followed him through his living room, past a white leather sectional sofa and a glass-and-chrome coffee table that held a small abstract sculpture. She wasn't too knowledgeable when it came to works of art, but this looked valuable.

"That's a Davis Stanford piece," Jordan said matter-of-factly.

Jill nodded, hoping he wouldn't guess how ignorant she was.

"White wine?"

"Please." Jill couldn't take her eyes off the view. The waterways of Puget Sound were dotted with white-and-green ferries. The islands—Bainbridge, Whidbey and Vashon—were jewellike against the backdrop of the Olympic Mountains.

"Nothing like Hawaii, is it?" Jordan asked as he handed her a long-stemmed wineglass.

"No, but just as beautiful in its own way."

"I'm going back to Oahu next week."

"So soon?" Jill was envious.

"It's another short trip. Two or three days at most."

"Perhaps you'll get a chance to go snorkeling again."

Jordan shook his head. "I won't have time for any underwater adventures this trip," he told her.

Jill perched on the edge of the sofa, staring down at her

wine. "I don't think I'll ever be able to separate you from my time in Oahu," she said softly. "The rest of my week seemed so…empty."

"I know what you mean."

Her heartbeat quickened as his gaze strayed to her mouth. He sat beside her and removed the wine goblet from her unresisting hand. Next his fingers curved around her neck, ever so lightly, brushing aside her hair. His eyes held hers as if he expected resistance. Then slowly, giving her ample opportunity to pull away if she wished, he lowered his mouth to hers.

Jill moaned in anticipation, instinctively moving closer. Common sense shouted in alarm, but she refused to listen. Just once she wanted to know what it was like to be kissed with real passion—to be cherished by a man. Just once she wanted to know what it meant to be adored. Her heart filled with delirious joy. Her hands slid up his chest to his shoulders as she clung to him. He kissed her again, small, nibbling kisses, as though he was afraid of frightening her with the strength of his need. But he must have sensed her receptiveness, because he deepened the kiss.

Suddenly it came to her. The same thing that had happened to Shelly was now happening to her. The phenomenon Aunt Milly had experienced sixty-five years earlier was coming to pass a third time.

The wedding dress.

Abruptly, she broke off the kiss. Panting, she sprang to her feet. Her eyes were wide and incredulous as she gazed down at a surprised Jordan.

"It's you!" she cried. "It really is you."

Six

"What do you mean, it's me?" Jordan demanded. When she didn't answer, he asked, "What's wrong, Jill?"

"Everything," she cried, shaking her head.

"I hurt you?"

"No," she whispered, "no." She sobbed quietly as she wrung her hands. "I don't know what to do."

"Why do you have to do anything?"

"Because…oh, you wouldn't understand." Worse, she couldn't tell him. Every time he looked at her, she became more and more convinced that Shelly had been right. Jordan Wilcox was her future.

But she *couldn't* fall in love with him, because she knew what would happen to her if she did—she'd become like her mother, lonely, bitter and unhappy. If she was going to marry, she wanted a man who was safe and sensible. A man like…Ralph. Yet the thought of spending the rest of her life with Ralph produced an even deeper sense of discontent.

"I'm not an unreasonable man," Jordan said. Then he

added, "Well, generally I'm not. If there's a problem you can tell me."

"It's not supposed to be a problem. According to Shelly and her aunt Milly, it's a blessing. I know I'm talking in riddles, but…there's no way you'd understand!"

"Try me."

"I can't. I'm sorry, I just can't."

"But it has something to do with my kissing you?"

She stared at him blankly. "No. Yes."

"You seem rather uncertain about this. Perhaps we should try it again…."

"That isn't necessary." But even as she spoke, Jordan was reaching for her, pulling her onto his lap. Jill willingly surrendered to his embrace, greeting his kiss with a muffled groan of welcome, a sigh of defeat. His arms held her close, and not for the first time, Jill was stunned by the effect he had on her. It left her feeling both unnerved and overwhelmed.

"Better?" he asked in a remarkably steady voice.

Unable to answer, Jill closed her eyes, then nodded. Better, yes. And worse. Every time he touched her, it confirmed what she feared most.

"I thought so." He seemed reassured, but that did nothing to comfort Jill. For weeks she'd played a silly game of denial. They'd met, and from that moment on, nothing had been the same.

She didn't, couldn't, believe in the power of the wedding dress; she scoffed at the implausibility of its legend. Yet even Mr. Howard, who'd never heard of Aunt Milly or her dress, had felt compelled to explain Jordan's past to her, had seen Jill as his future.

She'd spent only three days with Jordan, but she knew

more about him than she knew about Ralph, whom she'd been dating for months. Their day on the beach and the dinner with Andrew Howard had given her insights into Jordan's personality. Since then Jill had found it more difficult to accept what she saw on the surface—the detached, cynical male. The man who wore his I-don't-give-a-damn attitude like an elaborate mask.

Perhaps she understood him because he was so much like her father. Adam Morrison had lived for the excitement, the risks, of the big deal. He poured his life's blood into each business transaction because he'd never really acknowledged the importance of family, emotion, human values.

Jordan wouldn't, either.

Dinner was a strained affair, although Jordan made several efforts to lighten the mood. As he drove her home, Jill sensed that he wanted to say something more. Whatever it was, he left unsaid.

"Have a safe trip," she told him when he escorted her to her door. Her heart was pounding, not with excitement, but with trepidation, wondering if he planned to kiss her again.

"I'll call you when I get back," he told her. And that was all.

"I have a special fondness for this place," Shelly said as she slipped into a chair opposite Jill. They were meeting for lunch at Patrick's, a restaurant in the mall where Jill's branch of PayRite was located. Typically, she was ten minutes late. Marriage to Mark, who was habitually prompt, hadn't improved Shelly's tardiness. Jill often wondered how they managed to keep their love so strong when they were so different.

Patrick's had played a minor role in Shelly's romance

with Mark. Jill recalled the Saturday she'd met her there for lunch, and how amused she'd been at Shelly's crazy story of receiving the infamous wedding dress.

The way Jill felt now—frantic, frightened, confused— was exactly the way Shelly had felt then.

"So tell me everything," Shelly said breathlessly.

"Jordan stopped by. We had dinner. He left this morning on a business trip," she explained dispassionately. "There isn't much to tell."

Shelly's hand closed around her water glass, her eyes connecting with Jill's. "Do you remember when I first met Mark?"

"I'm not likely to forget," Jill said, smiling despite her present mood.

"Anytime you or my mother or anyone else asked me about Mark, I always said there wasn't anything to tell. Remember?"

"Yes." Jill thought of how Shelly's face would become expressionless, her tone abrupt, whenever anyone mentioned Mark's name.

"Well, when I told you nothing was happening, I was stretching the truth," Shelly continued. "There was plenty going on, but nothing I felt I could share. Even with you." She raised her eyebrows. "You, my friend, have the same look I did then. A lot has taken place between you and Jordan. So much that you're frightened out of your wits. Trust me, I know."

"He kissed me again," Jill admitted.

"It was better than before?"

"Worse!"

Shelly apparently found Jill's answer humorous. She tried to hide her smile behind the menu, then lowered it to say,

"Don't count on your feelings becoming any less complicated. They won't."

"He's going to be away for a few days. Thank goodness, because it gives me time to think."

"Oh, Jill," Shelly said with a sympathetic sigh, "I wish there was something I could say to help you. Why are you fighting this so hard?" She grinned sheepishly. "I fought it, too. Be smart, just accept it. Love isn't really all that terrifying once you let go of your doubts."

"Instead of talking about Jordan, why don't we order lunch?" Jill suggested a little curtly. "I'm starved."

"Me, too."

The waitress arrived at their table a moment later, and Jill ordered the split-pea soup and a turkey sandwich.

"Wait a minute," Shelly interrupted, motioning toward the waitress. She turned to Jill. "You don't even *like* split-pea soup. You never order it." She gave Jill an odd look, then turned back to the waitress. "She'll have the clam chowder."

"Shelly!"

The waitress wrote down the order quickly, as though she feared an argument was about to erupt.

"You're more upset than I realized," Shelly said when they were alone. "Ordering split-pea soup—I can't believe it."

"It's soup, Shelly, not nuclear waste." Her friend definitely had a tendency to overreact. It drove Jill crazy, but it was the very thing that made Shelly so endearing.

"I'm going to call Jordan Wilcox myself," Shelly announced suddenly.

"You're going to *what?*" It was all Jill could do to remain in her seat.

"You heard me."

"Shelly, no! I absolutely forbid you to discuss me with Jordan. How would you have felt if I'd called Mark?"

Shelly frowned. "I'd have been furious."

"I will be, too, if you say so much as one word to Jordan about me."

Shelly paused, her eyes wide with concern. "But I'm afraid you're going to mess this up."

Nothing to fear there—Jill already had. She reached for a package of rye crisps from the bread basket, and Shelly frowned again. That was when she remembered she wasn't any fonder of rye crisps than she was of split-pea soup.

"Promise me you'll stay out of it," Jill pleaded. "Please."

"All right," Shelly muttered. "Just don't do anything stupid."

"This is a pleasant surprise," Jill's mother said as she opened the front door. Elaine Morrison was in her late fifties, slim and attractive.

"I thought I'd bring over your gift from Hawaii," Jill said, following her mother into the kitchen, where Elaine poured them each a glass of iced tea. Jill set the box of chocolate-covered macadamia nuts on the counter.

"I'm glad your vacation went so well."

Jill pulled out a bar stool and sat at the counter, trying to look relaxed when she was anything but. "I met someone while I was in Hawaii."

Her mother paused, then smiled. "I thought you might have."

"What makes you say that?"

"Oh, there's a certain look about you. Now tell me how you met, what he's like, where he's from and what he does for a living."

Jill laughed at the rapid-fire questions.

Elaine added slices of lemon to their tea and started across the kitchen, a new excitement in her step. Finally, after all these years, her mother was beginning to overcome the bitterness her husband's obsession with business had created. She was finally coming to terms not only with his death but with her grief over his neglect.

Jill was relieved and delighted by the signs of her mother's recovery, but she had to say, "Frankly, Mom, I don't think you'll like him."

Her mother looked surprised. "Why ever not?"

Jill didn't hesitate. "Because he reminds me of Daddy."

Her mother's face contorted with shock, and tears sprang to her eyes. "Jill, no! For the love of heaven, no."

"I've been giving some thought to your suggestion," Jill said to Ralph a few hours later. Her nerves were in turmoil. The clam chowder sat like a dead weight in the pit of her stomach, and her mother's dire warnings had shaken her badly.

Ralph wasn't tall and strikingly handsome like Jordan, but he was a comfortable sort of man. He made a person feel at ease. In fact, his laid-back manner was a blessed relief after the high-stress, high-energy hours she'd spent with Jordan, few though they were.

Jordan Wilcox could pull together a deal for an apartment complex before Ralph stepped out of the shower in the morning. Ralph's idea of an exhilarating evening was doing the newspaper crossword puzzle.

Everything about Jordan was complex. Everything about Ralph was uncomplicated; he was a straightforward, honest man who'd be a good husband and a loving father.

"Are you saying what I think you're saying?" Ralph prompted when she didn't immediately continue.

Jill held her water glass. "You said something not long ago about the two of us giving serious consideration to making our relationship permanent and…and I wanted you to know I was…I've been giving some thought to that."

Ralph didn't reveal any emotion. He put down his hamburger, looked at her and asked casually, "Why now?"

"Uh…I'm going to be twenty-nine soon." She managed to sound calm, although she felt anything but.

She was the biggest coward who ever lived. But what else could she do? Her mother had become nearly hysterical when Jill had told her about Jordan. Her own heart was filled with trepidation. On the one hand, there was Shelly, so confident Jordan was the man for Jill. On the other was her mother, adamant that Jill would be forever sorry if she got involved with a workaholic.

Jill was trapped in the middle, frightened and unsure.

Ralph relaxed against the red vinyl upholstery. The diner was his favorite place to eat, and he took her there every time they dined out. "So you think we should consider marriage?"

It was the subject Jill had been leading up to all evening, yet when Ralph posed the question directly, she hesitated. If only Jordan hadn't kissed her. If only he hadn't held her in his arms. And if only she hadn't spoken to her mother…

"I missed you while you were away," Ralph said, his gaze holding hers.

Jill knew this was about as close to romance as she was likely to get from Ralph. Romance was his weakest suit, dependability and steadiness his strongest. Ralph would always be there by his wife's side. He'd make the kind of father who played catch in the backyard with his son. The kind of father who'd bring his wife and daughter pretty corsages on Easter morning. He was a rock, a fortress of permanence. She wished she could fall in love with him.

Jordan might have a talent for making millions, but all the money in the world couldn't buy happiness.

"I missed you, too," Jill said softly. She'd thought of Ralph, had wondered about him. A few times, anyway. Hadn't she mailed him a postcard? Hadn't she brought him a book on volcanoes?

"I'm glad to hear that," Ralph said. Then, clearing his throat, he asked, "Jill Morrison, will you do me the honor of becoming my wife?"

The question was out now, ready for her to answer. A proposal was what she'd been hinting at all evening. Now that Ralph had asked, Jill wasn't sure what she felt. Relief? No, it wasn't even close to that. Pleasure? Yes—in a way. But not a throw-open-the-windows-and-shout kind of joy.

Joy. The word hit her like an unexpected punch. Joy was what she'd experienced the first time Jordan had taken her in his arms. A free-flowing joy and the promise of so much more.

The promise she was rejecting.

Ralph might not be the love of her life, but he'd care for her and devote his life to her. It was enough.

"Jill?"

She tried to smile, tried to look happy and excited. Ralph deserved that much. "Yes," she whispered, stretching her hand across the table. "Yes, I'll marry you."

"What do you mean you're engaged to marry Ralph?" Shelly demanded. Her voice had risen to such a high pitch that Jill held the receiver away from her ear.

"He asked me tonight and I've accepted."

"You can't *do* that!" her friend shrieked.

"Of course I can."

"What about Jordan?" Shelly asked next.

"I'd already decided not to see him again." Jill was able to keep her composure, although it wasn't easy.

"If marrying Ralph is typical of your decisions, then I'd like to suggest you talk to a mental-health professional."

Jill laughed despite herself. Her decision had been based on maintaining her sanity, not destroying it.

"I don't know what's so funny. I can't believe you'd do something like this! What about Aunt Milly's wedding dress? Doesn't that mean anything to you? Don't you care that Mark, Aunt Milly and I all felt the dress should go to you? You can't ignore it. Something dreadful might happen."

"Don't be ridiculous."

"I'm not," Shelly said resolutely. "You can't reject the man destiny has chosen for you without consequences." Shelly's voice was solemn.

"You don't know that Jordan's the man," Jill said with far more conviction than she was feeling. "We both realize a wedding dress can't dictate who I'll marry. The choice is mine—and I've chosen Ralph."

"You're honestly choosing Ralph over Jordan?" The question had an incredulous quality.

"Yes."

There was a moment's silence.

"You're scared," Shelly went on, "frightened half out of your wits because of everything you feel. I know, because I went through the same thing. Jill, please, think about this before you do something you'll regret for the rest of your life."

"I have thought about it," she insisted. She'd thought of

little else since her last encounter with Jordan. Since her talk with Shelly. Since her visit to her mother's. She'd carefully weighed her options. Marrying Ralph seemed the best course.

"You have no intention of changing your mind, do you?" Shelly cried. "Do you expect me to stand by and do *nothing* while you ruin your life?"

"I'm not ruining my life. Don't be absurd." Her voice grew hard. "Naturally I'll return your aunt Milly's wedding dress and—"

"No," Shelly groaned. "Here, talk to Mark."

"Jill?" Mark came on the line. "What's the problem?"

Jill didn't want to repeat everything. She was tired and it was late and all she wanted to do was go to bed. Escape for the next eight hours and then face the world again. Jill hadn't intended to tell Shelly and Mark her news quite so soon, but there'd been a telephone message from them when she got home. She'd decided she might as well let Shelly know about her decision. Jill wasn't sure what kind of reaction she'd expected from her friends, but certainly not this.

"Just a minute," Mark said next. "Shelly's trying to tell me something."

Although Shelly had given the phone to her husband, Jill could hear her friend's frantic words as clearly as if she still held the receiver. Shelly was pleading with Mark to talk some sense into Jill, begging him to try because she hadn't been able to change Jill's mind.

"Mark," Jill called, but apparently he didn't hear her. "Mark," she tried again, louder this time.

"I'm sorry, Jill," he said politely, "but Shelly's upset, and I'm having a hard time figuring out just what the problem is. All I can make out is that you've decided not to see Jordan Wilcox again."

"I'm marrying Ralph Emery, and I don't think he'd take kindly to my dating Jordan."

Mark chuckled. "No, I don't suppose he would. Frankly, I believe the decision is yours, and yours alone. I know Jordan, I've talked to him a couple of times and I share your concerns. I can't picture him married."

"He's already married," Jill stated unemotionally, "to his job. A wife would only get in the way."

"That's probably true. What about Ralph—have I met him?"

"I don't think so," Jill returned stiffly. "He's a very nice man. Honest and hardworking. Shelly seems to think he's dull, and perhaps he is in some ways, but he...cares for me. It isn't a great love match, but we're both aware of that."

"Shelly thinks I'm dull, too, but that didn't stop her from marrying me."

Mark was so calm, so reassuring. He was exactly what Jill needed. She was so grateful she felt close to tears. "I want to do the right thing," she said, gulping in a quick breath. Her voice wavered and she bit her lower lip, blinking rapidly.

"It's difficult knowing what's right sometimes, isn't it?" Mark said quietly. "I remember how I felt the first time I met Shelly. Here was this completely bizarre woman announcing to everyone who'd listen that she refused to marry me. I hadn't even asked—didn't even know her name. Then we stumbled on each other a second time and a third, and finally I learned about Aunt Milly's wedding dress."

"What did you think when she told you?"

"That it was the most ridiculous thing I'd ever heard."

"I did, too. I still do." She wanted a husband, *but not Jordan.*

"I'm sure you'll make the right decision," Mark said confidently.

"I am, too. Thanks, Mark, I really appreciate talking to you." The more she grew to know her friend's husband, the more Jill realized how perfectly they suited each other. Mark brought balance into Shelly's life, and she'd infused his with her warmth and wit. If only she, Jill, could have met someone like Mark.

No sooner had she hung up the phone than there was a loud knock on her door. Since it was late, close to eleven, Jill was surprised.

Peering through the peephole, she gasped and drew away. Jordan Wilcox.

"I thought you were in Hawaii," she said as she opened the door.

"I was." His eyes scanned her hungrily. "This morning I had the most incredible feeling something was wrong. I tried to call, but there wasn't any answer."

"I…was out for most of the day."

He took her by the shoulders and then, before she could protest, pulled her into his arms.

"Jordan?" She'd never seen him like this, didn't understand why he seemed so disturbed.

"I just couldn't shake the feeling something was wrong with you."

"I'm fine."

"I know," he said, inhaling deeply. "Thank God you're safe."

Seven

"Of course I'm safe," Jill said, still feeling bewildered. Jordan's arms were tight around her and he buried his head in the curve of her neck, his breathing hard.

"I've never experienced anything like this before," he said, loosening his hold. His hands caressed the length of her arms as he moved back one small step. He studied her, his gaze intimate and tender. "I hope it never happens to me again." Taking her hand, he led her to the sofa.

"You're not making any sense."

"I know." He momentarily closed his eyes, then gave a deep sigh. He raised her fingers to his lips and gently kissed the back of her hand.

"It was the most unbelievable thing," he continued with a shrug. "I awoke with this feeling of impending doom. At first I tried to ignore it. But as the day wore on I couldn't shake it. All I knew was that it had something to do with you.

"I thought if I talked to you I could assure myself that nothing was wrong and this feeling would go away. Only I couldn't get hold of you."

"I was out most of the day," she repeated unnecessarily.

Jordan rubbed a hand down his face. "I tried to phone you at home and I couldn't get an answer. I don't know your cell number. So I panicked. I booked the next flight to Seattle."

"What about your business in Hawaii?"

"I canceled one meeting and left what I could with an assistant. Everything's taken care of." He sighed once more and sagged against the back of her sofa. "I could do with a cup of coffee."

"Of course." Jill immediately stood and hurried into the kitchen, starting the coffee and assembling cups and saucers in a matter of minutes. She was arranging everything on a tray when Jordan stepped up behind her.

He slid his arms around her waist and kissed the side of her neck. "I don't know what's happening between us."

"I'm...not sure anything is."

Jordan chuckled softly, the sound a gentle caress against her skin. "I'm beginning to think you've cast a spell over me."

Jill froze. *Spell* and *magic* were words she'd rather not hear. Even the smallest hint that the wedding dress was affecting him wouldn't change what she'd done. She'd made her decision. The dress was packed away in the box Shelly had mailed her, ready to be returned.

"I've never experienced anything like this," Jordan said again, sounding almost uncertain.

Jill should have been shocked. Jordan Wilcox had probably never felt confused or doubtful about anything in his adult life. She speculated that his emotions had been buried so deep, hidden by pride for so long, that he barely recognized them anymore.

"I think I'm falling in love with you."

Jill closed her eyes. She didn't want to hear this, didn't want to deal with a declaration of love. Not now. Not when she'd settled everything in her own mind. Not when she'd reconciled herself to never seeing him again.

"That's not true," Jordan countered, turning her around and into his arms. "I can't live without you. I've known that from the first moment we kissed."

"Oh, no..."

His amused laughter filled her small kitchen. "You said the same thing that night. Remember?" The smile faded as he gazed at her upturned face. His eyes, so gray and intense, seemed to sear her with a look of such power it was all Jill could do not to cry out and break off his embrace. She glanced away, chewing nervously on her lower lip, willing him to free her, willing him to leave.

His hands cupped her face, his thumbs stroking her cheeks. "You feel it, too, don't you?" he whispered. "You have from the very first. Neither one of us can deny it."

She meant to tell him then, to blurt out that she was engaged to Ralph, but she wasn't given the chance. Before she could utter a word, before she could even begin to explain, Jordan captured her mouth with his own.

His lips were hard and desperate as they claimed possession of hers, firing her senses to life. She moaned, not from pleasure, although that was keen, but from regret.

Ralph had kissed her that night, too. Jill had tried to reassure herself their marriage would work. She'd put her heart and her soul into their good-night kiss and hadn't felt even a fraction of what she did with Jordan.

It was so unfair, so wrong. She was marrying *Ralph,* she

reminded herself. But her heart, her foolish, romantic heart, refused to listen.

Nothing Jordan could say was going to change her plans, she decided, trying to think of Ralph and the commitment they'd made to each other a few hours earlier.

If only Jordan would stop kissing her. *Oh, please stop,* she begged silently as frustration brought burning tears to her eyes. If only he'd leave, walk out of her life forever so she could start forgetting.

But she had to push him out of her arms before she could push him out of her life. Yet here she was clinging to him, her arms curved around his neck. And she was holding on as though her very existence depended on it.

Jordan obviously felt none of her hesitation, none of her doubts, and soon, far too soon, Jill was returning his kisses with equal fervor. Raw emotion overwhelmed her until she was so weak she slumped against him, needing his support to remain upright. Her breath came in shallow gasps as his lips trembled against hers.

"Oh, Jill," he breathed, his voice a husky caress. "The things you do to me. I've frightened you, haven't I?"

"No." He had, but for none of the reasons he knew. She was terrified by the things he made her feel. Terrified by the rush of need and love that crowded her heart.

She hid her face in his shoulder, wanting to escape his embrace even as she submerged herself in it.

"I never knew love could be like this," Jordan said hoarsely. "I've never been in love, never experienced it before you." He rested his jaw alongside her cheek in a gesture of tenderness that moved her deeply.

Jill swallowed and blinked through a wall of tears. "Please..." She had to say something, had to let him know before he spoke again, before he convinced her to love him. She'd set her mind, her will, everything within her, to resist him and found she couldn't.

"I realize we haven't known each other long," Jordan was saying. "Yet it seems as if you've always been part of my life, always will be."

"No..."

"Yes," he countered softly, his lips grazing the side of her face. "I want to marry you, Jill. Soon. The sooner the better. I need you in my life. I need you to teach me so many things. Loving me isn't going to be easy, but—"

"No!" Abruptly she broke away from him. "Please, no." She buried her face in her hands and began to sob.

"Jill, what is it?" He tried to comfort her, tried to bring her back into his embrace, but she wouldn't let him.

"I can't marry you." The words, born of frustration and anger, were meant to be shouted, but by the time they passed her lips they were barely audible.

"Can't marry me?" Jordan repeated as though he was sure he'd misunderstood. "Why not?"

"Because..." Saying it became a nearly impossible task, but she forced herself. "Because...I'm already engaged."

She saw and felt his shock. His eyes narrowed with pain and disbelief as the color drained from his face.

"You're making it up."

"No, it's true." She held herself stiff, braced for the backlash her words would bring.

"When?" he demanded.

She heaved in a breath and squared her shoulders. "Tonight."

A shudder went through him as his eyes, dark and haunting, raked her face. Jill's throat muscles constricted at his tortured look, and she couldn't speak.

It took Jordan a moment to compose himself. But he did so with remarkable dexterity. All emotion fled from his face. For a breathless moment he just stared at her.

"I'm sure," he said finally, without any outward hint of regret, "that whoever it is will make you a far better husband than I would have."

"His name is Ralph."

Jordan grimaced, but quickly rearranged his features into a cool mask. "I wish you and…Ralph every happiness."

With that, he turned and walked out of her life. Just as she'd wanted him to…

Early the next morning, after an almost sleepless night, Jill put the infamous wedding dress in her car and drove directly to Shelly and Mark's. The curtains were open so she assumed they were up and about. Even if they weren't, she didn't care.

Keeping the wedding dress a second longer was intolerable. The sooner she was rid of it, the sooner her life would return to normal.

Jill locked her car and carried the box to the Bradys' front door. Her steps were impatient. If Shelly wasn't home, Jill swore she'd leave the wedding gown on the front steps rather than take it back to her apartment.

A few minutes passed before the door opened. Shelly stood on the other side, dressed in a long robe, her hair in disarray and one hand covering her mouth to hide a huge yawn.

"I got you out of bed?" That much was obvious, but Jill was in no state for intelligent conversation.

"I was awake," Shelly said, yawning again. "Mark had to go into the office early, but I couldn't make myself get up." She gestured Jill inside. "Come on in. I'm sure Mark made a pot of coffee. He knows I need a cup first thing in the morning."

Jill set the box down on the sofa and followed Shelly into the kitchen. Clearly her friend wasn't fully awake yet, so Jill walked over to the cupboards and collected two mugs, filling each with coffee, then bringing them to the table where Shelly was sitting.

"Oh, thanks," she mumbled. "I'm impossible until I've had my first cup."

"I seem to remember that from our college days."

"Right," Shelly said, managing a half smile. "You know all my faults. Can you believe Mark loves me in spite of the fact that I can't cook, can't tolerate mornings and am totally disorganized?"

Having seen the love in Mark's eyes when he looked at his wife, Jill could well believe it. "Yes."

"I'm glad you're here," Shelly said, resting her head on her arm, which was stretched across the kitchen table.

"You are?" It was apparent that Shelly hadn't guessed the reason for this unexpected visit, hadn't realized Jill was returning the wedding dress. Half-asleep as she was, she obviously hadn't noticed the box.

"Yes, I'm *delighted* you're here," Shelly said as her eyes drifted shut. "Mark and I had a long talk about you and Ralph. He seems to think I'm overreacting to this engagement thing. But you aren't going to marry Ralph—you know it and I know it. This engagement is a farce, even if you don't recognize that yet. Getting Ralph to propose is the only way you can deal with what's happening between you and Jordan. But you'd never go through with it. You're too honest. You won't let yourself cheat Ralph—because if you marry him, that's exactly what you'll be doing."

"He knows I'm not in love with him."

"I'm sure he does, but I'm also sure he believes that in time you'll feel differently. What he doesn't understand is that you're already in love with someone else."

A few hours earlier, Jill would have adamantly denied loving Jordan, but she couldn't any longer. Her heart burned with the intensity of her feelings. Still, it didn't change any-thing, didn't alter the path she'd chosen.

"Ralph doesn't know about Jordan, does he?"

"No," Jill said reluctantly. If she was forced to, she'd tell Ralph about him. Difficult as it was to admit, Shelly was right about one thing. Jill would never be able to marry Ralph unless she was completely honest with him.

Shelly straightened and took her first sip of coffee. It seemed to revive her somewhat. "I should apologize for what I said last night. I didn't mean to offend you."

"You didn't," Jill was quick to tell her.

"You frightened me."

"Why?"

"I was afraid for you, afraid you were going to ruin your life. I don't think I could stand idly by and let you do it."

"I fully intend to marry Ralph." Jill didn't know for whose benefit she was saying this—Shelly's or her own. The doubts were back, but she did her best to ignore them.

"Oh, I believe you intend to marry Ralph…now," Shelly said, "but when the time comes, I don't think it's going to happen. Neither does Mark."

"That isn't what he said when we talked." Mark had been the cool voice of reason in their impassioned discussion the night before. He'd reassured her and comforted her, and for that Jill would always be grateful.

"What he said," Shelly explained between yawns, "was that he was sure you'd make the right decision. And he is. I was, too, after he calmed me down."

"I've made my choice. There's no turning back now."

"You'll change your mind."

"Perhaps. I don't know. All I know is that I agreed to marry Ralph." No matter how hard she tried, she couldn't keep the breathless catch from her voice.

Shelly heard it, and her eyes slowly opened. "What happened?" Her gaze sharply assessed Jill, who tried not to say or do anything that would give her away.

"Tell me," she said when Jill hesitated. "You know I'll get it out of you one way or another."

Jill sighed. Hiding the truth was pointless. "Jordan came by late last night."

"I thought you said he was in Hawaii."

"He was."

"Then what was he doing at your place?"

"He said he had a feeling there was something wrong— and he flew home."

"There *is* something wrong!" Shelly cried. "You're engaged to the wrong man."

Unexpectedly, Jill felt defeated. She'd hardly slept the night before, and the tears she'd managed to suppress refused to be held back any longer. They brimmed in her eyes, spilling onto her cheeks, cool against her flushed skin.

"I'm not *engaged* to the wrong man," she said once she was able to speak coherently. "I happen to *love* the wrong one."

"If you're in love with Jordan," Shelly said, "and I believe you are, then why in heaven's name would you even consider marrying Ralph?"

It was too difficult to explain. Rather than make the effort, she merely shook her head and stood, almost toppling her chair in her eagerness to escape.

"Jill." Shelly stood, too.

"I have to go now...."

"Jill, what's wrong? My goodness, I've never seen you like this. Tell me."

Jill shook her head again and hurried into the living room. "I brought back the wedding dress. Thank your aunt Milly for me, but I can't...wear it."

"You brought back the dress?" Shelly sounded as though she was about to break into tears herself. "Oh, Jill, I wish you hadn't."

Jill didn't stay around to argue. She rushed out the front door and to her car. Her destination wasn't clear until she reached Ralph's apartment. She hadn't planned to go there and wasn't sure what had directed her there. For several minutes she sat outside, collecting her thoughts—and gathering her courage.

When she'd composed herself, blown her nose and dried her eyes, she walked to his front door and rang the doorbell. Ralph answered, looking pleased to see her.

"Good morning. You're out and about early. I was just getting ready to leave for work."

She forced a smile. "Have you got a minute?"

He nodded. "Come on in." He paused and seemed to remember that they were now an engaged couple. He leaned forward and lightly brushed his lips across her cheek.

"I should have phoned first."

"No. I was just thinking that this afternoon might be a good time for us to look at engagement rings."

Jill guiltily dropped her gaze and her voice trembled. "That's very sweet." She could barely say the words she had to say. "I should explain…the reason I'm here—"

Ralph motioned her toward a chair. "Please, sit down."

Jill was grateful because she didn't know how much longer her legs would support her. Everything seemed so much more difficult in the light of day. She'd been so confident before, so sure she and Ralph could make a life together. Now she felt as though she were walking around in a heavy fog. Nothing was clear, and confusion greeted her at every turn.

She took a deep breath. "There's something I need to explain."

"Go ahead." Ralph sat comfortably across from her.

She was so close to the edge of the chair she was in danger of slipping off. "It's only fair you should know." She hesitated, thinking he might say something, but when he didn't, she continued, "I met a man in Hawaii."

He nodded gravely. "I thought you must have."

His intuition surprised her. "His name… Oh, it doesn't matter what his name is. We went out a couple of times."

"Are you in love with him?" Ralph asked outright.

"Yes," Jill whispered slowly. It hurt to admit, and for a moment she dared not look at Ralph.

"It doesn't seem like a lot of time to be falling in love with a man. You were only gone a week."

Jill didn't tell him Jordan was in Hawaii only three days. Nor did she mention the two brief times she'd seen him since. There was no reason to analyze the relationship. It was over. She'd made certain of that when she told him she was marrying Ralph. She'd never hear from Jordan again.

"Love happens like that sometimes," was all she could say.

"If you're so in love with this other guy, then why did you agree to marry me?"

"Because I'm scared and, oh, Ralph, I'm sorry. I should never have involved you in this. You're a wonderful man and I care for you, I really do. You've been a good friend and I've enjoyed our times together, but I realized this morning that I can't marry you."

For a moment he said nothing, then he reached for her hand and held it gently between his own. "You don't need to feel so guilty about it."

"Yes, I do." She was practically drowning in guilt.

"Don't. It took me about two minutes to realize something was troubling you last night. You surprised me completely when you started talking about getting married."

"I surprised you?"

"To be honest, I assumed you were about to tell me you'd met someone else and wouldn't be seeing me anymore. I've known for a long time that you're not in love with me."

"But I believed that would've changed," Jill said almost desperately.

"That's what I figured, too."

"You're steady and dependable, and I need that in my life," she said, although the rationale sounded poor even to her own ears. True, if she married Ralph she wouldn't have the love match she'd always dreamed about, but she'd told herself that love was highly overrated. She'd decided she could live without love, live without passion—until Jordan showed up on her doorstep. And this morning, Shelly had told her what she already knew. She couldn't marry Ralph.

"You're here because you want to call off the engagement, aren't you?" Ralph asked.

Miserably, Jill nodded. "I didn't mean to hurt you. That's the last thing I want."

"You haven't," he said pragmatically. "I figured you'd call things off sooner or later."

"You did?"

He grinned sheepishly. "You going to marry this other man?"

Jill shrugged. "I don't know."

"If you do…"

"Yes?" Jill reluctantly raised her eyes to his.

"If you do, would you consider subletting your apartment to me? Your place is at least twice as big as mine, and your rent's lower."

Despite everything, Jill started to laugh. Leave it to Ralph, ever practical, ever sensible, to brush off a broken engagement and ask about subletting her apartment.

The week that followed was one of the worst of Jill's life. She awoke every morning feeling as though she hadn't slept. She was depressed and lonely. Several times she found herself close to tears for no apparent reason. She'd be reading a prescription and the words would blur and misery would grip her heart with such intensity she'd be forced to swallow a sob.

"Jill," her supervisor called early Friday afternoon, walking into the back room where she was taking her lunch break. "There's someone out front who wants to talk to you."

It was unusual for anyone to visit her at work. She immediately feared it was Jordan, but quickly dismissed that concern. She knew him too well. She was out of his life. The instant she'd told him she was engaged to Ralph, he'd cut her out, surgically removed all feeling for her. It was as if she no longer existed for him.

But as she'd been so often lately, Jill was wrong. Jordan

stood there waiting for her. His gaze was as hard as flint. Something flickered briefly in the smoky-gray depths, but whatever emotion he felt at seeing her was too fleeting for Jill to identify.

She'd had far less practice at hiding her own feelings, and right now, they were wreaking havoc with her pulse. With great effort she managed to remain outwardly composed. "You wanted to speak to me?"

A nerve twitched in his jaw. "You might be more comfortable if we spoke elsewhere," he said stiffly.

Jill glanced at her watch. She had only fifteen minutes of her lunch break left. Time enough, she was sure, for whatever Jordan intended. "All right."

Wordlessly, he walked out of the drugstore, obviously expecting her to follow, which she did. He paused beside his car, then turned to face her. A cool, disinterested smile slanted his mouth.

"Yes?" she said after an awkward moment. She folded her arms defensively around her middle.

"I need you to explain something."

She nodded. "I'll try."

"Your friend Shelly Brady was in to see me this morning."

Jill groaned. She hadn't talked to Shelly since the morning she'd dropped off the wedding dress. Her friend had phoned several times and left messages, but Jill hadn't had either the energy or the patience to return the calls.

"How she managed to get past security and my two assistants is beyond me."

It was a nightmare come true. "What did she say?" As if Jill needed to know.

"She rambled on about how you were making the worst

mistake of your life and how I'd be an even bigger fool if I let you. But, you know, if you prefer to marry Roger, then that's your prerogative."

"His name is Ralph," she corrected.

"It doesn't make any difference to me."

"I didn't think it would," she said, keeping her gaze lowered to the black asphalt of the parking lot.

"Then she started telling me this ridiculous story about a legend behind a certain wedding dress."

Jill's eyes closed in frustration. "It's a bunch of nonsense."

"It certainly didn't make too much sense, especially the part about the dress fitting her and her marrying Mark. But she insisted the dress also fits you."

"Don't take Shelly seriously. She seems to put a lot of credence in that dress. Personally, I think the whole thing's a fluke. You don't need to worry about it."

"*Then* she told me an equally ridiculous tale about a vision she had of you in Hawaii and how happy you looked. It didn't make any more sense than the rest."

"Don't worry," she said again. "Shelly means well, but she doesn't understand. The wedding dress is beautiful, but it isn't meant for me. The whole thing is ridiculous—you said so yourself, and I agree with you."

"That's what I thought—at first. A magic wedding dress is about as believable as a talking rabbit. I don't have any interest in that kind of fantasy."

"Then why are you here?"

"Because I remembered something. You had a wedding dress with you in Hawaii. When I asked you about it, you said a friend had mailed it to you. Then, this morning, Shelly arrived and told me why she'd sent you the dress. She told me the story of her aunt Milly and how she'd met her husband. She also said Milly had mailed the dress to her and she'd fallen into Mark Brady's arms."

"Did she leave anything out?" Jill asked sarcastically.

He ignored her question. "In the end I phoned Mark and asked him about it. I don't know Brady well, but I assumed he'd be able to explain the situation a little more rationally."

"Shelly does tend to get a bit dramatic."

"That's putting it mildly."

"I just wish she hadn't said anything to you."

"I imagine you do," he remarked dryly.

"What did Mark say?"

"We talked for several minutes. By this time Shelly was weeping and nearly hysterical, convinced she was saving us both from a fate worse than death. Mark was kind enough to inject a bit of sanity into the discussion. What it boiled down to is this."

"What?" Jill wasn't purposely being obtuse.

"Me confronting you. I'm here to ask you about Aunt Milly's wedding dress."

He could ask her whatever he wanted, but she didn't have any answers.

"Jill?"

She heaved a sigh. "I returned the dress to Shelly."

"She explained that, too. Said you'd brought it back the morning after my visit."

"It wasn't meant for me."

"Not true, according to Shelly...and Mark." He remained standing where he was, unwilling to divulge his own feelings.

"So you're going to go ahead and marry Roger."

"Ralph."

"Whoever," Jordan snapped.

"No!" she shouted, furious with him, furious with Shelly and Mark, too.

A moment of shocked silence followed her announcement. Several feet separated Jill from Jordan, and although neither of them moved, they suddenly seemed much closer.

"I knew that," he said.

"How could you possibly know?" Jill hadn't told anyone yet. Not Shelly and certainly not Jordan.

"Because you're marrying me."

Eight

All of Jill's defenses came tumbling down. She'd known they would from the moment she'd walked out of the lunchroom and confronted him. Known in the very depths of her soul that he'd eventually have his way. She didn't have the strength to fight him anymore.

He must have sensed her acquiescence because he moved toward her, pausing just short of taking her in his arms. "You will marry me, won't you?" The words were gentle yet insistent, brooking no argument.

Jill nodded. "I don't want…don't *want* to love you."

"I know." He reached for her then, drawing her into his embrace as though he were comforting a child.

It should have eased her mind that settling into his arms felt more natural than anything she'd done in the past week. A feeling of welcome. A feeling of rightness. And yet there was fear.

"You're going to break my heart," she whispered.

"Not if I can help it."

"Why do you want to marry me?" The answer evaded

her. A man like Jordan could have his pick of women. He had wealth and prestige and a dozen other attributes that attracted far more sophisticated and beautiful women than Jill.

The air between them seemed to pulse for a long moment before Jordan answered. "I've done some thinking about that myself. You're intelligent. Insightful. You feel things deeply and you're sensitive to the needs of others." He traced a finger along the line of her jaw, his touch light. "You're passionate about the people you love."

She should've been reassured that he seemed to know her so well after such a short acquaintance, but she wasn't. Because she knew that for a time she'd be a pleasant distraction. Their marriage would be like a toy to him. Then gradually, as the newness wore off, she'd be put on a shelf to look pretty and brought down when it suited his purposes. His life, his love, his personality, would be consumed by the drive to succeed, just the way her father's had been. Everything else would fade into the background, eventually to disappear. Love. Family. Commitment. Everything that was important to her would ultimately mean nothing to him.

"I want us to marry soon," Jordan whispered.

"I—I was hoping for a long engagement."

Jordan's eyes were adamant. "I've waited too long already."

Jill didn't understand what he meant, but she didn't question him. She knew Jordan was an impatient man. When he wanted something, he went after it with relentless determination. Now he wanted *her*—and heaven help her, she wanted him.

"A bride should be happy," he said, tucking his hand under her chin and raising her face to his. "Why the tears?"

How could she possibly explain? She loved him, although

she'd fought it with everything she had. She'd been willing, for a time, to consider marrying Ralph in her effort to drive Jordan from her life. Yet even then she'd known it was useless and of course so had Ralph. Nothing could save her. Her heart had been on a collision course with Jordan's from the moment she'd been assigned the seat next to his on the flight to Hawaii.

"I'll be happy," she murmured, silently adding *for a while*.

"So will I," Jordan said, his chest expanding with a breath and then a sigh that seemed to come all the way from his soul.

The small private wedding took place three weeks later in Hawaii at the home of Andrew Howard. Shelly was Jill's matron of honor and Mark stood up for Jordan. Elaine Morrison was there, too, weeping through the entire ceremony. But these weren't tears of joy. Her mother, like Jill, recognized Jordan's type and feared what it meant for her daughter's life, her happiness.

"Jill," Elaine had pleaded with her earlier that morning, before the wedding. "Are you sure this is what you want?"

Jill had nearly laughed aloud. With all her heart, with all her being, she longed to be Jordan's wife. And yet, if the opportunity had availed itself, she would've backed out of the marriage.

"He needs me." Repeatedly over the past few weeks, Jill had been reminded how much Jordan did need her. He didn't realize it himself, of course, not on a conscious level, but something deep inside him had acknowledged his need. And in her own way, Jill needed him.

Andrew Howard had seen that they belonged together. He'd been the first one to point it out to Jill. From the time

Jordan was a child, his life had been devoid of love. As an adult he'd closed himself off from emotion; he'd refused to allow himself to become vulnerable. That he should experience something as powerful as love for her in so short a time was close to a miracle. But then, Jill was becoming accustomed to miracles.

"All I want is your happiness," her mother had gone on to say, her eyes, so like Jill's, blurred with tears. "You're my only child. I don't want you to make the same mistakes I did."

Could loving someone ever be a mistake? Jill wondered. Her mother had loved her father, sacrificed herself for him even though, as the years went on, he'd barely seemed to reciprocate her love. And when he died prematurely, without warning, she'd become lost and miserable.

Jill knew she loved Jordan enough to put aside her fears, to bind herself in a relationship that might ultimately cause her pain. But she vowed she wouldn't lose her own identity. She wouldn't, couldn't, let Jordan's personality swallow her own.

He hadn't understood that in the beginning, despite her attempts to explain it. To him, Jill's desire to continue working after their marriage seemed utterly foolish. For what purpose? he'd asked. She didn't need the income; he'd made certain of that, lavishing her with gifts and more money than she could possibly spend. Her insistence on continuing her job resulted in their first real argument. But in the end Jordan had reluctantly agreed.

Andrew Howard had gone to a great deal of trouble to arrange their wedding, warming Jill's heart with his generosity. She'd come to understand that the older man looked upon Jordan as the son he'd lost. He was more than a mentor, far more than a friend. He was the only real family Jordan had—until now.

Flowers filled every room of Andrew's oceanfront home, their fragrance sweet in the summer air. An archway of orange blossoms stood outside on the lush green lawn that overlooked the roaring ocean. A small reception and dinner were to follow. Tables laid with white linen tablecloths were placed around the patio.

The warm wind whispered over Jill as Andrew Howard came to escort her into the sunshine where Jordan was waiting. Andrew paused when he saw her, his eyes vivid with appreciation. "I've never had a daughter," he said softly, "but if I did, I'd want her to be just like you."

Tears of love and gratitude gathered in her eyes. Her mother, fussing about Jill, arranged the long, flowing train of the dress, then slowly straightened. "He's right," Elaine said, stepping back to examine Jill. "You've never looked more beautiful."

It was the dress, Jill thought. The dress and its magic. She ran her glove along the bodice with its Venetian lace and row upon row of delicate pearls. The high collar was adorned with pearls, too, each one sewn on by hand. The skirt flared from her waist, the hem accentuated with a flounce of lace and wide satin ribbons.

Andrew Howard stood beside her mother as the minister asked Jordan and Jill to repeat their vows. Jill's gaze met Jordan's as she made her promises. Her voice, although low, was steady and confident. Jordan's eyes held hers with a look of warmth, of tenderness.

A magic wedding dress? The scenario seemed implausible. Yet here they were, standing before God, their family and friends, declaring their love for each other.

"You look so beautiful," Shelly told Jill shortly after the ceremony. "Even more beautiful than the day you first tried on the dress."

"My hair wasn't done and I didn't have on much makeup and I—"

"No," Shelly interrupted, squeezing Jill's fingers, "it's more than that. You hadn't met Jordan yet. It's complete now."

"What is?"

"Everything," Shelly explained with characteristic ambiguity. "Aunt Milly's wedding dress, you and Jordan. Oh, Jill," she whispered, her eyes brimming with tears, "you're going to be so happy."

Jill wanted to believe that—how she wanted to believe it!—but she was afraid. So afraid of what the future held for her and Jordan.

"I know what you're thinking," Shelly said, dabbing her eyes. "I loved Mark when I married him. I'd loved him for months, but deep down I wondered how long a marriage between us could last. We're totally different."

Jill smiled to herself. Shelly was right; she and Mark *were* different, but they were perfectly matched, balancing each other's strengths and weaknesses.

"I was sure my lack of domestic skills would drive Mark crazy, and at the same time I thought the way he organizes everything would kill our relationship. Did you know that man makes lists of lists? Even before I walked to the altar, I was worried this marriage was doomed."

"It's been all right, though, hasn't it?"

Shelly smiled. "It's been so easy—love does that, you know. Love takes something that's difficult and makes it feel so effortless. You'll understand what I mean in a few months."

Unfortunately Jill shared little of her friend's confidence. She was delighted that things had worked out between Shelly and Mark, but she didn't expect that kind of happiness for her and Jordan.

"When you think about it, it's not all that surprising," Shelly had gone on to say. "Take Aunt Milly and Uncle John for example. She's educated and idealistic, and John, bless his heart, was a realist and a mechanic with a grade-school education. Yet he was so proud of her. He loved her until the day he died."

"Mark will always love you, too," Jill said, smoothing the satin of the wedding dress.

"Jordan feels the same way about you."

Jill's heart stopped. It hit her then, for perhaps the first time—Jordan loved her. His love had guided Jill through her uncertainty. It had helped her understand what had led her to this point, helped her look past her mother's tears and her own doubts.

The small reception and dinner held immediately after the ceremony featured a light, elegant meal and a festive atmosphere. Jill met several of Jordan's business associates, who seemed both surprised and pleased for them. Even the Lundquists put in a jovial appearance, although Suzi was absent.

When it came time for them to leave, Jill kissed Andrew Howard's cheek and thanked him once more. "Everything's been wonderful."

"I lost my only son," he reminded her, his eyes momentarily aged and sad. "For years I've hungered for a family. After my wife died, and even before, I shut myself away, locked in my grief, and watched the world go on without me."

"You're being too hard on yourself," Jill told him. "Your work—"

"True enough," he said, cutting her off. "For a while I was able to bury myself in my company, but two years ago I realized I'd wasted too much of my life struggling with this grief. Soon afterward I decided to retire." His gaze wandered away from Jill and toward her mother, and he smiled. "I think the time might be right for me to make other changes, take the next step. What do you think, my dear?"

Jill smiled, too. Her mother needed someone like Andrew. Someone to teach her that love didn't always mean pain.

"I'd forgotten what it was like to be young," he said, now smiling easily. "I've known Jordan nearly all his life. I've watched him build a name for himself and admired his cunning. He's good, Jill. But he's a man without a family, and I suspect I see a lot of myself in him. The thought of him growing old and disillusioned with life troubled me. I want him to avoid the mistakes I made."

Funny how her mother had said basically the same thing to Jill a few hours earlier. "There are certain mistakes we each have to make," Jill returned softly. "It's the only way we seem to learn, painful as it is."

"How smart you are," Andrew said, chuckling. "Much too clever for your years."

"I love him." Somehow it was important Mr. Howard know that. "I have no idea whether my love will make a lot of difference, but…"

"Ah, that's where you're wrong. It will change him. Love does that, my dear, and he needs you so badly."

"How can you be sure I'll have any influence over Jordan's life? I'm marrying him because I love him, but I don't expect anything to change."

"It will. Just wait and see."

"How do you know that?"

His smile came slowly, transforming his face, brightening his eyes and relaxing his mouth. "Because," he said, clasping her hand in his own, "because it once changed my life, and I'm hopeful that it will again." He glanced at her mother as he spoke, and Jill leaned over to give him another quick kiss.

"Good luck," she whispered.

"Jill," Jordan called then, approaching her. "Are you ready?"

She looked at her husband of less than two hours and nodded. He was referring to their honeymoon trip, but she... she was thinking about their lives together.

"Hmm," Jill murmured as the first light of dawn crept into their hotel room. She yawned widely, covering her mouth with both hands.

"Good morning, wife," Jordan said, kissing her ear.

"Good morning, husband."

"Did you sleep well?"

Eyes closed, she nodded.

"Me, too."

"I was exhausted," Jill told him, smiling shyly.

"No wonder."

Although her eyes remained closed, Jill knew Jordan was smiling. Her introduction to the physical aspect of their marriage had been incredible, wonderful. Jordan was a patient and gentle lover. Jill had felt understandably nervous, but he'd been tender and reassuring.

"I didn't know it could be so good," she said, snuggling in her husband's arms.

"I didn't, either," he surprised her by saying. His lips were in her hair, his hands exploring her skin. "It's enough to make a husband think about wasting the morning in bed."

"Wasting?" Jill teased, a smile lifting the corners of her mouth. "Surely I misunderstood you. The Jordan Wilcox I've met wouldn't know how to waste time."

"It all has to do with the musical rest," he said seductively. "The all-important caesura. Who would ever have guessed something so small could change a man's entire life?" He kissed her with a hunger that moved her, then made love to her with a need that humbled her.

It was noon before they left the hotel room and one o'clock when they returned.

"Jordan," Jill said, blushing when he reached for her, "it's the middle of the day."

"So?"

"So…it's indecent."

"Really?" But as he spoke, he was lowering his mouth to hers. The kiss was intoxicating, and any resistance Jill might have felt vanished like ice in the sun.

She rested her palms against his shoulders as he kissed her again and again.

Unable to stop herself, Jill moaned softly.

Dragging his mouth from hers, he trailed kisses down the side of her neck. "There's that sightseeing trip you wanted to take," he reminded her. "To see the pineapple and sugarcane fields."

"It's not important. We could see them another time," she said breathlessly.

"That's not what you claimed earlier."

"I was just thinking…" She didn't get the opportunity to finish. Jordan's kiss absorbed her words and scattered the thought.

"What did you think?"

"That married people should occasionally be willing to change their plans," she managed to say.

Jordan chuckled, and lifting her gently into his arms, carried her to the bed. "I'm beginning to think married life is going to agree with me." His mouth found hers and gentleness gave way to urgency.

Five days later, when Jordan and Jill returned to the mainland, their honeymoon over, Jill was so deeply in love with her husband she wondered why she'd ever hesitated, why she'd fought so hard against marrying him.

The first person she called when they arrived at the penthouse was Shelly. Jordan had arranged to have her things moved there while they were away. Ralph lived at her previous apartment now and was elated with the extra space.

"Have you got time to meet an old friend for lunch?" Jill asked without preamble.

"Jill!" Shelly cried. "When did you get back?"

"About an hour ago." Although he hadn't said as much, she knew Jordan was dying to get to his office. "I thought I'd steal away for a few minutes and meet you."

"I'd love to see you. Just name the time and place."

Jill did, then kissed Jordan on the cheek while he was talking to his assistant on the phone in his study. He broke away, covered the mouthpiece with his hand and gave her a surprised look. "Where are you headed?"

"Out for lunch. You don't mind, do you?"

"No." But he didn't sound all that sure.

"I thought you'd want to go to the office," she said.

"I do." He wrapped his arm around her waist, bringing her close to his side.

"I know, so I thought I'd meet Shelly."

He grinned, kissed her lightly and resumed his telephone conversation as though she'd already left. Jill lingered at the door, waiting for the elevator. Part of her longed to stay with him, to hold on to the happiness before it escaped, before it was dispersed by everyday tensions and demands.

"Well," Shelly said a half hour later as she slid into the restaurant booth across from Jill, "how are the newlyweds?"

"Wonderful."

"I thought you'd be more tanned."

Jill blushed; Shelly laughed and reached for her napkin. "It was the same with Mark and me. I swear, we didn't leave that hotel room for three days."

"We made several short trips," Jill said, but she didn't elaborate on exactly how short their sightseeing ventures had been.

"Married life certainly seems to agree with you."

"It's only been a week," Jill reminded her friend. "That's hardly time enough to tell."

"I knew after the first week," Shelly said confidently, her face animated by a smile. "I figured if Mark and I survived the honeymoon, our marriage had a chance. Mark wanted to honeymoon at Niagara Falls, remember?"

"And you suggested a rafting trip through the Grand Canyon." Jill smiled at the memory. Mark preferred tradition, while Shelly craved adventure, but in the end, they'd learned what she and Jordan had already discovered. All that mattered was their marriage, their love for each other.

"We couldn't agree," Shelly continued. "I was seriously worried about it. If we were at odds over a honeymoon site, then what on earth would happen when it came to dealing with the really important issues?"

Jill understood what Shelly meant. She loved Jordan; of that there could be no doubt. Now she had to place her trust in their love, hope it was strong enough to withstand day-to-day reality. She was still fearful, but ready to fight for her marriage, to keep it safe.

Suddenly Shelly set aside the menu, pressed her hand against her stomach and slowly exhaled.

"Shell, what's wrong?"

Shelly briefly closed her eyes. "Nothing bad. I just can't stand to read about food."

"About food?" That made no sense to Jill.

"I'm two months pregnant."

"Shelly!" Jill was so excited she nearly toppled her water glass. "Why didn't you say something sooner? Good grief, I'm your best friend—I'd think you'd want me to know."

"I do, but I couldn't tell you until I knew for sure, could I?"

"You just found out?"

"Not exactly." Shelly reached for a small packet of soda crackers, tore away the cellophane wrapper and munched on one. "I found out before your wedding, but I didn't want to say anything then."

Jill appreciated Shelly's considerateness, her wish not to compete with Jill's important day.

"Actually, it was Mark who told me. Imagine a husband explaining the facts of life to his wife. I'm such a scatter-brain, I made a mistake. I miscalculated and didn't even know it."

As far as Jill was concerned, this baby certainly wasn't a mistake, and from Shelly's happy glow, her friend felt the same way.

"I was afraid Mark might be upset. Naturally we'd talked

about starting a family, but neither of us planned to have it happen so soon."

"He wasn't upset, though, was he?" Jill would've been shocked if Mark had been anything but thrilled.

"Not in the least. When he first told me what he suspected, I just laughed." She shook her head in mock consternation. "You'd think I'd know better than to question a man who sleeps with his daily planner by his side!"

"I'm thrilled for you."

"Now that I've adjusted to it, I can't wait. I'm looking forward to decorating the nursery and wearing maternity clothes and *everything*."

After the waitress had taken their order, Jill leaned back against the banquette cushion. "It happened just like you said it would," she said.

"What did?"

"Loving Jordan." Jill felt a little shy talking so openly about something so intimate. Although she and Jordan were married and deeply in love with each other, they never spoke of their feelings. Jordan was still uncomfortable with expressing emotion. But he didn't need to tell Jill he loved her, not when he went about proving it every way he knew how. She'd never pressured him, never demanded the words.

"The day we were married you told me love makes the difficult things seem effortless. Remember?"

Ever confident, Shelly grinned. "You're going to be so happy…" She paused, swallowed and reached for her napkin, dabbing her eyes. "I get so emotional these days, I can't believe it. The other night I found myself crying at a stupid television commercial."

"You? Seattle's drama queen? Impossible," Jill teased.

Shelly shook her head ruefully. "Yes, me." She began to laugh, and Jill joined in.

Laughter came easily since her marriage; it was all the happiness in her heart brimming over, spilling out. She'd never felt so carefree or laughed at so many silly things before.

When Jill returned from lunch two hours later, Jordan was gone. Exhausted from the flight and the excitement of the past week, she crawled into bed and slept, not waking until it was dark.

Rolling onto her back, she stretched luxuriously under the weight of the blanket and smiled, musing how thoughtful it was of Jordan to let her sleep.

She kicked aside the blanket and searched blindly for her shoes. Yawning, she walked into the living room, surprised to find it dark.

"Jordan?" she called.

She was greeted by silence.

Turning on the lights, Jill was shocked to discover it was after nine. Jordan must still be at the office, she supposed, her stomach knotting. Could it be happening so soon? Could he have grown tired of her already?

No sooner had the thought formed than the elevator doors opened and Jordan appeared. She didn't fly into his arms, although that was her first instinct.

"Hello," she greeted him, a bit coolly.

He was loosening his tie. "What time is it?"

"Nine-fifteen. Are you hungry?"

He paused, as though he needed to think about it. "Yeah, I guess I am. Sorry I didn't call. I didn't have a clue it was this late."

"That's okay," she muttered, although it really wasn't.

He followed her into the kitchen and slid his arms around her waist while she investigated the contents of the refrigerator.

"It won't be like this every night," he said, his words sounding very much like a promise her father had once made to her mother.

"I know," Jill said, desperately hoping that was true.

She couldn't sleep that night. Perhaps it was the long nap she'd taken in the middle of the afternoon; at least that was what she tried to tell herself. More likely, though, it was the gnawing fear that Jordan's love for her was already faltering. She tried to push the doubts aside, tried to convince herself she was overreacting. He'd been away from his office for a week. There must have been all kinds of important issues that required his attention. Was she expecting too much?

In the morning, she promised herself, she'd talk to him about it. But when she awoke, Jordan had left for the office.

Frowning, she dressed and wandered into the kitchen for a cup of coffee.

"Morning." Jordan's cook, Mrs. Murphy, a middle-aged woman with lively blue eyes and a wide smile, greeted her. Jill smiled back, although her cheerfulness felt a little strained.

"Hello, Mrs. Murphy, it's nice to see you again," she said, helping herself to coffee. "Uh, what time did Jordan leave this morning?"

"Early," the cook said with a disappointed sigh. "I was thinking Mr. Wilcox would stop working so hard once he was married. He hasn't even been home from his honeymoon twenty-four hours and he's already at the office at the crack of dawn."

Jill hated to disillusion the woman, but this wasn't Jordan's first trip to the office. "I'll see what I can do about giving him some incentive to stay home," Jill said, savoring her coffee.

Mrs. Murphy chuckled. "I'm glad to hear it. That man works too many hours. I've been telling my George that Mr. Wilcox needs a wife to keep him home at night."

"I'll do my best," Jill said, but she had the distinct feeling her efforts would make little difference. Checking her watch, she quickly drank the rest of her coffee and hurried into the bedroom to shower.

Within half an hour she was dressed and ready for work.

"Mrs. Murphy," she told the cook, "I'll be at work—Pay-Rite Pharmacy—if Jordan happens to call. Tell him I'll be home shortly after five." Jill wished she'd had the chance to talk to him herself; she knew he was going to be tied up in meetings and conference calls, so she was reluctant to interrupt. Still, she was more than a little distressed that within a week of their wedding she was communicating with her husband through a third party.

Despite everything, Jill enjoyed her day, which was busier than usual. The pharmacy staff took her out for a celebration lunch, and dozens of customers came by to wish her well. Many of the people whose prescriptions she filled regularly had become friends. In light of how her married life was working out, Jill was thankful she'd decided to keep her job.

By five she was eager to get home, eager to share her day with Jordan and hear about his. She was met by the aroma of cheese, tomato sauce and garlic, and followed it into the kitchen, where she found Mrs. Murphy untying her apron.

"Whatever you're cooking smells absolutely delicious."

"It's my lasagna. Mr. Wilcox's favorite."

Jill opened the oven door and peeked inside. She was famished. "Did Jordan phone?" she asked, her voice rising on a note of longing.

"About fifteen minutes ago. I told him you'd be home a bit after five."

No sooner were the words out than the phone rang. Jill saw Jordan's office number on call display and answered immediately.

"This is Brian Macauley, Mr. Wilcox's assistant," a crisp male voice informed her. "He's asked that I let you know he won't be home for dinner."

Nine

"Jill."

Her name seemed to come from a long way off. Someone was calling her, but she could barely hear.

"Sweetheart." The voice was louder now.

She snuggled into the warmth, ignoring the persistent sound. After hours and hours of forcing herself to stay awake, she'd finally given up and succumbed to the sweet seduction of sleep.

"Honey, if you don't wake up, you'll get a crick in your neck."

"Jordan?" Her eyes instantly flew open, and she saw her husband kneeling on the carpet beside her chair. She straightened, throwing her arms around his neck. "Oh, Jordan," she whispered, "I'm so glad you're home."

"With this kind of reception, I'll have to stay away more often."

Jill decided to ignore that comment. "What time is it?"

"Late" was all he said.

She kissed him, needing him, savoring the feel of his

arms around her. He looked dreadful. He hadn't been home for dinner in well over a week and spent all hours of the day and night at his office.

Although she'd asked him several times, Jordan's only explanation was that a project he'd been working on had developed problems. *A project.* For this he was willing to send both their lives into tumult; for this he was willing to place their marriage at risk. The upheaval had all but ruined the memory of their brief idyllic honeymoon. They'd been back in Seattle for two weeks now, and Jill hadn't been allotted a single uninterrupted hour of Jordan's time.

"Are you hungry?" She doubted he'd eaten a decent meal in days.

He shook his head, then rubbed his face wearily. "I'm more tired than anything."

"How much longer is this going to continue?" she asked, keeping her voice as steady as she could. She'd gone into this marriage with her eyes wide open. From the moment she'd met Jordan, she'd known how stiff the competition would be, how demanding his way of life was. She'd always known it would be difficult to keep their marriage intact. But she'd figured their love would hold the edge for at least the first couple of years.

Unfortunately she'd figured wrong. If anything, she'd underestimated the strength of his obsession with business and success. Jordan loved her; he might rarely have told her that, but Jill didn't need the words. What she did need was some of his time, his attention.

"I've hardly seen you all week," she reminded him. "You're gone before I wake up in the mornings. Heaven only knows what time you get home at night."

"It won't be much longer," Jordan said stiffly, standing. "I promise."

"Would it be so terrible if this project folded?"

"Yes," he returned emphatically.

"One failure isn't the end of the world, you know."

Jordan smiled wryly, and his condescension angered her.

"It's true," she said. "Did I ever tell you about trying out for the lead in the high-school play during my senior year?"

Jordan frowned. "No, but is this another story like the one about your piano-playing?"

Jill tucked her legs under her and rested one elbow on the chair arm. "A little."

Jordan sank down on the leather sofa across from her, leaned his head back and closed his eyes. "In that case, why don't you move directly to the point and skip the story?"

He wasn't being rude, Jill told herself, only practical. He was exhausted and in desperate need of rest. He didn't have the energy to wade through her mournful tale in search of a moral.

"All right," she agreed amicably enough. "You've probably already guessed I didn't get the lead. But I'd been so sure I would. I'd played major roles in several plays. In fact, I'd gotten every part I'd ever tried out for. Not only didn't I get this part, I wasn't even in the play, and darn it all, even now I think I would've done a good job of playing Helen Keller."

He grinned. "I'm sure you would have, too."

"What I learned from that experience was not to fear failure. I survived not playing Helen Keller, and later, in college, when I was awarded a wonderful role, it heightened my appreciation of that success." When Jordan didn't immediately respond, she added, "Do you understand what I'm saying or are you asleep?"

His eyes were still closed but his mouth lifted in a gentle smile. "I was just mulling over the sad history of your musical and acting careers."

Jill smiled, too. "I know it sounds ludicrous, but failure liberated me. My heart and soul went into my audition for that role, and when I lost, I felt I could never act again. It took me a long time to regain my confidence, to be willing to hazard another rejection, but eventually I was the stronger for it. When I decided to try out for a play in my freshman year of college, I felt as though I was somehow protected, because failure wasn't going to rock me the way it had earlier."

"So you wanted to be an actress?"

"No, I'm not much good at waiting tables."

Jordan didn't immediately catch her joke, but when he did, he laughed out loud.

"You know what they say about hindsight being twenty-twenty? In this case it's true. If failure hadn't taught me to appreciate success when I got it, I might have fallen into a nasty trap."

"What was that?"

"Thinking I deserved it, believing I was so talented, so gifted, so good that I'd never lose."

Jordan fell silent. Jill waited a moment, then said, "Mr. Howard told me something…about the shopping-mall project. I didn't say anything to you at the time because…well, because I wasn't sure he wanted me to."

She had Jordan's full attention now.

He straightened, his eyes searching hers. "What did he say?"

"He hasn't often gone in on construction projects with you, has he?"

"Only a handful of times."

"There's a reason for that."

"Oh?"

"You've never failed."

Jordan's head came up sharply. "I beg your pardon?"

Jill knew he found such thinking preposterous. If anything, his successes should have been an inducement to his financial supporters.

"Mr. Howard explained that he doesn't like to deal with a man until he's been devastated financially at least once."

"That makes no sense," Jordan returned irritably.

"Perhaps not. Since my experience in the financial world is limited to paying my bills, I wouldn't know," Jill admitted.

"Who's going to lend money to someone who's failed?"

"Apparently Andrew Howard," Jill said with a grin. "He told me the man who's lost everything is much more careful the next time around."

"I didn't realize you and Howard talked business."

"We didn't." She did her best to appear nonchalant. "Mostly we discussed you."

This didn't please Jordan, either. "I'd prefer to think I owe my success to hard work, determination and foresight. I certainly wouldn't have come as far as I have without them."

"True enough, but—"

"Is there always going to be a but?"

Jill tried to hold back a laugh. Actually she was enjoying this, while her tired husband was left to suffer the indignities of her insights.

"Well," he said shortly, "go on, knock down my argument."

"Oh, I agree your intelligence and dedication have played a large role in your success, but others have worked just as hard, been just as determined and shown just as much foresight—and lost everything."

Jordan scowled. "My, you're full of cheer, aren't you?"

"I don't want you to put so much store in this one project. If it falls apart, so what? You're beating yourself to death with this." She didn't mention what it was doing to their marriage.

He considered her words for a few seconds, then his face tightened. "I won't lose. I absolutely, categorically, refuse not to succeed."

"How much longer?" Jill asked when she could disguise the defeat and frustration she was feeling.

He hesitated, then massaged the back of his neck as though to ease away a tiredness that stretched from the top of his head to the bottom of his feet. "A week. It shouldn't be much more than that."

A week. Seven days. She closed her eyes, because looking at him, seeing him this exhausted, this spent, was painful. He needed her support now, not her censure.

"All right," she murmured.

"I don't like this any better than you do." Jordan stood and held her securely in his embrace, burying his face in the curve of her neck. "I'm a newlywed, remember. There's no one I want to spend time with more than my wife."

Jill nodded, because it would have been impossible to speak.

"I wish you hadn't waited up for me," he said, lifting her into his arms and carrying her into their bedroom. Without turning on the light, he settled her on the bed and lay down beside her, placing his head on her chest. Jill's fingers idly stroked his hair.

Words burned in her throat, the need to unburden herself, but she dared not. Jordan was exhausted. This wasn't the right time.

Would it ever be the right time?

There'd been so many lonely evenings, so many empty mornings. Every night Jill went to bed alone, and only when Jordan slipped in beside her did she feel alive. Only when they were together did she feel whole. So she waited night after night for a few precious minutes, knowing they were all he had to spare.

The even sound of Jordan's breathing told her he'd fallen asleep. The weight on her chest was growing uncomfortable, yet she continued to stroke his hair for several minutes, unwilling to disturb his rest.

She'd always known it would come to this; she just hadn't expected it to happen so soon.

A week. He'd promised her it would be over within a week.

And it would be—until the next time.

Jill awoke early the following morning, astonished to find Jordan asleep beside her. At some point during the night he'd rolled away from her and covered them both with a blanket. He hadn't bothered to undress.

Jill wriggled toward him and playfully kissed his ear. She knew she ought to let him sleep, but she also knew he'd be annoyed if he was late for the office.

Slowly he opened his eyes, looking surprised to see her there with him.

"Morning," she whispered, with a series of tiny, nibbling kisses.

"What time is it?" he asked.

"Almost eight." She looped her arms around his neck and smiled down at him.

"Hmm. An indecent hour."

"Very indecent."

"My favorite time of day." His fingers were busy unfastening the opening of her pajama top and his eyes blazed with unmistakable need.

"Jordan," she said breathlessly, "you'll be late for work."

"I fully intend to be," he said, directing her lips to his.

"It's happening already, isn't it?" Elaine Morrison said bluntly the next Saturday. She stood in Jill's living room, holding a china cup and saucer and staring out the window. The view of the Olympic Mountains was spectacular, the white peaks jutting against a backdrop of bright blue sky as fluffy clouds drifted past.

Jill knew precisely what her mother was saying. She responded the only way she could—truthfully. "Yes."

Elaine turned, her face pale, haunted with the pain of the past, the pain she saw reflected in her daughter's life. "I was afraid of this."

Until recently, Jill had found communicating with her mother difficult. After her husband's death, Elaine had withdrawn from life, hidden herself away in her grief and regrets. In many ways, Jill had lost her mother at the same time as she had her father.

"Mom, it's all right," Jill said in an attempt to reassure her. "It's only for the next little while. Once this project's under control everything will be different."

Jill knew better. She wasn't fooling herself, and she sincerely doubted she'd be able to fool her mother.

"I warned you," Elaine said, walking to the white leather

sofa and sitting tensely on the edge. Setting the cup and saucer on a nearby table, she turned pleading eyes to Jill. "Didn't I tell you? The day of the wedding—"

"Yes, Mother, you warned me."

"Why didn't you listen?"

Jill exhaled slowly, praying for patience. "I'm in love with him, just like you loved Daddy."

It seemed unfair to drag her father into this, her much-grieved father, but it was the only way Jill could explain.

"What are you going to do about it?"

"Mother," Jill sighed. "It's not as though Jordan's having an affair."

"He might as well be," Elaine replied heatedly. "Here it is, Saturday afternoon and he's working. One look at him told me he had the same drive and ambition, the same need for power, as your father."

"Mother, please... It isn't like that with Jordan."

The older woman's eyes were infinitely sad as she gazed at her daughter. "Don't count on that, Jill. Just don't count on it."

Her mother's visit had unsettled Jill. Afterward, she tried to relax with a book, but couldn't concentrate. The phone rang at six, just as it had every night that week. One of Jordan's assistants had called to let her know he wouldn't be home for dinner.

One ring.

Walking over to the phone, Jill stood directly in front of it, but didn't pick up the receiver.

Two rings.

Drawing in a deep breath, she flexed her fingers. Twice in the past couple of weeks, Jordan had phoned himself.

Maybe he'd be on the other end of the line, inviting her to join him for dinner. Maybe he was phoning to tell her he'd unscrambled the entire mess and he'd be home within the next half hour. Perhaps he was calling to suggest they take a few days off and vacation somewhere exotic, just the two of them.

Three rings.

Jill could feel her pulse throbbing at the base of her throat. But she didn't answer.

Four rings.

Five rings.

The phone went silent.

Her entire body was trembling when she turned away and walked into the bedroom. She sat on the bed and covered her face with both hands.

The phone began to ring again, the sound reverberating loudly through the apartment. Jill slapped her hands over her ears, unable to bear it. Each ring tormented her, pretending to offer hope when there was none. It wouldn't be Jordan, but his assistant, and his message would be the same one he'd relayed every night that week.

Making a rapid decision, Jill got her jacket and purse and hurried toward the penthouse elevator, purposely leaving her cell phone behind.

Not having any particular destination, she wandered downtown until she passed a movie theater and decided to go in. The movie wasn't one that really interested her, but she bought a ticket, anyway, willing to subject herself to a B-grade comedy if it meant she could escape for a couple of hours.

The movie actually turned out to be quite entertaining. The plot was ridiculous, but there were enough humorous moments to make her laugh. And if Jill had ever needed some comic relief, it was now.

On impulse she stopped at a deli and picked up a couple of sandwiches, then flagged down a taxi. Before she could change her mind, she gave the driver the address of Jordan's office building.

She had a bit of trouble convincing the security guard to admit her, but eventually, after the guard talked to Jordan, she was allowed inside.

"Jill," he snapped when she stepped off the elevator, "where have you been?"

"It's good to see you, too," she said, ignoring the irritation in his voice. She kissed his cheek, then walked casually past him.

"Where were you?"

"I went out to a movie," she said, strolling into his office. His desk, a large mahogany one, was littered with folders and papers. She noted dryly that he was alone. Everyone else was gone, but he hadn't afforded himself the same luxury.

"You were at a movie?"

She didn't answer. "I thought you might be hungry," she said, neatly stacking a pile of folders in order to clear one small corner of his desk. "I went to Griffin's and bought us both something to eat."

"I ate earlier."

"Oh." So much for that brilliant idea. "Unfortunately, I didn't." She plopped herself down in the comfortable leather chair and pulled a turkey-on-rye from the sack, along with a cup of coffee, setting both on the space she'd cleared.

Jordan looked as though he wasn't sure what to do with her. He leaned over the desk and shoved several files to one side.

"I'm not interrupting anything, am I?"

"Of course not," he answered dryly. "I was staying late for the fun of it."

"There certainly isn't any reason to hurry home," she returned just as dryly.

Jordan rubbed his eyes, and his shoulders slumped. "I'm sorry, Jill. These past few weeks have been hard on you, haven't they?"

He moved behind her and grasped her shoulders. His touch had always had a calming effect on Jill, but she wanted to fight it, wanted to fight her weakness for him.

"Jill," Jordan whispered. "Let's go home." He bent down and kissed the side of her neck. A shiver raced through her body and Jill breathed deeply, placing her hands over his.

"Home," she repeated softly, as if it was the most beautiful word in the English language.

"Jill!" Shelly's eyes widened when she opened the front door one evening a few weeks later. "What's wrong?"

"Wrong," Jill repeated numbly.

"You look awful."

"How kind of you to point it out."

"I've got it!" Shelly said excitedly. "You're pregnant, too."

"Unfortunately, no," she said, passing Shelly and walking into the kitchen. She took a clean mug from the dishwasher and poured herself a cup of coffee. "How are you feeling, by the way?"

"Rotten," Shelly admitted, then added with a smile, "Wonderful."

Jill pulled out a kitchen chair and sat down. If she spent another evening alone, she was going to go crazy. She probably should have phoned Shelly first rather than dropping in unannounced, but driving over here had given her an excuse to leave the penthouse. This evening she badly needed an excuse. Anything to get away. Anything to escape the loneliness. Funny, she'd lived by herself for years, yet she'd never felt so empty, so alone, as she had in the past two months. Even the conversation with Andrew Howard earlier in the evening had only momentarily lifted her spirits.

"Where's Mark?"

Shelly grinned. "You won't believe it if I tell you."

"Tell me."

"He's taking a carpentry class."

"Carpentry? Mark?"

Shelly's grin broadened. "He wants to make a cradle for the baby. He's so sweet I can hardly stand it. You know Mark, he's absolutely useless when it comes to anything practical. Give him a few numbers and he's a whiz kid, but when he has to change a lightbulb, he needs an instruction manual. I love him dearly, but when he told me he was going to build a cradle for the baby, I couldn't help it, I laughed."

"Shelly!"

"I know. It was a rotten thing to do, so Mark's out there proving how wrong I am. This is his first night, and I just hope the instructor doesn't kick him out of the class."

Despite her unhappiness, Jill smiled. It felt good to be around Shelly, to laugh again, to have a reason to laugh.

"I haven't talked to you in ages," Shelly remarked. "But then I shouldn't expect to, should I? You and Jordan are still on your honeymoon, aren't you?"

Tears sprang instantly to Jill's eyes, blurring her vision. "Yes," she lied, looking away, praying that Shelly, who was so happy in her own marriage, wouldn't notice how miserable Jill was in hers.

"Oh, before I forget," Shelly said excitedly, "I heard from Aunt Milly."

"What did she have to say?"

"She asked me to thank you for your letter, telling her about meeting Jordan and everything. She loves a good romance. Then she said something odd."

"Oh?"

"She felt the dress was meant to be worn one more time."

"Again? By whom?"

Shelly leaned forward. "You and Jordan were too wrapped up in each other on your wedding day to notice, but your mother and Mr. Howard got along famously. Milly wouldn't have known that, of course, but...it's obviously meant to be."

"My mother." Now that she recalled her conversation with Andrew at the wedding, it made sense. In the weeks since their return from Hawaii, she'd forgotten about it. He'd phoned Jill twice, but he hadn't mentioned Elaine, nor had her mother mentioned him.

"What do you think?"

"My mother and Mr. Howard?" Jill experienced a feeling of rightness.

"Isn't that incredible?" Shelly positively beamed. Until recently—the arrival of the wedding dress, to be exact—Jill hadn't realized what a complete romantic her friend was.

"But Mom hasn't said a word."

"Did you expect her to?"

Jill shrugged. Shelly was right; Elaine would approach romance and remarriage with extreme caution.

"Wouldn't it be fabulous if your mother ended up wearing the dress?"

Jill nodded and, placing her fingertips to her temples, closed her eyes. "A vision's coming to me now...."

Shelly laughed.

"I think we should call my mom and tell her that we both had a clear vision of her standing in the dress next to a distinguished-looking older man."

Once again, Shelly giggled. "Oh, that's good. That's really good." She sighed contentedly. "The dress definitely belongs with your mother. We'll have to do something about that soon."

Jill pretended her tears were ones of mirth and dashed them away with the back of one hand.

But the amusement slowly faded from Shelly's eyes. "Are you going to tell me what's wrong, or are you going to make me force it out of you?"

"I— I'm fine."

"No, you're not. Don't forget I know you. You've been my best friend for years. You wouldn't be here if something wasn't wrong."

"It's that crazy wedding dress again," Jill confessed.

"The wedding dress?"

"I should never have worn it."

"Jill!" Shelly exclaimed, then frowned. "I don't understand what you're saying."

"It clouded my judgment. I was always the romantic one, remember? Always a sucker for a good love story. When Milly first mailed you the dress, I thought it was the neatest thing to happen since low-fat ice cream."

"Not true! Remember how you persuaded me—"

"I know what I said," Jill interrupted. "But deep down, I could hardly wait to see what happened. When you and Mark decided to marry, I was thrilled. Later, after I arrived in Hawaii and you had the dress delivered to me, I kind of allowed myself to play along with the fantasy. I've wanted to get married for a long time. I'd like to have children."

"Jill," Shelly said, looking puzzled, "I'm not sure I follow you."

"I think I might even have felt a little…jealous that you got married before I did. I was the one who wanted a husband, not you, and yet here you were, so much in love. Somehow it just didn't seem fair." The tears slipped down her cheeks and she absently brushed them away.

"But you're married now and Jordan's crazy about you."

"He was for about a week, but that's worn off."

"He loves you!"

"Yes, I suppose in his own way he does." Jill didn't have the strength to argue. "But not enough."

"Not enough?"

"It's too hard to explain," she said. "I came over to tell you I've made a decision." As hard as she tried, she couldn't keep herself from sobbing, "I've decided to leave Jordan."

Ten

Shelly's eyes narrowed with disbelief. "You can't possibly mean that!"

Leaving Jordan wasn't a decision Jill had made lightly. She'd agonized over it for days. Unable to answer her friend, she pushed back her hair with hands that wouldn't stop shaking. Her stomach was in knots. "It just isn't going to work. I need some time away from him to sort through my feelings. I don't *want* to leave, but I'm afraid I'll just fall apart if I stay."

Shelly had never been one to disguise her feelings. Anger flashed from her eyes. "You haven't given the marriage a decent chance. It hasn't even been two months."

"I know everything I need to know. Jordan isn't married to me, he's married to his company. Shelly, you're my best friend—but there are things you don't know, things I can't explain about what's happening between me and Jordan. Things that go back to my childhood and being raised the way I was."

"You love him."

Jill closed her eyes and nodded. She did love Jordan, so much her heart was breaking, so much she didn't know if she'd survive leaving him, so much she doubted she'd ever love this deeply again.

"I don't expect you to understand," Jill continued, choking over the words. "I wanted you to know…because I'm going to be living with my mother for a while. Just until I can sort through my feelings and figure out what I'm going to do."

"Have you told him yet?" Shelly's voice sounded less sharp.

"No." Jill had delayed that as long as possible, not knowing what to say or how to say it. This wasn't a game, or an attempt to manipulate Jordan into devoting more time to her and their marriage. She refused to fall into that trap. If she was going to make the break, she wanted it to be clean. Decisive. Not cluttered with threats.

"You *do* plan to tell him?"

"Of course." She could never be so cowardly as to move out while Jordan was at the office. Besides, the sorry truth was that she might be gone for days before he noticed.

Confronting him wasn't a task she relished. She could predict his reaction—he'd be furious with her, more furious than she'd ever seen him. Jill was prepared for that. But in the end he would let her go as if she meant nothing to him. His pride would demand that.

"When do you plan to tell him?" Shelly asked softly, seeming to understand for the first time Jill's torment. A true sign of their friendship was that Shelly didn't ply her with questions, but accepted Jill's less-than-satisfactory explanation.

"Tonight." She hadn't packed yet, but she intended to do that when she got home.

Home.

The word echoed in her mind. Although the penthouse was so distinctly marked with Jordan's personality, it did feel like home. She'd only lived there a short while, but in the lonely weeks following her honeymoon with Jordan, she'd become intimately acquainted with every room. She was going to miss the solace she gained from looking out over Puget Sound and the jagged peaks of the Olympics. And Mrs. Murphy had become a special friend, almost like a second mother, who fretted over her and worried about the long hours Jordan worked. Jill would miss her, too. Although Jill hadn't mentioned it to the cook, she guessed that Mrs. Murphy wouldn't be surprised.

"You're sure this is what you want?" Shelly asked regretfully.

Leaving Jordan was the last thing Jill wanted. Yet it had to be done—and soon, before it was too late, before she found it impossible to go.

"Don't answer that," Shelly whispered. "The pain in your eyes says everything I need to know."

Jill stood and searched in her purse for a tissue. The tears were rolling freely down her cheeks now. She had to compose herself before she encountered Jordan. Had to draw on every bit of inner strength she possessed.

Shelly hugged her, and once again Jill was grateful for their friendship. They were as close as sisters, and Jill had never needed family more than she did right then.

The penthouse echoed with emptiness when she arrived home. Jill stood in the middle of the living room, then slowly moved around, skimming her hand over each piece of furniture. Her gaze gravitated toward the view, and she walked over to the window, staring into the night. Far below, lights flashed and glowed, but she was far removed from the brilliance. Far removed from the light…

Finally she entered the bedroom she shared with Jordan. Her breath came in shallow, painful gasps as she dragged out her suitcases and set them on the bed. Carefully, she folded her clothes and deposited them inside.

Several times she had to stop, clutching an article of clothing, crushing the fabric, until she composed herself enough to continue. Tears stung her eyes, but she refused to succumb to them.

"Jill?"

She froze. She hadn't expected Jordan to come home for several hours yet. They'd barely seen one another all week.

"Where are you going?" he asked.

Pulling herself together, Jill turned to face him. Jordan stood on the other side of the room, his expression confused.

"My mother's," she eventually said.

"Is she ill?"

"No…" Drawing a deep breath, hoping it would calm her frantic heart, she forged ahead. "I'm leaving for a while. I—I need to sort out my feelings…make some important decisions."

The fire that leapt into his eyes was filled with anger. "You plan to divorce me?" he demanded incredulously.

"No. For now, I'm just moving in with my mother."

"Why?"

Jill could feel her own anger mounting. "That you even have to ask should be answer enough! Can't you see what's happening? Don't you care? At this rate our marriage isn't going to last another month." She paused to gulp in a much-needed breath. "My instincts told me this would happen, but I was so much in love with you that I chose to ignore what was obvious from the first. You don't need a wife. You never have. I don't understand why you wanted to marry me because—"

"When did all this come on?"

"It's been coming on, as you say, from the minute we got home from our honeymoon. Our marriage has to be one of the shortest on record. One week. That's all the time you allotted to it. I need more than five minutes at the end of the day when you're so exhausted you can hardly speak. I wish I was stronger, but I'm not. I need more from you than you can give me."

"You might have said something to me earlier."

"I did. A hundred times."

"When?" he barked.

"I'm not going to get involved in a shouting match with you, Jordan. I won't sit by and watch you work yourself to death over some stupid project. You'd said ages ago that it'd be finished in a week. I was foolish enough to believe you. If this project is so important to you that you're willing to risk everything to keep it from folding, then fine, it's all yours."

"When did you tell me?" he asked a second time.

"Do you remember our conversation last night?" she asked starkly.

Jordan frowned, then shook his head.

"I didn't think you had."

The previous afternoon, Jill had been so lonely that she'd reached for the phone, planning to call Ralph to invite him to a movie. She'd nearly dialed his number before she remembered she was married. The incident had had a profound effect on her. She didn't *feel* married. She felt abandoned.

Forgotten. Unimportant. If she was going to live her life alone, she could accept that. But she wasn't interested in a one-sided marriage.

This time apart would help her gain perspective, show her what she needed to do. Explaining it to Jordan was impossible. But in time, a week perhaps, she might be able to tell him all that was in her heart.

"What was it you said last night?" Jordan wanted to know, clearly confused.

Jill neatly folded a silk blouse and put it in the suitcase. "I told you how I almost called Ralph to ask him if he wanted to see a movie…and you laughed. Remember? You found it humorous that your wife had forgotten she was a married woman. You didn't bother to understand what had led me to the point of wanting to call an old boyfriend."

"You're not making any sense."

"No, I suppose not. I'm sorry, Jordan. I wish I could explain it better. But as I already told you, I need more from our relationship than you can give me…"

"I've said this project would be settled soon. I'll grant you it's taking longer than I thought, but if you'd just be patient for a little while… Is that so much to ask? You'd think…" He hesitated, then jammed his hands in his pockets and marched across the room. "These past few weeks haven't been a picnic for me, either. You'd think a wife would be willing to lend her husband some support, instead of using threats to bully him into doing what *she* wants."

It didn't surprise Jill that Jordan assumed her leaving was merely a ploy. He didn't realize how serious she was.

"I can't live like this. I just can't!" she cried. "Not now, not ever. I want my children to know their father! My own was a shadow who passed through my life, and I couldn't bear my children to suffer what I did."

"This is a fine time for you to figure it all out," Jordan growled, his hold on his frustration and anger obviously precarious.

"If I could go back and change everything, I would… I would." Hurrying now, she closed her suitcases.

"Are you pregnant?" The question came at her like a bolt of lightning.

"No."

"You're sure?"

"Of course."

A moment of silence followed as she collected her purse and a sweater.

"Nothing I can say is going to change your mind, is it?"

"No." She took the handles of the two suitcases and pulled them off the bed. "If…if there's any reason you need to get hold of me, I'll be at my mother's."

Jordan stood there unmoving, his back toward her. "If you're so set on leaving," he said, "then just go."

"Jill, sweetheart." Her mother knocked lightly, then walked into the darkening bedroom. Jill sat on the padded window seat, her knees tucked under her chin, staring out the bay window to the oak-lined street below. Often as a child she'd sat there and reflected on her problems. But now her problems couldn't be worked out by staring out her bedroom window or by pounding on a piano for an hour or two.

"How are you feeling?"

"Fine." She wasn't ready to talk yet.

"I've made dinner," Elaine said, her voice sympathetic. There was a radiance about her these days. Andrew Howard had called almost daily since Jill had been living with her mother, although he didn't know about her separation from Jordan. Jill had sworn her mother to secrecy. The last Jill had heard, Andrew planned to fly to the mainland early the next month so he and Elaine could spend some time together. Jill was delighted for her mother and for Andrew. Her own situation, though, was bleak.

"Thanks, Mom, but I'm not hungry."

Her mother didn't argue, but sat on the edge of the cushion and leaned forward to hug Jill. The unexpected display of affection moved Jill to tears.

"You haven't eaten anything to speak of all week."

"I'm fine, Mom." Jill didn't want her mother fussing over her just now, and she was grateful when Elaine seemed to realize it. Elaine lovingly stroked Jill's hair, then got to her feet.

"If you need me…"

"I'm fine, Mom."

Her mother hesitated. "Are you going back to him, Jill?"

Jill didn't answer. Not because she didn't want to, but because she didn't know. She hadn't heard from Jordan even once in the week she'd been gone. A concerned Shelly had dropped by twice, unobtrusively leaving the wedding dress, in its original mailing box, on Jill's window seat. Even Ralph had called. But she hadn't heard from Jordan.

She shouldn't miss him this much. Shouldn't feel so empty without him, so lost. Jill had hoped their time apart would clear her thoughts. It hadn't. If anything, they were more confused than ever. Her musings were like snagged fishing lines, impossible to untangle.

She hadn't really expected him to get in touch with her,

but she'd hoped. Foolishly hoped. Although if he had, Jill didn't know how she would've reacted.

The doorbell chimed in the distance. A minute later Jill heard her mother talking with another woman. The voice wasn't familiar and Jill pressed her forehead to her knees, suddenly weary. Part of her had wanted the visitor to be Jordan. Fool that she was, Jill prayed that he'd be willing to put aside his pride enough to come after her, to convince her they could make their marriage work. She ached for the sight of him. Obviously, though, any move would have to come from her. But Jill wasn't ready. Not when her heart was in such turmoil.

"Jill?" Her mother knocked at her bedroom door again and opened it a crack. "There's someone here to see you. A Suzi Lundquist. She says it's important."

"Suzi Lundquist?" Jill repeated incredulously.

"She's waiting for you in the living room," her mother said.

Jill hadn't the slightest idea why Suzi would want to see her. Jordan had used her to ward off the younger woman's affections. Perhaps Suzi still loved Jordan and intended to rekindle the fire. But in that case, she wasn't likely to announce her plans to Jill.

After quickly changing her clothes, Jill went downstairs. Suzi was pacing the living room, her movements tense and agitated, when Jill appeared.

"I hope you're happy."

Jill blinked. "I beg your pardon?"

"He's done it, you know, and it's all because of you."

"Done what?"

"Given up the fight." Suzi was staring at her as though Jill was completely dense.

"I hate to seem ignorant, but I honestly don't know what you're talking about."

"You're married to Jordan, aren't you?"

"Yes." They stood several feet apart from each other, like duelists preparing to choose their weapons.

"Jordan's handed control of the firm to my father and brother," Suzi said impatiently.

"Isn't this rather sudden? When did all this happen?" Surely if Jordan was in a proxy fight, he would've said something to her. Surely he would have let her know. She'd only been away for a week. Nothing could have threatened his hold on the company in that short a time, could it?

"This proxy battle's been going on for months," Suzi snapped. "It all started while you and Jordan were on your honeymoon. He couldn't have chosen a worse time to leave. He knew it, too—that's what was so confusing. When he returned from Hawaii, he had a full-fledged revolt on his hands. Dad used that time against Jordan, buying shares until he controlled as large a percentage of the company as Jordan did. He wanted Jordan out as CEO and my brother in."

"What happened?"

"After months of gathering supporters, of buying and selling stock, of doing whatever he could to avoid a proxy fight," Suzi continued, "Jordan handed the whole thing over to my father, who'll hand it all to my brother on a silver platter. You met Dean, and we both know he doesn't have the leadership or the maturity to be a CEO. Within five years, he'll wipe out everything Jordan's spent his life building."

Jill didn't know what to say. Her immediate reaction was to argue with Suzi. Jordan would never willingly surrender control of his company. She didn't need the younger woman to tell her that Jordan had worked his entire adult life to build the company; he'd invested everything in it—everything.

Although it seemed a long time ago, she remembered that he'd told her about buying the controlling shares. He'd also said he'd soon be forced to battle to remain in power. Jill remembered what she'd said to him. She'd told him she couldn't imagine him losing.

"Jordan's resigned?" she repeated, breathless with disbelief.

"This morning, effective immediately."

"But why?"

"You should know," Suzi said harshly. "Because he's in love with you."

"What has that got to do with anything?"

"Apparently he felt it was either you or the company. He chose you."

"He sent you here to tell me?" That didn't sound like something Jordan would do. He preferred to do his own talking.

Suzi gave a short, humorless laugh. "You've got to be joking. He'd have my hide if he knew I was within a mile of you."

"Then why are you here?"

"Because I fancied myself in love with him not long ago. He was pretty decent about it. He could have used me to his own advantage if he'd wanted, but he didn't. Beneath that surly exterior is a real heart. You know it, too, otherwise you'd never have married him."

"Yes…" Jill agreed softly.

"He needs you. I don't know why you left him, but I figure that's between you and Jordan. He's not the kind of man who'd be unfaithful, so I doubt there's another woman involved. If anything, he's too honorable. If you don't realize what you've got, you're a fool."

Jill's emotions were playing havoc with her. Jordan had resigned! It was too much to take in.

"Are you going to him?" Suzi demanded.

Jill hesitated. "I, uh…"

Suzi shook her head. "If it's pride that's stopping you, I don't think you have anything to worry about. Eventually Jordan will come to you. It may take a while, though, if you're determined to wait him out."

"I'm going to him." Recovering somewhat, Jill looked at Suzi, struggling to speak. "I can't thank you enough for coming. I owe you so much."

"Don't thank me. I just hope you appreciate what he's done," Suzi muttered as she picked up her purse, tucking it under her arm.

"I do," Jill assured her, leading the way to the front door. No sooner had Suzi left than Jill went looking for her mother.

She found her in the kitchen. "I heard," Elaine said before Jill could explain the purpose of the other woman's visit. "It might not last, you know."

"I'm going to him."

Her mother's eyes searched Jill's face before she nodded. "I knew that, too."

As they embraced briefly, Jill whispered, "There's a box in my room, Mom. Shelly brought it over for you—and for Andrew Howard."

The drive into downtown Seattle seemed to take forever. It was rush hour and the only parking space she could find was in a loading zone. Without a qualm, she took it, then hurried toward Jordan's office. Luck was with her because the building hadn't been locked yet, but she was waylaid by a security guard. Fortunately, he was the same man she'd met earlier, and he let her stay.

"Has Mr. Wilcox left yet?" she asked.

"Not yet."

"Thank you," she said, sighing with relief.

She hurried to the elevator. Jordan's office was on the top floor. When the elevator doors opened, she ran down the wide corridor to the outer office where his assistants worked. No one was there, but the double doors leading into Jordan's massive office were open. He was packing the things from his desk into a cardboard box.

Jill stared at Jordan, unable to move or speak. He looked haggard, as though he hadn't slept at all during the week she'd been gone. Dark stubble shadowed his face, and his hair, ordinarily neat and trim, was rumpled.

He must have sensed her presence because he paused in his task, his eyes slowly meeting hers. His hands went still. The whole world seemed to come to a sudden halt. In that unguarded moment she read his pain and it became hers.

"You can't do it!" she cried, choking on a sob. "You just can't."

Jordan's face hardened and he seemed to clamp down on his emotions. He ignored her and continued packing up the objects from his desk. A smile, one that spoke more of sadness than joy, came into his eyes. "Your husband is unemployed as of five o'clock this afternoon."

"Oh, Jordan, why would you do such a thing? For me?

Because I left you? But you never told me... Not once did you explain, even when I pleaded with you. Didn't you trust me enough to tell me what was happening?" That was what hurt most of all, that Jordan had kept everything to himself. Not sharing his burden, carrying it alone.

"It was a mistake not to tell you," he admitted, the regret written clearly across his face. "I realized that the night you left. By nature, I tend to keep my troubles to myself."

"But I'm your *wife*."

He grinned at that, but again his smile was marked with sadness. "I'm new to this marriage business. Obviously I'm not much good at it. The one thing I was hoping to do was keep my business life separate from my personal life. I didn't want to bring my company problems home to you."

"But, Jordan, if I'd known, if you'd explained, I might have been able to help."

"You did, in more ways than you know."

Tears blurred Jill's eyes. She would have given everything she owned for Jordan to take her in his arms, but he stood so far away, so alone.

Jordan picked up a small photograph, one of their wedding day. He stared at it for a moment, then tucked it into the box. "I loved you almost from the day we met. Don't ask me to explain it, because I can't. After that first night, when we kissed on the beach, I knew my life would never be the same."

"Oh, Jordan."

"Being with you was like standing in the sun. I never knew how lonely I was, how my heart ached for love, how much I longed to share my life with someone...."

Tears ran unashamedly down Jill's face.

"The day we were married," he went on, "I swear I've never seen a more beautiful bride. I couldn't believe you'd actually agreed to be my wife. I vowed then and there that I'd never do anything to risk what I'd found."

"But to resign…" Trembling a little, nervous and unsure, Jill moved across the room to Jordan's side. He tensed at her approach, his expression a blend of undisguised longing and hope.

"I can't lose you," he said.

"But to walk away from your life's work?" What he'd done remained incomprehensible to Jill.

"I have a new life," he said, gently pulling her into his arms. He buried his face in her hair and inhaled deeply. "None of this means anything without you. Not anymore."

"But what are you going to do?"

"I thought we'd take a year off and travel. Would you like that?"

Jill nodded through her tears.

"And after that, I'd like to start our family."

Once again Jill nodded, her heart pounding with love and excitement.

"Then, when the time's right, I'll find something that interests me and start over, but I'll never allow work to control my life again. I can't," he said quietly. "You're my life now."

"You're sure this is what you want?" He'd given up so much.

She felt him smile against her hair. "Without a doubt. I don't need a business to fill up the emptiness in my life. Not when I have you."

"Oh, Jordan," she whispered, her throat tight. "I love

you so much." She squeezed her eyes shut and murmured a prayer of thanksgiving for the wonderful man she'd married.

"Shall we go home, my love?" he asked her.

Jill nodded and slipped her hand into his. "Home," she repeated. With her husband. The man she loved. The man she'd married.

* * * * *

Groom Wanted

To Wanda Roberts,
in appreciation of her many skills

One

Julia Conrad wasn't a patient woman at the best of times. She paced her office, repeatedly circling her high-gloss black-lacquer-and-brass desk. She felt so helpless. She should've gone to Citizenship and Immigration Services with Jerry rather than wait for their decision.

Rubbing her palms together, she retracted the thought. She was a wreck and the Immigration people would have instantly picked up on that and it could hurt their case. She couldn't help being anxious. The future of the company rested on the outcome of today's hearing. Ultimately she was the one responsible for the welfare of Conrad Industries, the business her grandfather had started thirty years earlier.

In an effort to calm herself she stared out the window. The weather seemed to echo her mood. There was a ceiling of black clouds, thunder roared and a flash of lightning briefly brightened the room. The lights flickered.

Julia's reflection was mirrored in the window and she frowned, mesmerized by the unexpected sight of herself. Her dark hair was swept back from her face and secured with a gold clasp. She wore a dark suit with a pale gray blouse, which—in her view, anyway—conveyed tasteful refinement. She *looked* cool, calm and collected, but inside she was a mass of tension and nerves. At thirty she had a pleasant face when she smiled, but she hadn't been doing much of that lately. Not in the past three years. Her cheekbones were high, her jaw strong, but it was her eyes that told the story. Her eyes revealed vulnerability and pain.

The image of herself distressed Julia and she hurriedly glanced away. Sighing, she circled her desk once more, silently praying for patience. She was determined to get the company back on its feet, to overcome the odds they faced. Jerry, her brother, had worked with her, sacrificing his personal life the way she had hers. They'd met with a handful of small successes. And now *this.*

Both Julia and Jerry were determined to revive Conrad Industries. Julia owed her father that much. Jerry had shown such faith in her by volunteering his services. If their situations were reversed, she wasn't sure she would've been so forgiving. But her brother had stuck by her through all the turmoil.

Slowly she lowered her gaze, disturbed by that revelation. However, she didn't have the time or the inclination to worry about it. If she ever needed a cool head and a cooler heart, it was now. Two years' worth of innovative research was about to be lost because they'd allowed the fate of the company to hinge on the experiments and ideas of one man. Aleksandr Berinski was a brilliant Russian biochemist. Jerry had met him some years earlier while traveling in Europe and convinced Julia he was the answer to their problems. Her brother was right; Alek's ideas would revolutionize the paint industry. Bringing him to the United

States had been a bold move on their part, but she hadn't been sorry. Not once.

Hiring Aleksandr Berinski from Russia and moving him to Seattle—it was the biggest risk Conrad Industries had ever taken. Now the fate of the company rested in the hands of a hard-nosed official.

Julia wondered again if she should've attended the hearing at the district office of Citizenship and Immigration. She'd done everything within her power to make sure Aleksandr's visa would be extended. She'd written a letter explaining his importance to the company and included documentation to prove that Aleksandr Berinski was a man of distinct merit and exceptional ability.

Jerry, who was a very good corporate attorney, had spent weeks building their case. Professional certifications, affidavits, a copy of Aleksandr's diploma and letters of reference filled Jerry's briefcase.

Her brother had told her there could be problems. It was often difficult to renew an H-2 visa, the type Aleksandr had been granted when he'd entered the United States. The H-2 is one of temporary employment. He'd warned her that if it looked as though employment might become permanent, then Immigration and the Labor Department would be reluctant to extend the visa.

On top of all that, the case had been assigned to a particularly difficult bureaucrat. Jerry had warned her that the agent hearing their case might decide Alek had applied for the temporary visa knowing the job was really permanent and refuse to grant an extension on principle.

She checked her watch again and exhaled with impatience. Only a few minutes had passed. Annoyed with herself for the uncharacteristic display of anxiety, she sat down on her white leather chair. Everything was neatly arranged on the polished black desk. A small marble pen stand was next to the phone. The address and appointment books were perfectly aligned with everything else. Behind the desk stood her computer table, the company website pulled up, its logo prominent. Julia liked to keep her office and her world under control.

When her phone rang, the sound caught her off guard. She grabbed the receiver. "Jerry?"

"Sis," Jerry's voice greeted her. "I'm on my cell. I thought you'd want to know the decision as soon as possible."

"Yes, please."

"I'm afraid it didn't go as well as we'd hoped. They've decided not to renew Alek's visa."

His words felt like a kick in the stomach. She closed her eyes and waited until the shock had passed. It wasn't as if she hadn't known the likelihood of this verdict. The fact that Aleksandr had no proof of a permanent residence in Russia didn't help. In the eyes of Immigration Services that was a red light indicating he didn't intend to return. Furthermore, she and Jerry were dealing with a large, complex bureaucracy. In a fit of worry, Julia had tried to contact the agency herself, reason with them. She'd spent nearly an hour on the phone and hadn't spoken to a single person. She was forced to listen to one recording after another. Press a number on the phone, listen, press another one, then another. She quickly became lost in a hopeless tangle of instructions and messages.

"When will he have to leave?"

"By the end of the week, when his current visa expires."

"That soon?"

"I'm afraid so."

"Jerry, what are we going to do?"

"I'll talk to you about it as soon as we get back to the office," her brother said in reassuring tones. "Don't worry, I've got a contingency plan."

Nice of him to mention it now, Julia mused. He might've said something this morning and saved her all this grief.

Ten minutes later, her intercom buzzed; her assistant announced that Jerry was in her outer office. Julia asked Virginia to send him in and waited, standing by the window.

Jerry entered and Aleksandr Berinski followed. Although Aleksandr had been working for Conrad Industries for nearly two years, she'd only talked to him a handful of times. Even those conversations had been brief. But she'd read his weekly reports and been excited by the progress he was making. If he was allowed to continue, Julia didn't doubt that his innovations would put Conrad Industries back on a firm financial footing.

Julia and Jerry, but primarily Julia, had taken on the impossible task of resurrecting the family business, literally from the ashes. Three years before, the plant and adjacent warehouse had been severely damaged by fire; fortunately, it hadn't spread to the lab and the offices. Because of the rebuilding they'd had to do, she'd decided the line of paints Aleksandr was developing would be called Phoenix.

To be so close to success and lose it all now was more than she could bear. For three long, frustrating years, she'd hung on to the business by wheeling and dealing, making trades and promises.

Being aggressive and hardworking had come naturally to her. Jerry possessed the same determination and had been a constant help. If she was cold and sometimes ruthless, she credited it to Roger Stanhope. She'd needed to be, but Julia didn't have any more tricks up her sleeve once Aleksandr returned to Russia.

She feared that losing the business would be a fatal blow to her grandmother. No one knew better than Julia how fragile Ruth's health had become these past few months.

"You said you have a contingency plan." She spoke crisply, the sound of her steps muffled by the thick wheat-colored carpet as she stalked back to her desk. She leaned forward and averted her gaze from Aleksandr's.

The man disturbed her in ways she didn't understand. He was tall and lanky with impeccable manners. His face wasn't handsome the way Roger's had been, but rawboned and lean. His eyes were dark, the brows arched slightly, and in him she read strength and character. Unwillingly she found her own eyes drawn to his, and the shadow of a smile crept across Aleksandr's face. She focused her attention on Jerry.

"There is one way," her brother said, with obvious reluctance.

"This isn't the time to play guessing games. Tell me what you're thinking," she snapped, hardly believing he could be holding something back. Jerry knew as well as she did what kind of predicament the company was in.

Her brother set down his briefcase and motioned toward the leather chair. "Perhaps you should take a seat."

"Me?" She noted that his voice was strained, which surprised her almost as much as his request.

"You, too, Alek," Jerry advised as he moved to the opposite end of her office.

Julia turned toward him and tried to read his features in the gloom of late afternoon. The storm had darkened the sky, stationing shadows around the room until it resembled a dungeon, Julia thought.

"Whatever you have to say, please say it, Jerry. You've never worried about phrasing before."

Jerry's eyes traveled from Julia to Aleksandr, and she saw that his cheeks were flushed. He sighed. "There's only one legal way I know to keep Aleksandr in the country." Slowly he leveled his gaze on Julia. "You could marry him."

"I was hoping you'd stop by and see me." Julia's grandmother, Ruth Conrad, spoke softly, stretching out one hand. She was sitting up in bed, her thin white hair arranged in a chignon of sorts. Ruth was pale, her skin a silky shade of alabaster, her eyes sunken now with age, revealing only a hint of the depth and beauty that had been hers in years past. She was frail and growing more so daily.

The cool facade Julia wore in her role with Conrad Industries quickly melted whenever she saw her grandmother. She sank gratefully into the chair next to the brass four-poster bed and slipped off her shoes, tucking her feet beneath her.

Visiting Ruth at the family home was an escape for her. She left her worries and troubles outside. Her world was often filled with chaos, but with Ruth she found calm; the day's tension was replaced by peace and solace.

The storm outside seemed far removed from this bedroom haven.

"The thunder woke me," Ruth said in a low voice, smiling weakly. "I lay back and I could hear huge kettledrums in the sky. Oh, how they rumbled. Then I had Charles open the drapes so I could look outside. The clouds billowed past like giant puffs of smoke. It was a marvelous show."

Julia took her grandmother's hand and released a slow, uneven breath. She glanced around the room, studying the treasures Ruth had chosen to keep nearby. A row of silver-framed pictures rested on the nightstand, next to several prescription bottles. There was one of her son—Julia's father—another of the family together, plus Ruth's own wedding portrait and a candid photo of her beloved husband, Louis. A chintz-covered Victorian chair sat in front of the fireplace, a wool afghan draped over the back for when Ruth felt well enough to venture from the bed. The round table beside the chair was covered with a dark velvet cloth. Julia's picture, one taken shortly after she'd graduated from college, was propped up beside the lamp. Julia looked away, unable to bear the naïveté and innocence she saw in that younger version of herself.

"I'm so pleased you stopped by," Ruth said again.

Julia came almost every day, knowing the time left with her grandmother was shrinking. Neither spoke of her death, although it was imminent. Julia was determined to do whatever she could to make these last days as comfortable and happy for her as possible. That was what kept Julia going day after day. She spent hours talking to her grandmother, telling her about Alek's ideas, the innovations he was currently working on, her own hopes for the company. They discussed the future and how the entire industry was about to change because of Alek's vision. Her grandmother had been as impressed with Alek as Julia was. Ruth had wanted to meet him, and Julia had asked Jerry to bring Alek over. From what she heard later, the two had been quite charmed by each other.

"I've been meaning to talk to you," Ruth whispered.

She sounded so weak. "Rest," Julia said urgently. "We'll talk later."

Ruth responded with a fragile smile. "I don't have much longer, Julia. A few weeks at the most...."

"Nonsense." The truth was too painful to face, yet much too persistent to ignore. "You're just tired, that's all. It'll pass."

Ruth's eyes drifted shut, but determination opened them a moment later. "We need to talk about Roger," her grandmother said insistently.

A muscle in Julia's neck tensed, and a cold shiver went down her backbone. "Not...now. Some other time. Later."

"Might not...have later. Best to do it now."

"Grandma, please..."

"He betrayed you, child, and you've held on to that grief all these years. Your pain is killing you just as surely as this heart of mine is draining away my life."

"I don't even think of him anymore." Julia tried to reassure her, although it was a lie. She struggled to push every thought of Roger from her mind, but that wouldn't happen until she'd completely rebuilt what he'd destroyed.

"Regret and anger are poisoning you like...like venom.... I've watched it happen and been too weak...to help you the way I wanted."

"Grandma, please, Roger is out of my life. I haven't seen him in over a year. What's the point of talking about him now?"

"He's gone...but you haven't forgotten him. He failed you."

Julia clenched her teeth. That was one way of putting it. Roger *had* failed her. He'd also betrayed, tricked and abandoned her. When she thought of how much she'd loved him, how much she'd trusted him, it made her physically ill. Never again would she allow a man into her heart. Never again would she give a man the power to manipulate her.

"The time's come to forgive him."

Julia closed her eyes and shook her head. Her grandmother was asking the impossible. A woman didn't forgive the things Roger had done. Roger, the company's onetime director of research and development—and Julia's fiancé—had taught her the most valuable lesson of her life. She wasn't going to turn her back on the humiliation he'd caused her. Forgive him? Out of the question. She'd rather bury herself in work, insulate herself from love, than forgive Roger.

"I want you to love again," Ruth said, but her voice was so frail Julia had to strain to hear. "I don't think I can die in peace, knowing you're so miserable."

"Grandma, how can you say that? Jerry and I are working hard to rebuild the company. We're on the brink of doing truly amazing things. I've told you about them and about everything Aleksandr's done. How can you say I'm miserable? These are the most challenging, exciting days of my life."

"None of that means much...not when you're still imprisoned in pain. I've waited all these years for you to break free and fall in love again. It hasn't happened. I...look at you—" she hesitated and tears moistened her faded eyes "—and my heart aches. I want you to marry, to discover the happiness I found. It's the only thing that's kept me alive. I've waited for your season of suffering to pass...."

"I'll never be able to trust another man."

"You must for your own sake."

"I can't, not after what Roger did. Surely you understand. Surely you—"

With what must have required supreme effort, Ruth raised her hand, cutting Julia off. "I've longed for the day you'd proudly introduce me to the man you love. I was hoping it would be Aleksandr.... He's such a dear man, and so brilliant. I'd also like Jerry to find a woman to love...." She paused. "I can't wait any longer. My time is short, so...very short." Her eyes drifted closed once more and her head slumped forward.

Julia sat quietly while the seeds of fear took root within her. Love again? Impossible. Something she refused to even consider.

Marriage. To Alek.

Twice in the same day someone had suggested she marry him. First Jerry, as a ridiculous solution to their problem with the Immigration people, and now her grandmother, as the answer to her pain.

Julia stood, her arms wrapped around her. Glancing over at Ruth, she realized her grandmother was asleep. The grandmother who'd loved and supported her all her life, who'd stood by her when the whole world exploded. When Ruth had lost her son and Julia her father, when the man who was supposed to love her betrayed them all.

Julia remembered a time, long past, when she'd been a child and a fierce thunderstorm had raged in the dead of night. Terrified, she'd raced down the hallway to Ruth's room and slipped into bed with her. Even then she'd known that was the safest place in all the world for her to be.

That security had always been with her. Soon she would lose her anchor, the person who'd guided and loved her. Ruth had never asked anything of her before. Julia didn't know how she could refuse now.

Julia's request came as no surprise. Aleksandr had been waiting for it since the scene in her office the day before. If he lived to be a wise, old man he doubted he'd ever understand this country he'd come to love. Nor was he likely to understand Julia Conrad. She was a woman encased in frost, a woman with a wounded soul. He'd recognized this from the moment they'd met. She was uncomfortable with him; he knew that from the way she avoided eye contact. He hadn't had much contact with her, and he suspected she preferred to communicate through her brother.

Julia's assistant let him into the office and announced his arrival. Julia was sitting at her desk writing. When he entered the room, she glanced up and smiled.

"Please, sit down," she said politely, motioning toward the chair on the other side of her desk. "I hope I'm not interrupting your work."

For a few seconds Aleksandr didn't trust himself to speak. Her pain was closer to the surface than ever before, almost visible beneath the facade she'd erected.

"I'm never too busy for you, Ms. Conrad," he said, bowing his head slightly.

Her features seemed perfect to him, her beauty so flawless it was chilling. He noted that her creamy skin was flushed but her eyes dark and clear as they studied him with equal interest.

"I thought it might be a good idea if we talked," she suggested haltingly.

He nodded. "About my work?"

She hesitated. Not answering, she stood and moved away from him, carefully placing herself in the shadows where it was more difficult to read her expression.

"Tell me how your experiments are progressing," she said, her hands clasped behind her back. He sensed her reserve—and her tension.

Aleksandr was well aware from the notes he'd received from her that Julia had read and understood his weekly reports. Nevertheless he humored her. The additives he'd been working on for Conrad paints had impressive capabilities. His first innovation had been a simple one. Once an exterior surface was painted, if the owner wished a different color at some later date, all he or she needed to do was wash the surface with another solution, one that would be available only through Conrad Industries. It was an approach that would work on homes, cars and lawn furniture.

His second innovation had been just as successful so far. He'd developed a blend of chemicals that, when applied to a surface, would completely remove the old paint. No more scraping or heating it. A spray of the solution would dissolve it away with a minimum of effort, without harmful effects or harsh chemicals to damage the environment.

Aleksandr gave Julia a detailed description of his most recent experiments. He regretted that he wouldn't be with Conrad Industries to see his work come to fruition, but there was nothing more he could do. He was sorry to be leaving America, especially since there was still such poverty and upheaval in his homeland.

He paused, awaiting her response.

"You're very close, then."

"Within a few months," he guessed.

Her brows arched with what he assumed was surprise and delight. Both emotions quickly left her expression as she looked away. Her eyes avoided his, and Aleksandr wondered privately how many hearts she'd broken. She held herself distant, the unattainable prize of many a man, the untouchable dream of loveliness.

"Aleksandr." She spoke with a casual familiarity, although as far as he could recall, it was the first time she'd addressed him by his first name. "We have a problem…as you know."

She moved toward him, her eyes wide, and when she spoke again it was in a whisper. "We're too close to lose everything now. I can't let it happen. My brother...came up with a solution."

Aleksandr's mind churned with confusion. She couldn't possibly be considering Jerry's suggestion that they get married, could she? Only a day earlier she'd scoffed at her brother for even mentioning something so preposterous. Alek hadn't been given a chance to comment.

"I've been thinking about Jerry's idea," she continued demurely, glancing over her shoulder at him as she returned to her desk. "It seems marriage is our only solution."

Aleksandr wasn't fooled by her demeanor; there wasn't a shy, retiring bone in that delectable body of hers. Julia Conrad was too proud and stubborn to play the role well. But there was no limit to her determination.

"Of course you'd be well compensated for your...contribution to Conrad Industries. Even more than we're currently paying you. We'd be happy to double your salary. Naturally it wouldn't be a real marriage, and when you've finished with your work, we'd obtain a quiet divorce. If you're agreeable, I'll have Jerry draw up a prenuptial agreement for us to sign."

Aleksandr was convinced that if there'd been any other way to solve the problem, Julia would have opted for it. She was offering him a pretend marriage, followed by a discreet divorce.

He frowned, disliking the fact that she was trying to bribe him with money. His wages were already far beyond what he could ever hope to make in Russia. Much of what he earned now he sent to his family, while he lived as frugally as possible.

"I understand there are several members of your family still in Russia," she said cautiously. "We might be able to help them immigrate to the States if we did decide to go ahead with this marriage."

At his silence, Julia added, "*If* that's something you'd care to consider—bringing your immediate family into the country. Is it?" she prompted.

Aleksandr's voice was strained when he spoke. "My sister is unmarried and lives with my mother, who is a widow." Unable to remain seated, he stood and walked to the window, his back to her. He felt a strong desire to take Julia in his arms, but he was painfully aware that there was no warmth in her, nor would she welcome his touch.

For two years Aleksandr had studied Julia Conrad. Outwardly she was often arrogant and sometimes sarcastic. But she wasn't entirely capable of hiding her softer side. Every now and then he caught puzzling, contradictory glimpses of her. She cared deeply for her employees and was often generous to a fault. Then there'd been the day, shortly after Alek had come to America, when he'd seen Julia with her grandmother.

Julia's facade had melted away that afternoon. If Alek hadn't seen it with his own eyes, he wouldn't have believed such a transformation was possible. Julia had glowed with joy and pride as she gave her grandmother a tour of the rebuilt facilities. Alek had watched from a distance—and had held on to that image of her ever since.

Marriage. He sighed inwardly. His religion didn't accept divorce and he refused to sacrifice his life and his happiness for a business proposition.

"I wish you'd say something," she said.

He returned to the chair and kept his features as expressionless as he could. "There's much we would need to consider before we enter into this agreement."

"Of course," she returned.

"Your money does not interest me."

She seemed surprised by his words. "Even for your family?"

"Even for my family." What he earned now was adequate. Julia wasn't the only one who was proud. Alek couldn't be bought. She, a woman who needed no one, needed him, and he appreciated what it had taken for her to approach him with this offer. Alek wasn't being completely unselfish, nor was he without greed. He had a price in mind.

"Then what is it you want?"

He shrugged, not knowing how to tell her.

Restlessly she came to her feet and walked away from him. He admired her smooth, fluid grace. She was a woman who moved with confidence, sure of herself and her surroundings. Usually. But at the moment she seemed sure of nothing and obviously that disturbed her.

"I don't know what to say," Aleksandr answered truthfully.

"Do you find the idea of marriage to me so distasteful?" she asked.

"No," he told her quietly. "You're lovely."

"Then what is it?"

"I don't want money."

"If it isn't money, then what? A percentage of my stock? A vice presidency? Tell me."

"You Americans regard marriage differently than we do in my country. There, when a man and woman marry, it is for many reasons, not all of them love. Nevertheless, when we marry it is for life."

"But you aren't in Russia now, you're in America."

"Americans treat marriage like dirty laundry. When it becomes inconvenient, you toss it aside. My head tells me I live in your country now, but my heart believes in tradition. If we marry, Julia, and it would be my wish that we do, there will be no divorce."

Her breath escaped in a rush and her dark eyes flared briefly.

Aleksandr ignored the fury he read in her and continued. "We both stand to gain from this arrangement. I will remain in the country and complete my experiments. You will have what you wish, as well. But there is a cost to this, one we should calculate now. The marriage will be a real one, or there will be no marriage."

Her gaze cut through him with ill-concealed contempt. "So you want more than the golden egg, you want the whole goose."

"The goose?" Aleksandr hadn't heard this story. He smiled. "In my family, goose is traditionally served at the wedding meal. I do not know about the golden egg, but you may keep that. I want only you."

Her voice was husky when she spoke. "That's what I thought."

The phone on her desk rang just then and Julia reached for it. "I said I didn't want to be disturbed," she said impatiently. Her face tightened as she listened. "Yes, yes, of course, you did the right thing. Put me through immediately." Several seconds passed. "Dr. Silverman, this is Julia Conrad. I understand you've had my grandmother taken to Virginia Mason Hospital."

Alek watched as the eyes that had been distressed and angry a moment earlier softened with emotion. She blinked, and Alek thought he might have noticed the sheen of tears.

"Naturally. I'll let my brother know right away and we'll meet you there as soon as we can. Thank you for contacting me so soon." She replaced the receiver, stood and started out of the room, apparently forgetting Aleksandr was there.

"Your grandmother is ill?" he asked.

She whirled around, apparently surprised at the sound of his voice, and nodded. "I...have to leave. I don't believe there's any need for us to discuss this further. I can't agree to your conditions. I refuse to be trapped in the type of marriage you're suggesting. I'd hoped we'd be able to work out some kind of compromise, but that doesn't seem possible."

"I'm disappointed. We would've had fine children."

She stared at him as if he'd spoken in his native tongue and she didn't understand a word he'd said. "Children?" she repeated. A sadness seemed to steal over her; she shook her head, perhaps to dispel the image.

"I will think good things for your grandmother," Alek told her.

She nodded. "Thank you." With what looked like hard-won poise, she turned and left the office.

Alek watched her go, and the proud way in which she carried herself tugged at his heart. He wished her grandmother well, but more importantly, he wished Julia a happy life.

Knowing his time in the States was limited to mere days, Aleksandr worked well past five, when his colleagues had all gone home. He felt it was his moral obligation to do everything within his power to see that the next series of experiments was performed to the standards he'd set for the earlier ones. He wouldn't be with Conrad Industries to oversee the ongoing research, and that bothered him, but he had no choice.

The laboratory was silent, and the footsteps echoing down the wide corridor outside his office were louder than they would otherwise have been.

He raised his eyes expectantly when Julia Conrad opened the door without knocking and walked inside. She was pale, her eyes darker than he'd ever seen them before.

"Julia," he said, standing abruptly. "Is something wrong?"

She looked sightlessly around, as though she didn't know where she was or how she got there.

"Your grandmother?"

Julia nodded and gnawed on her bottom lip. "She…she had another heart attack."

"I'm sorry."

Her eyes flew upward as if to gauge the sincerity of his words. For a lengthy moment she said nothing. Then she inhaled a shaky breath and bit her lip so hard, Aleksandr was afraid she'd draw blood.

"I…I've reconsidered, Mr. Berinski. I'll marry you under the conditions you've set."

Two

"I don't want an elaborate wedding." Julia folded her arms, moving to the far side of her office. Her brother was being impossible. "How could there even be time to arrange one?"

"Julia, you're not listening to me."

"I'm listening," she said sharply. "I just don't happen to like what I'm hearing."

"A reception at the Four Seasons isn't so much to ask."

"But a wedding with guests and this whole thing about wearing a fancy wedding dress is ridiculous! Jerry, please, this is getting out of hand. I understand marriage is the best solution, but I didn't realize I'd be forced to endure the mockery of a formal wedding."

Jerry gestured helplessly. "We've got to make this as credible as we can. Apparently you don't understand how important this is—and not just the wedding, either. That's only the first hurdle. You have to make everything appear as though you're madly in love. Nothing less will convince the Immigration people. If you fail… I don't even want to think about that."

"You've already gone through this." More times than she cared to count.

"Alek has to live with you, too."

This was the part that disturbed Julia most. Her condo was her private haven, the one place where she could be completely herself. She was about to lose that, too. "But why?" She knew the answer, had argued until Jerry was seething with exasperation. Julia didn't blame him, but this marriage was becoming far more complicated than she'd ever thought it would.

"Why?" Jerry shouted, throwing his hands in the air. "I've made everything as plain as I can. Alek isn't the problem, it's you. What I don't understand, Julia, is why you're being so difficult when we're the ones who stand to benefit from this arrangement."

"You're making Alek sound like a saint for marrying me." She frowned. "And I don't see *you* running for the altar." Jerry had recently ended yet another brief liaison.

He didn't answer right away, which irritated her even more. "Let's put it this way," he finally said. "Conrad Industries is gaining far more from this marriage than Alek ever will. And," he added, "my marital status is irrelevant."

Julia rolled her eyes at that. "I offered to pay him, and very generously, too," she said.

"You insulted him. The man has his pride, Julia. He isn't doing this for the money."

"Then why is he going through with it?"

Jerry shrugged. "Darned if I know."

His words reiterated that Alek wasn't getting any bargain by marrying her. "He wants to help his family," Julia reminded her brother. She remembered Alek mentioning a sister and his widowed mother. As the oldest son, Alek would feel responsible for taking care of his family. Julia had promised to do whatever she could to bring both his mother and his sister to the United States. This marriage provided plenty of incentives for Alek, she told herself, so she didn't need to worry about taking advantage of him.

"There's more to the man than meets the eye," Jerry muttered. "I'm convinced he's not interested in monetary gain. When he read over the prenup, he insisted on no stake in the company. We're about to make a fortune because of him, and he wants no part of it."

This discussion wasn't doing anything to ease Julia's conscience. "I agreed to the marriage," she said, not wanting to stray any farther from the subject than they already had. "But no one said anything about a wedding. I thought we'd make an appointment with a justice of the peace and be done with it." She walked over to her desk, opened the old-fashioned appointment book and flipped through the pages. "Friday at four is open."

"Julia," Jerry returned with a sigh. "As I've explained— we've got to make this as real as we can for obvious reasons."

"I've said Alek can move in with me." To Julia, that was a major concession. She wasn't pleased by it, nor did she feel good about tricking Alek. He'd insisted from the first that their marriage be real. He'd made it known that he intended to sleep with her; he also wanted children. Julia couldn't allow any of that. Alek didn't understand and neither did Jerry. Julia was incapable of love, the kind of trusting love a husband and wife shared. That possibility was dead, destroyed by Roger's treachery. Never again would she put her faith in a man. Alek expected her to be his wife in every way, but soon he'd learn the truth. Soon he'd know for himself how badly he was being cheated. Such deception didn't sit well with Julia, but there was no avoiding it.

While Julia admired Alek, she found herself nervous around him. He left her feeling naked, somehow. Exposed. He seemed to be able to look into her very soul. That didn't make sense, but she couldn't shake the suspicion that in some uncanny way he knew all there was to know about her.

"Immigration is going to ask about the wedding," Jerry went on. "We need proof that what prompted the marriage to Alek was nothing less than earth-shattering love. A hurried-up affair in some judge's chambers won't work. They're going to want evidence of your commitment and devotion to each other."

"A hurried-up affair at the Four Seasons will convince them of all that?" she asked sarcastically.

Jerry sighed again. "It looks better. Now, I suggest you go out and get yourself a fancy wedding dress while I make arrangements with Virginia. We'll deal with the caterers and the photographers and see to having the invitations hand-delivered."

"Jerry, this is crazy!" Julia protested. The idea of dressing up in an elaborate wedding gown, as if she were a loving bride on display, appalled her. Nor was she keen on posing for a series of photographs, like a new wife passionately in love with her husband. It was too much. "I can't go through with this," she said evenly.

"You've already agreed."

"To the marriage, yes, but not this...this circus. It's becoming a Hollywood production, a show for media attention."

"A show is what we need if we're going to fool the Immigration investigators," Jerry argued. "And trust me, Julia, this marriage will be investigated."

Julia walked over to the window and studied the street several floors below. In a moment of weakness, when her fears had been rampant and she was so deathly afraid of losing Ruth, Julia had gone to Alek and agreed to his terms. Even now she didn't understand what had prompted her. She was sick of analyzing it, furious with herself for being so weak. This morning, once her head had cleared, she'd realized it had all been a mistake. But by then Alek had contacted Jerry, who'd put everything in motion. Now, it seemed, there was no turning back.

Her intercom hummed before Virginia's efficient voice reached out to her. "Mr. Berinski is here to see you."

Julia looked at her brother in sheer panic. She wasn't prepared to deal with Alek just yet. They hadn't spoken since she'd consented to the marriage.

"Julia," Jerry prompted when she didn't respond.

"Send him in," Julia instructed her assistant, steeling herself for the confrontation.

No sooner had the words left her mouth than the door leading to her office opened. Alek walked in and his dark eyes shone brightly as he gazed over at her. A slow, seductive smile appeared on his lips.

"Good afternoon." Alek spoke to her brother first, then returned his attention to her. "Julia."

"Alek," she said briskly, surprised by how defensive she sounded.

He didn't seem perturbed by her lack of welcome. Last night she'd agreed to become his wife, accepting the stipulations he'd set. She'd been overwrought with anxiety, frightened and lost. Yet no matter how hard she argued with herself, Julia wouldn't change her mind...unless Alek wanted out. She was a woman of honor, a woman of her word. She knew he was the same way.

"I was just clearing the wedding arrangements with Julia," Jerry explained.

Alek's eyes refused to leave her. She felt her face heat and wished with everything in her that she *could* escape.

"I'd like some time alone with my fiancée," Alek said.

Julia sent Jerry a pleading glance, not wanting him to leave her. Jerry ignored the unspoken request, mumbled something under his breath and walked out of the room.

"You want to talk?" she asked abruptly. She rubbed her palms and walked away from him. Her shoulders felt stiff and her legs heavy.

"You're nervous."

Nervous. Terrified. Afraid. None of those words adequately described what Julia was experiencing. The situation had an eerie, unreal quality that she couldn't shake. Only a few years earlier she'd looked forward to being a happy bride. She'd dreamed of the day Roger would slip a wedding band on her finger and gaze down at her with love.

She felt a flash of unexpected pain, then forced herself to shake the image from her head.

"All brides are nervous," she said quietly in response to his question.

"How is your grandmother?"

"I'll be seeing her this afternoon…. Better, I believe." According to the nurse Julia had spoken with that morning, Ruth had slept restfully through the night. But that had been *after* Jerry had spoken to her and said Julia would be marrying Aleksandr Berinski. Her grandmother had only met Alek once, and that had been recently. He'd obviously made quite an impression, because his name had cropped up with alarming frequency ever since.

"Do you wish to cancel the wedding?" Alek probed.

Here was her chance, handed to her on the proverbial silver platter. All she needed to do was tell him that she hadn't been herself, that she hadn't been fully aware of what she was doing. She opened her mouth to explain it all away and found she couldn't. The words refused to come. While she was fumbling for a reply, he stepped behind her and rested his hands on her shoulders. He leaned forward, gently kissing the side of her neck.

Julia froze. It was the first time a man had touched her since Roger. She couldn't move, couldn't breathe. Alek didn't seem to notice. Sliding his arms around her, he brought her against him. His breath stirred shivers along her spine and a curious warmth crept into her blood.

Alek turned her around to face him. She wasn't given the opportunity to object as he pressed his mouth to hers. His lips moved slowly over hers. She wedged her hands between them, braced her palms against his hard chest and pushed herself free. Her lungs felt as though they were about to burst, and she drew in a deep breath.

Alek didn't seem offended or surprised by her actions. His eyes danced with mischief as they sought hers. Julia raised the back of her hand to her mouth and held it there. She burned with anger. He'd done this intentionally so she'd know he expected to touch her and kiss her often after the ceremony. She was to be his wife in every sense of the word and he wouldn't tolerate a loveless, sexless marriage. He wanted her and he was making sure she knew it.

What was she going to do?

* * *

Julia stood outside the bridal shop with all the thrill and anticipation of a long-overdue visit to the dentist.

She opened the door and walked inside, grateful the saleswoman wasn't busy.

"Hello."

"Hello," Julia said stiffly, fanning out the billowing chiffon skirt of a pale yellow bridesmaid's dress that hung from a rack.

"May I help you?" came the friendly voice.

Julia revealed her lack of enthusiasm with a noncommittal shrug. "I need a wedding dress for this Friday afternoon."

The shopkeeper was petite, hardly more than five feet tall with soft brown hair. The woman was a dreamer; Julia could see it in her eyes. She, too, had once worn that same look of innocence....

"The wedding is *this* Friday?"

"I know that doesn't give me much time," Julia said, feeling foolish. "It's one of those spur-of-the-moment things."

"Don't worry," the saleswoman assured her, hurrying toward a long rack of plastic-covered wedding dresses. "Spur-of-the-moment weddings are often the most romantic."

Julia had nothing to add. She could tell that this woman was more than a dreamer; she was also hopelessly sentimental. She had her head in the clouds when it came to love, and no doubt her attitude had been influenced by her job. She dealt with women who were deeply in love, women for whom the entire world was there for the taking.

Three years earlier, Julia had been one of them. Young, enthusiastic and so much in love she didn't recognize what should've been obvious.

"I'd like a very plain dress," she said forcefully, breaking off her thoughts.

"Plain," the woman repeated slowly.

"The plainer the better," Julia reiterated, strolling about the store.

"I'm afraid I have a limited selection of plain dresses."

That was what Julia feared. "Something simple, then."

"Simple and elegant?" she asked, grinning approvingly. "Would you like to look through this rack? Choose the designs that appeal to you, I'll get them in your size, and then you can try them on."

As far as Julia was concerned, this business with the wedding dress was a waste of time. She wanted it to be over and done with so she could head for the hospital and visit Ruth.

The saleswoman led her to the appropriate display of gowns. Julia shuffled through them quickly, making two selections. Neither dress really appealed to her.

"I'll try on these two," Julia said.

The woman made no comment as she went into the back room and returned a few minutes later with the two dresses in the correct size. She took them into the dressing room and placed them on the hook.

Julia obediently followed her inside. She undressed and slipped into the first dress. It was just as the saleswoman had promised. Simple and elegant. A straight skirt made of silk, a beaded yoke and cuffs. It looked fine, Julia supposed.

"No," the shop-owner said with certainty. "This one doesn't suit you."

"It looks…"

"No," the woman repeated. "Don't even bother to try on the next dress. It wouldn't suit you, either."

"Please, I don't have a lot of time."

"The dress is one of the most important aspects of your wedding. Every bride deserves to feel beautiful on her special day."

Julia didn't know why she felt like crying, but she did. Buckets of tears welled up inside her. She was grateful the woman didn't seem to notice. Brides deserved a whole lot more than feeling beautiful; they deserved to marry a man they loved. A man who loved them, too.

"Wait here," she instructed. She left the changing area and came back a moment later carrying a lovely ornate dress. The silk gown with pearls and sequins was anything but simple. Rarely had Julia seen a dress as intricate as this.

"Try it on," she said when Julia hesitated.

"I…I don't think I should."

"Nonsense. This dress was designed for someone with your body type. It's perfect. It arrived this afternoon, almost as though I'd sent away for it with you in mind."

"I don't know," Julia murmured. The woman held up the gown for her inspection. It was lovely, ten times more elaborate than the one she'd tried on earlier. Ten times more beautiful, too. It was the kind of dress a woman in love would choose, knowing her groom would treasure its beauty. Would treasure *her* beauty. A groom who'd cherish her devotion all his life. It was the style of dress she would've worn for Roger before she learned of his betrayal. Before she'd learned what a fool she'd been.

She wanted to argue, but one look convinced her that the woman would hear none of it. Not exactly sure why she'd allowed this stranger to dictate her actions, Julia put on the dress. The silk and taffeta rustled as it slid effortlessly over her hips. She kept her eyes lowered as she turned around and the shopkeeper fastened the small pearl closures down her back.

Julia felt strangely reluctant to look into a mirror, almost fearing her own reflection. When she did raise her eyes to the glass, she was startled at the beautiful young woman who gazed back at her. It took her a wild second to realize it was herself.

Gone were the lines that told of the bitterness and disappointment she'd carried with her since her father's death. The cool, disinterested look in her eyes had warmed. The calculating side of her personality faded, replaced by the woman she'd been before she'd fallen in love with Roger Stanhope. Open, trusting, naive—too young for her years.

Unable to look at herself any longer, Julia dragged her eyes away from the graceful reflection of the woman she'd once been. The woman Roger's deception had destroyed.

"It's perfect," the saleswoman was saying with a sigh of appreciation. "Just perfect. It's as if the dress was meant for you."

Julia opened her mouth to contradict the woman, but before she could voice her objection she looked at the mirror one last time. A few days earlier she'd caught a stormy glimpse of herself reflected in her office window. She'd disliked what she'd seen, the woman she'd become, cold, uncaring and driven.

She'd quickly abandoned her self-analysis and had concentrated on what was happening with Alek and Jerry at the Immigration office instead. The events of that afternoon had resulted in this farce of a wedding.

Alek had been adamant that there be no divorce. Julia had agreed to those terms, but not in the spirit he'd intended. If it weren't for these particular circumstances, Julia doubted she would ever have married. This would be her only wedding, her one chance to wear such a beautiful gown.

"I'll take it," she said, calling herself a fool even as she spoke.

"Somehow I knew you would." The saleswoman grinned broadly.

It took an additional twenty minutes, while the dress was wrapped up and the bill paid, before Julia was able to leave the shop. Nervously she glanced at her watch as she headed toward her parked car. She was already late and knew Ruth would be worried.

As often as she'd visited hospitals, Julia could never accustom herself to the antiseptic smell. She rushed down the polished hallway to the wing that housed her grandmother. She hated the thought of Ruth being here, away from her comfortable home and the pictures she loved and kept close to her side.

Ruth had tried repeatedly to prepare Julia for her death, but Julia refused to listen, refused to accept life without her adored grandmother.

Checking in at the nurses' station, Julia was left to wait until Velma Williams, the head nurse, returned. A striking arrangement of red, blue, yellow and white flowers overfilled an inverted straw hat on a corner of the long counter. Julia admired it as she stood there. A few minutes later, Velma was back and Julia was ushered to Ruth's side.

"Good afternoon," Julia whispered. She couldn't tell if Ruth was sleeping or simply resting her eyes. Her grandmother seemed to be doing more of both lately. There were various tubes and pieces of equipment attached to Ruth's body, monitoring her heart and administering drugs intravenously. Julia looked down on this woman she loved so much and had to force back her growing sense of alarm. It seemed to ring in her ears, announcing that the time was fast approaching when Ruth would no longer be with her.

The older woman's eyes gradually drifted open. "Julia, my dear, I'm so glad you're here. Come, sit with me."

Julia pulled up a chair and sat next to the high hospital bed. "How are you feeling?"

Ruth gestured weakly with her hand. "That's not important now. Tell me about you and Alek. How I've prayed for this day. How I've hoped you'd learn to love again."

"The wedding's on Friday afternoon." Julia half suspected her grandmother would find the timing suspicious, but instead Ruth smiled tenderly and a faraway look came into her tired eyes.

"Friday… It's a good thing you won't have a long engagement, because I doubt I'll last more than a week or two."

"Grandma, please don't say that. You're going to be around for years and years."

The weary smile didn't waver. "I won't see my great-grandchildren."

Julia wanted to argue with her, but she couldn't; there'd never be children for her and Alek because there would never be a real marriage. She suffered a slight twinge of guilt but pushed it aside as a luxury she couldn't afford.

"I'm sorry I'm late but I was trying on wedding dresses," Julia explained, injecting some enthusiasm into her voice. She was mildly surprised at how little effort it required to sound excited about the dress she'd bought at the bridal shop. She described it in detail and was pleased at the way her grandmother's eyes brightened.

"You and Alek will come see me after the ceremony, won't you?"

"Of course," Julia promised.

Ruth motioned toward the nurses' station. "He sent me flowers. He's a very thoughtful boy. Velma carried in the bouquet for me to see. Did you notice them?"

"*Who* sent you flowers?"

"Your Alek. An enchanting arrangement, and such a sweet thing to do. I like him, Julia. You've chosen well, my dear."

Julia was uncomfortable talking about Alek. He'd been foremost in her thoughts all day and she wanted to escape him, escape the memory of his gentle kiss.

"Tell me about your romance. You've been so close-mouthed about it all...yet I knew." Ruth's eyes closed slowly and she sighed. With what seemed to be a good deal of effort she opened her eyes again. "He's a special man, that one. Just hearing about you two gladdens my heart."

"Ah..." Julia hesitated, not sure what to say. "It all happened rather quickly...almost overnight."

"So I gathered." A spark appeared in Ruth's eyes. "Oh, how I adore a love story. Tell me more before I fall back asleep."

"Alek's green card was about to expire." Keeping everything as close to the truth as possible made this much easier.

"His green card," Ruth repeated. "Of course, I'd forgotten."

"He was going to have to return to Russia."

"And you realized you couldn't let that happen, didn't you?"

"I hadn't realized how important he was to me," Julia said, adding drama to her voice. "Jerry did everything he could to persuade the Immigration people to let Alek stay, but nothing he said convinced them. The three of us were talking and suddenly I understood how vital it was to me that Alek remain in the United States. I...don't think I could bear to go on without him." This was a stretch, but Julia knew what a romantic her grandmother was. If she was exaggerating the truth just a little, it was a small price to pay to satisfy Ruth.

"Julia, my sweet child." Her grandmother's delicate hand reached for Julia's and she squeezed her fingers. "I always trusted that in time you'd open your heart to love again. It took a special man like Alek. Be happy, my child. Promise me you won't let go until you've found your joy."

Julia wasn't sure she understood Ruth's words. They made little sense to her. She would have questioned her if Ruth hadn't chosen that moment to slip into a peaceful slumber. For several minutes Julia remained at her grandmother's side, taking in the solace she felt whenever she spent time with Ruth.

"Julia." The sound of her name, said with that soft European accent, caught her attention. She jerked around to find Alek standing in the doorway.

She got up abruptly, resenting his intrusion into these quiet moments. She walked toward the door, not wanting him to interrupt her grandmother's rest.

"What are you doing here?" she asked when they were well into the corridor.

The edge of his mouth lifted in a half smile. "I came to see you. There is much we need to discuss." He tucked her hand in the crook of his elbow and sauntered over to the elevator.

"I left the wedding arrangements in Jerry's hands. He'll look after everything. As far as I can see, there's nothing to discuss."

She saw the anger in him, in the prideful squaring of his shoulders and the way his mouth thinned.

"You want me, Julia, and you need me. I just wonder how long it will take before you realize this."

The arrogance of the man was beyond description. She glared at him. She needed no one, especially a man, and never a husband. She wanted to shout out the words, but a hospital corridor was the last place to do that.

Long seconds passed as they stared into each other's eyes.

"You need me," he said again.

"You're wrong," she returned defiantly. Conrad Industries needed him; she didn't.

Their eyes lingered and it seemed neither of them knew what to say or do next. Jerry had mentioned how proud Alek was, and she could see that colossal ego for herself. He released her arm and turned away.

He was several yards down the hospital corridor before Julia spoke.

"I *don't* need you, Alek," she called after him. She had to say something. They'd quickly make each other miserable if this friction between them continued. If he wouldn't make an effort, then it was up to her.

"So you've already said."

"But I *am* willing to admit we need each other."

Grinning, he turned back. His smile grew as he returned to her side. For a heartbeat, he said nothing. Then he lowered his mouth to hers and kissed her. His touch was as gentle as before. Light as air, it left her wondering if she'd imagined his kiss.

"Why did you do that?" she asked.

His smile was worth waiting for. "Because, my soon-to-be-wife, you deserved it." He brushed the hair away from her face. "For that matter," he said with a roguish grin, "so did I."

Three

The wedding ceremony was a nightmare for Julia. When it came time to repeat her vows, her throat closed up and she could barely speak. Not so with Alek. His voice rang out loud and clear, without the least hesitation.

Love and cherish.

Julia's conscience was screaming. She had no intention of loving Alek. She didn't want to love any man, because love had the power to hurt her, the power to break her. Julia had worked hard to blot it from her life. Love was superfluous, unnecessary, painful when abused, and her heart had yet to recover from her first experience with it.

Signing the final documents was even worse than enduring the ceremony. Her hand trembled as she wrote her name on the marriage certificate. Her eyes glazed with tears as she stared at the official document, all too aware of the lie she was living.

Jerry, her assistant and the minister all seemed unaware of her distress. She didn't know what Alek was thinking. His fingers pressed against the small of her back as though to encourage her. She continued to hold the pen and remained bent over the document long after she'd finished signing her name.

"May your marriage be a long and fruitful one," the minister was saying to Alek. Julia squeezed her eyes shut, drew in a steadying breath and straightened. She dared not look at Alek for fear he could read her thoughts.

Long and fruitful, Julia's mind echoed. A sob welled up inside her and she was afraid she'd burst into tears. This deception was so much more difficult than she'd ever imagined.

"Shall we join the others?" Jerry, who had served as Alek's best man, suggested, gesturing toward the door. Julia was grateful for an excuse to leave the room.

The reception was being held in a large hotel suite across the hall from where the wedding had taken place. Their guests were helping themselves to a wide array of hors d'oeuvres served on silver platters, and crystal flutes of champagne.

Julia was surprised by how many people had come on such short notice. Most were business associates, but several family friends were also in attendance. She had few friends left, allowing the majority of her relationships to lapse after her father's death.

Alek was at her side, smiling and cordially greeting their guests. He placed his arm casually around her shoulders. Julia stiffened at the unwelcome familiarity, but if he noted her uneasiness, he paid no heed.

"Have I told you how beautiful you look?" he whispered close to her ear.

Julia nodded. He hadn't been able to take his eyes off her from the moment she'd arrived in her wedding dress. Oddly, that depressed her, planning to deceive him the way she was. He was expecting more from this marriage than she was going to give him. She should've opted for the plain, simple, unadorned dress instead of the ornate one she'd chosen.

The minute she'd viewed herself before the wedding, she was sorry she'd bought this gown. Even Jerry had seemed dumbstruck when he went to escort her to Alek's side. He'd become especially maudlin with his compliments, which added to her stress. And her guilt.

"Could you *pretend* to love me?" Alek whispered. "Just for these few hours?" His warm breath against her skin sent shivers down her spine. "Smile, my love."

She complied obediently, her expression no doubt looking as stiff as it felt.

"Better," he murmured under his breath.

"How soon can we leave?"

Alek chuckled softly. "I know you're eager for me, but if we left too soon, it would be unseemly."

Julia's face burned with a wild blush, which appeared to amuse Alek even more. "Would you like me to get you a plate?" he offered.

She shook her head. Food held no appeal. "Do *you* want something?" she asked.

He turned to her, his eyes ablaze. "Rest assured, I do, but I'll get my dessert later."

Julia didn't think her knees would support her much longer. From obligation more than desire, she drank a glass of champagne. It must've been more potent than she realized because she felt giddy and light-headed afterward.

It was the dress, she decided. She wanted to change out of the wedding gown because it made her feel things she had no right to feel. With Alek standing at her side, she felt beautiful and wanted and loved when she didn't deserve or want any of it. She'd gone into this marriage for all the wrong reasons. She was uncomfortable, using Alek for her own gain, giving nothing of herself in return.

Until she'd stood before the preacher, marriage had been little more than a concept, an idea she didn't believe in. She hadn't expected a few words mumbled before a man of God to be so powerful. But she'd been wrong. Julia was shaken and uncertain afterward, as if she was mocking important human values.

"Jerry." She reached out to her brother and clasped his arm with both hands. "I've got to get out of here...."

He must have read the desperation in her eyes, because he nodded gravely. Whatever he said to Alek, Julia didn't hear. She assumed her brother would escort her from the room, but it was Alek who slipped his arm around her waist. It was her husband who led her out of the reception.

"Jerry is making our excuses," he explained.

She nodded. "I'm sorry," she whispered as he took her down the hallway to the changing room. "I don't know what happened."

"Are you feeling faint?"

"I'm fine now, thanks." Or she would be, once she was out of this dress and back in her own clothes. And once he removed his arm from her waist.... The walls seemed to close in around her. She wished Alek would leave her, but he stayed even when she reached the door leading to the changing room.

"We didn't kiss," Alek whispered. "Not properly."

Julia didn't bother to pretend she didn't know what he was talking about. When Alek was told to kiss his bride, Julia had made sure he'd merely given her a peck on the cheek.

Alek had been disappointed, and Jerry's eyes had revealed his frustration. A passionate kiss would've put the stamp of credibility on their act.

"You're not sick, are you?"

She could have lied, could have offered him countless excuses, but she didn't. "I'm fine," she said, just as she had a minute earlier.

"Then I'll kiss my bride."

Her first instinct was to put him off, to thwart him again, but a kiss seemed like such a simple way to ease her conscience. His touch had always been tender, as if he understood and appreciated her need for gentleness.

"Yes," she agreed breathlessly.

Her back was against the wall and his arms went around her waist. Unsure what to do with her own hands, she splayed them across his chest. He pulled her against him, and for a long moment he held her, as if savoring the feel of her in his arms.

The trembling returned and Julia closed her eyes. She could smell his cologne, feel his heart beat beneath her flattened palms. His breath echoed in her ears and rustled her hair.

His mouth met hers. His touch was light and brief. She tipped her head back and her eyes drifted shut as his mouth brushed hers again. And again. A sigh worked its way through her as his tongue outlined the shape of her mouth. After a series of nibbling kisses, he caught her lower lip between his teeth.

Julia held her breath, unable to respond. She was content to let him be the aggressor, to allow him to touch her and kiss her without fully participating herself.

But her lack of involvement obviously bothered Alek.

"Julia," he pleaded, "kiss me back."

Tentatively, shyly, her mouth opened to him and he moaned, then deepened the kiss. His arms tightened their hold and he slanted his mouth over hers. Strange, unwelcome pleasure rippled through her body.

She sighed at the sensations she experienced; she couldn't help it. She felt hot and shaky, as though she'd suffered a near miss, as though she'd stepped off a curb and felt the rush of a car passing by and come within inches of being struck.

Her hands, which had seemed so useless moments before, were buried in his dark hair. Her body, so long untouched, felt about to explode. She moved against him, clinging to him, fighting back tears.

The sound of someone clearing his throat broke the spell. Alek stilled, as did Julia. Slowly, reluctantly, she opened her eyes to find half of the reception guests lined up in the hall watching them.

Jerry stood in the background, smiling broadly. He gave her a thumbs-up, looking ecstatic. If they were hoping to fool their guests, they'd succeeded beyond her brother's expectations.

As though loath to do it, Alek released her. He seemed perturbed by the interruption and muttered something she didn't understand.

"I'll change clothes," she said, hurriedly moving into the room. She was grateful there was a chair. Sinking down onto it, she pressed her hands to her red face and closed her eyes. She felt as if she'd leapt off a precipice in the dark and had no idea of where she'd be landing. A kiss that had begun as a compromise had become something else. She'd been trying to soothe her conscience, but instead had added to her growing list of offenses, leading Alek to believe he should expect more.

Julia took her time changing. Fifteen minutes later she reappeared in a bright red flowered dress she'd found in the back of her closet. These days she dressed mostly in business suits—jackets, straight skirts and plain white blouses. The dress was a leftover from her college days. The design was simple and stylish.

Alek was pacing the hallway anxiously.

"I'm sorry I took so long."

His smile was enthusiastic. He touched her lips, still swollen from his kiss. The color hadn't faded from her cheeks, either; if anything, it had deepened with this fresh appraisal.

"I…promised my grandmother we'd stop in at the hospital after the reception," Julia said nervously. "I'd hate to disappoint her."

"By all means we will see her."

They said their farewells and left the reception. Julia knew the minute they walked into Ruth's hospital room that she'd been waiting for them. Her grandmother's smile was filled with love as she held her hands out to them.

Julia rushed forward and hugged her. She was reminded each and every time she saw her grandmother that Ruth was close to death. She clung to life, not for herself, but for Julia's sake. It hurt her to know Ruth was in pain. Why did those who were good always have to suffer? Why couldn't God spare her grandmother just a few more years? This day, her wedding day, had started a cauldron of emotions churning in her mind. She couldn't bear to think of what her life would be like without her grandmother.

It had been Ruth's kindness that had gotten her through

Roger's deception and her father's death. Otherwise, Julia feared she would've ended up in a mental ward.

Other emotions long buried and ignored came to the surface, as well. Kissing Alek had stirred up needs and desires she'd assumed were lost to her.

There were no answers, at least none she felt confident enough to face. Only myriad questions that assailed her on every front. She couldn't trust herself; her power to discern had been sadly lacking once and had cost her and her family dearly. She dared not trust herself a second time.

She was married to a man she didn't love, a man who didn't love her, either. To complicate everything, her grandmother was dying. This was what her life had come down to. A loveless marriage and a desperate loneliness.

When Julia released her grandmother, Ruth looked up and brushed the tears from Julia's cheeks. "You're crying?" she asked softly. "This should be the happiest day of your life."

Alek placed his arm around Julia's waist and helped her into the chair next to the bed. He stood behind her, his hands resting lightly on her shoulders. Julia pressed Ruth's hand to her cheek and held it there. Her grandmother seemed much weaker today.

"I remember when I married Louis," she said with a wistful smile.

Her grandfather had been dead many years now. He was only a vague memory to Julia, who guessed she'd been about seven or eight when he died.

"I was frightened out of my wits."

"Frightened?" Julia didn't understand.

"I wondered if I was doing the right thing. There were very few divorces in those days and if a woman happened to marry the wrong man, she was often sentenced to a miserable life."

"But I thought you'd known him for a long time."

Ruth arched one delicate brow. "A long time?" she repeated. "In a manner of speaking, you're right. But we'd only gone out on a handful of dates before we were married."

"I'd always assumed you knew Grandpa for years."

Ruth's hand stroked Julia's cheek. "It's true that in the early days Louis worked for my father at the paint company my family owned. I'd see him now and then when I dropped in at the office, but those times were rare."

Julia was enthralled. She knew her grandmother had deeply loved her grandfather, but she couldn't remember ever hearing the story of their courtship.

"When did you fall in love?"

"Louis stopped working for my father, and Dad was furious with him. They were both strong-willed men and it seemed they were constantly disagreeing. Louis started his own business in direct competition with my family's." She smiled whimsically. "It was a bold move in those depression years, before the war. He managed to keep his head above water, which infuriated my father even more. I think at that point Dad would've taken pleasure in seeing Louis fail." She paused and closed her eyes for a moment, as though to gather her strength.

"Then the war came and Louis joined the army. Before he left for England he came to the house. I thought he was there to see my father. Can you imagine my surprise when he said I was the one he'd come to see? He told me he was going overseas and he asked if I'd be willing to write him. Naturally I told him I would be, and then he did the strangest thing."

When Ruth didn't immediately continue, Julia prompted her. "What did he do?"

Ruth shook her head. "It was such a little thing and so very sweet, so much like Louis. He took my hand and kissed it."

Her grandmother's gaze fell to her hand, as if she still felt the imprint of his lips.

"As I look back on it," Ruth went on, "I realize that was when I lost my heart to Louis. You see, I don't believe he ever expected to return from the war. He loved me then, he told me much later, and had for a long time, but Louis was afraid Dad would never approve of him as my husband."

"How long was he away?"

"I didn't see him for three years, although I heard from him regularly. I treasured his letters and reread them so often I nearly wore them out. By the time he came home I was so deeply in love with him, nothing else mattered. My family knew how I felt and I feared the worst when Dad insisted on accompanying me to meet Louis's train."

"What happened?"

Ruth's smile was weak, but happy. "Dad offered to merge his business with Louis's. Even though Louis himself had been away, his small company had survived the war. Louis accepted, with the stipulation that both the company and I take on his name." She smiled again. "It was a...unique proposal. My father agreed without much hesitation—and I agreed with none at all. We were married less than a month later."

"What a beautiful story," Julia whispered.

"We had a wonderful life together, better than I dared dream. I'll never stop missing him."

Julia knew her grandmother had taken Louis's death

hard. For a long while afterward, she'd closed herself off from life. It was in those bleak years that Julia's father had wisely sent Julia and Jerry to spend the summers with their grandmother.

"You, my children," Ruth continued, turning to Alek, "will have a good life, too. Alek, be gentle with my lamb. Her heart's been bruised, and she can be a bit…prickly, but all she needs is love and patience."

"Grandma!"

Ruth chuckled and gestured with her hand. "Off with you now. You don't want to spend your wedding night with me."

"I love you," Julia murmured as Ruth settled back against the pillows. "Have a good sleep, and I'll call you in the morning."

"It was a privilege to spend this time with you," Alek said. Reaching for her grandmother's hand, he bent down and kissed it. "I would have liked your Louis," he told her. "He was a rare man of honor."

A smile coaxed up the corners of Ruth's mouth. "Indeed he was. When we first married, there was talk, there always seemed to be talk. Some folks said Louis had married me for my connections, for the money I would one day inherit. Few realized the truth. *I* was the fortunate one to be loved by such a man."

Julia looked at Alek, but when their eyes met, she quickly glanced away.

"Now go," Ruth urged. "This is your wedding night."

The words echoed in Julia's ears. Her grandfather had been a man of honor, but she clearly hadn't inherited his grit or his honesty. She planned to cheat Alek and he was about to learn exactly how much.

* * *

Julia had surprised him. Alek had misjudged this woman who was now his wife. For two years he'd studied her, astonished by her tenacity. Jerry had told him little of what had led to the company's financial problems. Ever since his arrival, he'd picked up bits and pieces of what had happened, but no one had explained the events that had brought near ruin. From what he understood, Conrad Industries had come very close to introducing a long-lasting exterior paint with a twenty-five-year guarantee. Jerome Conrad, Jerry and Julia's father, had been a chemist, too, and he'd been personally involved in developing it. The company was on the brink of making one of the most innovative and progressive advances in the industry. This high-tech development was expected to have a dynamic impact on sales and give Conrad Industries a badly needed financial boost. The company had been set for expansion, confident of success. Then a series of mishaps occurred.

This was the part that remained vague to Alek. He'd heard something about a burglary and a defection to a rival company. But by far the worst was a huge fire that had destroyed the lab and the warehouse. Not until much later had they learned the fire was arson.

An employee was suspected. That much he'd been told by Jerry. But there wasn't enough proof to prosecute whoever it had been. Shortly after the fire, Jerry and Julia's father had suffered a heart attack and died. It was then that Julia had taken over the company. They'd struggled for a year, trying to recover lost ground, before Jerry made the arrangements to bring Alek from Russia. Since that time he'd been working hard on implementing his ideas.

"You're very quiet," Julia commented, breaking into his thoughts.

He glanced over at his bride. Her nervousness didn't escape him. He wanted to do whatever was necessary to put her at ease. He'd enjoyed listening to the story of Ruth and Louis Conrad's love. It had touched his heart, reminding him of his own grandparents, long dead. They'd loved each other deeply and he could have asked for no finer heritage. His grandfather had died first and his grandmother had followed less than a year later. His mother claimed her mother-in-law had succumbed to a broken heart.

Julia shifted restlessly in the car. He caught the movement from the corner of his eye and wondered about this woman he'd begun to love. He'd been observing her for two years; he knew her far better than she could possibly grasp. And he'd known the instant Jerry had suggested they marry that he would accept nothing less than total commitment from her. He was not a man who did things by half measures. He looked forward to the time he would sleep with his wife. He'd sensed fire in her, but hadn't realized how hot the flames were until they'd kissed. Really kissed.

No woman had ever affected him as strongly as Julia. The kisses had enhanced his appetite for what was to follow. He would be patient with her. Careful and slow. Although every instinct insisted he take her to his bed now, do away with her fretting and worry so they could enjoy the rest of the evening together. He must be patient, he reminded himself.

"Where would you like to go for dinner?" he asked. He suggested a couple of his favorite restaurants.

"Dinner?" she echoed, as though she hadn't given the matter a second thought. "I…don't know."

"You decide."

"Would you mind if we went to my…our condo?" In one of their few practical conversations, they'd agreed that he'd move into her place; his own apartment had been a furnished rental, so there hadn't been much to bring over—just books, his computer, clothes and a few personal effects. He had a small moving company take care of it and continued to pay rent on the place so his sister, Anna, could eventually move in there.

Alek's nod was eager. She would relax there and—what was the American term—unwind? Yes, she would unwind so that when the time came for them to retreat to the bedroom, she'd be warm with wine and eager for his touch.

"We'll have to send out for something," Julia announced when they reached the high-rise condominium. It was situated in the heart of downtown Seattle on the tenth floor, overlooking Puget Sound. A white-and-green ferry could be seen in the distance. The jagged peaks of the Olympic Mountains rose majestically to the west. The day had been clear and bright, but now the sun was setting, casting a pink glow over the landscape.

"Send out?" he repeated, frowning.

Julia stood in the middle of her modern home and clasped her hands in front of her. "I don't cook much."

"Ah." Now he understood. "I am excellent in the kitchen." In the bedroom, too, but he couldn't say that without embarrassing her. She would learn that soon enough.

"You want to make our dinner?"

"Yes," he answered, pulling his attention from the magnificent view and following her into the kitchen. He liked her home. The living room was long and narrow with windows that extended the full length. The dining room and kitchen were both compact, as if their importance was minimal.

"Would you like a glass of white wine?" Julia asked him.

"Please." While she was busy with the wine, he explored his new home. A narrow hallway led to two bedrooms. The larger was dominated by a king-size bed, covered with a bright blue comforter and what seemed like a hundred small pillows. The scent of flowers, violets he guessed, hung in the air. The second bedroom was much smaller and the closet was filled with boxes. A quick examination revealed Christmas decorations.

He returned to the kitchen and took the wineglass from his wife's hand. Her eyes, so large and dark, appealed to him, but for what he wasn't sure. One thing was certain: Alek knew he couldn't wait much longer to make love to her.

Julia felt like a fox about to be released for the hunt. She would soon be cornered, trapped by her own lies. Alek didn't realize, at least not yet, that she had no intention of sleeping with him. So far he'd been patient and kind, but she couldn't count on his goodwill lasting.

"I found a couple of chicken breasts in the freezer," she told him. She felt as though she was in danger of swallowing her heart. She was pretending for all she was worth, acting the role of devoted wife, when she was anything but. "I'll make a salad."

He was searching through her drawers, stopping when he came across an old cloth dish towel. He tucked it at his waist and continued to survey her cupboards, taking out a series of ingredients.

He'd chopped an onion, a green pepper and several mushrooms by the time she dragged a stool to the counter. Perhaps she'd learn something about cooking from him. She'd seen Alek working in the laboratory. But now he astonished her with the familiar way he moved about her kitchen, as if this was truly his second home.

"When did you learn to cook?"

"As a boy. My mother insisted and I enjoy it."

"Thank her for me."

Alek paused and, glancing her way, smiled. "You can do that yourself someday. I'm doing what I can to arrange for her immigration to the States."

"If…there's anything I can do, please let me know."

He nodded, seemingly pleased by her offer.

Julia drank her wine and refilled both their glasses. Her mind was working at a frantic pace, devising ways of delaying the inevitable moment when he'd learn the truth. Her original plan had been to get him drunk. Two glasses of wine and she was feeling light-headed and a bit tipsy. Alek had consumed the same amount and was completely sober. He wielded a large knife without the slightest hesitation.

Her next thought was to appeal to his sense of honor. A strange tactic, she had to admit, coming from a woman who planned on cheating him out of an intimate relationship. He must recognize that she didn't love him. This was a business arrangement that profited them both; turning it into something personal could ruin everything.

The kiss. She must've been mad to let him kiss her like that. She'd done nothing to resist him. Instead she'd encouraged him, led him to believe she welcomed his touch.

She'd been shaken afterward. It shouldn't have happened. The very fact that she'd permitted him to hold her and touch her in such an intimate manner defeated her own purpose. Anger rose within her, not at Alek, but at herself for having let things go so far. Now he expected more, and she couldn't, wouldn't allow it. She was angry, too, about the enjoyment she'd found in his arms. It was as if she'd been looking for a way to prove herself as a woman, to show him—and everyone else—that she was more feminine than they'd suspected.

Her foolishness had only complicated an already difficult situation.

"More wine?" she asked nervously. The rice was cooking in a covered pot and the chicken was simmering in a delicious-smelling sauce. Alek appeared relaxed and at ease while Julia calculated how many steps it would take to reach the front door.

Alek shook his head. "No more wine for me."

"I'll set the table," she said, slipping down from the stool and moving into the dining room. Soon he'd know. Soon he'd discover what a phony she was. He'd learn that she was a liar and a cheat and a coward.

Her hands were trembling as she set the silverware on the table. She added water glasses, anything to delay returning to the kitchen. To Alek.

He'd filled up their plates when she walked back into the room. Julia didn't know if she could eat a single bite, and she watched transfixed as he carried their meal into the dining room.

"Julia, my love."

"I'm not your love," she told him coolly, leaning back against the kitchen counter.

His grin was slow. Undisturbed. "Not yet, perhaps, but you will be."

She closed her eyes, afraid to imagine what might come next.

"Let us eat," Alek said, taking her unresisting hand and leading her to a chair. With impeccable manners, he held it out for her, then seated himself.

"This is very nice," she said. The smells were heavenly. In other circumstances she would have appreciated his culinary skills.

"My sister is an excellent cook," he said casually. He removed the linen napkin from the table and spread it across his lap. "If you agree, she will prepare our meals once she arrives from Russia. She'll welcome the job and it'll simplify her receiving a visa."

"Of course…" Julia was more than willing to be generous with his family.

"You are nervous?" Alek asked, after several bites. Julia hadn't managed even one taste.

"Yes."

He grinned. "Understandably. Don't worry, I will be gentle with you."

Julia's heart plummeted.

"I admire you, Julia. It isn't any woman who would accept the terms of our marriage. You are brave as well as beautiful. I feel fortunate to have married you."

Four

Julia vaulted to her feet, startling Alek. Her hand clutched the pink linen napkin as though it were a lifeline, and her dark eyes filled with tears.

"Julia?"

"I can't do it! I can't go through with it... You expect me to share a bed and for us to live like a normal married couple, but I just can't do it. I lied...everything's a lie. I'm sorry, Alek, truly sorry."

"You agreed to my terms," he reminded her without rancor. She was pale and trembling and it disturbed him to see her in such emotional torment. He would have liked to take her in his arms and comfort her, but he could see she wouldn't welcome his touch.

"I was overwrought. I...I didn't know what I was doing. Everything happened so fast."

Alek considered her words and slowly shook his head. "You knew."

She retreated a couple of steps. "I've had a change of heart. It's understandable, given the circumstances."

It pained him to see her so distraught, but she'd willingly agreed to his stipulations, and there'd been ample opportunity for her to speak her mind before the wedding. Calmly he pointed this out.

"You didn't have to go through with the ceremony, but you did," he said. "You wanted this marriage, but you refuse to admit it even to yourself." He stared at her, demanding that she relent and recognize her foolishness. They were married, and she was his wife. There was no going back now.

"I...I felt I had no choice. Jerry was convinced that marrying you was the only way to keep you in the country. My grandmother's dying and she likes you, believes in you, and it seemed, I don't know, it just felt like the right thing to do at the time."

"But now it doesn't?" he asked calmly, despite his mounting frustration.

"No," she said emphatically. "It doesn't feel the least bit right."

Alek rubbed his hand over his chin as he contemplated her words. "You Americans have many sayings I do not understand. There is one expression I remember and it seems to fit this situation."

"What's that?"

"Hogwash."

Julia went speechless. Once she'd composed herself, she tilted her head regally and glared at him. Alek suspected she used this cold, haughty regard to intimidate those who dared to differ with her. A mere look was incapable of daunting him or distracting him from his purpose. It was apparent his bride had much to learn about him.

"Have you so little pride," she asked disdainfully, "that

you'd hold me to an agreement I made when I was emotionally distraught?"

Alek was impressed with her ability to twist an argument. "Pride," he echoed slowly. "I am a proud man. But what are you, Julia? Have you so little honor that you would renege on an agreement made in good faith and expect me to accept weak excuses?"

Her face reddened and she slumped into her chair.

"I've fulfilled my part of the bargain," he continued. "Is it wrong or unjust to expect you to live up to yours? I think not. You have what you wanted, what you needed. Therefore, shouldn't you satisfy *my* demands?"

She scowled at him and even though an entire room separated them, Alek could feel the heat of her outrage. "You ask too much," she muttered.

"All I ask is that you be my wife—share my life and bear our children."

Tears marked her pale cheeks. "You have every right to be angry, every right to curse me, but I can't be your wife the way you want."

"It's too late to change your mind." His voice was flat and hard. "We are married. You spoke your vows, you signed your name to the document. There is no turning back now. I suggest you forget this foolishness and finish your meal."

"Please try to understand. This isn't easy for me, either. I've been sick with guilt. I don't want to cheat you...I never wanted that."

Alek sighed, his patience shrinking. "You're beginning to sound like a disobedient child."

"You're correct about one thing," she said, gesturing beseechingly with her hands. "I should've said something sooner. I should never have gone through with the ceremony, but it's not too late. I'm saying something now."

"We are married." He sat down at the table and reached for his fork. He refused to give her the satisfaction of thinking her arguments had troubled him.

In abject frustration, Julia threw her hands in the air. "You're impossible!"

"Perhaps," he said readily enough. "But you are my wife and, as you yourself have agreed, you shall remain so."

Without another word she stormed out of the dining room. He heard her in the kitchen banging around pots and pans, but couldn't tell what she was doing. He finished his meal, although his appetite had long since deserted him.

He heard her trying to make a phone call, but whoever she called didn't answer. From his chair he witnessed her frustration when he saw her replace the receiver and lean her forehead against the wall.

His dinner finished, Alek returned to the kitchen to find Julia busily rinsing dishes and placing them in the dishwasher.

She ignored him for several minutes, until he said, "Shall we prepare for bed?"

Julia froze, then turned and stared at him. "Are you crazy?" Each word was spoken slowly, as if he didn't understand English.

"No," he answered thoughtfully. "I am a husband. Yours."

"I'm sorry, Alek," she said, her face pale, her voice shaking. "I know I should've spoken up before the ceremony.... I've put in a call to my brother. As soon as possible I'll make whatever arrangements are necessary to have our marriage annulled."

Alek didn't swallow the bait. Jerry Conrad was not only

his friend but an attorney and had sanctioned this marriage with his sister. In fact, he'd encouraged it from the beginning.

Although Jerry hadn't shared his concerns with Alek, he was convinced Julia's brother was worried about her. Whenever Jerry mentioned Julia's name his eyes clouded. After working with her these past two years, Alek understood her brother's anxiety. She was aggressive, domineering and driven. In themselves those weren't negative attributes, especially for a woman in a competitive business, but Alek had noticed something else. Julia Conrad had closed off her life from everything that didn't involve Conrad Industries. Perhaps he was a fool, but Alek saw this woman as a challenge. More than that, he liked Julia and with very little effort could find himself in love with her. Already he admired her and was attracted to her; he longed for the day she'd feel the same about him.

No, Alek reasoned, Jerry wouldn't give in to her dictates. He would be unemotional, reasonable. Alek knew they couldn't count on the same behavior from Julia. Smiling to himself, he decided he rather looked forward to the battle of wills.

Alek had met Jerry years earlier while the young American had traveled across Europe. Together they'd spent a restless day in a train station. Eager to learn what he could of America, Alek had questioned him and found they shared several interests. Alek had liked Jerry. They'd corresponded over the years and Alek had shared his frustration with his country and his work. Jerry had offered Alek employment soon after the fire that had nearly destroyed Conrad Industries. It had taken them almost a year to secure the necessary visa for him to live in the United States.

"Do you understand what I'm saying?" Julia asked. "I'm arranging an annulment."

"Yes, my love."

"I am *not* your love," she cried, sounding close to tears.

"Perhaps not now," he returned confidently, "but you will be soon. Sooner than you realize. Ah, Julia," he said, "we will have such marvelous children...."

Alek knew when her eyes drifted shut that she wasn't envisioning their offspring, but was desperately fighting to hold on to her temper. Once she accepted their marriage, he told himself, she would be a splendid lover. Already he'd experienced the passion that simmered within her. Soon, in her own time, she would come to him—and he'd be waiting.

Alek sauntered back into the living room, turned on the television and sat back to watch the nightly news.

No man had ever infuriated her more. Julia had needed every ounce of courage she'd ever possessed to confront him with the truth. But he'd been so blasé about it, as if he'd expected her to default on their agreement. As if he'd been calmly waiting for her to defy him.

Then to have him casually announce it was too late to change her mind? That was too much! She'd rather rot in jail than make love to such an uncaring, ill-tempered, scheming—

Suddenly she felt tired. If anyone had been scheming, she was the one. Exhaustion permeated her bones, and it was almost more than she could do to finish the dishes. Alek sat in her living room, watching television. Undaunted. Confident. Sure of himself.

"I'm going to bed," she said shakily, praying he wouldn't follow her.

Alek reached for the remote and turned off the television. He was on his feet, trailing her into the master bedroom, before she had time to protest.

"I'm very tired." Her eyes pleaded with him. If she couldn't reason with him, then perhaps she could evoke sympathy. Bottom-of-the-barrel compassion was all she had left.

"I'm tired, as well." He stood at the opposite side of her bed and unfastened the buttons of his shirt.

Julia felt like weeping. "You expect to sleep in here?"

"You are my wife."

"Please." Her voice cracked.

He didn't pause in his movements, tugging the shirt free from his waist.

"I can't sleep with you." Her words were low and barely audible.

He turned back the bed covers. "We are married, Julia, and we will share this room. You needn't worry that I will make any unwelcome…advances. I'm certain that in time you'll come to me. You will, you know, and when you do, I'll be waiting. I can be patient when the prize is of such high value."

The presumptuousness of the man continued to astound her. "I can't…sleep with you," she repeated.

"I am not a monster, Julia, but a man." He stopped and looked at her as if expecting her to argue further.

"I don't understand you," she cried, nearly hysterical. "I've cheated you and lied to you. Why do you still want me? You should be glad to be rid of me."

"You are my wife."

It demanded all of Julia's energy just to hold up her head.

This man confused her and she lacked the resources to go on arguing.

He pulled back the sheets and rearranged the pillows on his side of the bed, making certain she understood that he wouldn't be dissuaded.

"I can't think clearly," she said, holding her hands to her cheeks. "I'll sleep in the guest bedroom."

His disappointment was obvious. "You're sure?"

She nodded. "For now."

"As you wish, then."

Listlessly she moved around the foot of the single bed. She'd made a mess of this marriage from the beginning.

"Julia." His voice was softly accented and warmly masculine. Something in the way he said her name gave her pause.

"I'm so sorry," she said before he could speak. She could hear the tears in her voice.

"For what?"

She shrugged. For another failure. For dragging him into a loveless marriage with a cold, unwilling wife. For countless unconfessed sins.

"You've spent today and many others before it fighting yourself. You're weary of the battle, aren't you?"

Julia nodded. He was behind her, moving closer. She should leave now, walk away from him before he started to make sense, before he convinced her there was hope. She couldn't allow it to happen, because ultimately she would disappoint him. Even hurt him.

"I am your husband," he whispered once more as he turned her into his arms. "Let me carry your burdens and lighten your load. I'm here to be your helpmate, your friend, your lover. Let me take care of you, Julia. Let me love you."

As he spoke, his mouth was drawing closer and closer to hers, until their breath mingled.

As hard as she tried, Julia couldn't dredge up a single protest when his mouth settled firmly on hers. He kissed her the way a woman dreams a man will kiss her, with a tenderness that touched some long-hidden spark within her.

And then…he altered the kiss, making it hot and fierce. He buried his hands deep in her hair.

Alek sighed and her name spilled from his lips. His voice was filled with need. With unbridled desire.

"Be my wife."

Julia's eyes fluttered open. It took her a second to comprehend what he'd said. When she did, she stared at him, unable to speak. Her heart was pounding, tapping out a dire warning. One she should heed.

"I…need time."

He continued to hold her gaze. "All right."

Tears filled her eyes and she bit her lip. "You're getting the short end of the stick with me, Alek."

"Short end of the stick?"

She smiled softly. "It means you're getting less than you deserve."

"Let me be the judge of that. As I said, in time you'll come to me of your own accord. In time you'll want me as much as I want you."

"There are many things you don't know about me," she said, her words so low he had to strain to hear.

"Tell me."

She shook her head. "Just remember, I warned you."

He released her, maintaining their contact as long as possible. His hands slid down the full length of her arms and, catching her fingers, he held on to the tips with his own.

"Good night, my wife," he whispered, then turned away. "I shall be lonely without you."

Julia left the room quickly, knowing that if she stayed a moment longer, she'd end up in the bed next to Alek....

Julia found it surprisingly easy to avoid Alek. Their schedules were different and they drove to work in separate cars. She left for the office early, before he awoke. In the afternoons she visited her grandmother, then ate a quiet meal by herself. She was usually preparing for bed about the time Alek returned from the lab.

He was working long, hard hours, getting ready to put his latest research into production. From the weekly reports he sent her, she knew that they were speeding ahead; the marketing and distribution plans for Phoenix Paints were under way. The advertising blitz had yet to be decided, but that was coming. Everything looked promising.

But then, it had looked promising three years ago, too. Yet within the course of a single week she'd lost her father, been betrayed by the man she loved and nearly destroyed a business that had been in the family for four generations.

Julia had learned harsh but valuable lessons about promises. Probably the most painful lessons of her life. She'd come away convinced she could trust only a cherished few. Equally important, she'd learned never, ever to cash in on mere potential. The promise of a check in the mail wasn't money in the bank.

Dear heavens, she mused as she left the office, she was becoming very philosophical. Perhaps that was what marriage did to a woman.

Marriage.

Even the word sounded strange to her. She was married for better or worse. Married. After her tirade on their wedding night, when she'd pleaded, threatened and tried to reason with Alek, she'd decided he was right. There was no backing out now. They *were* married, for better or worse.

Her decision was prompted by a certain amount of pride. Jerry had made sure the news of their wedding was carried by the local newspapers. The business community and their acquaintances would know about her marriage. It would be acutely embarrassing to seek an annulment so soon after the ceremony.

Mentally she added vanity to her growing list of character defects.

"Julia," Ruth said weakly when she entered the hospital room, "what are you doing here?"

Julia grinned as she leaned forward to kiss her grandmother's pale cheek. "It's good to see you, too."

"Alek will never forgive me."

"Alek is hard at work," she assured Ruth.

"But you're newlyweds."

Julia's gaze skirted past her grandmother's. "He's been so busy lately. I'd rather spend time with you than go home to an empty apartment."

"I worry about you," Ruth said, her voice growing weaker.

"Worry?" Julia repeated. "There's no need. Our schedules are hectic just now. Coming here is the best thing for me.... That way, when Alek gets home, I'm calm and relaxed."

"Good. He's such a dear boy. You married well.... I so want you to be happy—it's what you deserve. Your season of pain is past now that you have Alek."

Julia wanted to avoid the subject of her husband. "Would you like me to read to you?"

"Please. From the book of Psalms, if you would?"

"Of course." Julia reached for the well-worn Bible and

sat in the chair next to her grandmother's bed and began. She read long past the moment Ruth had fallen asleep. Long past the dinner hour. Long past the time she should leave for home.

The night was hot and muggy, the air heavy. Her air-conditioning system must not be working properly because it felt like the hottest night of the year. Even her skimpy, baby-doll pajamas seemed clammy and constricting.

Sleep seemed just beyond her grasp no matter how hard she tried to capture it. The night was still and dark, and she flopped from her side to her back, then onto her side once more, attempting to find the touch of a cool breeze. But there was none.

Another hour passed and she gave up the effort. Getting out of bed, she moved into the living room, standing in front of the window. A few scattered lights flickered from Puget Sound. The last ferry crossing before dawn, she guessed, on its way to Winslow on Bainbridge Island.

The lights from Alki Point gleamed in the distance.

Julia had no idea how long she stood there, looking into the still, dark night. Raising her arms high above her head, she stretched, standing on her toes. The thin fabric of her pajama top rustled. Her hair felt damp and heavy and she lifted the long tresses from the back of her neck. She shook her head, sending a spray of hair in a circle around her face.

She heard the briefest of noises behind her and whirled around to see a shadow unfold from the chair. Alek stood. He wore only the bottom half of his pajamas and his hard chest glistened in the muted light.

"Alek," she said breathlessly.

"I couldn't sleep, either," he told her.

"How…long have you been here?" she demanded.

"I wasn't spying on you, if that's what you're insinuating."

"I...you startled me, that's all."

"Come sit with me."

She shook her head again and watched as his jaw tightened at her refusal.

"We're married," he reminded her. "You can't ignore me the rest of your life. We made a bargain, which has yet to be fulfilled."

Why he chose to bring up the subject of their marriage now, Julia didn't know. They'd lived peacefully together for nearly two weeks, barely seeing each other, rarely talking. She'd almost convinced herself they could continue like this forever.

"I don't want to talk about our marriage."

She sensed that his irritation turned to amusement. "No, I don't imagine you do," he said.

"I'm sorry...I didn't mean to snap at you. It's just that I didn't realize you were here."

"Fine. I forgive you. Now sit and we can talk."

Julia hesitated, then decided it would do more harm than good to refuse him. She sank onto the sofa across from him. Holding a decorative pillow to her stomach helped ease her discomfort over her state of undress, although not by much.

"How is your grandmother?"

"About the same. I talked to her doctor this afternoon and he said..." She paused, biting her lip. "He said we shouldn't expect her to return home."

"Is she in pain?"

"Yes, sometimes, although she tries to hide it from me. Listen, do you mind if we don't talk about Ruth, either?"

"Of course not. I didn't mean to bring up a subject that causes you distress."

Julia lowered her eyes. "It's just that…she's so important to me. Ruth's all the family Jerry and I have left."

"Your mother died years ago, didn't she?"

Julia wasn't surprised he knew that, since he and Jerry had been friends since her brother's college days, when they'd met in Europe. "When I was fifteen, and as you probably recall, my father," she added, "died three years ago… shortly after the fire."

Silence stretched between them. Julia's pressure on the pillow increased. Even in the darkened room, she could feel his smoldering gaze move caressingly over her. He wanted her and was growing impatient. Her heart pounded with dread and some other emotion. Regret? Perhaps…yearning?

"Please don't look at me like that," she begged. It seemed as if his eyes were about to devour her. He wanted her to know how much he longed to make love to her. The memory of his kisses returned to haunt her and she tried to dispel the image before it took root in her mind and her heart.

"You're very beautiful."

She'd heard those meaningless words before. Beauty was fleeting and counted for little of real value in life. Being outwardly attractive hadn't made her a better judge of character. It didn't do one iota of good as far as her grandmother's health was concerned. If anything, it had been a curse, because it attracted the wrong kind of man.

"This makes you sad?"

She shrugged. "Beauty means nothing."

"You are wise to recognize that."

"Then why do you mention it?"

"Because you were not beautiful, not in the same way, when we first met. It's only recently that I've come to appreciate that you are a real woman."

A real woman. Julia nearly laughed aloud.

"This is what makes being married to you and not sleeping with you so difficult. Have you reconsidered yet, my love? Come with me, share my bed."

"I…can't, please don't ask me." Her response was immediate. Tossing the pillow aside, she leapt to her feet, needing to escape. "Good night, Alek."

He didn't answer and she didn't look back as she rushed to her room. Her heart was roaring in her ears when she reached the bed. Not for the first time she felt like the fox in an English hunt, and the baying of the hounds was closing in on her.

"Julia."

She nearly fell off the bed when she looked up and found Alek framed in her doorway. Her breath froze in her lungs.

"Someday you won't run from me."

"I wasn't running from you." It was a lie and they both knew it, yet Julia persisted in claiming otherwise.

His smile was more than a little cocky. "Someday you will come to me voluntarily."

She wasn't going to argue with him. He watched her closely in the muted moonlight and she studied him with equal intensity. She suddenly realized her top had inched up and exposed her breasts. Furiously she tugged it down, glaring at him as though he'd purposely arranged the immodest display.

He smiled roguishly at her. "As I said earlier, you are very beautiful." Then he turned and left.

After a sleepless, frustrating night, Julia was in no mood to deal with a long list of complicated problems. Virginia, her middle-aged assistant, looked apologetic when Julia arrived at the office early the next morning.

"Please get my brother on the line when you can," Julia said. Her mind was made up. She wanted out of this farce of a marriage.

"He's already called for you." Virginia hugged a file folder against her chest. "He asked that you call him the moment you got here."

Julia reached for her phone and punched out the extension. Jerry answered on the first ring. "Come down to my office," he said impatiently.

"Now?"

"Right now."

"What's wrong?"

"You'll find out soon enough."

This morning was quickly going from bad to worse, much like her life. She paused, catching herself. Her thoughts hadn't always been this negative. When had it started? The wedding? No, she decided—long before then. Three years before... She wondered why she was so aware of it now.

She rounded the corner that led to the suite of offices her brother occupied on the floor below her own.

"Jerry, what's this all about?" she asked before she noticed Alek. She halted when she saw her husband sitting in one of the visitor's chairs, waiting for her.

"Sit down." Her brother motioned toward Alek.

Julia did as he asked. Jerry paced back and forth behind his desk. "I was contacted this morning by the Immigration people. I knew this would happen, I just didn't expect it to be quite so soon."

"We're being investigated?" Alek murmured.

Jerry nodded. "The two of you are going to have to

convince them you're madly in love. Do you think you can do it?"

Julia saw that he focused his gaze on her. "Ah…"

"Yes," Alek responded without hesitation.

"Julia, what about you?"

"Ah…" She'd never been good with pretense.

"She'll convince them." Alek revealed far more confidence in her than she had in herself. "It won't take much effort." He reached for her hand, gripping it in his own. "All we need is a little practice, isn't that right, Julia?"

Five

Only seconds earlier Julia had decided she wanted to end this charade of a marriage, no matter what the price. Just when it seemed that very thing was about to happen, she discovered herself willing to do whatever was necessary to keep their relationship intact.

Counseling. That was what she needed, Julia thought. Intensive counseling. She wasn't an indecisive woman; that would be a death knell for someone in her position. Generally she knew what she wanted and went after it with a determination that left everyone in her wake shaking their heads in wonder.

It was Aleksandr who managed to discomfit and confuse her. It was Alek who made her feel as though she was walking through quicksand.

"Julia?" Jerry turned the full force of his attention on her. "Can you do it?"

Both men were studying her. Could she pretend to be in love with Alek? Pretend her happiness hinged on spending the rest of her life with him? Could she?

"I…I don't know."

"Shall I repeat what's at stake here?" Jerry muttered.

It wasn't necessary; he'd gone over the consequences of their actions when he'd proposed the idea of marrying Alek in the first place. The government did much more than frown upon such unions. There was the possibility of jail time if they weren't able to persuade the Immigration department of their sincerity.

"Julia knows," Alek assured Jerry calmly. "Isn't that right?"

She lowered her eyes. "I'm fully aware of what could happen."

"That's fine and dandy, but can you be convincing enough to satisfy the Immigration people?" Jerry demanded.

She nodded slowly, thoughtfully. It wasn't just a question of being able to pull this off with the finesse required; it also meant lowering her guard, opening her heart to the truth. She was attracted to him, both physically and emotionally. Otherwise she wouldn't have participated in or enjoyed the few times they'd kissed. The most important factor wasn't her ability to fool Immigration, but resurrecting the shield protecting her against the pull she felt toward Alek.

To complicate matters, the attachment she felt was growing stronger every day. She often found herself thinking about him. Hard as it was to admit, Julia had discovered she enjoyed his company and looked forward to the short time they spent together in the evenings.

"You're sure?" Jerry asked, sounding as if he thought she was anything but.

"Positive," she said, chancing a look in Alek's direction. He caught her eye and smiled reassuringly. Taking her hand, he squeezed her fingers.

"We'll do just fine," Alek said to Jerry. "Wait and see. What both of you fail to realize is that Julia and I *did* marry for love."

"Stop pacing," Alek said, more testily than he intended. The Immigration officer was due in fifteen minutes and Julia was understandably nervous. Unable to sit still, she stalked the living room.

"Walking helps take my mind off the interview," Julia snapped back.

The tension between them was thick enough to slice and serve for dinner. That would hurt their case more than anything they said or did. The man or woman doing the interview would sense the strain immediately and count it against them.

"You should know more about me," Julia said, whirling around to face him as if this was a new thought. "The brand of toothpaste I use and stuff like that."

"Don't be ridiculous."

"I'm not…. That's exactly the kind of questions he'll ask."

"Julia, my love," he said patiently, "a man doesn't pay attention to such things. Now relax."

"How can you be so calm?" Julia shrugged, raising both hands. "Our future hinges on the outcome of this meeting. There's a very real possibility I could go to jail for involving myself in this…marriage." Her arms seemed to have lost their purpose and fell lifelessly to her sides. "I'm not the only one who has a lot at stake with this. Your mother and sister's plans depend on the outcome, as well. Didn't you mention you've already seen to the necessary paperwork for them?"

"I'm aware of the consequences."

"Then how can you be so *calm?*"

"Very simple, my love." He said this evenly and without emotion as he leaned forward, clasped her around the waist and brought her down into his lap.

Julia struggled at first. "Stop," she said, wriggling against him. "What are you trying to do?"

He let her struggle, but her efforts were weak. His arms were around her and he felt her yielding. Taking advantage of her acquiescence, he brushed his face against her hair. She'd left it down, at his request, and he gathered the length of it in his hands, loving its clean jasmine scent.

"Alek, are you insane?"

He dropped a trail of moist kisses along her throat and shoulder. "That's better," he whispered as her tight muscles relaxed. "Much better."

"I…I don't think we should be doing this."

"What?" he asked as his hand caressed her back in a slow, soothing motion. "This?" He eased her against the chair until her hair spilled over his arm. A sigh escaped her as he pressed his lips to hers.

Julia felt hot, then cold and shaky in his embrace, but no more so than he. They'd kissed a handful of times and each had been a battle for him. His wife had balked at his touch in the beginning, then gradually she'd opened herself to him until he was so needy he ached.

This time the skirmish between them was over even before it started. Julia accepted his kiss with little more than a token protest. Perhaps she was ready for more….

He broke off the kiss and told her how badly he needed her. He pleaded with her as only a man who needs his wife can implore. It wasn't until he saw the confusion in her eyes that he realized he'd spoken in his native tongue. His English was hopeless just then.

Julia's fingers were digging into his shoulders. He felt the rapid beat of her heart and heard the ragged echo of her breath as it rasped in his ear.

The doorbell chimed and Alek would have ignored it if Julia hadn't frozen and then jumped from his lap as though she'd caught fire.

"Oh, my goodness," she cried. Her face was a rich shade of red as she swept back her hair. "The interviewer is here." She stared at him as if he had the magical power to make everything right.

"That would be my guess."

"Alek." Her voice shook as she quickly adjusted her clothes. "I'm scared."

"Don't be. Everything will be fine," he said. He gave her a moment to fuss with her hair before he stood, kissed her lightly on the lips and answered the door.

Although Alek appeared outwardly composed, he was as shaken as Julia. And not because their future hung in the balance. His head reeled with the aftershock of their kissing. A few kisses, he'd thought, to take the edge off their nervousness. In another five minutes, he would've carried her to his bed....

"Hello," Alek said, opening the door to admit a lanky, official-looking gentleman. He wore a crisp business suit and from the tight set of his mouth, Alek guessed he would brook no foolishness. His expression was sharp and unfriendly.

"Patrick O'Dell," he said.

"My name is Alek and this is my wife, Julia," Alek said.

Julia stood on the far side of the room, her smile fleeting

and strained. "Welcome to our home, Mr. O'Dell. Would
you care to sit down?"

"Thank you." He moved into the living room and didn't
pause to look at the view. Indeed, there might not have
been one for all the notice O'Dell took. He sat on the re-
cliner they'd recently vacated and set his briefcase on the
coffee table.

Alek walked over to Julia's side and held her hand in his.
Together they ventured to the sofa opposite the interviewer
and sat down.

Mr. O'Dell removed a file from his briefcase. He scanned
the contents, then frowned with clear disapproval. "How
did you two meet?"

"Through my brother," Julia said quickly. "He'd met Alek
several years earlier while he was in Europe. They corresponded for a number of years and then after the fire..."
She hesitated and turned to Alek.

"Jerry offered me a job in this country almost three years
ago. I've lived here for the past two."

"Tell me about your work."

Alek answered the questions thoroughly, while mini-
mizing his importance to Conrad Industries. No need to
raise suspicions.

"Alek is a gifted biochemist," Julia added with unnecessary enthusiasm. "The company was nearly ruined a few
years back following the fire I mentioned. I don't know what
would've become of us if it hadn't been for Alek."

Although he smiled, Alek was groaning inwardly. Julia
was offering far more information than necessary. He
wished now that they'd gone over what they planned to
say. Jerry had advised them to do so, but Alek had felt

spontaneity would serve them better than a series of practiced responses.

"In other words, you needed Mr. Berinski."

"Yes, very much so." Julia was nothing if not honest.

"Do you continue to need him?" the interviewer pressed.

"No," Alek answered before Julia could.

"I disagree," she returned, looking briefly at Alek. "I find we need him more than ever now. The new line of paints Alek's been working on for the past two years is ready to be marketed. That's only the beginning of the ideas he's developing."

Alek's concern mounted as O'Dell made a notation. Julia really was as bad at pretense as she'd claimed.

"My husband has worked hard on this project. He deserves to reap the fruits of his labors." Fortunately, Julia didn't stumble over the word *husband*. She'd said it a number of times since their marriage and it always seemed to cause her difficulty.

"You give me more credit than I deserve, my dear," he murmured, feeling they'd dug themselves into a pit.

"Nonsense," Julia said, obviously warming to her subject. "Alek is a genius."

Another notation.

Alek squeezed Julia's fingers, willing her to stop speaking, but the more he tried to discourage her, the more she went on.

"If you two held each other in such high esteem, why did you wait until Alek's visa had almost expired before you agreed to marry?"

"Love isn't always planned," Julia answered quickly. "No one completely understands matters of the heart, do they? I know I didn't." She glanced shyly toward Alek.

"I understand why the Immigration department is suspicious of our marriage," Alek added. "We realized you would be when we decided to go ahead and marry. It didn't make any difference."

Another notation, this one made with sharp jagged movements of his pen.

There were several more questions, which they answered as forthrightly as possible. Alek was uncertain of how well they were coming across. He'd rarely heard Julia sound more animated and, to his surprise, sincere. When he'd first learned of the interview, his biggest concern had been Julia, but now he suspected she'd be his strongest asset.

If he was forced to return to Russia, Alek would go, because he had no other choice. He hadn't dwelled on the consequences, refusing to allow any negative suggestions to enter his mind. He realized as they were speaking how much he'd hate to leave Julia.

"I think that answers everything," O'Dell said, closing his file and placing it back in his briefcase.

The unexpectedness of his announcement caught Alek off guard.

"That's all?" Apparently Julia was as astonished as he was. "You don't want to know what brand of toothpaste Alek uses or about his personal habits?"

The official smiled for the first time. "We leave that sort of interrogation for the movies. It's obvious to me that you two care deeply for each other. I wish all my assignments were as easy."

"Will I need to sign anything?" Julia asked.

"No," O'Dell said as he stood. "I'll file my report by the end of the week. I don't believe there's any reason for us to be in further contact with you. I appreciate your agreeing to see me on such short notice."

Alek stood in order to escort Mr. O'Dell to the door. Julia seemed to be in a state of shock. She sat on the sofa, her mouth hanging open, staring up at the official with a baffled, uncertain look.

"Thank you again for your trouble," Patrick O'Dell said when Alek opened the front door.

"Julia and I should be the ones thanking you."

The two men exchanged handshakes. Alek closed the door with relief and leaned against the frame. He slowly expelled his breath.

"Julia." He whispered her name as he returned to the living room. She hadn't moved. "We did it."

She nodded as though she was in a trance.

"You were fantastic."

Her eyes went to him and she blinked. "Me?"

"You were straightforward and honest. At first I was worried. I thought you were giving him far more information than necessary. Then I realized that was what convinced him. You acted as though you had nothing to hide. As if our staying married meant all the world to you. It wasn't anything *I* said or did, it was you."

"Me?" she repeated again, sounding close to tears.

Alek knelt down in front of her and took her hands. "Are you all right?"

Sniffling, she shook her head. The ordeal had been a strain, but he was surprised by her response. Julia wasn't the type of woman to buckle easily. Nor did she weep without provocation. Something was definitely going on.

"What's wrong?" he asked tenderly, resisting the urge to take her in his arms.

Tears filled her eyes and she made an effort to blink them away. "I think I'll go lie down for a while. I'm sure I'll be fine in a few minutes."

Alek didn't want her to leave. He was hoping they could pick up where they'd left off before they were interrupted by O'Dell's arrival. The craving she'd created in him had yet to be satisfied. He wanted her to share his bed. She was his wife. They belonged together.

Alek had learned enough about Julia to know that she'd come to him in her own time, when she was ready and not before. He prayed he had the patience to wait her out.

As she lay in her bed, pretending to nap, Julia realized it wasn't until the Immigration official had stood to leave that she'd recognized how sincere she was in what she'd told him. She'd answered the questions as candidly as possible, becoming more fervent the longer she spoke. It had suddenly struck her that Alek was as important to her personally as he was to the company. Perhaps more so. That came as an unexpected shock.

He'd been patient and loving and kind. His kisses stirred her soul. That sounded fanciful, overdramatic, but she was at a loss to explain it otherwise.

Heaven help her, she was falling in love with him. It wasn't supposed to happen this way. She didn't *want* to love him, didn't want to care about him. After Phoenix Paints was launched and he'd established his mother and sister in the country, she wanted Alek out of her life. That was what she'd planned. Involving her heart would be both foolish and dangerous. She'd already learned her lesson when it came to trusting a man. Roger had taught her well.

"Julia?" His voice was a whisper. She kept her eyes

closed, not wanting Alek to know she was awake. Afraid he might want to resume what they'd started…

Her face filled with color at the memory of their kisses. She couldn't believe the liberties Alek had taken with her earlier that afternoon. Worse, liberties she'd encouraged and enjoyed. She would be forever grateful that Mr. O'Dell had arrived when he had.

Julia had eventually drifted off. Because of her nap, she was unable to sleep that evening. Hoping to sidestep any questions from Alek, she'd gone to the hospital to visit Ruth later in the afternoon.

The condo was empty when she returned and Julia guessed Alek had gone to the lab to work. Feeling somewhat guilty, she microwaved her dinner, hoping he'd pick up something for himself while he was out.

He wasn't back by the time she showered and readied for bed. She should've been grateful; instead she found herself waiting for him. It was nearly eleven when she heard the front door open. Light from the kitchen spilled into the hallway outside her bedroom as he rummaged around, apparently looking for dinner.

A second bout of guilt didn't improve her disposition. Knowing next to nothing about cooking should prove beyond a doubt what a terrible wife she was. Another, more domesticated woman would have been knitting by the fireplace, awaiting his return with a delectable meal warming in the oven. Forget that it was summer; this imaginary dutiful wife would have a cozy fire roaring anyway.

Then, when he'd eaten, she'd remove her housecoat and stand before him dressed only in a sheer nightie.

But Alek hadn't married the ideal wife; instead he was stuck with her.

"Julia?"

She was so surprised by the sound of her name that she lifted her head from the pillow.

"I hope I didn't wake you."

"No...I hadn't gone to sleep yet." She sat up in bed and tugged the sheets protectively around her.

His shadow loomed against the opposite wall like...like some kind of fairy-tale monster. But try as she might, Julia couldn't make him into one.

"How's your grandmother?" he asked.

She shrugged hopelessly. It became more apparent with every visit that Ruth wouldn't last much longer. A part of Julia clung to her grandmother and another part struggled to release Ruth from this life and the pain that accompanied it.

"You were at the lab?"

Alek nodded.

"Is it really necessary for you to work so many hours?"

Alek crossed his arms and leaned against the doorjamb. "Work helps me deal with my frustration."

He didn't need to clarify his answer. Julia knew he was referring to the sexual disappointment of their marriage.

When she didn't respond, he sighed and added, "I know why everything went so smoothly with the Immigration official. You, my dear wife, are in love with me."

The audacity of the comment was shocking. "I'm what?"

"In love with me," he repeated.

"You're badly in need of some reality therapy," Julia said, making her words as scathing as she could. "That's the most ridiculous thing you've ever said."

"Wait, I promise you it'll get better. Much better."

"Much worse, you mean," she said with an exaggerated yawn. "Now if you don't mind, I'd like to get some sleep."

"Later. We need to talk."

"Alek, please, it's nearly midnight."

"You've already admitted you hadn't been to sleep."

"Exactly," she said. "And I need my rest."

"So do I."

"Then leave it until morning," she suggested next.

"You're my wife. How long will it take before you live up to your end of our bargain?"

"I…already explained I need time…to adjust to everything. Why are you doing this?" she cried, furious with him for dragging out a subject she considered closed. "I refuse to be pressured into making love just because you've got an overactive libido."

"Pressured," he echoed, and a deep frown formed. He rubbed his hand over his face, sighing audibly. "I've been waiting for you since our wedding night. You agreed that we'd be married in every sense of the word."

"It's only been a few weeks," she protested.

"Ah, but you love me. You proved it this afternoon. There's no need to wait any longer, Julia. I need you, and you need me." With a knowing smile, he turned and walked away.

The comment irritated her so much she couldn't bear to let it go unanswered. Grabbing her pillow with both hands, she threw it after him. It hit the doorframe with a soft thud that was barely discernible. She knew Alek heard it, however, because he started laughing.

The following morning, as was her habit, Julia rose early and stood barefoot in the kitchen while she waited for the first cup of coffee to filter into the glass pot. The aroma pervaded the kitchen.

"Morning." Alek spoke groggily from behind her.

Julia's eyes flew open. Normally Alek didn't get up until after she'd left for work. "Morning," she greeted him with little enthusiasm.

"Did you sleep well?"

No. "Fine. How about you?" Her attention remained focused on the coffeepot. She didn't dare turn around to confront her rumpled, groggy husband. Knowing he was only a few feet behind her activated her imagination. His hair was probably unkempt and his eyes drowsy, the way hers were. He'd look sexy and appealing.

"Julia," he whispered, moving forward. He slipped his arms around her waist and nuzzled her neck. "We can't go on like this. We're married. When are you going to recognize that?"

She braced her hands against his, which were joined at her stomach. His lips located the pulse pounding at the side of her neck and he kissed her. Small, soft kisses...

Julia's breath caught in her throat. "Alek, please, don't."

"Stop?" He raised his head as though she couldn't have meant it.

"Yes."

"I couldn't sleep for want of you," he whispered.

Her throat felt as dry as a desert. Speaking was impossible.

"All I could think about was how good you tasted and how much I wanted to hold you and kiss you again," he went on.

The coffee had finished brewing, but Julia couldn't make herself move.

"I know you want me, too. Why do you torture us like this?"

"I...have to get to work." Each syllable was a triumph.

"Let me make love to you," Alek urged, his mouth close to her ear.

"No. We can't. I…I'll be late for work." She didn't wait for him to argue with her, but rushed toward her bedroom. Toward sanity.

By the time Julia reached her office, she was in a terrible mood. She blamed Alek for this. As much as she wished it, she wasn't made of stone. She was flesh and blood. A woman. When he kissed her and touched her she experienced a certain sexual yearning.

It was inevitable. A mere physiological reaction. It meant nothing. He insisted she was in love with him, but Julia knew that was just talk. Sweet talk, with a single purpose. To seduce her.

Julia had been seduced before, by an artful master. In comparison, Alek was so much more honest and, therefore, easier to defend herself against. She refused to give in to his pressure, subtle or otherwise. As for misleading him, she had, but only to a limited degree.

Furious now, she marched into her office, reached for her phone and dialed Jerry's extension. "Can you come up?"

"Yes. Is everything okay?"

"No."

Jerry paused. "I thought things went hunky-dory with the inspector."

"They did, as far as I know. This has to do with Alek."

"I'll be right up," her brother said.

She was pacing her office with precise steps when he arrived. Julia stopped, angry with herself, feeling close to tears and not understanding why.

"What's wrong?" he asked, his concern evident in his eyes.

"I…there's a problem."

"With what?"

"Whom," she corrected. "Aleksandr Berinski."

Jerry frowned, then sighed with resignation. "What's he done?"

"Everything… Listen, I don't want to get into this. Let me make this as plain and simple as I can. I think it's time he moved out of the condo. One of us has to and it's either him or me."

Six

"You want Alek out of your condo?" Jerry repeated.

"You heard me the first time," she said impatiently. "Our marriage has been sanctioned by the government. What reason do we have to continue this charade?"

"Julia…"

She'd heard that tone all too often. "Jerry, I'm not in any mood to argue with you." She walked around her desk and claimed her seat. Reaching for a file from her in-basket, she opened it. "I'll leave the arrangements in your hands."

"Do you plan to talk this over with Alek?"

She hadn't thought of that. "It…won't be necessary. He'll get the picture once he hears from you."

"I won't do it."

Her brother's refusal caught her attention as nothing else could have. "What do you mean, you won't do it?"

"First, I won't have you treating Alek as though he's… some pest you're trying to get rid of."

"It wouldn't be like that," she insisted, realizing even

as she spoke that Jerry was right. She couldn't treat Alek this way.

"Secondly," her brother said, "it'd be crazy to throw everything away now. You think that just because you've passed some interview with an Immigration official, you're in the clear. Think again, Julia. That's exactly the kind of thing the government's expecting."

"They won't know."

"Don't count on it. They make it their business to know."

"Jerry, please." She rarely pleaded with her brother. "The man's impossible.... I've done my duty. What more do you expect of me?"

"Alek is your husband."

"You're beginning to sound just like him! He frightens me.... He makes me feel things I don't want to feel. I'm scared, Jerry, really scared." Close to tears, she covered her mouth, fearing she'd break down.

"I don't know what to do," Jerry said with a sympathetic shrug. "I wish I did, for your sake. Alek's, too."

With nothing left to say, he returned to his own office.

Her mood didn't improve when two hours later Alek unexpectedly showed up. He walked into her office without waiting for her assistant to announce him. Julia happened to be on the phone at the time and she glanced up, irritated by the intrusion. Alek glared at her, and every minute she delayed appeared to infuriate him further.

He began to pace, pausing every other step to turn and scowl in her direction.

Julia finished her conversation as quickly as she could without being rude—and without letting him believe he was intimidating her.

"You wanted something?" she asked calmly as she replaced the receiver.

Anger was etched on his features. "Yes, I do. I understand you spoke to Jerry this morning about one of us moving. I want to know what's going on in that head of yours."

Julia folded her hands on her desk. "It seemed the logical thing to do."

"Why?"

She stood, feeling at a distinct disadvantage sitting. "It makes sense. The only reason we were living together was for show because—"

"We're living together, my dear wife, because we're married."

"In name only."

He muttered something blistering in Russian, and Julia was grateful she couldn't understand him.

"You deny your vows. You abuse my pride by involving your brother. You ask for patience and then stab me in the back."

"I...explained on our wedding day that I need time. I let you know you were being cheated in this marriage. You can't say I didn't warn you." Contacting Jerry had been wrong, she saw now. But she was frightened and growing more so each day. No longer could she ignore the powerful attraction she felt for Alek. No longer could she ignore his touch. He was chipping away at the barrier she'd erected to protect herself from feelings. From love. He was working his way into her life and her heart. She had to do something.

"You are my *wife*," Alek shouted.

Julia closed her eyes at the anger in his voice.

"I'm not a very good one," she whispered.

"We are married, Julia. When will you accept that?" He turned away from her and stalked to the door.

"I...don't know if I can."

At her words, he spun around.

They stood no more than a few feet apart, yet an ocean might have lain between them. He was furious with her and she with him.

"I may never be your wife in the way you want." Julia didn't know what drove her to say that.

And yet, at the same moment, she realized she wanted him. Needed him. And that frightened her half to death.

"You're afraid, aren't you?" he asked as if he could read her thoughts. "Afraid you aren't woman enough to satisfy me. That's what's behind all this, isn't it? That, and the fact that you're afraid to trust another man. But I'm not like the one who hurt you, Julia, whoever he was. I'm not like him at all. I respect you—and I want you. Which, if you're honest, is how you feel about me, too."

Stricken, Julia closed her eyes. It felt as if he'd blinded her with the truth, identified her fears, hurled them at her to explain or reject.

"Julia?"

She sobbed once, the sound nearly hysterical as she backed away from him.

"I didn't mean..." he began.

She stopped him by holding out her arm.

He cursed under his breath, and reaching for her, drew her into his arms. She didn't resist. Without pause he lowered his head and covered her mouth, sealing their lips together in a wild kiss. The craziness increased with each impatient twist of their heads, growing in frenzied desperation.

Her breasts tingled and her body grew hot as his powerful hands held her against him. It was where she wanted to be....

His hands were busy with the zipper at the back of her straight, no-nonsense business skirt. It hissed as he lowered it. Julia made a token protest, which he cut off with a bone-melting kiss.

"I'm through fighting you," he whispered. "Will you stop fighting me?"

He gently brought his mouth back to hers. They were so close Julia felt as if they were drawing in the same breath, as if they required only one heart to beat between them.

Sobbing, she slid her arms around his neck and buried her face, taking deep, uneven breaths. Not understanding her own desperate need, she clung to him as a low cry emerged from her lips. The grief she felt was overwhelming. She was lamenting the wasted years, when she'd closed herself off from life. Ever since her father's death and Roger's betrayal, she'd lived in limbo, rejecting love and laughter. Rejecting and punishing herself.

"Julia," Alek whispered, stroking her hair, "what is it?"

She shook her head, unable to answer.

"Say it," he told her softly, sitting in her chair and taking her with him so she was nestled in his lap. "Tell me you need me. Tell me you want me, too."

She sobbed and with tears streaming down her face, she nodded.

"That's not good enough. I want the words."

"I...need you. Oh, Alek, I'm so scared."

He held her, kissed her gently, reassured her while she rested her head on his shoulder and cried until her tears were spent.

"I don't know why you put up with me," she finally gasped.

"You don't?" he asked, chuckling softly. "I have the feeling you'll figure it out soon enough, my love."

Her intercom hummed and Virginia's voice echoed through the silence. "Your nine-thirty appointment is here."

Her eyes regretfully met Alek's.

"Send whoever it is away," Alek urged.

"I...I can't do that."

"I know," he said, and kissed the tip of her nose. He released her slowly.

Just when Julia was convinced her day couldn't possibly get any more complicated, she received a call from Virginia Mason Hospital. Her grandmother had slipped into a coma.

Jerry was away, so she left a message for him and for Alek, canceled her appointments for the rest of the day and drove directly to the hospital.

Julia realized the instant she walked into her grandmother's room that Ruth's hold on life was tenuous, a slender thread. Her heart was failing, and Julia felt as though her own heart was in jeopardy, too.

In the past few years she'd faced a handful of crises, starting with the fire that had nearly destroyed the business and their family. Her father's death had followed. Immediately afterward she'd realized Roger had used her, had sold out her family. And her.

Ruth, her beloved Ruth, was dying, and Julia was powerless to stop it. She was terrified. For the past months she'd watched helplessly as her grandmother's health deteriorated.

Sitting at Ruth's bedside now, Julia could almost hear the older woman's calming voice. "My death is inevitable—"

the unspoken words rang in her head "—but not unwel-come."

Silently Julia pleaded with her grandmother to live just a little longer, to give her time to adjust, to grant her a few days to gather her courage. Even as she spoke, Julia recognized how selfish she was being, thinking of herself, of her own pain. But she couldn't make herself stop praying that God would spare her grandmother.

"You have walked through your pain," the silent voice continued. "The journey has made you wiser and far stronger than you know."

Julia wanted to argue. She didn't feel strong. Not when it seemed Ruth was about to be taken from her. She felt pushed to the limits, looking both ways—toward despair in one direction and hope in the other, toward doubt and faith.

An hour passed as Julia struggled with her grief, refusing to let it overwhelm her. Fear controlled her, the knowledge that if she gave in to her grief, she might never regain her sanity.

"Please," she pleaded aloud, praying Ruth heard her. It was the selfish prayer of a frightened child.

Jerry arrived, pale and shaken. "What happened?"

Julia shrugged. Their grandmother's physician, Dr. Silverman, had been in earlier to explain the medical symptoms and reasons. Most of what he'd said had meant only one thing. Ruth was close to death.

"She's in a coma," Julia answered. "I talked to her doctor earlier. He's surprised she's hung on this long."

Her brother pulled out a chair and sat down next to Julia. "I love this old woman, really love her."

"What are we going to do without her, Jerry?"

Her brother shook his head. "I don't know. We'll make do the way we always have, I suppose."

"I'm going to miss her so much." Julia heard the tears in her voice.

"I know." He reached for Julia's hand and gently squeezed it. "Alek phoned. He'll be here as soon as he can."

Julia instinctively wanted Alek with her. She'd never needed him like this before. That thought produced another regret. Alek was devoted to her and she didn't deserve it. She'd treated him terribly and yet he loved her.

Her grief, fed by her burning tears and broken dreams, was overwhelming. She couldn't sit still; she stood and started pacing, then returned to her chair.

They sat silently for another hour. She did what she could to make her grandmother more comfortable. She held Ruth's hand, read her favorite passages from Scripture, stroked her forehead.

"I have to go." Jerry spoke from behind her.

Understanding, Julia nodded. She loved her brother and knew he was grieving in his own way. She was grateful he was leaving; she preferred this time alone with Ruth.

"When will you go home?" he asked.

"I don't know yet."

The next thing she heard was the sound of the door closing. Being alone was a relief and a burden. Julia recognized the inconsistency of her reactions. Never had she craved Alek's company more, and yet she wanted these hours alone with her grandmother, sensing that it would be the last time they'd be together.

She found it ironic that hope and despair could feel the same to her.

The nurses came in a number of times. One encouraged

her to take a break, go have some dinner, but Julia refused. She was afraid to leave, fearing that once she did, her grandmother would quietly release her hold on life.

Leaning her forehead against the side of the hospital bed, Julia must have dozed because the next thing she knew Alek was there.

"How is she?"

"There's been no change."

Alek sat down next to Julia. "Have you had dinner?"

"I'm not hungry."

Alek nodded and when he spoke again it was in his own language, which had a distinct beauty. Whatever he was saying seemed to please her grandmother because Ruth smiled. At first Julia was convinced she'd imagined it, which would've been easy enough to do. But there was no denying the change in Ruth's ashen features.

"It's midnight, my love."

Julia glanced at her watch, sure he was mistaken. She must have slept longer than she'd realized.

"Come," he said, standing behind her, his hands on her shoulders. "I'll drive you home."

She shook her head, unwilling to leave.

"You aren't doing her any good, and you're running yourself down, both physically and mentally."

"You go ahead," she said. "I'll stay a little longer."

She heard the frustration in his sigh. "I'm not leaving without you. You're exhausted."

"I'm afraid to leave her," she whispered brokenly. The time had come for the truth, painful though it was. Julia was surprised she'd chosen to voice it to Alek and not her brother.

"Why?" her husband inquired gently.

She was glad he was standing behind her and couldn't see the tears in her eyes. "If Ruth dies, when she dies, a part of me will go with her." The best part, Julia feared. Something would perish in her own heart. Her faith in God and in herself would be shaken, and she wondered if this time the damage would be beyond repair.

"Do you wish to bind her to this life, this pain?"

"No," Julia answered honestly. Yet she held on to Ruth fiercely.

A part of Julia had died with her father. It had been joy. Trust had vanished afterward when she realized everything he'd told her about Roger was true. She hadn't wanted to believe her father, had argued with him, fought with him. It was while they were shouting at each other that he'd suffered the heart attack that had prematurely claimed his life.

Joy had faded from her soul that afternoon, replaced by guilt. In the years since, she'd made a semicomfortable life for herself. She wasn't happy, nor was she unhappy. She buried herself in her work, the desire to succeed propelling her forward, dictating her actions. Her goal was to undo the damage Roger had done to the company. First she would rebuild Conrad Industries to its former glory and then continue on the course her father had so carefully charted.

She was making progress, not only with the company, but with her life. Encouraged by Ruth, Julia was just beginning to recapture some of the enthusiasm she'd lost. She could laugh occasionally, even joke every now and then.

It had seemed impossible that she'd ever again feel anything but the weight of her sadness. Then, without being aware of the transformation, she realized she was feeling again, and it had started after her marriage to Alek.

Now here she was, trapped in pain and fear, and it was too soon. Much too soon.

"Come." Alek took her by the shoulders.

She followed because she didn't have the strength to resist. Leaning forward, she kissed Ruth's cheek and felt the tears run down her own.

Alek gently guided his wife from the hospital room. He kept his arm around her, wanting to lend her his strength. She would never admit she needed him, never confess she was pleased he'd come to be with her. He'd been at the airport that afternoon, dealing with the Immigration people, working out the final details of his sister's entry into the country. He'd been torn between his duty to his sister and Julia.

Alek found he was weary of this constant battle between them. She fought him at every turn, cheated him out of her love. Yet he'd begun to love her and was more determined than ever to win her heart.

He knew only bits and pieces of the past. Even Jerry seemed reluctant to discuss Julia's relationship with Roger Stanhope.

Whenever his friend mentioned the other man's name, Jerry's mouth tightened and anger flashed in his eyes. Because he was often so involved with his own work, Alek couldn't interact with other staff members as much as he would've liked. Recently he'd made a point of doing so.

Over lunch that afternoon, he'd casually dropped Roger Stanhope's name and was astounded by the abrupt silence that fell over the small gathering.

"If you want to know about Roger, just ask Julia," someone suggested.

It sounded like an accusation, which puzzled Alek. From the little he was able to surmise, Roger had been blamed for the fire, although presumably nothing was proven or he'd be in jail. Questions abounded. The answers, like so much else in his marriage, would come with time.

Julia was silent on the ride from the hospital to their home. Alek led her into the condo and toward the guest bedroom, where she chose to sleep.

She sat on the edge of the bed like a lifeless doll.

"Would you like some help undressing?" he asked her.

She shook her head. "No, thanks."

He left her, but not because he wanted to.

Venturing into the kitchen, he made a pot of tea. Julia needed something hot and sweet. When the tea had finished steeping, he returned to her room and knocked lightly on the door.

"Come in."

She'd changed clothes and was dressed in a sexless pair of cotton pajamas.

"I made tea." He carried in a cup and saucer, and set them on the nightstand by her bed.

She stared at the cup as if she'd never seen anything like it before.

"I don't know if you remember, but I told you yesterday that my sister was arriving this afternoon. I was at the airport meeting Anna and then drove her to my old apartment. That's why I couldn't come to the hospital until late. Anna will be here tomorrow morning."

"Why are you so good to me? I don't deserve it…not after the way I've treated you. Not after the things I've said."

He had no answer for her because the truth would only enhance her distress. He loved her as any husband loved his wife. In time she'd recognize and accept it. But she wasn't ready yet.

Alek peeled back the covers of her bed and fluffed up the pillow. She stood behind him, her breathing labored, as if she was struggling not to weep.

"Alek." His name was a mere whisper. "Would you mind...would you sleep with me tonight? Just this once?"

The desire that invaded his body came as a greater shock than her request. From the first night of their marriage, Alek had been waiting for her to voluntarily invite him to her bed. He hadn't imagined it would happen this way, when she was emotionally distraught.

In the same instant, Alek recognized that she wasn't offering him her body. She was seeking his comfort. It wasn't what he wanted, but it was a small step in the right direction and he'd take whatever Julia was willing to give him.

He reached for her hand, kissed her fingers and then moved to the doorway where he switched off the light. Darkness filled the room. He heard the mattress squeak as she slipped beneath the sheets. Then he walked back to the bed, stripped off his clothes and joined her.

It was the sweetest torture he'd ever known to have Julia move into his waiting arms. She cuddled her soft, feminine body against his, molding herself against him, her satiny smooth leg brushing his. She released one long sigh as her head nestled on his chest and was instantly asleep.

Asleep.

Alek grinned mockingly to himself and wrapped his arm around her shoulders. He listened to the even sound of her breathing and after a few moments, kissed the crown of her head.

So this was to be his lot. Comforter. Not lover or husband,

but consoler. His body throbbed with wanting her. Holding her so close, yet unable to really touch her, was the purest form of torment Alek had ever endured.

He didn't sleep and was grateful he hadn't, because Julia stirred suddenly, apparently trapped in a nightmare. She thrashed around until he managed to hold her down.

"No," she sobbed and twisted away from him. Her nails dug into his flesh.

"Julia," he whispered, "wake up. It's just a dream."

She raised her head from the pillow, looked into his eyes and frowned. Rubbing a hand over her face, she looked again as though she expected him to have disappeared.

"It's all right," he whispered soothingly. "I'm here."

He could feel her heart racing. Her eyes met his in the darkness and he saw her confusion. It was on the tip of his tongue to remind her she'd invited him into her bed. But he didn't. Instead he plowed his fingers into the thickness of her hair and brought her mouth to his.

She welcomed his kiss without hesitation, without restraint, moaning. She flattened her palms against his chest, then sighed when they'd finished kissing. A sigh that spoke of satisfaction. And confusion.

His body was on fire, but he didn't press her for more. She snuggled against him and draped her arm around him, nestling back into their original position. Her hand was restless as it leisurely roamed across his chest.

Her face angled toward his, her eyes shining in the dark. Alek couldn't resist kissing her again. He couldn't force himself to draw too far away from her. They were so close, physically and emotionally, he wanted this moment to go on forever.

A soft lullaby came to him. He didn't have much of a

singing voice, but this was a song his mother had sung to him as a child when he was troubled. Julia wouldn't understand the words, but they would soothe her spirit as they had his.

After the first verse, she released a long, trembling sigh. A few minutes later, she was sound asleep once more.

Alek followed her shortly afterward.

Julia opened her eyes and felt the unbearable weight of her sadness crushing her. Ruth was dying. She rolled over and, despite her sadness, realized it wasn't grief that was pressing her down, but Alek.

Alek! In a sudden panic, she vainly tried to recall the events from the night before. Oh, no, she'd asked him... asked him to sleep with her. She'd been distraught. She hadn't known what she was doing and now he'd think, he'd assume she wanted him to make love to her...that she'd welcome him to her bed every night.

Scrambling to her feet, she backed away from him, her hand at her breast.

"Julia?"

Her heart leapt into her throat. She'd hoped to slip away without waking him.

"Good morning."

"'Morning," she said shyly.

"Did you sleep well?"

Julia nodded and glanced down as the tears sprang readily to her eyes.

"Julia?" He reached for her hand, pulling her back to the bed. She sat on the edge and he slid his arms around her. Words weren't necessary just then. She was grieving and Alek was there to comfort her. She placed her hands over his and their fingers entwined.

"Thank you," she whispered when she could form the words. She leaned back, relaxing into his warmth. He kissed her hair and she turned abruptly and flung her arms around his neck, holding him for all she was worth.

He spoke to her, and she smiled softly when she realized it was in Russian. He seemed to forget she didn't understand him. It didn't matter. She knew what he was saying from his tone—that he was there, that he loved her.

For the first time, the thought didn't terrify her.

Sometime later, Julia dressed, although she had trouble holding back the tears. She finished before Alek did and wandered into the kitchen, intent on starting a pot of coffee. She stopped short when she caught sight of a woman working in her kitchen.

"Good morning," the woman said, struggling with the language. "I am Anna, Alek's sister."

Seven

"Hello, Anna." Julia had forgotten Alek's sister was coming that morning. "Welcome to America."

"Thank you." Alek's sister was small and thin with brown hair woven into a braid. Her eyes were so like Alek's, it was as if Julia were staring into her husband's own dark gaze. Her smile was warm and friendly and despite this awkward beginning, Julia liked her immediately.

"My English is poor, but I'm studying every day."

"I'm sure you'll do just fine," Julia said, wondering why Anna was staring at her.

"I will cook your breakfast."

"Thank you."

"Eggs and toast?"

"Yes, please," Julia answered and hurried into the bathroom. By the time she entered the kitchen, she understood Anna's concern. There'd been tears in her eyes, and Alek's sister must have assumed they'd been arguing. Julia hoped to find a way to reassure her that wasn't the case.

Her breakfast was on the table. Generally she ate on the

run, usually picking up a container of orange juice and a muffin at the local convenience store on her drive to the office. When Alek had suggested they hire his sister as a housekeeper and cook, Julia had readily agreed. It was a way of helping his family. A way of repaying her debt to him. A way of eating regular meals herself.

It wasn't until she sampled the fluffiest, most delicious scrambled eggs she'd ever tasted that Julia realized Anna was the one doing her and Alek the favor.

She was reading over the morning paper when Alek appeared in the kitchen, smartly dressed. He poured himself a cup of coffee while his sister spoke enthusiastically in Russian.

"English," Julia heard him say. "You must speak English."

"This country is so beautiful."

"Yes," Alek agreed, pulling out the chair across from Julia and sitting down. She ignored him, concentrating on the paper.

"Did you phone the hospital?" Alek asked.

"Yes…there's been no change. I'm going into the office this morning."

"You'll let me know if you hear anything?"

"Of course."

His eyes met hers and he smiled. Julia found herself responding, treasuring this understanding between them, this sense of trust they'd stumbled upon. But it frightened her. When Alek recognized her reserve, he sighed and mumbled something she didn't catch.

Anna responded to him in Russian. Naturally Julia couldn't understand the words, but it sounded very much as if her sister-in-law was upset with him. She offered Julia a sympathetic look as she hurried out the door.

Alek returned his attention to Julia. "She thinks I caused your tears this morning. Suffice it to say, she wasn't pleased with me."

"Did you tell her about Ruth?"

"No. Not yet."

"But—"

Alek leaned forward to place his finger on her lips. "Don't worry about my sister. Or me."

It was a mistake to go into the office; Julia realized that almost immediately. There were several pressing matters that needed to be taken care of before she could spend any more time at the hospital. Appointments to reschedule, work to delegate. Julia resented every minute away from her grandmother. She found herself impatient to get back to the hospital. Her relationship with Alek concerned her, too.

Sitting at her desk, Julia supported her face on her hands. She'd been so sure this marriage would never work. Now she wasn't sure of anything. She needed Alek, and he'd come to her, held her, comforted her. She'd given him plenty of reasons to turn away from her. But when the opportunity came to comfort her, he'd come, willingly, unselfishly.

Each day, Julia felt herself weakening a little more, giving in to the attraction she felt for Alek. Every day he found some small way of dismantling the protective barrier around her heart. He was slowly, methodically, exposing her to the warming rays of the sun.

And yet…Julia wanted to shout that she didn't *need* a man in her life, didn't want a husband. Silently she did, forcing his image from her mind—with only limited success.

It was while she was trying not to think of Alek, to concentrate on the tasks before her, that he casually strolled into her office.

"I thought we should talk," he said, dropping into a chair as if he had every right to be there.

"About what?" She pretended to be absorbed in reading her latest batch of correspondence.

"Last night."

He sounded so flippant, so glib, as if their sleeping in the same bed had all been part of his game plan from the start. She'd conveniently fallen into his scheme without realizing it. His attitude infuriated her.

"It was a mistake," she informed him sharply. "One that won't be repeated."

"I suppose it was too much to hope you'd think other-wise," he said with a beleaguered sigh. "If you don't want to accept the truth, then I'll say it for you. It felt good to hold you in my arms, Julia. I'm here if you need me. I'll always be here for you. If you believe nothing else about me, believe this."

Julia felt her chest tighten as he stood and, without wait-ing for her to comment, walked out of her office. She didn't understand this man she'd married, and wasn't sure she ever would. She'd rewarded his kindness by cheating him out of the kind of marriage he'd expected, the marriage she'd agreed to. She'd insulted him and hurt his pride. Not once, but time and again.

Julia didn't want to love Alek. Love frightened her more than any other emotion, even pain. She pulled a little more inside herself, blocking Alek from her heart, because it was only then that she felt safe.

Removing the slim gold band from her finger, she stared at it. She put it back on her finger, wondering if she'd *ever* understand Alek, then doubted it was possible when she had yet to understand herself.

She spent nearly two hours clearing her desk and her schedule before she was free to leave for the hospital.

Her heart grew heavy as she walked down the long corridor that led to her grandmother's room. She didn't stop at the nurses' station, didn't ask to talk to Ruth's physician. Instead she went directly to the woman who'd helped her through the most difficult period of her life.

As Julia silently opened the door and stepped inside, she felt tears burn the backs of her eyes. Her grandmother appeared to be asleep. Ruth's face was pale, but she seemed more at peace now, as if the pain had passed.

Tentatively Julia stepped over to her grandmother's bed and took her hand. She held it to her own cheek and pressed it there. Slowly Julia closed her eyes.

As soon as she did, it felt as if Ruth were awake, waiting to speak with her.

"Don't be sad," Ruth seemed to be saying. "I don't want you to grieve for me. I've lived a good, long life. You were my joy. God's special gift to me."

"No, please," Julia pleaded silently. "Don't leave me, please don't leave."

"Julia, my child. You have your whole life ahead of you. Don't cling to the past. Look instead to the future. You have a husband who adores you and children waiting to be born. Your life is just beginning. So much love awaits you, more joy than you can possibly imagine now. Your pain shall reap an abundant harvest of life's treasures. Trust me in this."

"Treasures," Julia whispered. She couldn't look past the present moment to think about the future. Not when her heart was breaking.

Tears ran unrestrained down her face and she felt her grandmother's presence reaching out to comfort her, a last farewell before she set out on the journey before her.

Julia didn't know how long she stood there, holding on to Ruth's hand. She realized as she looked up at the monitor registering her grandmother's heartbeat that it had gone silent. Ruth had quietly slipped from life into death with no fuss, no ceremony, as if she'd been awaiting Julia's arrival so she could leave peacefully.

Julia had known it would be impossible to prepare herself emotionally for this moment. Ruth's death wasn't a shock; she'd been ill for years. Julia had been aware that each day could be her grandmother's last. She'd accepted the inevitability of Ruth's passing as best she could. But nothing could have prepared her for the grief that slammed against her now. Nothing.

Collapsing into the chair, Julia cried out, the sound a low, anguished wail as she swayed back and forth.

A nurse came, so did a doctor and several other health professionals. Julia didn't move. She couldn't. The sobs racked her shoulders and she hid her face in her hands. And slowly rocked with grief.

Someone led her from the room. She sat in the private area alone, desolate, inconsolable.

Jerry and Alek arrived together. Jerry spoke with the hospital officials while Alek wrapped Julia in his arms and held her against him as she wept until she had no more tears.

She needed him and was past pretending she didn't. Her own strength was depleted. Clinging to Alek, she buried her face in his chest, seeking what solace she could. When her father died, she'd been numb with guilt and grief. The tears hadn't come until much later.

He held her close and she was grateful for his comfort, for his willingness to share her grief.

They seemed to be at the hospital for hours. There were papers to sign and a hundred different decisions to make. Jerry went with her and Alek to the funeral home, where arrangements were made for Ruth's burial.

Julia was surprised by the calm, almost unemotional way she was able to deal with the details of the funeral. The flowers, the music, discussing the program with first the funeral home director and then the family's minister, Pastor Hall.

It was dark by the time they'd finished. Jerry, solemn and downcast, walked out to the parking lot with her and Alek.

"Do you want to come back to the condo with us?" Julia asked, not wanting to leave her brother alone. Unlike her, he'd return to an empty house. Ruth's death had shaken him badly. He didn't express his grief as freely as she had.

Jerry shook his head. "No, thanks."

"Anna has dinner ready and waiting," Alek said.

"I'll pick up something on the way home," he assured them both. "Don't worry about me."

Alek drove through the hilly streets that led to their condominium. "How are you feeling?" he asked, when he opened the front door for her.

"Drained." The emotions seemed to be pressing against her chest. She was mentally and physically exhausted; her fatigue was so great she could barely hold up her head.

Alek guided her into the kitchen. She hadn't eaten since breakfast, hadn't thought about food even once. The smells were heavenly, but she had no appetite.

He brought two plates from the oven and set them on the table.

"I'm not hungry," she told him. "I'm going to take a bath." She half expected him to argue with her, to insist she needed nourishment. Instead he must have realized she knew what was best for herself right now.

One look in the bathroom mirror confirmed Julia's worst suspicions. Her eyes were red, puffy, and her cheeks were pale, her makeup long since washed away by her tears. She looked much older than her thirty years. About a hundred years older. She looked and felt as if she'd been hit by a freight train.

Ruth was gone, and other than Jerry she was alone in the world. She was grateful for Alek's assistance during this traumatic day, but in time he'd leave and then she'd be alone again.

Running her bathwater, she added a package of peach-scented salts and stepped into the hot, soothing water. She leaned against the back of the tub and closed her eyes, letting the heat of the bath comfort her.

Children waiting to be born.

She didn't know why that phrase edged its way into her mind. There would be no children because there would be no real marriage. She was more determined than ever not to cross that line, especially now, when she was most vulnerable. She'd hurt Alek enough, abused his gentleness, taken advantage of his kindness.

He was standing in the hallway outside the bathroom waiting for her when she finished. "I'm fine, Alek," she said, wanting to reassure him, even if it wasn't true.

"You're exhausted. I turned back the sheets for you."

"Thank you."

He ushered her into the bedroom as if she were a child. In

other circumstances, Julia would have resented the way he'd taken control of her life, but not then. She felt only gratitude.

She slid beneath the covers, nestled her head against the pillow and closed her eyes. "Alek," she whispered.

"Yes, my love?"

"Would you sing to me again?"

He complied with a haunting melody in his own language. His voice was clear and strong, and even though she couldn't understand the words, she found it beautiful and soothing. She wanted to ask him the meaning, but her thoughts drifted in another direction. Toward rest. Toward peace.

Julia woke with a start. She didn't know what had jarred her awake. The room was dark, although the hall light offered little illumination. The digital clock on the nightstand informed her it was nearly 1:00 a.m. As her eyes adjusted, she realized Alek was sitting beside her in a chair, his legs stretched out before him and his head cocked at an odd, uncomfortable angle.

"Alek?" she whispered, propping herself up on one elbow.

He stirred immediately and straightened. "Julia?"

"What are you doing here?"

"I didn't want you to be alone."

"I'm fine," she said again.

"Do you want me to sing to you?"

Hot, burning tears filled her eyes at his tenderness, his concern. She shook her head. What she needed was to be held.

"Julia, my love," he whispered, moving from the chair to the edge of the bed. His hand smoothed the hair from her face, his touch as gentle as if she were a child in need of re-assurance, which was exactly the way Julia felt.

"Why do you have to be so wonderful?" she sobbed. "Why are you so good to me?"

His lips touched her forehead, but he didn't answer.

"I'm a rotten wife."

He laughed. "You haven't given yourself a chance yet."

"I've treated you terribly. You should hate me."

"Hate you?" He seemed to find her words amusing. "That would be impossible."

"Will you lie down with me? Please?" The words were out before she could censor them. It was a completely self-ish request. "I…need you, Alek." She added this last part for honesty's sake, to ease her conscience.

He kissed her, his mouth locating hers unerringly in the near-dark. Although his kiss was light, she knew it was his way of thanking her for admitting the truth.

He stood and stripped off his pants and shirt. Julia lifted the covers and moved over as far as she could in the nar-row bed.

Despite sleeping in his embrace the night before, she felt strangely shy now. He put his arm around her shoulders and brought her close. He was warm and real and felt so alive that she trembled when she laid her head on his chest. His heart was pounding strong and steady against her ear.

"Can you sleep now?" he whispered.

"I…think so. What about you?"

"Don't worry about me."

That didn't answer her question, but she didn't press him. "We kissed last night, didn't we?"

He rubbed his chin across her hair. "Yes." She heard the strain in his voice and felt unusually pleased. She tilted her head back so that she was looking into his warm, dark eyes. Only a few inches separated their mouths.

"Would you...mind—" she hesitated and moistened her lips "—kissing me again?"

His breathing stopped abruptly and his eyes narrowed as if he wasn't sure he should trust her. Julia didn't blame him.

Rather than waiting for his permission, she arched toward him until their lips met. Their kiss was sweet and undemanding. She was breathing hard when they finished, but so was he.

He kissed her again, a little deeper, a little more intensely. Then a lot more intensely.

Julia sighed as his mouth left hers, their bottom lips clinging momentarily. "Oh, Alek." She sighed, and a trembling kind of response made its way through her body.

She said his name again, more softly this time. "I want to make love."

She watched him closely and noted the different emotions flashing in his eyes. He wanted her, too; there was no question of that. He wanted her and had from the beginning of their marriage. He'd made certain she knew how much. Yet he hesitated.

His eyes gradually changed and told her another story. They darkened with doubt, which won over the needy, sensual look she'd seen in him seconds earlier.

"Julia." He breathed her name, his tone regretful. "Not now."

"Why not?" She knew she sounded defensive and couldn't help it. He'd demanded she share his bed from the first night of their marriage.

But when she finally agreed to fulfill her part of their bargain, he rejected her. It made no sense. And it angered her.

"I'd feel as if I was taking advantage of you."

"Shouldn't I be the judge of that?" she said irritably.

"Right now, no."

Stunned, she jerked her head away. His fingers came to her face, resting on her cheek, directing her gaze back to his.

"I want you, Julia, don't ever doubt that. But I refuse to put my own needs before yours. You're confused and hurting. There's nothing I'd like more than to—" He stopped. "I'm sure you understand."

She nodded.

He kissed her briefly, then tucked his arm around her and brought her even closer to his side. His lips were in her hair. "When we make love, I don't want there to be any regrets in the morning."

Julia smiled and kissed his bare chest. "No one told me you were so noble."

"No one told me, either," he muttered disparagingly.

The way he said it with a deep, shuddering sigh led her to believe that if anyone had regrets in the morning, it would be her husband.

Content now, she curled up against him and shut her eyes. She'd prefer it if they made love, but being in his arms would satisfy her for now.

Alek envied Julia her ability to sleep. For weeks he'd been waiting for his wife to come to him, to fulfill her wedding vows by her own choice. Yet when she invited him to her bed, held her arms softly around him, he felt compelled to do the honorable thing.

Honor. But at what price? His body throbbed with need. His heart ached with love. No woman had led him on a finer chase. No woman had challenged him as much as his wife. No woman had defied and infuriated him more than Julia.

She'd been hurt and angry at his refusal, then seemed to accept the wisdom of his words. Wisdom, nothing! He was a fool.

Maybe not, he decided after a moment. Perhaps he *had* been wise. Only time would tell.

He felt Julia stir some time later and was surprised to realize it was morning. Slowly he opened his eyes to discover her face staring down at his, studying him. "Good morning," she whispered.

He waited, thinking she might be angry at finding him in bed with her, but she revealed none of the outrage she had the morning before. Still, her eyes were clouded and her grief was evident.

"Did you sleep well?" he asked.

She nodded shyly, her gaze avoiding his. "What about you?"

"As well as can be expected." He stretched his cramped arms and yawned loudly. They were fools, the pair of them. His sister had said as much yesterday morning. They were sleeping in a single bed when there was a perfectly good king-size bed in the other room.

Alek didn't have a single excuse to offer his sister and finally told her to mind her own business. But Anna was right.

"Thank you, Alek," Julia said, climbing out of bed. Her face was turned away from him.

"For what, staying with you?"

"No…well, yes, that, too, but for…you know, not…"

"Making love to you?"

She nodded. Reaching inside her closet, she took out a set of clothes and held them in front of her as if to shield her body from his view. She'd spent most of the night cuddling against him. He'd felt every inch of her creamy smooth skin; there wasn't anything left to hide. It didn't seem right to point that out, however.

"The next few days are going to be very busy. I'll be spending a lot of my time finishing up the funeral arrangements and…and going through Ruth's things, so we probably won't see much of each other for a while."

She didn't need to sound so pleased at the prospect, Alek mused.

By the time he'd showered and dressed, Julia had already left the condominium. His sister was eyeing him critically, clearly displeased about something.

"What's wrong with Julia?" Anna asked in an accusatory voice. "She looks as if she was crying."

Naturally it would be his fault, Alek thought, ignoring his sister's glare.

"Her grandmother died," he explained and he watched as Anna's eyes went soft with sympathy.

"You love this woman."

"She's my wife." He saw now that it was a mistake to have hired his sister. It was obvious that she was going to be what Jerry called "a damned nuisance."

"You did not marry her for love."

"No," he admitted gruffly, resenting this line of questioning. He wouldn't have tolerated it from anyone else and Anna knew it.

"She knows that you did not love her. This is why she sleeps in the small bed."

"Thank you, Dear Abby."

"Who?"

"Never mind," Alek said impatiently. He grabbed a piece of toast from the plate and didn't wait for the rest of his breakfast. He turned to leave the room.

"Aleksandr," she said sharply, stopping him. "You've become very American." Her face relaxed into a wide smile. "I think this is good. You teach me, too, okay?"

"Okay," he said, chuckling.

Sorting through Ruth's possessions proved to be far more difficult than Julia had expected. Her grandmother's tastes had been simple, but she'd held on to many things, refusing to discard life's mementos.

Disposing of her clothes was the easiest. Julia boxed them up and took them to a shelter for the homeless. It was the little things she found so difficult. A token from the Seattle World Fair, an empty perfume bottle that had long since faded. The photographs. She could never part with the photographs.

Julia had no idea her grandmother had collected so many snapshots. The comical photos Ruth sent Louis Conrad while he was away fighting in the Second World War made her smile.

Julia came across a packet of pictures that caused her to laugh outright. Her grandmother, so young and attractive, was poised in a modest-looking swimsuit in front of a young soldier's photograph. It had to be Julia's grandfather, but she'd never seen pictures of him at that age.

The whole thing must have been rather risqué for the time. Julia guessed Ruth had been giving Louis a reason to come home. Heaven knew it had worked.

Julia studied the picture and sat for several minutes remembering the love story Ruth had told her. It was sweet and innocent, unlike now when sex so often dominated a relationship.

Except for her marriage, she thought defeatedly. It was

difficult to believe she could've been married to Alek this long without making love.

He'd been eager for the physical side of their relationship—until she'd revealed the first signs of wanting him, too. How typical of a man.

"Oh, Alek," she breathed, holding her grandmother's picture. "Will there ever be a way for us?"

In her heart she heard a resounding *yes*. But the voice wasn't her own, nor was it Alek's. It came from Ruth.

The day of the funeral, Julia wore a black dress and an old-fashioned pillbox hat with black netting that fitted over her face.

Julia hadn't slept well the past few nights and the fatigue was beginning to show. She'd made a point of coming home late, knowing Alek would be waiting for her. She'd mumble something about being tired and close her bedroom door, slipping into bed alone.

She'd spent the past two nights wishing Alek was there with her. She cursed her foolish pride for not approaching him. But she was afraid that once she did, she'd ask him to make love to her again, and this time she wouldn't take no for an answer.

The limousine delivered Julia, Jerry and Alek to the Methodist church where Ruth had worshiped for a number of years. Jerry and Alek climbed out first. Alek offered her his hand as Julia stepped out of the car. A small group of mourners had formed on the sidewalk outside the church, awaiting the family's arrival. Julia's gaze quickly scanned the crowd, then stopped abruptly.

There, seeking her eyes, stood Roger Stanhope.

Eight

Julia hesitated, one foot on the curb, the other in the limousine. Crouched as she was, she felt in danger of collapsing. Roger had dared to show up at her grandmother's funeral! The man had no sense of decency, but that didn't come as any surprise.

Although Alek couldn't have known what was happening, he leaned forward, put his arm around her waist and assisted her to an upright position.

His eyes were filled with concern. Julia's heart was beating double time and her head was spinning. She was afraid she might faint.

"I…I need to sit down."

"Of course." With his hand securely around her waist, Alek led her into the church vestibule. A row of wooden pews lined the wall and Alek encouraged her to take a seat.

"What's wrong?" Jerry asked.

Julia couldn't answer. "Water…could you get me a glass of water?"

Jerry hurried away and returned a moment later with

her drink. Other friends were beginning to arrive and after taking a moment to compose herself, Julia stood.

How dare Roger come to her grandmother's funeral! He'd done it to agitate her, and his unscrupulous ploy had worked. Julia had never been so close to passing out. Not even the day her father had— She pushed the thought from her mind, refusing to dwell on anything that had to do with Roger.

Jerry caught sight of their former employee, and his mouth thinned with irritation. "You saw him, didn't you?"

Julia nodded.

"I'll have him thrown out."

"Don't," she said. Roger wasn't worth the effort. "He'll cause a scene. Besides, I think Ruth would've gotten a kick out of it. We tried everything but a subpoena to talk to him after the fire, remember?"

"I'm not likely to forget."

"Who would've believed he'd end up coming to us?"

"Not me," Jerry agreed.

Alek didn't say anything, but Julia was well aware of his presence at her side. She wasn't fooled; he took in every word of the exchange between her and her brother.

"Point out this man to me," Alek said to them both. "I will see to his removal."

Jerry glanced at Julia, looking for her consent. She thought about it a moment, then decided she wouldn't give Roger the satisfaction.

"Don't kid yourself, Julia, he's up to something," Jerry warned.

"I'd be a fool if I didn't know that," she returned testily. She'd been duped by Roger once and it wasn't a mistake she cared to repeat. She knew his methods and wouldn't be taken in a second time.

The three of them had gathered in the back of the church and were unaware of anyone else until Pastor Hall approached them and announced they were ready for the service to begin.

Julia had known this ordeal would leave her emotionally depleted. Several times during the funeral she felt close to tears, but she held them at bay, taking in deep, even breaths. Her fingers were entwined with Alek's and she appreciated more than ever that he was with her. His presence lent her the strength she needed to get through the heartrending experience of saying goodbye to the woman she loved so dearly.

Anna sat nearby, and despite the solemnity of the occasion, Julia thought she saw Jerry cast her several interested glances.

From the church they traveled to the north end of Seattle to the cemetery where Ruth would be buried in the plot next to her beloved Louis.

Julia was surprised by how many people came. The day was bright and clear and the sky a pale shade of blue she'd only seen in the Pacific Northwest.

There were so many lovely bouquets of flowers. The group of mourners gathered under the canopy at the cemetery. Julia, Jerry and Alek were given seats, along with a few of Ruth's more elderly friends. Pastor Hall read from his Bible and the words were familiar ones since Julia had read them so often to Ruth herself.

Her heart felt as if it would shatter into a thousand pieces as the casket was slowly lowered into the ground. Alek must have sensed her distress because he placed his arm around her shoulders. The tears sprang from her eyes and she quietly sobbed her last farewell.

Afterward, the assembly met at Ruth's home. Charles, who'd been with the family for years, had insisted on having it there, although it demanded extra work on his part. The meal was catered, but several friends brought dishes themselves. A wide variety of casseroles, as well as salads, cheeses and sliced meats, were served.

Julia and Jerry stood by the doorway and greeted their visitors, thanking each of them for their love and support. Julia received countless hugs. Anna had a felt uncomfortable about being among so many strangers and had left, with Julia's fervent thanks for attending the service.

Various family friends recounted stories involving Ruth and Louis, and before she realized it, Julia found herself smiling. Her grandmother had been a wonderful, generous, warmhearted woman. Julia didn't need others to tell her that, but their comments reaffirmed what she'd always known.

The gathering broke up into small groups of mourners. Every available seat in the living room and formal dining room was taken. Julia assisted Charles in seeing to the guests' comfort.

She was filling coffee cups when Roger spoke from behind her. "Hello, Julia."

It was fortunate that she didn't empty the steaming coffee into someone's lap. Roger had apparently sneaked into the house through the back door, because Jerry would never have allowed him in the front.

"Hello, Roger," she said as unemotionally as she could.

"I'm sorry to hear about your grandmother."

"Thank you." Her words, if not her tone, were civil.

"Julia, Julia," he said with an injured sigh, "isn't it time for us to let bygones be bygones? How often do I have to tell you it was all a horrible mistake? It seems a shame to rehash something that happened so long ago, don't you agree?"

"I'm sure it wasn't a mistake. Now, if you'll excuse me, I have to see to my guests."

Roger surprised her by taking her arm and stopping her. Her gaze flew back to him and she wondered how she could ever have thought herself in love with him.

He was handsome, but his good looks were so transparent that she was shocked she hadn't seen through his guise sooner. She'd learned a good deal about character in the past few years, and that thought, at least, comforted her.

"I suggest you let go of my wife's arm," Alek said. He was angry. Julia could tell by how heavy his accent had become.

Roger looked puzzled, as if he didn't understand.

"And I suggest you do as he says," Julia said.

Roger released her arm. He held up both hands for Alek's inspection. "I heard you were married," he said, continuing to follow her as she filled yet another coffee cup. Alek came after Roger and the three of them paraded across the room.

"Why you chose to marry a Russian is beyond me. I figured you were smarter than to involve yourself with some foreigner."

Julia didn't dignify that comment with a reply. Instead she introduced the two men. "Roger Stanhope, meet Aleksandr Berinski."

"Ah," Roger said sarcastically, "and I thought he was your bodyguard."

"I am," Alek said in a less heavy accent. "Touch my wife again and you'll be sorry. We *foreigners* have effective ways of making our point."

"Alek," Julia admonished with a grin.

Roger seemed to take the threat as some kind of joke. "I'm truly sorry to hear about your grandmother," he went on.

"Thank you." The coffeepot was empty and Julia returned to the kitchen with both Roger and Alek in tow. If it hadn't been such a sad occasion, Julia would've found the antics of the two men funny.

"I'd like to take you to lunch sometime," Roger said, leaning against the kitchen counter as Julia prepared another pot of coffee. "We could talk over old times."

"Great. I'd love it. Do you mind if I bring the arson investigator?"

"Julia won't be having lunch with you," Alek said before Roger could react.

"I'm sorry, Roger, I really am, but my husband is the jealous sort. You've started off on the wrong foot with him as it is. Don't press your luck."

"Julia, sweetheart," Roger said meaningfully, "it's time for us to clear the air."

"The air will be much clearer once you leave," Alek muttered. "Perhaps you would allow me to show you the door?" He advanced one menacing step, then another.

"Ah…" Roger backed up, hands raised. "All right, all right. I'll go."

"I thought you'd see matters my way," Alek said.

Roger cast an ugly look in his direction. He straightened the cuffs of his starched white shirt and wore an injured air as he left the house through the back door.

Julia's gaze followed Roger. "That really wasn't necessary, you know."

"Ah, but it gave me pleasure to send him."

Her smiling eyes met his. "Me, too."

"Tell me about this man. You loved him?"

She felt her amusement drain away. She was surprised no one had ever told Alek about her fateful relationship with

Roger. But she'd dealt with enough grief for one day and didn't feel like delving into more.

"Another time?" she asked.

Alek seemed to require a moment to think over his response. "Soon," he told her. "A husband needs to know these things."

She agreed with an unenthusiastic nod.

Alek was leaving the kitchen when she stopped him. "I'll tell you about Roger if you tell me about the women in your life."

This, too, seemed to give him pause. "There's never been anyone but you," he said, then grinned boyishly.

The gathering broke up an hour or so later. Julia insisted on staying to help Charles with the cleanup. Jerry and Alek were helpful, too, stacking folding chairs, straightening the living room and carrying dirty dishes into the kitchen.

By the time Alek unlocked the door to their home, Julia felt drained.

"Sit down," Alek said, "and I'll make you a cup of tea."

"That sounds heavenly." She kicked off her shoes and stretched out her tired legs, resting her feet on the ottoman. Alek joined her a few minutes later, bringing a china cup and saucer.

He sat across from her.

"I don't think I'll ever stop missing her," Julia whispered, after her first sip of tea. Now that she wasn't so busy, the pain of losing Ruth returned full force. "She's left such a large void in my life."

"Give yourself time," Alek said gently.

Julia looked over at her husband and her heart swelled with some emotion she couldn't quite identify. Possibly love.

That frightened her half to death, but she sensed that with Alek there was the chance of feeling safe and secure again.

He'd been so good to her through the difficult weeks of Ruth's illness and death, even when she'd given him ample reason to be angry with her.

"When was the last time you ate?" he asked unexpectedly.

Julia shrugged. "I don't remember."

"You didn't have anything this afternoon."

"I didn't?" There'd been so much food, it seemed impossible that she hadn't eaten something.

"No," Alek informed her. "I was watching. You saw to everyone but yourself. I'll make you dinner."

"Alek, please," she said, trailing him into the kitchen. "That isn't necessary."

"It'll be my pleasure." Lifting her by the waist, he sat her effortlessly on the stool next to the kitchen counter. "You can stay and observe," he said. "You might even learn something."

Relaxed now, Julia smiled.

Alek looked at her for a moment. "You don't do that often enough," he said, leaning toward her and dropping a kiss on her lips.

"Do what?" she asked in surprise.

"Smile."

"There hasn't been much reason to."

"That's about to change, my love."

She leaned her chin on her hands. The sadness she'd carried with her all these weeks seemed to slide off her back. "You know, I think you're right."

Alek, who was beating eggs, looked over at her and grinned. "Anna said something to me the other morning.

As her older brother I'm guilty of not listening to my sister as often as I should. This time, I did—and I agree with her."

"I like Anna very much."

"She feels the same way about you. She told me you were wise not to let me make love to you."

Julia lowered her gaze, uncomfortable with the topic.

"When we married I wasn't in love with you," Alek confessed. "You weren't in love with me. This is true?"

Given no option but the truth, Julia nodded.

"My heart tells me differently now." He put the bowl down and moved to her side. With one finger, he raised her chin so her eyes were level with his own. "I love you, Julia, very much."

She bit her trembling lower lip. "Oh, Alek..." Tears blurred her vision until his face swam before her.

"This makes you sad?"

"This terrifies me. I want to love you...I think I already do, but I don't trust myself when it comes to falling in love."

Alek frowned. "Because of this man you saw today?"

"Roger? Yes, because of Roger."

"I am not like him. You know that."

"I do." Logically, intellectually, she understood, but emotionally—that was harder. That was a risk....

Alek slipped his arms around her and Julia was struck not for the first time by the incredible beauty she saw in him. Not merely the physical kind. Oh, he was handsome, but that wasn't what captivated her. She saw the man who'd held and comforted her when her grandmother died. The man who'd sung her to sleep. The man who'd refused to take advantage of her even when she'd asked him to do so.

They stared at each other, and Julia knew the exact moment Alek decided to make love to her. It was the same moment she realized she wanted him to—wanted it more than anything.

His mouth sought hers in a hungry kiss. "I love you," he whispered against her lips.

"I love you, too," she echoed, so lost in his kiss that she couldn't speak anything but the truth. She'd tried to fool herself into believing it wasn't possible to trust a man again. Alek was different; he had to be. If she couldn't trust *him,* there was no hope for her.

He took her by the waist as he lifted her from the stool. Her feet dangling several inches off the floor, he carried her out of the kitchen and into the bedroom, kissing her, nibbling at her lips.

Julia tipped her head back in an effort to gather her scattered wits. Her breath came in short bursts, her lungs empty of air. Feeling seemed more important than breathing. Alek's touch, which was most important of all, brought back to life the desire that had lain dormant in her for years.

He lay with her on the king-size bed, bringing his mouth to hers, revealing sensual mysteries with his lips and tongue. He was sprawled across her, pinning her to the bed.

"You're so beautiful," he whispered. "You make me crazy."

"Love me," she told him, her arms around his neck. Just as she'd known she would, Julia felt safe with Alek. And she felt sure, of him and of herself.

"I do love you, always." He lowered his mouth to hers again. His kiss was sweet as his hands fiddled with the zipper at the back of her dress. Growing impatient, he rolled her onto her side, turning with her in order to ease it open. He removed the dress, along with her bra and panties.

Then his own clothes came off....

* * *

Afterward, neither spoke. Alek kissed her repeatedly and Julia kissed him back, in relief and jubilation. Her season of pain had passed just as her grandmother had claimed it would. She'd found her joy in Alek.

They slept, their arms around each other, their bodies cuddling spoon-fashion. Alek tucked his leg over hers and pressed close to her back.

Julia woke first, hungry and loving. She turned over so that her head was nestled beneath Alek's chin.

"Hmm."

"You awake?"

"I am now," he muttered drowsily.

"I'm hungry. Do you want to order out for dinner?"

Alek grinned. "I was going to cook for us, remember?"

Julia scooted closer, wrapping her arms around his neck, her fingers delving into his thick hair. "I think you should conserve your strength for later," she advised, bringing his mouth down to hers.

Gentle flames flickered over the gas logs in Julia's fireplace while they lounged on the floor, the remains of a boxed pizza resting nearby on the plush, light gray carpeting. Alek had found a bottle of wine and poured them each a glass.

"You're quiet," Alek commented.

Julia leaned back her head and smiled up at him. They couldn't seem to be apart from each other, even for a moment. Not just then. His touch was her reality.

His arms tightened around her. "Any regrets?"

"None."

He kissed the side of her neck. "Me, neither."

"I thought you'd gloat. Our making love is a real feather in your cap, isn't it?"

"I care nothing for feathers. All I want is my wife." He stroked his chin across the top of her head. "Are you still hungry?"

Julia patted her stomach. "Not a bit. Are you?"

"Yes. I'm half-starved."

The odd catch in his voice told her it wasn't food that interested him. He went still, as though he feared her response. Looking up at him, she stared into his eyes and smiled. "I have a feeling I've awakened a monster," she teased.

Alek pressed her down into the thick carpet, his eyes seeking hers. "Do you mind?"

"No," she whispered, untying the sash to her silk robe. "I don't mind at all."

Alek's mouth had just touched hers when the phone rang. He froze and so did Julia.

"Let it ring," she suggested, rubbing her hands over his chest, loving the smooth feel of his skin.

"It could be important." Reluctantly his eyes moved from her to the phone.

"You're probably right," Julia said, although she was far more interested in making love with her husband than talking on the phone.

"I'll get it." He scrambled across the floor and grabbed the receiver. "Hello," he said impatiently.

Julia followed, kneeling beside him. Leaning forward, she caught his earlobe between her teeth.

"Hello, Jerry," he said curtly.

Julia playfully progressed from his ear to his chin, then down the side of his neck.

"Yes, Julia's right here." He seemed winded, as if he were under strain.

"It's for you." He handed her the phone.

Julia took it, her eyes holding his. "Hello, Jerry," she said in a clear, even voice. "You caught me at a bad moment. Would you mind if I called you back in say…half an hour?"

"Ah…sure." Her brother obviously wasn't pleased, but Julia didn't really care.

"Thanks." She hung up the phone. "Now…"

"A bad moment?" Alek repeated, struggling to hide a smile. "Or a good one?"

"Definitely a good one," she said. "At least from my point of view."

"And mine, too…"

Nearly thirty minutes passed before Julia returned her brother's call.

"Hello, Jerry," she said, when he answered the phone. "I'm sorry I couldn't talk earlier."

"What's going on over there, anyway?"

"Sorry. We were busy."

The pause that followed was full of meaning. "Ah. I see. So," he said smugly, "how do you like married life now?"

"I like it just fine." She felt embarrassed to be discussing her love life with her brother even in the vaguest way. "Why are you calling? Is there a problem?"

"Yes, there is." Jerry's voice sharpened. "It's Roger."

Julia groaned inwardly. Would she never be rid of him? "What's he up to now?"

"I told you he was after something when he showed up for the funeral."

"We both know he didn't come out of respect," Julia agreed.

"I got a call from a friend who said he's heard Roger's been asking a lot of questions about Phoenix Paints."

"What did your friend learn?" A cold chill skittered down Julia's spine. Three years ago she'd handed Roger their latest fomula—the biggest advance in house paint in over thirty years. A month before Conrad Industries' new line of paints was scheduled to hit the market, their plant burned to the ground. Within a matter of weeks Roger had left the company, and Ideal Paints was marketing Conrad Industries' new product.

Because of the fire, it was impossible to meet the demand for their innovation, while Ideal Paints was capable of delivering paint to every hardware store in the country.

"My friend? He couldn't find out very much."

"Let's double security around the plant," Julia suggested.

"I've already done that."

"Who has Roger contacted?" she asked, pushing the hair from her forehead. They wouldn't allow him to steal from them again.

"I don't know." Jerry sounded equally concerned.

"Should we bring in a private investigator?"

"For what?"

"Tracking phones calls. See if he's getting information from any of our employees. We could have him watched. What do you think?"

"I don't know what to think. This is crazy. It's like a nightmare happening all over again. How soon did Alek say the new product would be ready for marketing?"

"Soon. He's been working a lot of hours."

"I figure we should move ahead as quickly as possible,

don't you? I'll see what I can do to schedule a meeting with the marketing folks. The sooner we can get our new paint on the store shelves, the better."

"Okay. Let me know if you hear anything else," Julia said.

"I will," Jerry promised.

They said a few words of farewell and when she replaced the receiver, she sighed.

"What was that all about?" Alek asked.

Julia shook her head, not wanting to explain, because explaining would mean telling him about her relationship with Roger. That was something she wanted to avoid, at least for now.

"These lines," he said, tracing his finger along the creases in her brow, "are because of Roger Stanhope, aren't they?"

Julia nodded.

"That's what I thought. Tell me about him, Julia. It's time I knew."

Nine

"Julia," Alek urged when she didn't immediately respond.

"Roger was just a man I once knew and trusted...several years ago. He proved he wasn't trustworthy. Can we leave it at that?"

"You loved him?"

Admitting it hurt her pride. Mixed in with all the regrets and the guilt was shame. Her only crime had been loving a man who didn't deserve it. A man who'd used her and shocked her with his betrayal, so much so that she'd refused to believe he was responsible for what had happened until her father had literally shoved the evidence at her. Even then she'd made excuses for him, unable to accept the truth. Her father had become so exasperated with her that he'd... Julia turned her thoughts from that fateful day when her life had become a living nightmare.

"Yes, I loved him," she answered finally. "It was a mistake. A very bad one."

"*What* was your mistake?" Alek probed gently.

"It's too complicated. But rest assured, I learned my lesson."

"And what was that?"

"That...love sometimes hurts."

Alek studied her for a moment, but what he was hoping to see, Julia could only speculate.

"Love doesn't always bring pain," he said. "My love will prove otherwise." He kissed her with a compassion that brought tears to her eyes. She managed to blink them back and offer him a look of gratitude.

"Come," he said softly, lifting her into his arms. "It's time for bed."

At dawn Alek was suddenly awake. Moonlight waltzed across the bedroom walls and the room was silent.

A chime rang the hour from the anniversary clock Julia kept on top of her bookcase. It was only 5:00 a.m. and he *should* be exhausted. But he was drained, sated, happy. His wife slept contentedly at his side, her slim body curled against his. He kissed her cheek, grateful Julia was married to him.

He'd wanted to ask her more about Stanhope, but he could see the raw anguish the man's name brought to her eyes, and even satisfying his curiosity wasn't worth causing her additional pain.

Alek knew very little of this man, but what he did know, he didn't like. He'd seen the way Roger had reached for Julia, placing his hand on her arm as though he had a right to touch her, to make demands. Alek didn't like the way the other man had looked at her, either, with a leer, as if he could have her with no more than a few persuasive words.

Alek hadn't thought of himself as jealous, but the quiet

rage he'd felt when he found Roger Stanhope pestering Julia couldn't be denied.

The man was a weakling. Stanhope relied on his sleek good looks, his flashy smile and compelling personality instead of intelligence, honest work and business acumen.

Alek wasn't fooled. Roger Stanhope was an enemy. Not only of Julia's, but Jerry's, as well. Julia hadn't explained the telephone conversation she'd had with her brother, even when he'd asked.

Although she'd tried to make light of Jerry's call, Alek had caught snatches of the conversation, enough to know she was worried. She'd been unable to disguise her distress. Stanhope wasn't worth one iota of anxiety. As Julia's husband, it was up to Alek to make sure that the man who'd betrayed her and her family wouldn't be allowed to do so again.

Alek was gone when Julia woke and she instantly experienced a surge of disappointment. One look at the clock explained Alek's absence. The last time she'd slept past ten had been as a teenager.

Nevertheless, she missed him. A slow smile spread over her lips. She'd married quite a man. Obviously he worked with as much energy and enthusiasm as he made love.

She climbed out of bed and threw on her robe. Since it was Saturday, and her week had been hellish, she intended to relax. There would be problems enough to deal with on Monday morning. The desire to rush into her office today was nonexistent.

She was knotting the belt on her pink silk robe as she wandered into the kitchen. Anna was there, busily whipping up something delicious, no doubt.

"Good morning, Anna."

"Good morning." Alek's sister stopped what she was doing and brought Julia a cup of coffee.

Being waited on was a luxury that would soon spoil her. "I'll take care of myself," Julia told her, not unkindly. "You go back to whatever you're doing." She walked over to the counter and on closer examination saw that the contents of Anna's bowl resembled cookie dough. A sample confirmed her guess. Oatmeal raisin, she thought.

"Yum."

Anna grinned at the compliment. "Alek asked me to bake them this morning for your picnic."

Julia paused halfway across the kitchen floor. "Our picnic?"

"Yes, he left a note asking me to pack a basket of food. He gave me a long list of everything he wants."

"Where is he?" Julia asked, adding cream to her coffee. "Do you know?"

Anna shook her head as she resumed stirring the thick batter. "No. He had some errand. He doesn't tell me much. I'm only his sister."

"He doesn't tell me much, either," Julia added with a short laugh. "I'm only his wife."

Anna giggled. "He should be back soon. He said you were very tired and wanted to be sure you slept as long as you needed. I'm very sorry about your grandmother."

"Thank you—I'm sorry, too," Julia said, breathing in deeply at the fresh stab of pain she felt at the mention of Ruth's death. That pain would be with her for a long while. Losing her grandmother had left a wide, gaping hole in her heart. Alek's love had helped her begin to heal, but she would always miss Ruth.

Sitting down at the table with the morning paper, Julia tried to focus her attention on the headlines. Soon the words blurred and ran together. The tears came as an unwelcome surprise, and she bent her head, hoping Anna wouldn't notice.

The sound of the front door opening announced Alek's return. Julia hurriedly wiped the tears from her cheeks and smiled up at him. She hadn't fooled him, she realized, but it didn't matter. He strolled over to her, his eyes full of love, and kissed her deeply.

Julia had trouble not losing herself in his kiss. It would have been so easy to let it lead to something more....

Alek glanced impatiently over his shoulder at his sister. "I'll give her the rest of the day off," he whispered.

"Don't be silly."

The hunger in his eyes told her how serious he was. He raised her effortlessly from her chair, sat down and held her in his lap.

"You slept late?" he questioned, smoothing the hair away from her face.

"Very late. You should've gotten me up."

"I was tempted. Tomorrow I will have no qualms about waking you."

"Really?" she asked, loving him so much it felt as if she could hardly contain it. She saw Anna watching them and could tell that Alek's sister was pleased at their closeness. "We're going on a picnic?"

"Yes," Alek said, his face brightening.

"Where?"

"That's a surprise. Bring a sweater, an extra set of clothes and a…" He hesitated, as if searching for a word, something he rarely did. "A kite."

"Kite…as in a flying-in-the-wind kite?"

He nodded enthusiastically.

"Alek," she said, studying him, "Are you taking me to the ocean?"

"Yes, my love, the ocean. And," he added, "we're leaving our cell phones and BlackBerries behind."

Julia had no problem with that directive.

Within fifteen minutes they were on their way. Anna's basket was tucked away in the backseat, along with an extra set of clothes for each of them, several beach towels, a blanket—and no fewer than five different kites, all of which Alek had bought while he was out.

He drove to Ocean Shores. The sun shone brightly and the surf pounded the sand with a roar that echoed toward them. The scent of salt stung the air. Sea gulls soared overhead, looking for an opportune meal. There were plenty of people, but this was nothing like the crowded beaches along the Oregon and California coasts.

Alek parked the car and found them an ideal spot to spread out their blanket and bask in the sunshine. Julia removed her shoes and ran barefoot in the warm sand, chasing after him.

"This is *perfect*," she cried, throwing out her arms. "I love it."

Alek returned to the car for their picnic basket and the kites and joined her on the blanket. He looked more relaxed than she could ever remember seeing him. He sank down beside her and stretched out with a contented sigh.

The wind buffeted them and a minute later, Alek moved, positioning himself behind her. He wrapped his arms around her and inhaled slowly, drawing the salty air into his lungs.

Julia did the same, breathing in the fresh clean scent of the sea.

"It's so peaceful here," she murmured. There were a number of activities going on around them, including horseback riding, kite flying, a football-throwing contest, even a couple of volleyball games, but none of those distracted her from the serenity she experienced.

"I thought you'd feel this way." He kissed the side of her neck.

Julia relaxed against his strength, letting him absorb her weight.

"My mother often brought Anna and me to the Black Sea after our father was killed."

Julia knew shockingly little about her husband's life before he came to the United States. "How old were you when he died?"

"Ten. Anna was seven. It was 1986."

"How did he die?"

It seemed an eternity passed before Alek spoke, and when he did his voice was low. "He was murdered. I don't think we will ever know the real reason. They came, the soldiers, in the middle of the night. We were all asleep. I woke to my mother's screams but by the time I got past the soldier guarding the door, my father was already dead."

"Oh, Alek." Julia's throat tightened with the effort to hold back tears.

"We learned from someone who risked his life to tell us that the KGB suspected my father of some illegal activity—we never heard the details. It made no sense to us since my father was a loyal Communist. Like me, he worked as a chemist."

"Oh, Alek. How terrible for all of you."

"Yes," he agreed, "and it nearly destroyed my mother. If it hadn't been for Anna and me, I believe my mother would have died, too. Not at the soldiers' hands, but from grief."

"What happened afterward?"

"My mother had to support us. Both Anna and I did everything we could to help, but it was difficult. Because I was a good student, I was given the opportunity to attend university. It was there that I met my first Americans. I couldn't believe the freedom and prosperity those students told me about. I've always been good with languages—Anna, too. Soon afterward, I started learning English. After I met Jerry, he sent me books and CDs. He was my link to America."

"Were you surprised when he asked you to come and work for Conrad Industries?"

"Yes."

"Did Jerry ever tell you about his beautiful younger sister?" Julia prodded.

"In passing."

"Were you curious about me?"

"No."

She poked him in the ribs and was rewarded with a mock cry of pain.

"I'm more curious now," he said, laughing.

"Good."

His hand edged beneath her blouse.

"Alek!"

"I'm just wondering how fast I can make you want me."

"Fast enough. Now, stop. We're on a public beach."

He sighed as though her words had wounded him. "Maybe we should get a hotel room."

"We could have done that in Seattle. Since we're at the beach and the day is gorgeous, let's enjoy ourselves."

"Julia," Alek said sternly, "trust me, we would enjoy ourselves in a hotel room, too."

Smiling, she leaned back her head to look at him. "No one told me you were a sex fiend."

"You do this to me, Julia, only you."

"I promise I'll satisfy your, uh, carnal appetite," she assured him with a grin. "And I'm a woman of my word."

"I must not be so selfish," Alek said, and the teasing quality was gone from his voice. "I didn't bring you here to make love, I brought you here to heal. After my father was killed, my mother made weekly trips to the beach with Anna and me. It was a time of solace for us, and it helped us heal. I hoped it would help you, too."

"It does," Julia said, looking out at the pounding surf.

"You must forgive my greed for you."

"Only if you forgive my greed for you." The lovemaking was so new, they were eager to learn everything they could about each other, eager to give and to receive. Julia didn't fool herself into believing this kind of desire could continue. If it did, they might both die of sheer exhaustion.

"I want you to relax in my arms," Alek said, "and close your eyes." He waited a moment. "Are they closed?"

She nodded. The sounds that came at her were intense. The ocean as it slapped against the shore, the cry of the birds and the roar of scooters as they shot past her, kicking up the sand. The smells, carried on the wind, were pungent.

"Now open your eyes."

Julia obeyed and was overwhelmed by the richness of the colors around her. The sky was blue with huge puffy clouds. The water was a sparkling green that left a thin, white, frothy trail on the sand. Every color was vibrant, every detail. Julia's breath caught in her throat at the beauty before her.

"Oh, Alek, it's so lovely."

"My mother did that with Anna and me, but I think she was doing it for herself, too. She wanted us to see that life could be good, if we looked around at the world instead of within ourselves."

Julia knew that was what she'd been doing these past few years, looking at the darkness and the shortcomings within herself. Under such intense scrutiny, her faults had seemed glaring. It was little wonder that she'd been so miserable.

"Alek," she said, with her discovery, "thank you, thank you so much."

They kissed, and it was as if his love was absolution for all that had gone before and all that would come later. She turned in his embrace and slipped her arms around his neck. When they'd finished kissing, they simply held each other.

Alek knew his relationship with Julia had changed that afternoon by the ocean. Things between them were different now. More open, more trusting. They'd had fun, too—childish, uncomplicated fun—something neither of them had done in years. They'd flown kites, run through the surf, eaten Anna's sandwiches and cookies, feeding each other bites.

Sunday evening, the day after their venture to the beach, Alek needed to run down to the lab. When he told Julia, she offered to go with him, as if even an hour apart was more than she could bear.

Her willingness had taken him by surprise.

"You're sure?" he asked.

"Of course. It'll do me good to get out."

They listened to classical music on the way across town. Security had been increased at the plant, with extra guards posted; Alek gave them a friendly nod. Julia went with him into his office. He found the notes he needed and brought them home.

"Would you like some coffee?" she asked once they'd returned.

"Please." Her desire to indulge him with small pleasures was something of a surprise, too, a pleasant one.

While he read over his calculations, Julia was content to sit at his side, absorbed in a novel. He couldn't remember a time when she'd voluntarily sat still. Her body always seemed to be filled with nervous energy. That was gone from her now and in its place had come a restfulness.

"I'm not looking forward to work in the morning," she said when Alek was finished. Leaning against him, she stretched her legs out along the sofa and heaved a giant sigh. "These past few days have been so wonderful. I don't feel ready to deal with the office again."

"Will you always work, Julia?"

"I…don't know. I hadn't thought about it. I suppose I will until after the children are born at any rate, but even then I'll still be involved in the management of the company."

"Then you wouldn't mind if we had a family."

"No, of course I wouldn't mind. Did you think I would?"

"I wasn't sure."

"Then rest assured, Mr. Berinski, I want your children."

Alek felt his heart expand with eagerness. "So you'd like a family," he said. "Could we work on this project soon?"

"How soon?" she whispered.

He fiddled with the buttons of her shirt. "Now," he said, aware of the husky sound of his voice.

Julia sighed that womanly sigh he'd come to recognize as a signal of her eagerness for him. "I think we might be able to arrange that."

"Julia, my love," Alek said with a groan, "I'm afraid I'll never get enough of you. What have you done to me? Are you a witch who's cast some spell over me?"

Julia laughed. "If anyone's cast a spell over anyone, it's you over me. I'm lonely without you. If we can't be together, I feel lost and empty. I never thought I could love again, certainly not like this, and you've shown me the way."

"Julia." He rasped her name and, folding her over his arm, bent forward to cover her soft reaching mouth with his. The kiss revealed their need for each other. He heard Julia's book fall off the sofa and hit the floor, but neither cared. His hands were busy with her shirt and once it was open, she twisted around to face him.

"I vote for the bed this time."

"The bed," he said mockingly. "Where's your sense of adventure?"

Julia laughed softly. "It was used up in the bathtub this morning. Did you know it took me twenty minutes to clean the water off the floor?"

He carried her into their bedroom, kissing her all the while.

Afterward, they lay on the bed. Julia was sprawled across him. Every now and then she kissed him, or he kissed her. Alek had never known such contentment in his life. It frightened him. Happiness had always been fleeting, and he wasn't sure he could trust what he'd found with Julia. His hold on her tightened and he closed his eyes and discovered he couldn't imagine what his life would be like without her now. Bleak and empty, he decided.

When Jerry had first suggested this marriage, Alek had set his terms. He wasn't a believer in the staying power of love. It had always seemed temporary to him, ephemeral, and it came at the expense of everything else. Alek couldn't claim he'd never been in love before. There'd been a handful of brief relationships over the years, but each time he'd grown bored and restless. He was a disappointment to his mother, who was hoping he and Anna would provide her with grandchildren to spoil.

How perceptive his sister was to realize he hadn't loved Julia in the beginning. He hadn't expected to ever truly love her. He'd offered her his loyalty and his devotion, but had held his heart in reserve. She had it now, though, in her palm. His heart. His very life.

Julia lay across her husband's body and sighed deeply, completely and utterly content. She'd never known a time like this with a man. A time of peace and discovery. His talk of children had unleashed long-buried dreams.

They hadn't bothered to use protection. Not even once. They each seemed to pretend it didn't matter, that what would be would be.

Pregnant.

She said the word in her mind as though it was foreign to her, and in many ways it was. A few weeks ago she would've sworn it was impossible; after all, she didn't intend to sleep with her husband. *That* had certainly changed, and now, thoughts of a family filled her mind and her heart. Perhaps it was because she'd so recently lost Ruth and because one of the last things her grandmother had said was about children "waiting to be born."

After so many years of pain, Julia hardly knew how to

deal with happiness. In some ways she was afraid to trust that it would last. She'd been happy with Roger—and then everything had blown up in her face. The crushing pain of his deception would never leave her, but she'd lost the desire to punish him. Conrad Industries' success would be revenge enough. There might not have been sufficient evidence to charge him, but people in the business suspected him. They talked. That meant he wasn't likely to be hired by any other company once he left Ideal Paints—or they fired him. After what had happened, no one else would trust him. Without realizing what he was doing, he'd painted himself in a corner. She smiled at her own pun.

"Something amuses you?" Alek asked, apparently having felt her smile.

"Yes…and no."

"That sounds rather vague to me."

"Rest," she urged.

"Why?" he challenged. "Do you have something…physical in mind?"

Julia grinned again. "If I don't, I'm sure you do. Now hush, I'm trying to sleep."

"Then I suggest you stop making those little movements."

Julia hadn't been conscious of moving. "Sorry."

He clamped his hands on her hips. "Don't be. I'm not."

Julia resumed her daydream. A baby would turn her world upside down. She'd never been very domestic. If her child-rearing skills were on the level of her cooking skills, then she—

"Now you're frowning." Alek murmured. "What's wrong?"

"I…I was just thinking I might not be a very good

mother. I don't know anything about babies. I might really botch this."

He took her head between his hands and brought her mouth to his. "You're going to be a wonderful mother. We'll learn about this together when the time comes. Agreed?"

Julia sighed loudly. "You're right. As a logical, practical businessperson I know it, but as a woman, I'm not so sure."

"Listen, woman, you're making it impossible to nap. As far as I can tell, there's only one way to keep you quiet." With his arms around her waist, he turned her onto her back and nuzzled her neck until Julia cried out and promised to do whatever he said.

Monday morning, Julia arrived at the office before eight. Virginia, her assistant, appeared a few minutes after she did, looking flustered.

"I'm sorry, I didn't realize you were planning to be here quite so early. If I had, I would've come in before eight myself. I'll get your coffee right away."

"Don't worry about it," Julia said, reaching for the stack of mail in her in-basket. Her desk was neatly organized, and she was grateful Virginia had taken the time to lighten her load.

"I read over the mail and your emails and answered everything I could," Virginia said. "I hope that's okay."

"Of course. I'm grateful for your help."

Virginia hurried out to the lunchroom, returning a few minutes later with a steaming cup of coffee. "I'm sorry but there doesn't seem to be any cream. I'll send out for some."

"I can live without cream," Julia said absently, turning on her computer. "Would you ask my brother to drop in when it's convenient? And please contact my husband and see if he could meet me for lunch." She'd left while he was in the shower and had forgotten to leave him a note. "I meant to ask—" She stopped, realizing she probably already had a luncheon appointment. "That is, if I'm not tied up."

"You were scheduled to meet with Mr. Casey, but I wasn't sure if you'd feel up to dealing with him your first day back. I took the liberty of rescheduling the luncheon for Tuesday."

Virginia knew Doug Casey, their outside counsel, was one of her least favorite people, and she smiled her appreciation. "Thanks."

"I'll get right back to you," Virginia said. True to her word, she returned a few minutes later. "Your brother will be down shortly and your husband suggests you meet at noon at Freeway Park."

"Great." She turned back to her computer and didn't hear Virginia leave her office.

Jerry hurried into her office. "I'm worried about Stanhope," he said immediately. "I think he's up to something. I've got a private investigator following him. If he makes contact with any of our people, we'll know about it."

Julia rolled a pen between her palms. "I can't believe any of our employees would sell us out, can you?"

Jerry tensed. "After what happened last time, who's to tell?"

"Let me know the second you hear anything."

"I will. The investigator's going to make regular reports."

Her brother left, and Julia was involved with a large stack of correspondence when she noted the time. She stopped in the middle of a dictation.

Virginia raised her head, anticipating Julia's next move.

"We'll continue this after lunch," she said, standing and

reaching for her purse. "I won't be back until after one. Cover for me if need be."

"Of course." Virginia was on her feet, too, and Julia felt her scrutiny.

"Is something wrong?" she asked the older woman.

"No," Virginia said with a shy smile. "Something's very right."

"Oh?" Julia didn't understand.

"I don't think I've ever seen you look happier."

Ten

Freeway Park was one of Seattle's many innovative ideas. A large grassy area built over a freeway. Green ivy spilled down the concrete banks, reaching toward the road far below.

At noon, many Seattle office workers converged on the park to enjoy their lunch in the opulent sunshine. Each summer the city offered a series of free concerts. Julia didn't know if there was one scheduled for that afternoon, but nothing could have made her day any more perfect than meeting her husband.

She saw Alek from across the grass and started toward him. He'd obviously seen her at the same time because he grinned broadly and moved in her direction.

"Did you bring anything for lunch?" he asked, after they kissed briefly.

Eating was something Julia often failed to think about. "Oh, no, I forgot."

"I thought as much. Luckily you have a husband who knows his wife. Come, let's find a place to sit down."

"What'd you buy?" she asked, pointing at the white sack in his hand.

"Fish and chips. Do you approve?"

"Sounds great." She *was* hungry, she realized, which had become a rarity. Generally she ate because it was necessary, not for any real enjoyment. Anna was sure to change that. Alek's sister cooked tempting breakfasts and left delicious three- and four-course dinners ready to be served when they got home. By the end of the year, Julia predicted she'd gain weight—from all the wonderful food…and because by then she'd likely be pregnant. The thought produced a deep sense of excitement.

Alek found a spot for them on a park bench. He set the white bag between them and lifted out an order of fish-and-chips packed in a cardboard container.

"Are you trying to fatten me up?" she teased.

His eyes twinkled. "You know me almost as well as I know you."

"Indeed I do." She laughed.

"But the question is," Alek said, eyeing her speculatively, "do you like me?"

It was an effort to pull her gaze away from his magnetic eyes. "More each day," she answered honestly.

An electric moment passed before Alek spoke. "You won't be working late tonight, will you?"

"No. Will you?"

He shook his head. "I plan to be home at five-fifteen."

"That early?" She usually didn't leave the office until after six.

"I'll be lucky to last that long," he whispered.

There was no missing his meaning. Julia's body went into overdrive. She'd never thought of herself as a highly sexual person, but in that instant she knew she had to do *something* to appease the overwhelming urge she had to make love with her husband.

"Alek...would you mind kissing me?"

He blinked, then bent his head, meaning only to brush her lips, she suspected, but that wouldn't be enough to satisfy her. Not anymore. She touched his lips with her tongue, teasing and taunting him.

A deep moan came from low within his throat, which aroused her as nothing ever had before. The kiss deepened and deepened until they were completely lost in each other.

She wrenched her mouth from his, gasping. "Five-fifteen," she said when she could manage to speak.

"I'll be there."

Jerry was waiting in her office when Julia returned from lunch. Without greeting her, he announced, "Roger's made contact with someone from the lab."

Julia was stunned into speechlessness. "How do you know?" she asked when she could. There was a cold, sinking feeling in her stomach.

"Rich Peck."

"Who's Rich Peck?"

Jerry spun around and glared at her. "The private eye I hired. Rich traced the phone numbers that came into Roger's home for the past several days."

"How did he do that?"

"Julia," Jerry said, clearly exasperated with her, "that isn't important right now. What *is* important is that someone from Conrad Industries contacted Roger. They used the phone from the lab."

"But...who?"

"That's the point. It could've been any number of people. The phone's used by nearly everyone on staff. What I'm saying is that we've got a traitor on our hands."

Julia found that hard to believe. Almost everyone who was employed at the lab had been with them three years earlier. Their dislike of Roger was well-known. After the fire it had taken months to rebuild, and Julia had tried to keep as many employees on the payroll as possible during that time, in order not to lose her trained and loyal help. There were at least twenty who'd been with Conrad Industries fifteen years or longer. The strain on the budget crippled the company financially. And nearly every employee had hung on, counting on the promise of reimbursement once Julia could get the company back on its feet.

Julia appreciated their sacrifice. And their trust. Her father had recently died, and to say she was inexperienced would've been an understatement. The company was on the verge of bankruptcy. It was one of the bleakest times in Julia's life and in the company's history.

Ruth's faith in her to pull the company out of financial disaster had helped Julia survive that grim period.

The idea that someone working in the lab was selling her out now—it seemed impossible. She refused to believe it. Refused to accept it.

"What do you think we should do?" Jerry asked.

Julia walked over to the window and stared down at the street ten floors below. Cars and people looked miniature and seemed to be moving in slow motion. It was as if she was staring at another world that had no connection to her own.

"Nothing," she said after a moment. "We do nothing."

"But…"

"What *can* we do?" she demanded impatiently. "All we have is the knowledge that someone contacted Roger. Should we haul every employee in for questioning by Peck, hoping his expertise at grilling fifty-year-old men and women will flush out whoever wants to betray us?"

"We could have Alek scout around and—"

"No," she said quickly, interrupting him. "Alek is as much a suspect as anyone else."

"Don't be ridiculous! Alek's poured his whole life into this project. You don't think *he'd* betray us."

"No, I don't," she agreed readily enough. "But that doesn't change the facts. Roger had every reason to hope Conrad Industries would prosper, too, and look what he did."

"But Alek…"

"Alek is a suspect, like everyone else. I warn you, Jerry, don't say a word to him. Not a single word."

Her brother stared at her. "He's your husband. You don't even trust your own husband?"

"You're right," she admitted. "I don't. You can thank Roger for that. I wouldn't trust my own mother after the lesson Roger taught me. If you think I'm coldhearted, then fine. I'd rather have you think poorly of me than hand over the fate of this company to a man who could destroy us."

Making love to his wife was probably the most fabulous sensation Alek had ever experienced. Perhaps it was because she'd withheld herself from him for so long that he treasured the prize so highly. Julia was open, honest and genuine.

Alek had never lost control of himself with another woman, but he had with Julia. She was fast becoming as necessary to him as the air he breathed. He wanted her, and that need was growing at an alarming rate.

Every time they were intimate, she gave him a little more of herself. A little more of her trust. A little more of her heart and soul.

He glanced at his watch and frowned. It was well past the time they'd agreed to meet. Knowing Julia, she'd probably got caught up in her work and let the time slip away from her.

He waited another ten minutes before calling her office. Her assistant answered.

"This is Alek. Has Julia left the office yet?"

"No." Virginia sounded surprised. "She's still here. Would you like me to connect you?"

"Please." He waited a moment before Julia came on the line.

"Hello," she said absently. Alek could picture her sitting behind her desk with her reading glasses at the end of her nose.

"Do you know what time it is?"

"Five-forty. Why?"

"We had an appointment, remember?" He lowered his voice. "I've got a deck of cards and—"

"A deck of cards?"

He wasn't sure what he heard in her voice, but it wasn't amusement. It troubled him, but he didn't have time to analyze it just then. "Yes, I recently heard about this American card game that I want to play with you."

"A *card* game?"

"Strip poker. Sounds like fun. I've got everything ready. How much longer are you going to be?"

"Oh, Alek, listen, I'm really sorry, but I could be at the office another hour or more. Everything from last week is piled up on my desk. I really shouldn't leave."

"I understand." He didn't like it, but he understood. "My game can wait, and it looks like I'll have to, as well." He was hoping for a little sympathy, or at least a sigh of regret, but he received neither.

Julia was keeping something from him. He heard it in her voice, felt it as clearly as if it were a tangible thing.

Julia didn't arrive home until nearly nine. It would be too much to ask that Alek *not* be there waiting for her. She didn't know how she was going to look him in the eye.

A headache had been building from the moment Jerry had left her office. Everything in her told her Alek would be the last person who'd sell them out. It would make it much easier to believe in him if she hadn't so staunchly defended Roger to her father. She'd been wrong once and it had nearly cost her sanity.

Alek greeted her at the door. Without a word he drew her into his arms and hugged her. She was swallowed in his embrace, surrounded by his love, and she soaked it up, needing it so badly.

"Tell me what's troubling you," he said.

She had no choice but to sidestep the question. "What makes you think anything's wrong?"

"I'm your husband. I know you," he said, echoing his comment from that afternoon. But then he'd been teasing; now his statement sounded like the simple truth.

"I've got a terrible headache."

He studied her as if he wasn't sure he should believe her, although it was true enough. Her temples throbbed and she was exhausted. "Did you have dinner?" she asked, wanting to turn the subject away from herself.

"No, I waited for you. Are you ready?"

Her appetite was nil. "I'm not very hungry. If you don't mind, I'd like a bath." She left him without giving him a chance to respond.

The hot water was soothing and a full thirty minutes passed before she could bring herself to leave the tub. She dressed for bed, craving the oblivion of sleep. But Alek was waiting for her when she finished. He seemed to anticipate her every need, which increased her guilt.

He followed her into the bedroom. "Would you like me to rub your temples?" he asked, sitting on the edge of the bed.

"You'd do that?"

He seemed surprised by her question. "Of course. There's nothing I wouldn't do for you."

"Oh, Alek," she moaned.

"Come," he said, sitting on their bed, his back against the headboard, his legs stretched out. "Rest your head on me and I'll massage your forehead. Would you like me to sing to you again?" He reached for the light at the side of the bed and turned it off.

"Please." The meaning of the words he was singing was beyond her, but she loved the deep, melodic sound of his voice. As he sang, his nimble fingers gently soothed the throbbing pain in her head. She was sleepy when he finished. Lifting her head from his lap, he began to leave her. It was then that Julia realized how much she wanted him to stay.

"Don't go," she pleaded softly. "Come to bed with me."

"For a few minutes," he agreed with obvious reluctance. He undressed in the dark and slipped beneath the sheets, then gathered her in his arms.

Alek held her for a long time and she savored these moments of closeness as the warmth of his love stole over her.

Alek alleviated the feelings of abandonment and loss she'd felt since Roger's betrayal, since her father's death and now her grandmother's. He loved her as no man ever had.

Julia was restless. She didn't understand why she couldn't sit still. Then again, she could. It was only natural to be nervous, considering the phone call she'd received earlier that morning. It had been a week since Jerry had hired Rich Peck and now Rich had phoned wanting to give them his first weekly report. Since Jerry was out for the afternoon, Julia had agreed to meet with the investigator herself.

Virginia announced his arrival and Peck entered her office. He was tall and wiry, and much younger than she'd expected. Perhaps thirty, if that.

"Hello," he said, stepping forward and shaking her hand.

"Please sit down," Julia invited.

He took the chair on the other side of her desk. "This Stanhope fellow is an interesting character," he began. "I've been tailing him for nearly a week. I managed to get photos of just about everyone he's met. My guess is that whoever's leaking information to him is a woman. Once you get a look at the photographs you'll understand why. He's quite the ladies' man."

This wasn't news to Julia.

Rich brought out a folder thick with photographs, reached for a small pad and flipped through the first couple of pages.

"He had several business lunches, as best as I can tell. Although we've got a twenty-four-hour tail on him, there are certain periods of time we can't account for."

"I see. Do you think he knows he's being followed?"

Rich snickered. "The guy hasn't got a clue. He's way too arrogant. He lives on the edge, too. I talked to his landlady and learned he's two months behind on his rent. It's happened before. His credit rating's so full of holes he couldn't get a loan if his life depended on it."

"What about his position with Ideal Paints? Is that secure?"

"Who knows? From what I've been able to find out, he doesn't have many friends. He seems to get along all right on the job. As for what he does with his money, that isn't hard to figure out. The guy goes out with a different woman every night. He seems to get his kicks showing off what a stud he is."

This, too, didn't come as any surprise to Julia. Roger liked to refer to himself as a "party animal."

"Go ahead and look through those photos and see if there's anyone you recognize. Take your time. I've got them stacked according to the day of the week. Thursday of this week is on top. He left his apartment about ten. He seemed to be in a hurry and got to his office around ten-fifteen. He didn't leave again until four, and then came out a side entrance. My tail noted that some girl came out the front of the building directly afterward and seemed to be looking for someone. Our guess is that he was escaping her.

"He waited around ten or fifteen minutes and then left. He went home, changed his clothes and was out again by six. He picked up some chick and they went to dinner. He spent the night with her."

That, too, was typical.

"Wednesday…" Rich continued as Julia flipped through the photographs. "Again he was late to the office. He arrived about ten and left again at eleven-thirty. He drove to Henshaw's, that fancy restaurant on Lake Union."

Julia nodded; she knew it well. An eternity earlier it had

been one of their favorite places. The food was delicious and the ambience luxurious but not overpowering.

"Whoever he was supposed to meet was waiting for him outside. I assume this was a business lunch. The guy he was meeting was angry about something. The two of them exchanged words outside the restaurant. We got several excellent photos. It looked for a moment like they were going to have a fistfight. Frankly, Stanhope was smart to avoid this one. The guy would've pulverized him in seconds."

Julia flipped to the next series of pictures. Her gaze fell on Alek's angry face and she gasped.

Rich's attention reverted from the tablet to her. "You recognize him?"

Julia felt as if she was going to vomit.

"Ms. Conrad?"

She nodded.

"An employee?"

Once again she nodded. "Yes," she managed. "An employee. You can leave the rest of the photographs here and I'll go through them later. You've done an excellent job, Mr. Peck." She stood and ushered him to the door. "Jerry will be in touch with you sometime later this afternoon. I believe you've solved our mystery."

"Always glad to be of service."

"Thank you again."

Julia collapsed against the door the instant it was closed. Her stomach twisted into a knot of pain. This *couldn't* be happening. This couldn't be real. She felt nauseous and made a dash to her wastepaper basket, where she threw up her lunch. She was kneeling on the floor, her trembling hands holding her hair away from her face, when Virginia walked into the office.

"Oh, dear! Are you all right?"

Julia nodded.

"Let me help you," Virginia said. With her hand under Julia's elbow, she raised her to her feet. "You need to lie down."

"Could...would you see if you could find my brother for me?"

"You don't want me to call your husband?"

"No," she said forcefully, "get Jerry. Have him come as soon as he can.... Tell him it's an emergency."

Her legs were unstable and she slumped into her chair. In the past three years Julia had received a number of lessons in pain. Roger had been her first teacher, but his tactics paled when compared to Alek's. It would've been easier to bear if Alek had aimed a gun at her heart and pulled the trigger.

It took her brother twenty minutes to reach her office; he must've been in the middle of something important when Virginia called. As she waited she gazed sightlessly at her desk. She should be sobbing hysterically; instead, she found herself as calm and cool as if the man who'd been betraying her and her brother was barely more than an acquaintance.

Jerry rushed into her office, apparently having run at least part of the way, because his face was red and he was breathless.

"Virginia said it was an emergency."

"I...I was being a bit dramatic."

"Not according to Virginia. She wanted to know if she should phone for an ambulance. You're pale, but otherwise you look fine."

"I'm not, and you won't be, either, once you take a look at these." She handed him the series of three photographs.

The blotchy redness faded from Jerry's face and he blanched as he studied Rich Peck's photographs.

"Alek?" he breathed in disbelief.

"It appears so."

"There's got to be some explanation!"

"I'm sure there is." There always was. Something that would sound logical and persuasive. She'd been through this before and knew all there was to know about betrayals of trust. When she'd confronted Roger, he'd worn a hurt, incredulous look of shock and dismay. He'd angrily declared his innocence, told her it was all a misunderstanding that he'd be able to clear up in a matter of minutes, given the opportunity. Because she loved him so desperately and because she wanted to believe him so badly, she'd listened. In the end it all seemed credible to her and she'd defended him because she loved and trusted him. She loved and trusted Alek, too, but she'd been wrong before, so very wrong, and it had cost her and her family dearly.

"What are you going to do?" Jerry asked in a whisper. He hadn't recovered yet. He continued to stare at the photographs as though the pictures themselves would announce the truth if he studied them long enough.

"I don't know," she said unevenly.

"You aren't going to fire him, are you?"

"I don't know yet."

"Julia, for the love of heaven, Alek's your *husband*."

"I don't know what I'm going to do," she repeated. "I just don't know."

Jerry rubbed a hand over his face and inhaled deeply. "We should confront him, give him the opportunity to explain. It's possible that he's got a very good reason for meeting Roger. One that has nothing to do with Phoenix Paints."

"Jerry, you were ten before you stopped believing in Santa Claus. Remember? There's only one reason Alek would contact Roger and we both know it."

"That doesn't make any sense," he argued. "Alek has more reason for Phoenix Paints to succeed than anyone. His career hinges on the success of our new line. Why would he deliberately sabotage himself? He spent years researching these developments." His eyes pleaded with her.

"If you're looking to me for answers, I don't have any. Why do any of us do the things we do? My guess is that he's out for revenge."

"Revenge? Alek? Why? We've been good to him, good to his family, and he's been good to us. He doesn't have any score to settle."

"Dad was good to Roger, too, remember? He was the one who gave Roger his first job. Dad hired him directly out of college when he could've taken on someone with far more experience. If we're looking for reasons Alek would never do this, we'd be putting blindfolds over our own eyes."

Jerry watched her for several minutes. "I'm going to talk to him."

Julia folded her arms around her waist and nodded.

"Do you want to come with me?"

"No! I couldn't bear it. Not again." She squeezed her eyes shut and her body swayed with the pain. "I can't believe this is happening."

"I can't believe it is, either."

"Why do I continually fall for the wrong kind of man? There must be something wrong with me."

Jerry walked to her window and stared out. His shoulders moved in a deep sigh. "We're overreacting."

"Maybe," Julia agreed. "But I have that ache in the pit

of my stomach again. The last time it was there was when Dad forced me to face the truth about Roger."

"The least we can do is listen to his explanation."

Julia shook her head. "You listen, I…can't." She didn't want to be there when Alek made his excuses. She'd let her brother handle this because she was incapable of dealing with it.

Jerry's eyes narrowed. "It's been a long time since I've seen you so…detached."

"Let me guess," she returned sarcastically. "Could it have been following my breakup with Roger?"

"This is different. You're married to Alek."

"That means it's a little more involved, a little more complicated than before, but it's not really so different. Until… this is resolved it would be better if Alek didn't come into work. Tell him that for me."

"Julia…"

"Tell him, Jerry, because I can't. Please." Her voice cracked. "It's just until this is settled. Alek will understand."

"But you aren't going to listen to his explanation?"

"No. You listen to what he has to say, but don't argue his case with me. I tried that with Dad, remember? I was so certain Roger was an innocent victim of circumstances."

Her brother looked older, as though he'd suddenly aged ten years. Julia understood. She felt old herself. And sick. Her stomach felt decidedly queasy.

Jerry left and her stomach pitched again. Automatically she reached for the wastepaper basket.

Julia left the office an hour later, her cell phone turned off. She wasn't sure where she intended to go, but she knew she couldn't stay at work any longer. She started walking with no destination in mind and ended up at the Pike Place

Market. People were bustling about and, not wanting to be in a crowd, she headed for the waterfront. Not the tourist areas, but much farther down where the large cruise vessels docked.

She walked for hours, trying to sort through her emotions, and eventually gave up. She was in too much pain to think clearly.

She didn't cry. Not once. She figured this numbness was her body's protective device.

It was well past dark and she'd wandered into an unsafe area of town. She finally realized she had to make her way home.

When she reached her building, the security man looked surprised to find her arriving so late. He greeted her warmly and held open the heavy glass door for her.

The elevator ride up to her apartment seemed to take forever, but it wasn't long enough. Soon she'd face her husband.

She'd barely gotten her key into the lock when the door was wrenched open. Alek loomed above her like a bad dream.

Eleven

She saw the same signs in Alek that she'd seen in Roger. The indignation. The hurt, angry look that she could believe such a terrible thing of him. As if *she* were the betrayer. As if she were the guilty one.

Roger had turned the tables on her with such finesse she didn't realize what was happening until too late. Julia studied her husband and if she didn't know better would've believed with all her heart that he'd never betray her.

"Where have you been?" Alek demanded. "I've been worried sick."

"I went for a walk."

"For five hours?"

She moved past him. "I should've phoned. I'm sorry, but I needed to think."

Alek followed her. "Why didn't you come to me yourself? Instead you sent Jerry." His voice revealed his pain. "I don't deny talking to Roger Stanhope, but at least give me the chance to explain why."

"You *can't* deny seeing him since we have the evidence,"

she responded lifelessly. "You called him, too, from the lab. We know about that, as well."

If he was surprised, he didn't show it. "I called him because I wanted him to stay away from you. He wouldn't listen. Our meeting at Henshaw's was an accident, he was arriving just as I was leaving. He taunted me, said he could have you back anytime he wanted. He said other things, too, but I don't care to repeat them. Ask the man you hired to take photographs what happened that day. Stanhope and I nearly got into a fistfight."

Julia desperately wanted to believe that he was telling the truth about his motives. Her heart yearned to trust him. But this was like an old tape being played back again and the memories it brought to the surface were too compelling to ignore.

"That man Stanhope is slime. I won't have him anywhere near you," Alek said heatedly. "If you want to condemn me for protecting you, then you may. But I would rather rip out my own heart than hurt you."

He was saying everything Julia longed to hear. She pressed her hands to her head, not knowing what to do. "I have to think."

He nodded, seeming to accept that, but he was hurt and she felt his pain as strongly as her own. Rather than continue a discussion that would cause them both grief, she showered and dressed for bed.

Alek appeared in the doorway to the guest bedroom when she'd finished. "Anna left you some dinner."

"I'm not hungry."

"You're too thin already. Eat."

"Alek, please, I'm exhausted."

"Eat," he insisted.

Julia's appetite was gone. She'd thrown up her lunch and hadn't eaten since. Unwilling to argue with him, she went into the kitchen, took the foil-covered dinner plate warming in the oven and sat down at the table.

His sister had cooked veal cutlets, small red potatoes and what looked like a purple cabbage stir-fry. Even after sitting in the oven for hours, the food was delicious. Julia intended to sample only a few bites to appease Alek and then dump the rest in the garbage disposal, but she ended up eating a respectable amount of food. When she'd finished, she rinsed off her plate and retired to the guest room. Alone.

In the morning, Julia woke to the sound of Anna and Alek talking in the kitchen. They were speaking in Russian and it was apparent that Anna was upset.

Donning her robe, Julia wandered in and poured herself a cup of coffee. Anna eyed her with open hostility.

"My brother would not do this thing," she said forcefully.

"Anna," Alek barked. "Enough."

"He loves you. How can you think he would ever hurt you? He is a man of honor."

"It isn't as simple as it seems," Julia said in her own defense. Anna didn't understand, and she didn't expect her to.

Alek said something sharp and cold in Russian, but that didn't stop Anna from turning to Julia once more. "You do not know my brother. Otherwise you wouldn't believe he could do this terrible thing."

Alek reprimanded his sister harshly. Julia didn't need to understand Russian to know what he was saying.

Anna responded by yanking the apron from her waist, throwing it on the kitchen counter and storming out of the apartment.

"I apologize for my sister's behavior," Alek said after she'd left. He was so formal, so stiff and proud. He hesitated, as if trying to find the words to express himself. "There is a meeting with the marketing people this afternoon. It is a very important discussion. I need to be there to answer questions. If you'd rather I wasn't, I'll see if someone can take my place."

Julia felt incapable of making any decision, even a straightforward one like this.

"I suggest you attend it, too," he said. "If you feel I am doing or saying anything that would hurt Conrad Industries, then you can stop me. I suggest Jerry be there, as well."

"Alek, please try to understand how awkward this is."

"Come to the meeting," he urged.

"All right," Julia agreed reluctantly.

He told her the time and place, and afterward they were silent. Julia thought with a kind of sad whimsy that she could hear the sound of their heartache, like the loud ticking of a clock. She was sure Alek heard it, too. After a few minutes, he left the condo.

Rarely had Julia ever felt more alone. Her thoughts depressed her. She dressed, determined to act as if life was normal until they resolved this problem.

It wasn't until she was at the office that she made a clear decision, her first sensible one since this whole nightmare began.

She pulled the phonebook out of her desk drawer, swallowed hard, praying she could pull this off, and then, with a bravado she didn't feel, dialed Roger Stanhope's number.

"Mr. Stanhope's office," came the efficient reply.

"This is Julia Conrad for Mr. Stanhope."

"One moment, please."

A short time passed before Roger's smooth voice came over the wire. "Julia, what a pleasant surprise."

"I understand you met with my husband." Preliminary greetings were unnecessary.

"So you heard about that?"

"Alek told me. I'm calling you for your own protection. Alek meant what he said about you staying away from me. If you value your neck, I advise you not to try contacting me again." Her heart was in her throat, pounding so loudly she was sure he must be able to hear it.

"I think there must be some misunderstanding," Roger said in an incredulous tone. "I did meet with your husband. Actually, he's the one who contacted me, but your name didn't enter into the conversation. He wanted to talk to me about Phoenix Paints. He was hoping the two of us could strike some kind of deal. Naturally Ideal Paints is very interested."

"Good try, Roger, but it won't work."

He laughed that slightly demented laugh of his, as though she'd said something hilarious.

"I guess we'll just have to wait and see, won't we?" he added sarcastically.

Julia hung up the phone.

She sat there for several minutes with her hand on the receiver. When she found the strength, she stood, walked out of her office and directly past her assistant's desk.

"Ms. Conrad, are you feeling all right? You're terribly pale again."

Julia shrugged. "I'll be fine," she said, more brusquely than she'd intended.

"Have you thought about seeing a doctor?"

Julia didn't know any physician who specialized in treating broken hearts. Virginia frowned at her, waiting for a reply. "No, I don't…need one."

"I think you do. I'm going to make an appointment for you and ask for the first available opening. We can't have you walking around looking as if you're going to faint at any moment."

Julia barely heard her. She walked farther into the hall-way to the elevator and rode down to her brother's office.

Jerry stood when she walked in. "Julia! Sit down. You look like you're about to keel over."

If her brother was commenting on her appearance, she must resemble yesterday's oatmeal. "I'm fine," she lied.

"Do you need a glass of water?"

She shook her head. She hadn't come to discuss her health.

"I'm getting you one anyway. You look dreadful."

Julia pinched her lips together to bite back a cutting com-mentary, and didn't succeed. "How nice of you to say so."

Jerry chuckled and left his office, returning with a paper cup of water. He insisted Julia drink it, which she did. To her surprise she felt better afterward. But then, it was prob-ably impossible to feel any worse.…

"I imagine you're here to find out what Alek said," Jerry murmured. "He claims he confronted Roger and told him to leave you alone. I wish I'd done it myself."

"I talked to Roger myself."

Jerry froze and his eyes narrowed suspiciously. "You talked to Roger?"

"This morning."

"What did he say?" Jerry demanded. "Never mind, I can guess." He started pacing then as if holding still was more than he could manage. "Naturally he wasn't going to tell you what Alek actually said. What did you expect him to say, anyway? That he was shaking in his boots with fear? How could you do anything so stupid?"

"I…"

"I thought you were smarter than that!"

"Roger claims Alek tried to strike a deal with our strongest competitor," Julia said, trying hard to control her temper.

"I don't believe that for a minute."

Neither did Julia, not really, but she was so desperately afraid. She needed Jerry to confirm her belief in Alek, needed the reassurance that she wasn't making the same tragic mistake a second time.

"Don't you realize you're playing directly into Roger's hands? This is exactly what he was hoping would happen. He *wants* you to distrust Alek. You certainly made his day."

"I…hadn't thought of it like that," Julia admitted reluctantly. She was a fool not to leave the detective work to Rich Peck.

"You contacted Roger even knowing the kind of man he is, and expected him to tell the truth. You've done some stupid things in your time, Julia, but this one takes the cake."

Julia bristled. "The cake came three years ago, Jerry," she reminded him. "Complete with frosting, don't you remember? That was when I trusted Roger, when I believed in love and loyalty."

"You believe Alek, don't you?"

"Yes…" She did, and yet she had no confidence in her own judgment.

Jerry's eyes narrowed. "Then why'd you contact Roger?"

"Because I hoped…I don't know, I thought he might let something slip."

"He did that, all right, another pile of doubts for you to deal with." He rammed his hand through his hair. "Why on earth would you do anything so asinine?"

"I wish you'd quit saying that."

"It's true. Now are you going to believe in Alek or aren't you?"

With all her heart, she *wanted* to trust her husband, but she'd been badly hurt before. She'd zealously defended Roger, even when faced with overwhelming proof of his betrayal. Her faith in him had nearly destroyed her family.

"I take it you didn't fire him, then?" she asked.

"No. I won't, either. If you want him out of here, then you're going to have to do it yourself. I believe him, Julia, even if you don't."

"Jerry, please, try and understand. This is like waking up to my worst nightmare. Don't you think I *want* to believe him? So much that it's killing me."

"I can see that." He sighed. "Just leave it for now, Julia. Time will tell if he's being honest with us or not. For the record, I'm sure he is."

"I can't let the fate of the company ride on your instinct and your friendship with him. I can't take that kind of risk. I have no choice but to ask for his resignation."

Jerry's fists clenched at his side. "You can't do that."

"I'm the president of this company, I can do as I please." She didn't want to get hard-nosed about this, but her first obligation was to protect their family business. Jerry was silent as he absorbed her words. "So you're going to pull rank on me."

"I didn't mean it like that. The last thing we need to do now is argue with each other."

"If you ask Alek to go…"

"Jerry, please, I have to, don't you see?"

"If you ask for Alek's resignation," he started again, "you'll receive mine, as well."

Julia felt as if her own brother had kicked her in the stomach. "It's funny," she said unemotionally, "I remember saying those very same words to Dad three years ago. I believed Roger, remember?"

"A week," Jerry said. "We'll know more in another week. All I ask is that you give him the opportunity to prove himself."

"As I recall, I said something along those lines to Dad, too."

"Alek isn't Roger," Jerry said angrily. "What's it going to take to convince you of that?"

"I know he's not," she said vehemently. "Maybe it would be best if I was the one who resigned."

"Don't be ridiculous. Just give this time. If Alek sold us out, then there's nothing we can do about it now. The deed's done. It isn't going to hurt us any to sit on our doubts for the next few days. Promise me you'll do that."

"All right," Julia said. "One week, but then it's over, Jerry. Unless there's incontrovertible proof that Alek's telling the truth. If not, he goes and I can return to running this company the way it's supposed to be run."

Jerry's smile was fleeting. "I promise you, it's going to be different this time."

She stood to leave, then recalled her conversation with her husband that morning. "Alek mentioned an important meeting with marketing this afternoon." She gave Jerry the particulars. "He said he'd like us both to be there. Can you make it?"

Jerry nodded. "With a bit of juggling. You're going, too?"

"Yes," she said, but she wasn't looking forward to it.

* * *

Alek waited for Julia and Jerry to arrive. He watched the door anxiously, glancing repeatedly at his watch. Jerry was the first to show up; he walked into the conference room and took the chair next to Alek. Apart from them, the room was still empty.

"You talked to her?" Alek didn't need to explain who he meant.

Jerry nodded. "I've never seen her like this. It's tearing her apart."

"It hasn't been easy on any of us. I wish I knew how to clear my name. Julia would barely listen to me. It's as though she's blocked out everything and everyone, including me."

"It would be a lot easier if she were a man," Jerry muttered.

Alek arched his brows and laughed for the first time in days. "No, it wouldn't."

"Yeah, it would. I hate to stereotype, but maybe then she'd listen to reason. Sometimes I forget my sister is a woman— she clouds the issues with emotion."

Personally Alek had no trouble remembering Julia was female. "Not all women have been betrayed the way she was," he said. "I understand her fears, but at the same time I want her to believe what I say because she loves me and knows me well enough to realize I'd never do anything to hurt either of you. Until she does, there's nothing I can do."

"I don't know what Julia believes anymore and she doesn't either," Jerry said after a moment. "I talked her into giving the matter a week."

"A week," Alek repeated. "Nothing can happen in that short a time. The paint won't reach the market for another two to three weeks at the earliest."

"Unfortunately, there's more than that to consider from her point of view," Jerry said.

"She's miserable," Alek added. "She doesn't eat properly, she's working herself to death and she's sleeping poorly." In truth he wasn't in much better shape himself.

He loved Julia, but he couldn't force her to trust him, he couldn't demand that she believe him. She would have to come to those conclusions herself. In the meantime he was left feeling helpless and hopeless, and worst of all, defenseless. She was judging him solely on her experience with another man, one who'd hurt and betrayed her.

"I thought Stanhope was out of our lives once and for all," Jerry was saying. "I should've figured he'd be back since we're on the brink of a major product breakthrough. We should've been prepared."

"No one could have known."

"I should have," Jerry said, his lips thinning with annoyance. "Only this time Roger knows he doesn't have a chance of stealing anything, so he's undermining our trust in each other."

The marketing people rushed in with their displays. Most of what they'd be reviewing was geared toward television and radio advertising. The magazine ads had been done a month earlier and would be coming out in the latest issues of fifteen major publications.

The advertising executive glanced at his watch. Alek sighed. Jerry did, too. Everyone in the room was waiting for Julia.

"Virginia, please, I have a meeting with marketing."

"But I've got Dr. Feldon's office on the line. If you could wait just a few minutes."

Julia looked pointedly at her watch while her assistant haggled for the first opening in Dr. Feldon's already full appointment schedule.

"That'll be fine, I'll make sure she's there. Thank you for your help."

"Well?" Julia said when Virginia hung up.

"Five o'clock. The doctor's agreed to squeeze you in then."

Julia nodded. She wished now that she'd put her foot down about this appointment issue. A doctor wasn't going to be able to tell her anything she didn't already know. She was suffering from stress, which, given her circumstances, was understandable.

"You won't forget now, will you?" Virginia called after her as Julia headed for the elevator.

"No, I'll be there. Thank you for your trouble."

"You do what Dr. Feldon says, you hear? We can't have you getting sick every afternoon."

Julia grinned. The never-married Virginia was beginning to sound like a mother. "I'll see you in the morning," Julia said. "Why don't you take an early afternoon?" she suggested. "You deserve it for putting up with me."

Her assistant looked mildly surprised, then nodded. "Thank you, I will."

Every head turned when a breathless Julia burst into the conference room. "Sorry I'm late," she muttered, sitting in the chair closest to the door.

The marketing director smiled benignly and walked over to a television set that had been brought in for the demonstration. "I thought we'd start with the media blitz scheduled to air a week from this Thursday," he said as he inserted a DVD.

Julia couldn't help being aware of Alek. His eyes were on her from the moment she'd entered the room. She expected to feel his anger; instead she felt his love. Tears clogged her throat. It would've been less painful if she'd found him with another woman than to learn he'd been talking to Roger, no matter what his reason.

"Our ad agency tested this twenty-second commercial and is very pleased with its effectiveness."

The figure of a man and a woman came onto the screen. The husband was on a ladder painting the side of a house. The woman was working on the lawn below, painting a patio table with four matching chairs. Two children played serenely on a swing set in the background. The music was a classical piece she recognized but couldn't immediately name. The announcer's well-modulated voice came on but Julia couldn't hear what he was saying.

The room started to spin. The light fixtures faded in and out as though someone was controlling a dimmer switch. She thought she heard a woman cry out but even that seemed to be coming from far away.

When she regained consciousness, Julia found herself on the floor. She blinked up at the ceiling. Alek was crouched over her, his arm supporting the back of her neck. His eyes were filled with anxiety.

"What happened?" she asked.

"You fainted," Jerry said. He was kneeling beside her, holding her hand, patting it gently. "I'll say this for you, Julia, you certainly know how to get a man's heart going. You keeled right over."

"Where is everyone?"

"We had them leave. Alek and I will review the commercials later."

"I don't understand it," she said, struggling into a sitting position. "One moment I was perfectly fine and the next thing I knew, the room started whirling."

"I'll get her some water," Jerry said.

He left the room and Alek slid his arm behind her back, helped her into an upright sitting position and held her against his chest. She braced her hands against his ribs, intent on pushing herself free.

"No," he said, kissing her temple. "You can mistrust and hate me later, but for right now let me hold you."

"That's the problem," she whispered. "I believe you."

"Right now, we won't speak of this again. You've worked yourself into a state of collapse."

"I don't know what happened here, but I'm sure it's nothing important. I've just been overstressed, that's all."

Jerry returned with the water. "Why is it I'm always getting you water?" he joked, handing her a paper cup. "You'd think I'd gone to college to be a water boy instead of an attorney."

"I'm sorry," she said, pressing her hand to the side of her head. "I didn't mean to create such a commotion."

"Should we take her back to her office?" Jerry asked, looking at Alek.

"No, I'll take her home."

"If you don't mind, I prefer to make my own decisions," Julia stiffly informed them both. They made it sound as if she were a piece of furniture they couldn't decide where to place.

Leaning against the back of a chair, she stood. She felt a bit unstable, but that dizziness quickly passed. "I'm fine. You two go about your business and I'll go about mine."

"Julia, for heaven's sakes, would you listen to common

sense? You just fainted," Jerry informed her, as if she hadn't figured it out yet.

"I know that."

"Let Alek take you home."

"No."

"I think she'd feel more comfortable if you took her," Alek suggested.

"I *fainted*," she told both men, "I didn't have a lobotomy. Let me assure you, I'm perfectly capable of making my own decisions, and I'm not leaving my office until I'm finished with what I need to do."

"Some of those decisions should be questioned," Jerry snapped.

"Jerry."

"Shut up, Alek, this is between me and my sister. She's an emotional and physical wreck because of this mess and to complicate matters she decides to play detective herself."

"I don't understand."

"Jerry, could we discuss this another time?" Julia asked pointedly.

"No. Alek has a right to know. Tell him."

"Julia?" Alek turned to face her. "What's Jerry talking about?"

She flashed her brother a scathing look. "It's nothing."

"Fine, I'll tell him. Julia had the bright idea of calling Roger Stanhope herself and playing this crazy game with him. She said she knew about the meeting between the two of you."

Alek's gaze narrowed. "And what did Stanhope say?"

"You can well imagine."

"I didn't believe Roger," Julia said. "I never did." Jerry was right, contacting Roger hadn't been the smartest thing she'd ever done, but she was desperate.

"What my sister failed to remember is that Roger isn't stupid. She was fishing for information and he knew it, so he made up this ridiculous story about you trying to strike a deal with Ideal Paints."

Alek released a one-word expletive.

"It's driving her crazy," Jerry continued. "She looked terrible when she came to see me this morning."

Julia watched her husband. He was distancing himself from her, physically and emotionally, freezing her out.

"She must make her own decision and I must make mine." Without another word, Alek turned and left the conference room.

"I wish you hadn't said anything to him about my talk with Roger."

"Why not? He had a right to know."

Her lack of faith—and the fact that she'd acted on it—had hurt Alek. She'd seen it in his eyes and in the way he'd stiffened and moved away from her. Covering her face with her hands, Julia slowly exhaled.

"I have to go," she whispered. "I'll talk to you tomorrow."

Julia's head was pounding as she walked out of the conference room. She checked the time, wanting to know how long she had before her appointment with Dr. Feldon. The physician had been treating her family for the past fifteen years and knew Julia well.

She arrived at his office at one minute past five and was ushered directly into the exam room. His nurse asked her a series of questions.

"Basically, I've been under a lot of stress lately," Julia explained. "This afternoon the craziest thing happened. I fainted. Me! I can't believe it."

After taking her temperature and her blood pressure, Dr. Feldon's nurse asked for a urine sample.

Minutes later, she was joined by Dr. Feldon. His hair was grayer than the last time she'd seen him and he was a little thicker around the waist.

"Julia, it's good to see you, although I wish it were under different circumstances. Now tell me what the problem is."

The tears came as a surprise and an acute embarrassment. "I…I'm just not myself lately. There's been so much happening with the company and I've been so stressed, and today I fainted right in the middle of a marketing meeting. I gave my husband and my brother quite a scare."

"Yes, I heard you got married. Congratulations."

She smiled weakly in response.

Dr. Feldon reached for a tissue and pressed it into her hand. "How are you feeling now?"

She had to stop and think about it. "A little woozy."

"And emotional?"

She nodded, paused, then blew her nose.

"I'd say this is all normal, my dear. Most pregnant women experience these symptoms."

Twelve

"Pregnant?" Julia repeated in a shocked whisper. "You mean all this, the nausea and the fainting spell, is because I'm going to have a baby?"

"No, I think the stress you've talked about is complicating the symptoms."

"But I don't have morning sickness."

"A good many women don't. Some have what you might call afternoon sickness instead. My guess is that you're one of those."

"I should've realized...." Julia began, wondering why she hadn't recognized her condition herself.

"As you probably know I stopped delivering babies several years back. I can recommend an excellent obstetrician. I'll have my receptionist make an appointment for you, if you'd like. Her name is Dr. Lois Brandt and my patients who've had babies delivered by her have been very pleased."

"Yes, that would be fine." Julia was both excited and surprised, although heaven knew she had no right to be. "How...far along do you think I am?"

Dr. Feldon chuckled. "My estimate is about two weeks."

She nodded, knowing it couldn't be much more than that, astonished, too, that her pregnancy could be detected so early.

"I'm going to prescribe prenatal vitamins and have you start watching your diet. According to those ridiculous charts the insurance companies put out, you're about five pounds underweight. Don't skip meals, and make an effort to eat from the major food groups every day. Plenty of fresh fruit and vegetables," he emphasized.

Smiling, Julia nodded. Dr. Feldon made it sound as if she were pregnant with a rabbit instead of a baby.

She left the office a few minutes later, her step lighter. *A baby.* She was going to have a baby. Alek would—

Alek.

Her thoughts came to a skidding halt. This complicated everything tenfold. There was far more at stake now than before. There was far more involved. They'd introduced a tiny being into the equation.

Julia's steps slowed. She wasn't sure what to do or say to him, if anything. At least, not yet. He had a right to know, but Julia wasn't convinced now was the time to tell him.

She returned to her condominium and let herself in. Two steps into the entry, she nearly stumbled over a large leather suitcase.

She heard movement in the master bedroom and walked down the hallway leading to it. Alek stood inside the walk-in closet, carefully removing his clothes from their hangers. Another large leather suitcase yawned open on top of the bed.

"Alek? What are you doing?"

He continued his work without looking at her. "It should be obvious."

"You're moving out," she whispered and the truth hit her like a slap of icy rain. Alek was leaving.

"I knew you'd figure it out sooner or later." He walked over to his suitcase and carefully folded his shirts and placed them inside.

"Where will you be living?"

"I don't know yet. I don't believe there's any reason for us to stay in touch after I move out."

"What about at the office? I mean—"

"As of four-thirty this afternoon I am no longer an employee of Conrad Industries."

Julia's heart froze at what his words implied. "I see.... You're going to work for Ideal Paints."

He whirled around to face her. "No, Julia, I am not going to work for the competition. I know it means nothing to you, but the Berinski word of honor is all I have to offer you as proof. On the grave of my father, I swear I would never do anything to hurt you or Jerry. That includes betraying you to Ideal Paints or any other of your competitors." He spun back around and resumed his task, his movements abrupt and hurried as if he was eager to be on his way. Julia didn't want him to leave, but she couldn't ask him to stay, either.

"Why now?" she asked, sitting on the edge of the bed. She wasn't sure her shaky legs would support her. She felt as if she was about to burst into tears, which would have embarrassed them both.

"I'd hoped that given time you'd see the truth, but I no longer believe that's possible."

"Why not?"

"If you believe Stanhope's word over mine, then I have to accept that you're not capable of recognizing the truth when you hear it."

Julia had no argument to give him, although her doubts

and fears were beginning to mount. "Do you want a divorce?"

He went still for a moment, as if the question required some consideration. "That's up to you. I told you once that my religion forbids it."

Julia relaxed a little, but not much.

"I can't live with you, Julia, and I can't see ever living with you again."

"It wasn't so bad, was it?" she said, looking for something, anything, to bring them back together, to force him to acknowledge his love for her. She was tempted to tell him her news, but if he stayed, she wanted it to be because he loved her and not because she'd trapped him.

"No, Julia, living with you wasn't bad—if you don't mind a porcupine for a wife."

She sucked in her breath at the pain his words caused.

His shoulders sagged and he exhaled sharply. "I shouldn't have said that. I apologize."

"I've hurt you, too."

He didn't respond, but she knew she *had* hurt him. He was intent on his packing and refused to look up. He closed the suitcase, then dragged it from the bed and carried it into the other room, setting it beside the first one.

"If you forget anything, where would you like me to send it?" she asked, hoping to appear helpful when she was actually looking for a means of staying in contact.

He frowned, then said, "Give it to Anna. She'll know where I am." He paused. "I trust you're willing to let her go on working here? Until she gets another job? She hopes to be hired as a translator soon."

She nodded. "Yes. Of course. But…I think you might be acting a bit hastily, don't you? Why don't you give it some thought?" This was as far as she was willing to go. She wouldn't ask him to stay, wouldn't plead with him or make an issue of his going. Those choices were his.

"There's nothing to think about," he told her stiffly. "Goodbye, Julia." He added something softly in Russian, then opened the door, reached for his suitcases and walked out of the condominium. And her life.

Julia stood for a moment, so stunned and feeling so bereft that she couldn't move. Or breathe. Or think. Those abilities returned slowly. Taking small, deliberate steps, she walked into the living room, collapsing onto the white leather sofa.

She'd had the most dreadful day. Within the space of a few hours, she'd fainted, learned she was pregnant and been abandoned by her husband. The prospects for the future didn't look bright. Except for the baby...

The phone rang fifteen minutes later and Julia grabbed it, thinking, praying, it was Alek. "Hello," she answered quickly.

"Julia, have you seen Alek? You've got to talk some sense into him! I just got back to my office and found his letter of resignation. What do you know about this? Listen, don't answer that, just put him on the line. I'll convince him he's overreacting."

"I can't," she said, biting her lower lip. "I really wish I could, but...Alek's not living here anymore."

"What do you mean?"

"He moved out. He was packing when I got home."

"Why didn't you stop him?"

"How?"

"Oh, I don't know," Jerry said with heavy sarcasm. "Maybe you could've told him you believe in him and trust him. You might've thanked him for working two long years on the project that's going to take this company's profit line right off the page. You could even have told him you love him and didn't want him to go."

Julia, who was crying softly by then, sniffled. "Yeah, I guess I could."

"Do you believe him now?"

"I...don't know. I think I do, because not trusting him hurts too much."

Jerry swore under his breath, then sighed loudly. "You've got a really bad sense of timing. Did anyone ever tell you that?"

"No," she said, wiping the tears from her cheek.

"Go to him, Julia," Jerry advised, "before it's too late."

"It's already too late," she whispered. "I don't know where he is and he didn't want to tell me."

The following morning, Julia was waiting for her sister-in-law. "Good morning, Anna," she said when the woman arrived.

Alek's sister frowned and didn't respond. She walked over to the broom closet, took out her apron and tied it around her waist, all the while ignoring Julia.

"I guess you heard that Alek moved out?" Julia asked, following her.

Still Anna didn't acknowledge her. She opened the refrigerator and removed a carton of eggs.

"Do you know where he is?"

"Of course. He is my brother."

"Would you mind telling me?"

"So you can hurt him more? So you can think terrible things of him? So you can insult his honor? No, I will not tell you anything about my brother."

"I love him," Julia whispered. "I've just been so afraid. You see, three years ago I loved a man who betrayed my

family and me. I believed him when I shouldn't have. I defended him, and my father and I got into a terrible argument and my father...while we were fighting he suffered a
heart attack. He died and I felt so incredibly guilty. I blamed
myself." Anna had turned to face Julia, her face white and
emotionless. "Can you understand why it was so difficult
for me to believe Alek? Can you see why I'm skeptical after
all the things that have happened?" Tears were very close
to the surface, but she held them back, crumpling a tissue
in her hand until it was a small wad.

"My brother would never betray you."

"I know that. In a way, I've always known that."

"Alek isn't this other man."

"I realize that, too, but...because of my experience with
this...other man, I made a mistake and gave Alek reason to
believe I doubted him." She stopped, because arguing her
case with Alek's sister wasn't going to help.

She dressed for work with no enthusiasm. In another ten
days, Phoenix Paints would be on sale to the public. Conrad
Industries had developed a whole new kind of paint, several kinds, in fact, thanks to her father's dream and Alek's
genius. Somehow it all seemed empty now. The purpose
that had driven her all these years meant nothing without
Alek at her side.

Jerry was waiting in her office. "Did you find out where
he's staying?"

Julia shook her head. "His sister wouldn't tell me. I don't
blame her. If our positions were reversed, I wouldn't tell
her, either."

"I'll get Rich on it right away."

"No," she said quietly. "Leave Alek his pride. I've robbed
him of everything else." She walked around her desk and
sat down. Reaching for her desk calendar, she flipped the

pages ahead eight months. "I'm going to need some extensive time off soon."

"We all need a vacation, Julia."

"This is going to be more than a two-week vacation, Jerry. I'll need maternity leave."

Alek sat at a table in the library, where he came to spend part of every day. He'd moved into another small furnished apartment, near Anna's, and came here to read—and primarily to escape his own four walls. Books were his comfort, his consolation.

Perhaps that was his problem. He knew more about books than people. He had badly bungled his marriage. It'd been over a week since he'd seen Julia. Two weeks since he'd moved out of their condominium—*her* condominium, he corrected.

He'd seen her interviewed on a local television station the day Phoenix Paints hit the market. She'd looked pale and so beautiful he hadn't been able to take his eyes off the television screen. Long after her face vanished from view, he'd continued to stare at the television, not even seeing.

She'd answered the reporter's questions, explained her father's vision for the paint industry and how Alek had seen it to fruition. Alek had been surprised that she'd mentioned his name, credited him with the innovations. Paints that changed color, paints developed for easy removal, paints that were guaranteed to last into the next generation.

Alek thought long and hard about what she'd said, wondering if she was trying to tell him something. If she was, he'd missed it. He was worried about her; she looked drained, but jubilant. Jerry was with her and had responded to some of the questions.

Alek closed the book he was reading. He relied on Anna

for information about Julia, but his sister had grown stubborn, refusing to give him the detailed answers he sought. She seemed to think that if he was so curious, he should talk to Julia himself.

Alek considered her suggestion. He'd left because he couldn't tolerate her mistrust.

His gaze fell onto his swollen, bruised knuckles and he flexed his hand. Standing, he returned the book to the shelf and picked up his jacket. It was raining outside, a cold, persistent drizzle. His hair was drenched by the time he'd gone a single block.

It was while he was passing a large parked van that he glanced at the side mirror—and caught the reflection of a man in a beige raincoat behind him. He'd seen this same man in the library. Alek wondered. It would be foolish to believe he was being followed. Then again, he'd lived in a country where it wasn't uncommon for citizens to disappear and never be heard from again.

He stepped into an alley and waited. The man casually strolled past and continued down the walkway. Alek expelled his breath, thinking he'd become fanciful. Then again, it wouldn't be beneath Stanhope to hire someone to injure him.

No, he decided, Stanhope was just the type to have someone else do his dirty work for him.

Alek walked for several blocks until he reached the Seattle waterfront, which had become one of his favorite places. The fish and chips were excellent and there was a covered eating space along the pier. It was late afternoon, and he hadn't eaten since breakfast, so he purchased a double order and carried it onto the farthest end of the dock. Here he could look out over the water; he enjoyed viewing the nautical activity on Puget Sound. He claimed a picnic table and sat down to enjoy his dinner.

He was lost in thought, apparently, because he didn't notice the man in the raincoat until he was directly in front of him.

"I guess I'd better sit down and introduce myself," the man said. He held out his hand. "Rich Peck."

Alek stood and they exchanged handshakes. "Hello. Alek Berinski."

"You figured out I was following you, didn't you?" Uninvited, Peck sat down at the table, across from Alek.

Alek shrugged. "I had my suspicions."

"Huh," Peck muttered, "I must be getting sloppy."

"There was a reason you've been tracking my movements?"

Peck grinned, that cocky grin Alek often saw in American men. "There generally is a reason. And it usually involves someone paying me. Rather handsomely, I might add."

Alek looked at him, confused. "Are you saying Roger Stanhope paid you to follow me?"

"Stanhope? Don't bet on it. The man hasn't got two dimes to rub together. Oh, by the way, I heard about your little skirmish with him. Provoking him into taking the first swing was smart. I heard he tried to hit you from behind. The man's a sleaze. Are you pressing assault charges against him?"

"No, I decided I'd punished him enough. I know one thing for sure. He'll stay out of Julia's life now. He knows what will happen to him if he doesn't."

"Listen, Stanhope's got more problems than you know," Peck went on to say. "He'll be happy to stay away from anything to do with Conrad Industries for the next fifteen years. If he lives that long, which I personally doubt. He borrowed money from the wrong kind of people, if you know what I mean."

"You know a lot about this…slimeball." That was an American expression Alek found particularly fitting.

Peck shrugged. "I was paid to learn what I could. The guy's an open book. You, on the other hand, weren't so easy to track down. Your sister wouldn't tell me a thing. She pretended she didn't understand English."

"Who hired you to follow me?" Alek was growing bored with this detailed speech.

"Sorry, but that's privileged information."

"Julia?" His heart pounded hard with excitement.

"Nope. My lips are sealed. But I can tell you it *isn't* her. She doesn't know anything about this, although what I'm supposed to tell you concerns her."

Alek was beginning to think he didn't like Peck as much as he initially had. "Then tell me."

Peck arched his brows at Alek's less than patient tone. "First, let me ask you a couple of questions."

"I don't have time for this." Alek surged to his feet and stalked away. He half expected Peck to follow him, but when the investigator didn't get up, he slowed his pace.

Alek had gone a block before he recognized his mistake. His impatience had cost him what he'd wanted most, information about Julia. He turned back, walking at a fast clip. He need not have worried; Peck was sitting at the table, enjoying the fish-and-chips dinner Alek had hastily left behind.

Alek stood over him and Peck licked his fingers. "I thought you might have a change of heart."

"Tell me."

"No problem. There's something Jerry thought you'd like

to know about his sister. She's going to be a mother. If I understand correctly, that means you're about to become a daddy."

Alek felt as if he'd had his legs knocked out from under him. He literally slumped onto the picnic table. "When?"

"Don't know. But I don't think she's very far along. A month, maybe two."

"Have you seen her? Is she healthy?"

Peck shrugged. "The last time I did, she was a little green around the gills."

Another crazy American idiom, one that made no sense to him at all. "Green gills? What does that mean?"

"You know, a little under the weather."

Alek's confusion increased. "Say it in plain English, please."

"Okay, okay. She's sick every afternoon. Jerry says it's like watching Old Faithful. About three-fifteen her assistant leads her to the ladies' room so she can lose her lunch. It's perfectly normal from what I understand. Not that I know much about pregnant women."

Alek felt as if someone were sitting on his chest and the weight kept increasing. A baby. *His* baby. Julia was going to have his baby.

He stood up again, frowning. He had a right to know, and the news shouldn't have come from his brother-in-law, either. Julia should have told him herself.

A low, burning anger simmered in his blood. He was angry, angrier than he'd been in a long time, and he wasn't about to let this go.

"You tell Jerry something for me," Alek muttered.

"Sure."

He paused. He didn't have any cause to be angry with

Jerry. His friend had taken the initiative and sent Peck to tell him what he should've been told from the beginning—by Julia. And he himself had been avoiding Jerry, at least for now—*because* of Julia.

"You wanted me to pass something along to Jerry?" Peck pressed.

"Yeah," Alek said, feeling the beginnings of a smile. "Tell him I think he's going to make a very good uncle."

Julia took another bite of her celery stalk, then set it back on the plate. Her attention wavered from her book for only an instant while she reached for a slice of apple.

The manual, one she'd recently picked up at a bookstore, described the stages of pregnancy week by exciting week. She kept the book hidden from Anna and brought it out in the evenings. By the time Junior was ready to be born, she'd practically have the whole three hundred pages memorized.

She called the baby Junior, although she didn't know yet if it was a boy or a girl. Funny, only a couple of weeks ago she hadn't even known she was pregnant, and now it seemed as though the baby had always been a part of her.

At night, she slept with her hand on her stomach. She talked to Junior, carrying on lengthy conversations with her unborn child.

Jerry and Virginia had become ridiculously vigilant. Julia swore her assistant suffered more from her bouts of afternoon sickness than Julia did herself. And Jerry. She smiled as she thought about her brother and how solicitous he'd become. He was constantly asking after her health. He'd even gone so far as to contact Dr. Feldon about her daily bouts of afternoon sickness.

She had been to see Dr. Brandt and liked the young, attractive woman very much. Thanks to her and the pregnancy book she'd recommended, Julia understood far better the changes that were taking place within her body.

She tried not to think about Alek, tried not to dwell on how much she missed him. Or the mistakes she'd made in her brief marriage. Sooner or later she'd have to get in touch with him. She needed to tell him about the baby. And to thank him. Phoenix Paints had taken the market by storm. A national television network had called today wanting to do a news piece on the ideas behind the innovative paints.

She owed Alek so much and she'd treated him so poorly.

She hadn't asked Anna his whereabouts since that first morning. His sister didn't volunteer any information about Alek even when Julia asked. Julia didn't think Anna had forgiven her yet for hurting her brother.

She pressed her hand to her stomach and whispered, "Your daddy is a wonderful man, Junior. He's going to love you so much."

She took another bite of the celery stalk and turned the page of her text. Labor and delivery. She'd read this chapter first, the same night she'd bought the book, wanting to learn everything she could on the subject.

When she did deliver Junior, she hoped Alek would be there to coach her. From what she'd seen of Jerry, he wouldn't last ten minutes in a delivery room. And Virginia wouldn't be able to take watching her in pain, Julia was convinced of that.

When she'd finished her snack, Julia moved into the living room to exercise. She turned on the television and inserted the low-impact prenatal aerobics DVD. Ten minutes later she was huffing and puffing and sweating enough to dampen the gray T-shirt she wore.

"I hope you appreciate this," she told the baby.

After a full thirty minutes, she went into the kitchen, got a glass from the cupboard and gulped down some water. After that, she grabbed a pencil and marked the schedule posted on the refrigerator. Anna thought it was a diet sheet and it was. Sort of. Julia listed the food she ate, plus her water intake. Eight glasses a day, no excuses.

That was another interesting aspect of her condition. Her life was now ruled by how long it would take her to reach a bathroom. She'd considered having one installed in her office because it was so disruptive to hurry down the hall every hour, and sometimes more often. The eight glasses of water didn't help matters.

She was feeling better, though, and for that Julia was grateful. The first couple of weeks after Alek had moved out she'd felt as if she were living in a nightmare. She did what needed to be done, performed her duties, ate, worked and slept, but did it all with a low-grade sense of dejection—and with an air of expectancy. She couldn't seem to let go of the idea that Alek would come into her office one day the way he used to. It was the hope of seeing him again, of telling him about the baby, that had kept her going. That and, of course, her happiness about the baby.

The doorbell rang and Julia ripped the sweatband from her forehead. It was probably Jerry, who'd taken to checking up on her in the evenings.

But it wasn't. When she opened the door, Alek stood before her, looking more furious than she'd ever seen him.

Thirteen

"Alek." Julia couldn't say anything more. He looked wonderful, while she must have resembled a towel that had been sitting at the bottom of the dirty-clothes hamper.

"I just heard you're pregnant. Is that true?" His eyes were hard as granite. He was furious with her and didn't bother to disguise it.

"It's true."

"You might have told me. I played an important role in this event."

"Yes, I know, it's just that..." She realized she'd left him standing in the hallway outside the condo. Opening the door wider, she said, "Come inside, please."

"You weren't going to tell me about the baby?" He was frowning.

"Of course I intended to tell you!"

"When?"

"Would you care to sit down?"

"No, just answer the question."

Julia ignored the demand in his voice. "Would you like something to drink?"

"Just answer the question!"

"There's no reason to yell. I was going to tell you, how could I not? This baby is as much a part of you as of me. How could I keep something this important from you?" She hoped that would appease him.

"That's my question exactly." Alek's hands were knotted into fists at his sides. Julia wanted to think that meant he was restraining himself from holding her—not simply expressing his frustration.

She started to walk into the kitchen. He hesitated, then followed her. She poured a glass of water for him and then one for herself and set them down on the kitchen table.

"Anna knew?"

"No. I couldn't tell her. I was afraid she'd say something to you." Her explanation didn't satisfy him; if anything, his scowl darkened.

Julia pulled out a chair and sat. Alek did, too. Avoiding his probing eyes, she lowered her gaze to her water glass. "I'm drinking two quarts of water every day now. Eight full glasses… I'm keeping track of my intake on that sheet on the fridge."

"The baby needs water?"

"In a manner of speaking, I guess, but actually it's me the doctor's concerned about."

"Why is the doctor concerned?"

She hadn't said this to alarm Alek. It was just conversation, a way to ease the tension between them. "I'm perfectly healthy, Alek. Don't look so worried."

"Then why is your doctor concerned?"

"That's her job. She keeps a close eye on my health and the baby's. So far I'm having a perfectly normal pregnancy. That's what my doctor says. So does the book." She reached across the table for the manual she'd read from cover to cover three times over. "Junior's doing just great."

"Junior?"

"That's what I call him...or her."

The anger had faded and in its place Julia saw a love and devotion so deep it wounded her. To think she'd abused that love and mistrusted his word. Her throat grew thick. Tears filled her eyes.

"Julia."

She looked away. "Don't worry, it's all part of this pregnancy thing. I'm very emotional. The other night I started crying over a TV ad." She didn't tell him it was the one for Phoenix Paints. The tears had come because she'd realized how much she missed her husband.

Alek passed her his handkerchief.

"Thanks." She dabbed her eyes. "Look on page fifty-three. It explains why a woman's more likely to cry when she's pregnant."

Alek flipped through the pages until he found the one she'd mentioned. He scanned the text and nodded.

"How have you been feeling?"

She shrugged. "All right, I guess. I don't get sick in the mornings the way most women do. I usually get nauseous around three-thirty in the afternoon. I don't know why I bother with lunch since it comes right back up again."

"Have you had any other problems?"

"No," she was quick to assure him. "Actually, I've been feeling great. And the nausea should be over soon." She smiled. "You'll be proud of me. I've been eating well, with lots of fresh fruit and vegetables." She stopped when she noticed the way he was staring at her. "Is something wrong?"

Alek's eyes left hers and he shook his head. "Never mind."

"No, tell me, please."

He hesitated and Julia felt a jolt of fear. She'd read about this, in the very book that rested on the table between her and Alek. Some men were turned off by their wives during pregnancy.

"You are more beautiful than ever," Alek whispered.

Julia bit her lower lip and a sigh trembled through her.

"That disappoints you?"

"I'm not beautiful, Alek. Judging by the way Jerry and my assistant are constantly fussing over me, I must look awful."

Emotion produced a second quivering sigh. "I've missed you so much," she admitted. "I wanted to tell you about the baby right away.... I learned I was pregnant the afternoon you moved out. I came home from the doctor's office to find you packing."

"And you didn't tell me then?" he bellowed.

"Would it have changed anything if I *had* told you?" she asked calmly.

"Yes," he answered, then lowered his gaze. "I don't know."

"I'd hurt you and was hurting so badly myself. If I'd told you about Junior then, I was afraid it might sound like blackmail."

"You realize now that I would never betray you?"

"I knew it then, I always knew it...in my heart. I just did a poor job of showing you. I couldn't get past my own fears." A tear ran from the corner of her eye. "No words can ever express how sorry I am for the pain I caused you. When we got married, I didn't expect to fall in love with you. I'd steeled myself against it. I'd been in love once before and, as you know, the experience cost me and others dearly.

"A green-card marriage seemed workable. I was determined not to involve my heart, but day after day you treated me with love and affection, chipping away at my defenses no matter how much I fortified them.

"When Ruth died... I don't think I would've survived that time without you. Your comfort and love meant the world to me. I'll always treasure our day at the beach."

She stopped to catch her breath and to keep her voice from cracking. "This much is a fact—I love you, Alek, and I'm deeply sorry for the pain I caused you. I swear I'll never doubt you again." Tears fell unheeded from her eyes.

"Don't cry, Julia."

She noticed he didn't call her *my love* the way he so often had in the past. Covering her face with her hands, she wiped away the moisture, expelled a sigh and forced herself to smile. "I know it's a lot to ask, but could you ever find it in your heart to forgive me for contacting Roger?"

"If you can forgive me for letting my pride stand in the way."

"Your pride? Oh, Alek, I trampled over it a hundred times, and still you loved me. I didn't know how to deal with love and I made so many mistakes."

"I made my own mistakes."

"I asked Anna about you countless times, but she refuses to talk about you. I don't think she's forgiven me for hurting you."

"Ah, my sister," Alek said slowly. "She played the same game with me. I asked her about you so often, she finally told me that if I was so curious, I should go ask you myself."

"She was right, you know. Neither of us had any business putting her in the middle, pumping her for information about the other."

"I agree. But I still don't like it that you didn't tell me about our baby."

Julia thought her heart would melt at the tender way he said *baby*. Alek was going to be a wonderful father. She hadn't gone into this marriage with any great expectations; she hadn't thought she'd be married long, despite her undeniable attraction to him. Falling in love with Alek had come as a delightful surprise.

His gentleness, his patience, his comfort had seen her through that bleak time surrounding Ruth's final days and the dark weeks that followed. Without him, she would have become lost and tormented. How wise of Ruth to recognize the type of man Alek was. To recognize that he would become her compass, guiding her toward happiness.

"I would've eventually found a way of getting in touch with you," Julia said. "Soon, too.... I don't know how much longer I would've been able to keep this baby to myself." She stopped talking, realizing Alek had come to her because he'd learned of her condition. Slowly she raised her eyes to his. "Who told you I was pregnant?"

If Jerry had known where Alek was all this time, she'd have a few words to say to him.

"Does it matter?"

"Yes."

"All right, if you must know, a private detective told me."

"You hired a detective to—"

"No, Jerry was the one who did the hiring. A man named Peck. Your brother thought it was my right to know about the baby."

It didn't escape Julia's notice that he still hadn't referred to her as his love.

"I see," she said. "And now that you know, what do you expect to happen?"

He frowned. "That depends on several matters."

"Yes?" she pressed when he didn't elaborate. "What sort of matters?"

"I'll expect to be a major part of our child's life."

Julia nodded in full agreement; she was hoping he'd be a major part of her life, too. "I'd like that. Is there anything else?" she asked when he didn't continue.

Alek seemed to need time to think over his response. "I'd very much like to be your husband," he finally said, "to live with you and love you and perhaps have another child. Would this be agreeable to you?"

She threw her arms around his neck with such fervor that she nearly toppled the chair he was sitting on.

"Be careful, my love…."

"Say that again." She choked out the words through her tears. "Call me your love. Oh, Alek, I've missed hearing that so much. Wait, kiss me first." She had so many requests he obviously didn't know which one to comply with first. It didn't take him long, though, to direct her mouth to his.

"My love."

"Oh, Alek."

"Julia."

Their names were trapped between two hungry mouths. Between two eagerly beating hearts.

Their mouths strained toward each other. Julia felt the emotion rise within her. She'd missed him so much, more than she dared to admit even to herself. He was speaking to her in Russian, short snatches of words between frantic kisses.

She tightened her arms around his neck.

He surprised her by standing and carrying her into the bedroom. "You are so romantic," she told him, languishing in his arms.

"I plan to get a whole lot more romantic in about thirty seconds." His intentions were clear as he lovingly placed her on the bed.

"Oh, good.... Hurry, Alek, I've needed you so much."

He stripped while she watched him, marveling at his maleness and his readiness for her. Sitting up, Julia struggled out of her T-shirt and tossed it aside. Her tennis shoes came next. "I really should shower," she commented as the spandex pants flew in the opposite direction.

"No time now," Alek said. "Later, we'll shower together."

"But I just finished a workout."

"And you're about to start another," he said.

Long minutes later, they were exhausted, panting in each other's arms, their bodies linked, their hands and hearts entwined.

"I love you, Alek."

"You are my love," he returned as their bodies thrilled, excited and satisfied each other.

Julia slept in her husband's arms afterward, her head on his chest. When she stirred into wakefulness, she found his hand pressed against her abdomen and heard him communicating in whispers to his child. Since he was speaking Russian, she could only speculate on what he was saying.

He noticed her looking at him and smiled shyly. "I told him to be good to his mother."

"Him?"

"A daughter would please me just as well." He smiled. "Someday a young man will come to me and thank me for having fathered such a beautiful daughter. Wait, and you'll see that I'm right."

"Someday a young woman will come to me and tell me our son is totally awesome, or whatever expression is popular at the time." She wrinkled her nose. "They change every few years, you realize."

"I sometimes go crazy with the things you Americans say. Your strange idioms and slang—they're constantly changing."

"Don't worry, you'll catch on. I'll help you."

"Awesome," he said with a mischievous grin.

They showered and Julia dressed in a thick terry-cloth robe and padded barefoot into the kitchen. "I don't know about you, but I'm starved."

Alek grinned again. "I see your appetite has increased."

It was true. "I suppose it has." She opened the refrigerator and took out a container of ice cream and served them both large bowls.

"Should we call Jerry?" Julia asked. "We seem to owe him a great deal."

"No, I don't want to share you with anyone just yet. Tomorrow will be soon enough. We'll invite him and Anna," he said, and Julia nodded delightedly.

They sat in the living room, cuddled against each other, eating their ice cream. "The late news is on," Julia commented. "Okay with you if I turn it on?"

"Of course." He took the empty bowl and set it aside. Then he brought her back against him. His roving hands distracted Julia from her intention and she gasped at the sensation that shot through her.

"I keep up with current events as much as I can," she

said, trying to get her mind *off* the subject at hand. "I missed the earlier newscast because I had a doctor's appointment."

Alek's eyes widened with concern.

"It was the dentist, don't worry." She leaned forward to pick up the remote control. The screen flared to life just as the sportscaster began the latest update on the Mariners. It was heavenly to sit quietly with Alek's arms around her.

"I will take our son to baseball games," Alek announced, "and the library."

"I hope you intend to take your daughter and your wife while you're at it."

"Whoever wishes to go," he said, as though their family was already complete and they were making ordinary, everyday plans.

Julia smiled to herself.

After the sports news, they watched the five-day weather forecast. "I hope it rains every day," Alek whispered close to her ear. "That way I can keep you in the apartment, or better yet, in our bed."

"I've got news for you," Julia whispered, kissing his lips, still cold from the ice cream. "You don't need an excuse to take me to bed. In case you haven't noticed, I'm crazy about you."

"I noticed," he said with a satisfied smile. "And I approve."

Soon they were kissing again. They would have continued, Julia was certain, if the newscaster hadn't returned to announce the breaking news stories of the day.

"Ideal Paints, a national paint manufacturer based here in Seattle, has declared bankruptcy. As many as three hundred jobs have been lost."

Julia was stunned. "I knew they were having financial difficulties," she said, breaking away from Alek. "But I didn't realize it was that serious."

"They couldn't hope to compete with Conrad Industries any longer," Alek told her. "Stanhope hurt them, but it took them three years to feel the effects. Their whole developmental program came to a halt after he sold them the formula for guaranteed twenty-five-year paint. They had the latest advance without having gone through the learning process, without the trial and error that comes with any major progress. It set them back."

Julia had never thought of it in those terms. What she did remember was something Ruth had told her years earlier, when revenge and justice had ranked high on her list. Her grandmother had insisted time had a way of correcting injustices, and she'd been right.

"I wonder what'll happen to Roger," she said absently, almost feeling sorry for him.

"He's finished in the business world," Alek said calmly. "It's a well-known fact he sold out Conrad Industries. No company's going to risk hiring an employee with questionable loyalty and ethics. He'll be lucky to find any kind of job."

"Everything's come full circle," Julia said, leaning into her husband's strength. He wrapped his arms around her waist and she pressed her hands over his. "Everything I lost has been returned to me a hundredfold."

Alek kissed her neck. "Same for me."

"I didn't know it was possible to be this happy. Only a few years ago I felt as if my whole life was over, and now it seems to get better every day." Leaning back, she reached upward for her husband's kiss.

* * * * *

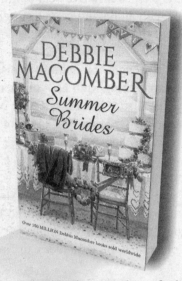

Finding love was never easy...

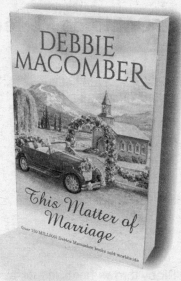

The alarm on Hallie McCarthy's biological clock
is buzzing. She's hitting the big three-0 and
there's no prospect of marriage, no man in sight.
But Hallie's got a plan. She's giving herself a
year to meet her very own Mr Right...

Except all her dates are disasters. Too bad she can't
just fall for her good-looking neighbour, Steve
Marris—who's definitely *not* her type.

HARLEQUIN®MIRA®
www.mirabooks.co.uk

MILLS & BOON®

It's Got to be Perfect

IT'S GOT
TO BE
Perfect

UNCORRECTED
PROOF COPY

HALEY HILL

* cover in development

When Ellie Rigby throws her three-carat engagement ring into the gutter, she is certain of only one thing. She has yet to know true love!

Fed up with disastrous internet dates and conflicting advice from her friends, Ellie decides to take matters into her own hands. Starting a dating agency, Ellie becomes an expert in love. Well, that is until a match with one of her clients, charming, infuriating Nick, has her questioning everything she's ever thought about love...

**Order yours today at
www.millsandboon.co.uk**

Loved this book?
Let us know!

Find us on **Twitter @Mira_BooksUK**
where you can share your thoughts, stay up
to date on all the news about our upcoming
releases and even be in with the chance of
winning copies of our wonderful books!

Bringing you the best voices in fiction

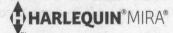